PRAISE FOR GENERATION SHIP

"*Generation Ship* is a ferocious story of human desperation, boiling with tension and betrayal."

—Sunyi Dean, author of *The Book Eaters*

"*Generation Ship* has the brilliant political complexity of *The Expanse* and the American government, while keeping the fun and excitement of *Dark Matter*. Thoughtful, well-written, deep, and engaging. Familiar to fans of sci-fi and of Mike Mammay's voice while watching him take us in a new direction with his craft and storytelling."

—R. R. Virdi, author of *The First Binding*

"Michael Mammay's *Generation Ship* is a masterclass in political science fiction. A political chess match filled with absolute page-turning tension that culminates in an ending that manages to be both bittersweet and hopeful. This was a book that will be stuck in my head for a while."

—K. B. Wagers, author of the NeoG Series

"Mammay writes compellingly and convincingly about the complex, imperfect, and rocky nature of political and personal change set against the backdrop of a generation ship counting down to its hoped-for destination and what that will mean for everyone aboard."

—Kate Elliott, author of *Unconquerable Sun*

"Political sci-fi done right! *Generation Ship* offers a captivating look at an authentic spaceborne civilization aboard a nascent powder keg. Cleverly written, topical, and compelling with a relatable cast of diverse characters, deeply personal stakes, and twisty plot elements that will keep you on your toes."

—J. S. Dewes, author of the Divide series

"A riveting political drama that had me on the edge of my seat wondering if humanity would survive itself. Tense, twisty, and deeply human—my favorite Mammay novel so far!"

—Bethany Jacobs, author of *These Burning Stars*

THE MISFIT SOLDIER

"Highly recommended."

—*Library Journal* (starred review)

"Gas is a snarky, sharp-witted protagonist whose reckless decisions are balanced by bold confidence and luck—and a lively group cast of supporting characters who make up his crew. In a story packed with quippy dialogue and cinematic action, Mammay deftly blends military sci-fi with edge-of-your-seat heist elements."

—Ren Hutchings, author of *Under Fortunate Stars*

"*The Misfit Soldier* is a goddamned delight. Mammay masterfully blends heist and military SF in the schemes of a sergeant—bent on rescue, with a side of smuggling—whose best weapon is his wit, not his power armor. Han Solo meets *Halo* meets *Ocean's Eleven*, and more fun than all three."

—K. Eason, author of *Nightwatch on the Hinterlands*

"*The Misfit Soldier* is an action-packed, engrossing read that has just enough military sci-fi trappings to dress the set, but the far more interesting action is what takes place between the characters on that set as they seek out a place to survive. You don't have to be a fan of space marines to enjoy this book (though their power armor *is* pretty cool), and Mammay has shown obvious growth as an author, with this being his most intriguing work yet."

—*Lightspeed* magazine

"*The Misfit Soldier* is *Starship Troopers* meets *Saving Private Ryan* with a dash of *Ocean's Eleven*. A fun, fast-paced Military-SF space adventure. As with all of his books, I highly recommend."

—Zac Topping

COLONYSIDE

"Highly recommended for readers who like their heroes cynical, their mystery twisted, and their sf thought-provoking."

—*Library Journal* (starred review)

"*Colonyside* by Michael Mammay is an incredible and deeply captivating read that puts an outstanding and enjoyable protagonist on a high-stakes, mysterious adventure. This latest novel from Mammay is an amazing third entry in one of the best science fiction thriller series out there."

—Unseen Library

SPACESIDE

"Highly recommended for military sf lovers, who will savor his perspective and probably want to buy the man a drink."

—*Library Journal* (starred review)

"*Spaceside* is a worthy sequel to *Planetside* and Mammay once again successfully delivered another highly entertaining page-turner. The cleverly mixed mystery and military sci-fi element made this relatively small book packed with a strong impact, and I highly recommend it to readers who are looking for a fast-paced mystery/sci-fi read."

—Novel Notions

"This is another wonderfully addictive, fast-moving book from Michael Mammay. Corporate intrigue, interplanetary politics and military action are blended into a cohesive whole that is both satisfying and great fun."

—SFCrowsnest

"Wow, just wow. This was another exceptional book from Mammay, who has once again produced a fantastic science fiction thriller hybrid with some amazing moments in it. . . . *Spaceside* is an incredible second outing from Michael Mammay, who has a truly bright future in the science fiction genre."

—Unseen Library

PLANETSIDE

"This was a brisk, entertaining novel. . . . I was reminded a bit of some of John Scalzi's Old Man's War novels."

—SFFWorld

"A tough, authentic-feeling story that starts out fast and accelerates from there."

—Jack Campbell, author of *Ascendant*

"Not just for military SF fans—although military SF fans will love it—*Planetside* is an amazing debut novel, and I'm looking forward to what Mammay writes next."

—Tanya Huff, author of the Confederation and Peacekeeper series

"*Planetside* is a smart and fast-paced blend of mystery and boots-in-the-dirt military SF that reads like a high-speed collision between *Courage Under Fire* and *Heart of Darkness*."

—Marko Kloos, bestselling author of the Frontlines series

"The book was an enjoyable read and would likely sit well with any fan of military SF looking for an action-thriller to browse while lying in the sun at the beach."

—Chris Kluwe for *Lightspeed* magazine

"If *Cold Welcome* and *Old Man's War* had a love child you might get something like *Planetside*. And it would be, and is, pretty damn awesome. I would say it's awesome for a debut novel, but that isn't nearly praise enough. It's just plain awesome."

—Reading Reality

"In *Planetside* Mammay mixes a brevity of prose with feeling of authenticity that would be remarkable in many experienced authors, let alone in a debut novel. Definitely the best military sci-fi debut I've come across in a while."

—Gavin Smith, author of the Bastard Legion and Age of Scorpio series

GENERATION SHIP

ALSO BY MICHAEL MAMMAY

GENERATION SHIP

MICHAEL MAMMAY

HARPER Voyager
An Imprint of HarperCollins*Publishers*

GENERATION SHIP. Copyright © 2023 by Michael Mammay. All rights reserved. Printed in the United States of America. No part of this book may be used or reproduced in any manner whatsoever without written permission except in the case of brief quotations embodied in critical articles and reviews. For information, address HarperCollins Publishers, 195 Broadway, New York, NY 10007.

HarperCollins books may be purchased for educational, business, or sales promotional use. For information, please email the Special Markets Department at SPsales@harpercollins.com.

Harper Voyager and design are trademarks of HarperCollins Publishers LLC.

FIRST EDITION

Designed by Angie Boutin

Title page background © Jarn Aui/shutterstock.com

Library of Congress Cataloging-in-Publication Data has been applied for.

ISBN 978-0-06-325298-1

23 24 25 26 27 LBC 5 4 3 2 1

For those who look to the future, not the past

GENERATION SHIP

PROLOGUE

||||||||||||||||||||||||||||||||

Promissa Probe DS-8723-1A

ARRIVAL IN PROMISSA ORBIT
AND ATMOSPHERIC ENTRY

<Transmission> Atmospheric entry. Data send 1428.

<Function> Atmospheric analysis. Deploy.

<Data> Received.

<Data> Received.

<Data> Received.

<Error> Unauthorized inquiry.

<Data> Received.

<Error> Unauthorized inquiry.

<System Fault> Main power overload.

<Transmission> Data send 1429.

<Error> Unauthorized inquiry.

<System Fault> Emergency power overload.

<Transmission> Error. Power overload. Transmission failed.

<System Fault> Offline

<System Fault> Offline

<System Fault> Offxxxxxxxx . . .

<CHAPTER 1>

SHEILA JACKSON

||||||||||||||||||||||||||||||||||||||||||||||||||||||||||||||||||||

140 CYCLES UNTIL ARRIVAL

Dr. Sheila Jackson reached across her desk to the button that darkened the window between her office and the open workspace of her department. It barely qualified as an office, as she could almost touch two of the walls without leaving her chair, and the other two weren't far off. She still appreciated it. She'd earned it when, at age thirty-seven, she became the second-youngest deputy director in the almost 250-year history of the ship's science department. In the science and medicine division, led by Dr. Lavonia Carroway, only deputy directors and the director herself rated private workspaces— a luxury in a place where privacy was at a premium. As it happened, Lavonia had her office right next door out of tradition. The first director had been a space explorer, and while directors since had come from many different fields, the office had stayed. As with most days, that office was currently empty. Lavonia was a medical doctor by training and didn't have much use for the day-to-day management of space exploration.

At least not for now. With the message waiting on her computer, Sheila had a feeling that might change. Depending on the data, a *lot* of people might find new interest in space exploration, and Lavonia wasn't one to miss out on an opportunity for attention.

Technically, Sheila wasn't supposed to be here. The ship had rules about shifts, and working too long was theoretically as big a crime as not working long enough—work-life balance, and all that. But that rule applied more to subordinates than bosses, and for all intents and purposes, Sheila was the boss of her own little fourteen-person empire. Nobody would report her for getting in an extra hour. Most of that empire had departed at the ship-wide chime that signaled the end of first shift. The department did keep coverage around the clock, and two people still manned the large work area outside her office, but they were used to her and wouldn't disturb her unless there was an emergency—and there just weren't that many space exploration emergencies.

At least not usually. The message in her inbox might change that.

She leaned back in her high-quality office chair, which was bolted to the deck, letting her feet come off the ground slightly in the low gravity. The science department was four levels up—or more accurately, in—from the residential deck, and the gravity monitor in the outer area constantly displayed 0.53g. It was only 10 percent lower than her living space, but she could swear she felt it, even though the people in charge of such things said she couldn't. She rolled her shoulders and called up the first-ever live data from a probe in orbit around the second planet in the Zeta Tucanae system. A planet commonly called Promissa. Prom for short.

The probe could transmit only a little data to the ship at a time, since they were something like .06 light-years away, which required an extremely tight beam. They had been traveling at 11 percent of light speed at their fastest, but had been slowing for twenty-seven days, and Sheila didn't even know their current velocity. But the computers did, and they compensated. Even so, they would get only a split second of transmission time before they lost the signal. It was part of what made space exploration from a fast-moving ship challenging.

Much of the data they had was still centuries old—information that scientists with giant telescopes had discovered back on Earth before they departed. Even now, with their first probe arriving, she wouldn't get much in this first of what should be many reports. But what she did get . . . it could be the most important discovery to date in the 253-year-long mission.

Opening the message, she scanned the single chart: the atmospheric composition of the planet. The computer had run the numbers already, of course, but that didn't stop her from checking them manually. She knew the parameters by heart at this point, and she held her breath as she read the first new analysis of Prom's atmosphere in more than two centuries. The information gleaned all the way from Earth had been promising—they wouldn't have launched if it wasn't. It had indicated that the planet was 97 percent likely to support human life. Good odds—enough to launch the first-ever colony ship—but now, just over a hundred days out from arrival, that 3 percent chance that it *wouldn't* support life loomed larger.

But this, the data in front of her now, would be more accurate by over an order of magnitude. She skipped over the major components, oxygen and nitrogen. They knew with pretty high confidence those to be close to 20 percent and 79 percent, respectively. Argon read at just under 1 percent. She read through each of the trace elements, moving her finger across her screen as she did to be absolutely sure she had them right. She almost squealed. The trace elements accounted for just over one tenth of 1 percent of the atmosphere, but the wrong things in just the right amounts could doom an otherwise breathable atmosphere.

This probe was saying they didn't.

The planet, from an atmosphere perspective, would support human life.

Sheila found herself on her feet without realizing how she got there, and she forced herself to sit back down. She took three slow, cleansing breaths and then checked the data again, line by line.

It wasn't until the second time through that she saw the anomaly. She'd been focused on the data, but this was in the transmission message itself:

Unexpected truncation of data. Error code 5xB27.

Her heart started pounding to the point where she could hear it in her ears. What error was that? She opened a file and looked up 5xB27.

Loss of signal.

Okay. That could be normal. Maybe this was just the signal loss they'd expected due to the ship's high velocity. But the computer would compensate for that, wouldn't it? She was pretty sure. She put that behind her for a second, however, and forced herself to look at the figures again, and then bounced it off what the computer models said. They agreed with her.

She had it right. She picked up the comm and hit the first contact in her list.

The other end picked up almost immediately. "Dr. Carroway."

"Boss, it's Sheila. We got a report from our first probe. You're going to want to see it."

"You know it's really hard for me to enforce work hour standards when one of my own deputies won't follow them."

Sheila could almost hear Lavonia shaking her head and was glad that she hadn't opted for a video call. "This is important."

"It's always important."

Sheila shoved down her frustration and kept her voice level. "I have the atmospheric composition from Prom."

"I'll be right there." The connection went dead.

Four and a half minutes later Sheila's door slid open to reveal her boss standing there in a workout version of the vac suits that everybody wore on the ship. It fit snugly and featured athletic footwear, but it would still seal in an emergency and would fit to any of the helmets stored in brightly marked lockers throughout the ship. Lavonia stepped inside and held up one hand for silence, waiting until the door slid all the way closed before she spoke. "Don't mind the clothes. I was headed down to the workout level. A place where you yourself will go, immediately after we finish here."

"Yes, ma'am." Health regulations required every resident of the ship to spend ninety minutes per day on one of the outer levels of the ship where the gravity reached 0.90g or higher. Many used that time for workouts, but Sheila came up with every possible excuse to avoid it when she could. Thankfully there were recreational areas, reading nooks, and food shops on those levels as well, to accommodate the less athletically minded of the crew. "Sorry to bother you. I could have given you the data over the comm."

"No, you did the right thing. I don't want this widely released until we know what we're dealing with. What have you got?"

Sheila handed her a printout, and Lavonia raised her eyebrows. Hard copies were extremely rare. "This is significant enough that I didn't want to forward a digital file. It's currently isolated within our department, as per protocol on communications received from outside," said Sheila.

"Right. Smart." Lavonia glanced over the data. "I can see that all the values are inside what the computer is giving as expected ranges, so all the component elements are in line. Other than that, what am I looking at?"

"The key numbers are methane at 0.00013 percent and CO_2 at 0.0341 percent, though to really gain everything we need from that data we'll need iterative readings across multiple seasons, especially due to the high axial tilt of the planet, which will likely exacerbate the seasonal impact on the—"

"Okay," said Lavonia, cutting her off. "But what's it *mean*?"

Sheila paused and bit back her frustration before speaking again, purposefully slowing herself. Sure, she was excited, and maybe talking a little faster than normal, but this was important data, and as the head of science Lavonia should understand that. But Sheila didn't want a confrontation. And besides, most days she appreciated her boss not involving herself in space exploration. "Sorry. Where should I start?"

"Break it down for me in layman's terms. I'm going to have to go to the governor with this, so he needs to be able to understand it."

"It looks good. Really good." Sheila braced herself for more criticism.

"We'll probably need to give him more than that. Can you explain in basic terms what the methane and CO_2 levels mean for us? Focus on the implications to the mission."

Sheila hesitated, wondering if her boss didn't know. "Uh . . . sure. At 0.00013 percent and 0.0341 percent respectively, the methane and CO_2 levels are lower than those recorded back on Earth—"

"Hold on. Methane is 0.00013 percent of the atmosphere?"

"Right."

The other woman studied her, one hand holding the paper, the other on her hip. "And something that small is the key takeaway?"

Sheila hesitated again, unsure where to go with the question. "I mean . . . there are other things. Helium is a touch high at 0.0016 percent, but it's still within acceptable parameters."

"But you mentioned methane first, because it's the most important."

"Yes," said Sheila. "In conjunction with the CO_2, it presents the best evidence that the planet supports life. That it probably already *does* support life."

"Intelligent life?"

"There's no way to know that yet," said Sheila, her hands moving with increasing enthusiasm.

"But it will definitely support *us*."

"Well," she hedged, "there are still factors beyond the atmosphere. We need a temperature study by region in conjunction with a geographic survey to make sure that the extremes that are likely due to the axial tilt will support human life in any regions also conducive to agriculture and horticulture."

"When will we have that?"

"Well . . ." After finally seeing some excitement from her boss, Sheila hesitated at telling her the bad news.

"Go ahead. Tell me." Lavonia handed the printout back.

"I don't know when we'll have more data. There was an anomaly—"

"What kind of anomaly?" It said something about Lavonia that she immediately seemed more focused at the mere hint of a problem.

"There was an error message at the end of the data . . . a loss of connection. I don't know whether that means that it cut off that transmission, or if we've lost comms with the probe altogether."

"When will we know?"

"The next scheduled message would be in about twenty hours. If we hear from it, we'll know a lot."

"And if we don't?"

Sheila considered it carefully. She hated speaking off the cuff without all the facts, but Lavonia didn't have the patience for her to run all the different permutations. "If we've lost connectivity, I can't be sure when we'll get more information. This is our first probe, and I don't know if this problem is isolated or indicative of a wider issue, but . . ." She paused, waiting for her boss to interject, but she didn't, so Sheila continued: "At a minimum, if we've lost this one—and again, we aren't sure we have—we're looking at a couple of weeks at least until the next one arrives. But after that, more should arrive in pretty short order, so we'll have redundancy."

Lavonia nodded. "Redundancy is good. But I've got to talk to the governor, so what can we say for sure *today*? Bottom-line this for me."

Sheila thought about it, trying to determine what she could say that would satisfy her boss despite their limited information. "Okay. From a data perspective, you know that we've maintained that the planet is 97 percent likely to support colonization?"

"Yes. We teach that to children."

"Right. That number is now over 99 percent."

Lavonia grunted. "That's it?"

"What? What do you mean?"

"That's not much."

Sheila paused, now unsure if her boss was serious or just trying to spin her up, but nothing in their history suggested that the older woman had a sense of humor. At the same time, they'd just learned that their odds of finding a livable planet had increased by fortyfold. How could she miss that? "What . . . what do you mean, not much? This is huge."

Lavonia leaned to the side, her shoulder against the wall. "Okay, you're the expert. If you say so."

If I *say so?* Math *says so!* "I absolutely do. I can't wait to tell my team. They're going to be so excited—"

"What? No! This stays between you and me."

"What?" Vaguely, Sheila realized her mouth was hanging open. "This is scientific data. My people need it for their work, and they should have it before any kind of news announcement. We especially need to look into what happened to the communications."

Lavonia shook her head. "It's hypothetical data, and until it's verified, not a word. The last thing we need is people getting their hopes up for something, and then us finding out that we made a mistake—"

"But it's not hypothetical. The data is clear—"

Lavonia raised a hand, cutting her off. "Let me put it a different way. The data may be clear. It may be science. But the decision on whether to release that data to the public is a political one, and we're not going to make that decision without briefing the governor first. Is that clear?"

Sheila took a deep breath in through her nose, trying to hold back her emotions. This was the most important discovery of her lifetime—of *anyone's* lifetime on the ship—and she couldn't tell anybody about it. It wasn't clear at all—what did politics have to do with facts? Yet when she spoke, it was barely more than a whisper. "Yes, ma'am."

Lavonia stared her down for a few more seconds, and then her face softened. "Look. I know this is important to you, and I know it affects other things that your team does."

"Not just my team. All the science subdirectorates. The implications for xenobiology are—"

"I get that," said Lavonia, cutting her off. "But can you imagine what would happen if word got out about a failure of communications with the first probe without the proper context? There could be a panic."

Sheila considered it. She hadn't thought of it that way, but now that she had, she could see it. She still wanted to argue, though. They could issue a statement, *provide* the context. But they'd know more about the loss of communications in a day. She could certainly wait that long. "Okay. I hear you."

Lavonia softened her voice. "I promise, you can tell your people before there's a public announcement, just as soon as the governor approves it."

Sheila nodded, hoping that she wasn't being set up. Part of her couldn't help but believe that Lavonia wanted to politicize the announcement to further her own ambitions, but was that fair? The announcement *would* cause a commotion on the ship, and it did make sense to let the governor know so that he could be prepared for that. He'd be a key part of managing expectations, and his team could help tell the story in an accurate and responsible manner.

"Are we okay?" asked Lavonia.

"We're good."

Lavonia nodded once. "Good. I'll let you know when it's time to brief the governor. I'll try to make it soon. Until then, we keep it to ourselves."

"Yes, ma'am."

"Good." Lavonia opened the door and left.

Sheila stood there for at least a minute, stunned. *What just happened?*

Within five minutes she'd had the discovery of a lifetime, panic at an error message, and an exchange where she learned she couldn't talk about either of them. Her mind was whirling at the speed at which it had all transpired. But then she did what she always did: She wiped it away and focused on the task at hand. Focused on the science and what she'd do with it. She could leave the politics to her boss, who would be happy to deal with it. For her part, she needed to send additional commands to the probe, so she sat down and pulled up the program that let her do that. Even though new commands wouldn't reach it for several weeks, Sheila was excited, and she needed to order an extra set of diagnostics to confirm or deny the error message. There would be more probes with more capabilities in the coming days, but for now she had what she had, and she'd work with that. If she still had contact, they'd get soil samples, water vapor readings at a bunch of different places, wind speeds, and temperature readings. And that didn't even begin to account for later probes that would focus on the critical area of microbial science. So many tasks.

She should have had help. She had a team that planned the requirements for the drones and wrote the code to execute them, but she couldn't tell them what she needed without violating Lavonia's gag order. She'd have to write the code herself.

That was okay. She didn't really want to go to the full-grav deck for a workout anyway. She sent a quick message off to Alex, telling him not to expect her for dinner, and she buried herself in her work.

<CHAPTER 2>

EDDIE DANNIN

|||||||||||||||||||||||||||||||||||||||||||||||||||||||||||||||||||||

135 CYCLES UNTIL ARRIVAL

Eddie Dannin slammed a set of vise grips into her tool satchel and made an exaggerated show of dropping the whole thing on the deck. The soundproofing in the floor kind of ruined the effect she had hoped for. At nineteen, she was the youngest person on shift by at least five years, and the others looked at her with a mixture of annoyance and pity. It wasn't her first outburst.

"You get assigned to customer service again?" asked Niko. He was a tall man, at least thirty years older than her, but one of the few people she genuinely liked in the division. Or on the ship, for that matter.

"Yes. *Again*. You want to trade?"

"No way," said Niko. "I'm working air duct preventative maintenance. Nice and clean, and nobody complaining. I'll be wearing earbuds all day, watching bots as they spray antifungals, and I'll be done two hours early." He left unsaid that customer service was the worst job, filled with unpredictable tasks and whiny people who were just as likely to fill out a complaint on you as give a simple thanks.

"This is bullshit. I'm going to go talk to Walter." Walter was the director of maintenance, their boss, and, most significant at the moment, the man who made the daily work schedule.

"You know you're wasting your time," said Niko, as he slung his satchel over his shoulder then ran his hand through his thick, graying hair.

"It's not a waste," said Eddie. "I haven't bothered him in a while, and I don't want him to forget how much I despise him."

Niko half chuckled. "Not much chance of that." He lifted his arm, and Eddie bumped her elbow against his as she passed in the typical greeting.

Eddie made her way out of the locker room where they stored their coveralls and tools and down a short corridor to Walter's office. She pressed her thumb to the pad and the door slid open.

"How many times have I told you to stop hacking my entry pad?" Walter didn't look up from his screen, which was mounted on a wall bracket over his cluttered desk. A light sheen of sweat showed through his close-cropped hair, almost shiny in the small, well-lit room.

"I don't know, eight or ten times, maybe." It had obviously been a rhetorical question, but Eddie found it amusing to answer anyway. It was an ongoing battle with them. He would change the coding on his door, and she would immediately break it. Now she blocked it so her boss couldn't close it on her.

"Yet you keep doing it."

"I figure when you get sick enough of it, you'll finally approve my transfer to engineering. By the way, it's been three months, so I submitted another request." He was going to say no, but she'd keep asking until she died.

"Answer's still no." And in that, his word was final, and the reason why transfers didn't happen. They required approval of the department director, and he had no incentive to allow it. It meant training a new person, which meant work. And Walter wasn't willingly signing up for more work.

Never mind that it would be good for the ship, which was supposed to be everyone's priority.

"Come on, Walter. You know I've got the skills for it. I'm better than half their division." Truth was that she was better than almost all of them, but it seemed too much like bragging to say so. Engineering and maintenance were related, but engineering worked on the critical ship functions—the power plant, the navigation—while maintenance worked on everything else. The stuff to keep the people alive and happy. More important, engineering worked outside the ship. In space. Eddie dreamed of doing space walks while her living nightmare continued to be fixing showers in people's living quarters and being made to feel like shit for it.

"We've been over this. I'm not trading you because we need you in *this* division." It was such a bullshit answer, but he was nothing if not consistent.

"If you need me so bad, explain this." Eddie held out her tablet with the day's work assignments.

"What?"

She pretended to look at the list of customer service tasks that she'd already memorized. "Let's see. You've got me doing a repair to a personal entertainment unit, replacing a light in somebody's room that they could change themselves, changing four intake filters for an air recirculator in the entertainment division's work area . . . ooh, that's a biggie, there."

He didn't change his tone to meet hers, even though she was right on the line of insolence. "So? They're all jobs that need to be done."

"Right. All jobs that I could have done when I was seven. You say you need me, but you give me all the crap jobs. There's a problem with the drip irrigation system on the grain farm level. Why not give me that?" It wasn't engineering, but it promised to be complicated and directly impacted the lives of everyone on the ship.

"Because I gave that to Rex and Becka."

"I'm better than both of them combined, and you know it."

"And I don't care. They have seniority. Seriously, how often do we have to go over this?"

Eddie wanted to scream. That was the point. "Until you change the policy."

Walter sighed and made an exaggerated show of looking at his screen. "Would you look at that? It's three past the hour. You're already behind for the day. I'd hate to have to dock you for not finishing your assigned work."

"Oh no. However will I make up the time with such complex tasks on my chart?"

"You know your problem, Eddie? You only think about yourself."

It was a powerful reprimand on the ship, where everybody relied on one another to live, but it didn't stop her from saying, "You know your problem, Walter?" She stepped out and closed the door. "You suck," she finished once he couldn't hear her. Because as much as she detested the man, he could make her life even more miserable than it already was. Some lines she could cross, some she couldn't.

Department directors had way too much authority.

AFTER MAKING HER WAY DOWN TWO LEVELS TO ONE OF THE RESI-dential decks, she walked several minutes to reach room E1014. She hit the buzzer, and then stood there tapping her foot as she waited for an answer. Despite playing it tough with Walter, she really did have a time schedule. If she blew it and had to push a task to the next day, it would give him more ammunition the next time they fought. He could even put it on her official record and dock her lux pay, though he rarely did. Walter preferred to keep his own journal of who owed him what for which infraction so he could lord it over them later. After a few more seconds she opened her tablet to get the key code. Nobody was around, which made sense. This part of the living area belonged to the science types, and most of them worked main shift. She keyed the override code and the door opened.

A tall, pretty woman wearing only a towel stared at her, her hair wet and hanging across her face, nearly obscuring one of her eyes in a cute way.

"Oh . . . sorry, Lila." Eddie looked down at the floor, heat rushing to her face. "I . . . uh, I buzzed, and when you didn't answer, I figured you were on shift."

"It's no issue, Eddie. It's my free day and I had my workout early. I was just getting a shower, so I didn't hear you buzz." Each living compartment had a small shower in the corner that put out thirty seconds of water a day per person, though one could spend some of their monthly luxury credits and get more time, if they wanted.

"Okay. Sorry." Eddie couldn't meet her eyes, looking at the wall instead. It was painted lavender and had yellow highlights, and Eddie thought for the hundredth time that she should do something with her own walls, which were still the standard puke green. Although that was exactly the color of her feelings at the moment.

Of everybody it could have been, it had to be Lila.

Perfect, gorgeous, didn't-know-Eddie-existed Lila. "I didn't know this was your place. I have a work order for your PED." Each room had a personal entertainment device that played music, videos, games, and allowed access to content from across the ship. Common rooms had more impressive systems, but the ship's designers a million years ago had believed that people needed their alone time, too.

"There's nothing wrong with it." A wry smile crept across Lila's lips, lighting her face and making her even cuter, if that was possible.

Eddie frowned and looked at her tablet. "You submitted a work order, and the system diagnostics checked it and confirmed the fault."

"I know," said Lila. "I disconnected a wire. Don't be mad. Please? I needed an excuse to get you to my room."

Eddie's heart skipped a beat. "Wha . . . what do you mean?"

"I need a favor. I want to hire you for one of your, um, off-duty jobs."

Eddie's face fell, but she tried to recover quickly. Of course Lila had asked her there for business. What else would it be? "I don't know what you're talking about."

"Come on, Eddie. You're not fooling anybody. You're the best black market hacker on the ship."

Eddie frowned. She hadn't thought everybody knew, but if someone as clean as Lila had the info, then everybody else probably did, too. She'd have to watch that. But she didn't see any reason to deny it if Lila already knew. "Even so, that's after hours. I'm on the clock."

"And my work order will take thirty seconds to fix, leaving you plenty of time to do my other job. Please? For me?"

Eddie sighed. She could have said no . . . at least she told herself she could have. Truthfully, she wasn't sure she believed it. "What do you need?"

"Yay!" Lila bounced with joy, and Eddie smiled despite herself. "I need to be able to access my work files from my system here in my room."

The smile left Eddie's face, replaced by confusion. "You don't need a hack for that. Just put in a request. It's perfectly legal."

"Except my boss won't approve the request," said Lila. "She's adamant that we only work eight hours a day."

"That monster!" Eddie put her hands to her face, hiding from the fake horror of a boss that actually cared about people.

"Come on, Eddie. Be nice. There's a job opening up—a promotion—in under a year. Three of us are up for it, and I need to work harder if I'm going to beat the others."

"Must be nice to get merit-based promotions."

"Yeah, we get them to an extent," said Lila, missing Eddie's tone. "But only when there's an opening. And if I miss this one, it's *years* until the next opportunity. There are only fourteen people in my division and only one over the age of sixty. The system sucks. So come on, will you help me?"

"I can't," said Eddie. "I've got fourteen minutes left on this job, and what you're asking will take thirty."

"You can work fast. I know you can do it."

"Nope. You rush a hack, you get caught. I really can't do it."

Lila gave an exaggerated sigh followed by a pout. "Please?" She cocked her head to one side and smiled.

Eddie stared for a few seconds, then averted her eyes, feeling the heat rush to her face for a second time. "I can't. Really. I have a schedule." But even she could hear the crumbling of her will in her voice.

Lila came closer, the scent of her lavender soap—another luxury purchase—drifting before her.

"What are you doing?" Eddie's voice quavered.

"You look tense. Maybe I could rub your shoulders as you work."

Eddie knew Lila was manipulating her—she must know Eddie liked her—but her brain was too addled at the moment for her to do anything about it. Finally she managed a thought. "How are you even going to pay for it? I know you don't have scrip."

The ship had two types of money: luxury credits, which were legal and on the record, and scrip, which was technically illegal, though nobody enforced the rule unless it got to be a problem. Scrip drove the shadow economy, and Lila was too clean to get anywhere near that.

"I have something else," said Lila.

Eddie's breath caught. "What's that?"

"I've got three tablets of star. I'll trade you, straight up."

"*You* have star," said Eddie, snapping back to reality. Star was half muscle relaxer, half hallucinogen, and fully illegal, and currently the rage among young people in certain sectors. Eddie could sell one tablet and make nearly enough to make the job worth it.

"I work in the science division. Who do you think makes it?"

Interesting. "I can't take advantage of you. That's too much for this job. Give me two tabs and I'll owe you some change once I sell them. And put some clothes on. I need to concentrate."

"Great!" She bounced over to the drawers mounted under the bed, and Eddie allowed herself a long look before turning to the computer. "My guest passcode is—"

"Don't worry about it," said Eddie. She'd already engaged her virtual keyboard and entered the system, bypassing the local security. Lila's terminal was a standard model—well below what Eddie herself had—but it would do for a simple job like this one. Each division had its own subnetwork, so she'd have to break into science's. She didn't have an existing hole there because she'd never gone into that division before, so it would take a bit more time. It would have been easier to access it using Lila's protocols, but if she did that and somebody caught it, they'd trace it back to Lila—and despite her surprising access to drugs, the woman wasn't shipwise enough to hold up under questioning.

It took her almost fifteen minutes of rapid-fire coding to get into the system, and when she got there, she found a mess. "What *is* this?" she said, half to herself. "This division needs some new coders. It's half-assed."

"What is?" asked Lila.

Eddie started. The other woman hadn't spoken while Eddie worked, and Eddie had almost forgotten she was there. "It looks like instructions to a probe, but it's messy code, and it's not where it should be."

"We have probes out to look at Prom, but we haven't heard back from them yet," said Lila. "Can I see that?"

Eddie gestured the taller woman over. Lila put one hand on her shoulder, and Eddie could feel the heat from her.

"Holy shit," said Lila.

"Is it Prom?" asked Eddie. Information about their destination was hard to come by, and she'd have been interested even if it hadn't excited Lila.

"We're communicating with probe One Alpha."

"We *were* communicating with it. Look here, there's an error message saying that the connection terminated. And . . ." She scrolled through more data. "Yeah, that's the end of it. It never reestablished."

"Holy shit," said Lila. "That seems . . . big. Even the fact that we've heard from it at all should be news, but there's been nothing about that in the division reports." She paused, and began pacing as she thought. "Can you see what it *did* send?" Lila stared at the screen with such longing that Eddie would have done anything to make her happy at that moment.

"Probably," said Eddie. "Give me some space?" Lila took a step back but hovered. "Boom. Here it is. It came in five days ago. Looks like—"

Lila almost shoved her out of the way in her haste to see the screen. "Oh. Wow. It's data on the atmosphere." She went quiet, studying.

"What's it mean? Is it good?"

Lila looked at her and smiled, then put one hand on each side of Eddie's head and pressed their foreheads together for a moment, before pulling away. Her voice almost broke when she spoke. "It's good. It's *so* good. Why haven't they released this?"

Warning bells sounded in Eddie's head, that sense she got when something very wrong was about to happen. "We shouldn't have done this."

"What do you mean?" asked Lila.

"I can't give you access right now. Not with this going on. Normally nobody would trace an incursion for something like this—personal access of your own files. But this?" Her hacker's sixth sense was blaring alarms in her head, and Eddie gestured to the screen. "People will look for someone who accessed this."

"But I need—"

"Look, Lila, I'll come back once it's safe and give you the access you paid for. I promise. But right now, I need to make this look like nobody was ever here. You have to trust me."

"What is it?" said Lila, the light gone from her face. She took a half step back. "We're not going to get in trouble, are we?"

"Pfft. No. We're not going to get caught. I've got this." She tried to inject confidence into her voice that she didn't completely feel.

When Eddie left Lila's room twenty minutes later, she glanced at her tablet. Thirty-seven minutes behind schedule. Shit. Walter would have a party with that. She'd have to skip lunch to make up the time.

<CHAPTER 3>

MARK RECTOR

||||||||||||||||||||||||||||||||||||||||||||||||||||||||||||||||||

13Ø CYCLES UNTIL ARRIVAL

Mark Rector walked through the corridor next to his partner, Diana Vasquez. The stun stick that was his badge of office was bumping against his leg in the relatively high 91 percent gravity of the upper agriculture deck. He'd never used the weapon other than in training, but having it made him comfortable. His partner, in contrast, got on his fucking nerves.

"I hate these high-grav decks. What are we doing down here, anyway?" asked Vasquez.

"We're being seen. Community engagement. It's a key tenet of effective community policing."

They had this conversation once a week. His response was right out of the security officer's study guide, which Vasquez never read. He didn't mention that, first because it was useless to try to get her to study, and second because her failure to do so improved his chance at the next promotion. Not that she was a threat, but still. When there would be only one potential promotion in the next decade, why risk it?

"Being seen by whom? The potato plants? I feel like they're doing fine without us."

"Think of it this way," said Rector. "We're getting our high-grav time in now, so we don't have to do it when we're off duty."

"Whatever," said Vasquez. "If we have to be in high-grav, let's at least get to a deck where I can get a cup of coffee. I've got a hangover."

"Sure." Rector knew better than to mention that she always had a hangover. That conversation never failed to degenerate. Seven years working six days a week with the same partner—one of the drawbacks of such a small security force—and he could pretty much predict where every conversation would lead as soon as it started. His comm vibrated, and he checked the message. "Hey, we've got a call."

"Just tell me it's somewhere inward, in lower gravity."

"It is. Residential deck. Maintenance personnel's corridor."

"What is it? Fight?" asked Vasquez hopefully. They didn't get many calls—maybe two or three a week—and the ones they did get tended toward the mundane. Disputes over property, missing items, lovers' quarrels, that sort of thing. People tended to police themselves most of the time. Either that or they didn't report things. Rector wasn't naïve enough to ignore the organized crime on the ship, but if people didn't report, then it wasn't his problem. He didn't see himself as apathetic. He was just a realist. Some things handled themselves and didn't need to be made official.

"No." Rector checked the message again, to make sure he'd read it correctly. "Mrs. Applebaum failed to show up for her Departure this morning."

"That can't be right," said Vasquez. "I went to her going-away party four days ago. It was totally normal. Nothing at all suggesting she'd bail." Everybody had a party on their seventy-fifth birthday, a culmination of a year of celebration where they didn't work. Four days later, they went in to medical and they were put to Sleep, which was a nice way of saying *prepped for the recycler.*

"You know her?"

"Nah. I was a plus-one. They had free booze."

"Huh. Well she didn't show up at medical." He flicked the message to her with a finger.

Vasquez studied it. "Weird."

"Yeah," said Rector. It *was* weird. Nobody missed their appointment. From their first day of school they learned the necessary sacrifices one had to make for the ship, and this was a big one. The population was capped at eighteen thousand. For new children to be born, the elderly had to feed the recycler. Not doing one's part . . . that was the height of irresponsibility. It just wasn't fucking done.

"She probably just got drunk and overslept," said Vasquez. "Did anyone check that?"

"I don't know." Rector doubted it, though. Who could oversleep on the day of their scheduled death? Vasquez, maybe.

"Well let's go," said his partner. "Lower gravity awaits. We can stop and grab a coffee on the way."

IT TOOK THEM ALMOST FIFTEEN MINUTES TO REACH THE J CORRIDOR of the residential deck where Mrs. Applebaum lived, and Vasquez had sulked the whole way because they hadn't stopped for coffee. They'd had to wait on two separate elevators and then walk a good distance around the deck. No single elevator ran all the way from the outer part of the ship to the inner. Rector didn't know why, and he only rarely thought about it, but he knew his way around the ship, since Secfor traveled more of it than most. Probably more than anyone other than maintenance. For a regular worker, it was possible to go through their entire life while visiting only five or six decks total. Not many people lived that way, but somebody probably had at some point in the ship's two-and-a-half-century history.

"You hear that?" said Rector, as they approached the room.

"No. Hear what?"

"It's quiet."

"Nobody's around. Of course it's quiet."

Rector reached down and checked his stun stick, which hadn't moved. The small population occupied only a tiny part of the huge ship at any given time, so it wasn't uncommon to find an empty corridor, but this particular one being devoid of life made him uncomfortable. It felt off.

He pushed the buzzer on J0933 and waited. No response. He pushed it again, then pounded on the door with his fist. "Mrs. Applebaum?"

"She's not here," said Vasquez. "I'll hit the override."

"Yeah," said Rector, though he wasn't willing to concede that she wasn't there. As Secfor they could override most of the doors on the ship, though in practice they rarely did. Something in his gut didn't let him hesitate this time.

"Wouldn't it be ironic if we went in and found her body?" Vasquez keyed in her passcode then put her thumb to the pad. Nothing happened. "What the flip. It's not working."

"What? Let me try." He edged past his partner and entered his code and pressed his thumb to the pad. Nothing.

"I told you it wasn't working."

Rector pounded on the door again. "Mrs. Applebaum!" Down the hall, a few doors slipped open, and heads popped out.

"You mind keeping it down? I've got to work next shift," called one man, enough doors away that Rector couldn't identify him.

"There's something wrong with the door. We need to call maintenance," said Rector.

Vasquez gestured up and down the corridor. "You think that's going to work? This *is* maintenance. They live here." She was right, of course. Divisions mostly lived in adjacent apartments, and they were firmly in maintenance territory.

"So?"

Vasquez shook her head. "So they broke the door on purpose. She's in there, and they don't want us to get to her."

"They wouldn't do that."

"Okay," said Vasquez. "What's your explanation then?"

Rector hesitated for a few seconds, realizing he was probably wrong. They *shouldn't* do that. Nobody ever *had* done that. But what other explanation fit? A handful of people had joined them in the hallway but kept their distance and just watched. He took out his comm and called headquarters. "We need a system override on a door . . . J0933. Our local override isn't working."

"Stand by," came the response. Several seconds passed. "Something is wrong with the system. I can't operate it from here, either. It must be the door itself. You want me to call maintenance?"

Rector glanced around. A few more people had joined the gathering, which had a decidedly unfriendly demeanor. "They're here. We . . . uh . . . don't think that's going to help."

"You're the regulations guy," said Vasquez. "What do the rules say we do here?"

"I just did it," said Rector. He got back on his comm and called maintenance. "This is Security Officer Rector. Put me in contact with the head of the maintenance department. It's official business."

"Hold please."

Rector drew his lips into a thin line while he waited and tried not to make eye contact with what was now around a dozen people milling in the hall. Vasquez ignored them, too, as if by some sort of mutual unspoken thought.

"Walter Krasnov here," said a new voice.

"This is Security Officer Rector. One of your personnel was scheduled for Departure today, and she failed to make her appointment. Applebaum."

"What's that got to do with me? She came off my books five years ago when she was transferred to general services. Just like everyone who turns seventy."

Rector paused, letting his retort pass. Of course he knew that, and he suspected that Krasnov was being a dick on purpose. When he spoke, he did it in his most official-sounding voice. The director could make a lot of trouble for Rector if he stepped out of line. "We believe she has locked herself in the room and sabotaged the door. What it has to do with you is that I need someone from your department to get it open, highest priority."

"Hold on." After half a minute Krasnov spoke again. "Diagnostics confirm that there's a problem. Somebody recoded the door."

"Can you fix it?" asked Rector.

"I have people who can, but they're out on jobs. Give me ten minutes and I'll have it open."

"You want us to wait here?"

"You can wait wherever you want. I'll have your access restored in ten minutes." Krasnov cut the connection.

"Great," said Vasquez. "We've got time to get coffee."

"We need to stay here," said Rector. The last thing he was going to do was leave and let Mrs. Applebaum sneak out. If somebody had recoded the door, who knew what else they'd done? He used his device to check the feed from the closest camera, waved, and saw it reflected on his screen. That was working, but that didn't mean it would keep working if they left.

"Why don't you just leave her alone?" called a woman, standing with another woman and a man several meters back.

"Ma'am, you know why," said Rector. "We live in a limited-resource situation. Mrs. Applebaum continuing to live means that someone else can't."

"That's cricket shit," said the man. "We're like a hundred days from the planet. Now that we know for sure that it's livable, the rules need to change."

"What are you talking about?" asked Rector. He read his daily updates without fail, and he'd seen no announcement about the planet. Certainly nothing about it being livable. That's not something he would have forgotten. He glanced at Vasquez, but she wasn't paying attention, instead lost in her device.

The woman flipped her hand at him in a moderately offensive gesture. "You hall walkers. You don't even know what's happening on the ship you're supposed to patrol."

"Look, ma'am, I can tell you're upset, but there's no reason to be rude. We're just doing our jobs, enforcing the rules that you all know." He spoke loudly, intending his words for all the gathering personnel, including the ones just now straggling up. He was trying to come up with another line of reasoning when the door to J0933 slid open.

"Just leave her alone," shouted a new voice, but Rector couldn't identify the man. He edged back a step toward the door, trying to keep an eye on the gathering crowd and look inside at the same time.

"Mrs. Applebaum?" Rector kept his voice calm as he stepped into the room. It was double size—fifty cubic meters, twice the twenty-five allocated per person—though the call had indicated that Mrs. Applebaum lived there by herself. Maybe she had had a partner who wasn't with the ship any longer. He didn't have the time to look it up and didn't want to ask. The walls were clean white, giving the room an air of brightness, while blue accents gave it some color. It smelled vaguely of cleaning fluid.

"Leave me alone." A woman sat on the made double bed, hands behind her back. She had light brown skin with only the wrinkles around her eyes and at the corners of her mouth belying her age. She could have easily passed for ten years younger.

"Mrs. Applebaum, you know you have to go."

"I won't. I won't do it. I've lived on this ship for seventy-five years, and I'll be damned if I'm leaving it when we're finally reaching our destination."

"Mrs. App—"

"I'll do any job. I'll volunteer to go on the first landing party. Someone has to go down and see if it's safe. I'll be a human test subject!"

Rector kept his face impassive, just like the book said to do when dealing with an unreasonable person. It wasn't the type of thing that Secfor usually dealt with, but of course they were trained for it. He was supposed to stick to the facts. "I'm sorry, Mrs. Applebaum. There is no provision for that."

"There needs to be," she said. "I want a hearing with the governor."

"Rector, we've got a problem out here. You need to hurry up." Vasquez's voice held urgency in it, but Rector ignored her and kept his focus on Mrs. Appelbaum. He stepped toward the older woman slowly, trying to look unthreatening.

She stood and pulled a small knife from behind her back, the kind one might use to cut fruit. She brandished it at Rector, though it shook in her hand. Rector took a step back and put one hand up to forestall her, letting his other hand slowly creep toward his stun stick. He slipped it free from its holster, thumbed it on, and struck, all in one motion, just like in training. He caught the woman on her thin forearm and the knife clattered to the floor. Her body twitched for a moment in a standing position before slumping to the deck.

"He killed her!" a man's voice shouted from the door.

"Stay back," yelled Vasquez, but she was being pushed through the door into the room.

"Murderer!" yelled a woman.

"She's not dead," shouted Rector, not liking the desperation in his own voice. "I just stunned her." He reached out to Mrs. Applebaum's neck to check her pulse, an active gesture to show that she was fine. He couldn't find it. *Oh shit oh shit oh shit.* She hadn't hit her head when she fell. He'd have seen that. He set his weapon on the deck and used two hands, supporting her head with one and feeling for her pulse with the other.

Nothing.

This is bad. He couldn't think for a moment. People were still shouting at the door, but their words didn't penetrate the cloud around his mind.

"Rector. Rector!" Vasquez yelled his name.

"Yeah," he said.

"What's going on? We need to get her and get out of here. *Now.*"

Rector picked up his stun stick, checked to make sure it was recharged, and stood. "Everybody stand back!"

"Block the door!" shouted a wide-shouldered man at the front of the group, exhorting the others. They were crowded around now, blocking the only exit. Rector strode briskly toward the door and touched his stun stick to the vocal man's shoulder. The big man twitched, fell back against the doorjamb, and slid to the floor, toppling back out into the corridor where people had to move to get out of his way.

"Let's go," he said to Vasquez. They had to get out of there before the crowd regrouped, before they learned the truth about Mrs. Applebaum.

"What's going—"

"Let's go!" He cut Vasquez off, grabbed her by the wrist and pulled her though a gap that had developed around the fallen man. Once clear, he ran, trusting that she would keep up. He didn't stop until he reached the elevator and the door closed behind him.

Shit. This definitely wasn't going to help his chances for promotion.

<CHAPTER 4>

JARRED PANTEL

129 CYCLES UNTIL ARRIVAL

Governor Jarred Pantel sat in his large, carpeted office behind his large, bolted-to-the-deck faux-wood desk. Dr. Lavonia Carroway, the director of science and medicine, sat in an uncomfortable chair across from him. Ten days prior, she had, along with Sheila Jackson, given him a brief on the atmosphere of Promissa and the loss of communication with their first probe. Despite that bad news, today's meeting promised to be a good deal less pleasant. To that end, he didn't speak for almost half a minute, intentionally letting the silence grow awkward.

Carroway fidgeted. He was okay with that. She probably expected him to yell at her, which he wasn't going to do, but he didn't mind her being uncomfortable. The way the charter was written, department directors didn't report to him, but things had changed over time, and now, when the governor called, directors responded. At least they did unless they wanted their resources cut. Pantel liked to reinforce that concept every chance he got. It kept things on the ship more orderly when departments worked for the common good instead of their own interests.

"So go ahead," he said finally.

"What do you want me to say?" Carroway scowled at him, looking less nervous and more perturbed.

"You could start with explaining how the data that I specifically asked you to keep quiet is now common knowledge around the ship," said Pantel. "That might be a good beginning."

"I have no idea." She met his stare and didn't break it, even when he held it a few seconds too long. She had more backbone than he remembered, which would normally be a good thing. Here it was damned inconvenient.

He blinked first, deciding that she was telling the truth. "Who else knew?"

"Only me and Sheila Jackson."

"So if you didn't leak it, it had to be her," said Pantel.

"I don't think so, Governor. I specifically forbade it, and Sheila isn't one to break the rules. She didn't like my order, but she's compliant."

Pantel considered that. "She struck me as someone who puts science before politics. You don't think that might motivate her to share the information?"

"She *definitely* puts science before politics. Before everything, I imagine. It's all she thinks about. But I don't think she'd go against me so openly. There's no doubt that she *wants* to share the information. She told me as much. But she doesn't have the guts."

"So if not her, then who?"

"I don't know. Someone else had to have accessed the file. I've got my internal IT people looking for potential security breaches, but I'm kind of limited there because if I tell them exactly what I'm looking for, I confirm that the information is important. Right now, news about the planet is only rumor," she said.

"A rumor that almost started a riot. And hey, bonus, there's video. Have you seen the video?"

"You can't blame me for a brain-dead security officer waving around a stun stick like he's a hero in a bad action movie."

She was right about the outcome not being her fault. He was just frustrated.

"I'm sorry. You're right. The riot wasn't your fault. But *you* lost control of the data."

Carroway started to speak, but apparently thought better of it. Smart woman. He wasn't going to allow her the last word, regardless. Right now, he needed her to fall in line for the good of the ship, and that meant recognizing her failure and being willing to do what it took to make things right again.

Pantel took a cleansing breath and thought for a few seconds before speaking. He needed to get this situation under control, and he needed to do it fast. There was enough discontent on the ship without giving people something else to protest about. But he had to walk a fine line with Carroway. He'd made it clear that her mistake wasn't acceptable, and now he needed her back on his side. "Here's what you're going to do. Call off your people looking for the network breach. I'll assign someone to do that—someone we can trust." He meant someone *he* could trust, but she didn't need to know that part.

"Will do," she said.

"You're going to get a call from my PR department. They are going to arrange a time for you to give a statement on camera. You will give short remarks and say that we have initial data and it looks promising, but we can't validate the accuracy of it until we get more reports. Give a vague timeline of four to eight weeks. Understood?"

"Yes, Governor."

"You won't answer further questions, no matter who asks."

"Of course not."

"What about Jackson? Is she going to be a problem?"

"I can keep her under control," said Carroway.

"Good. See that you do. Thanks," he said.

She stood and let herself out.

A few seconds later a side door opened, and Marjorie Blaisdell entered. She had a strong jaw and tightly cropped hair with a peak in the front and wore a form-fitting vac suit that was just a little tighter than necessary. She looked like she was about forty, though Pantel knew she was on the other side of fifty. As she walked toward him her steps were virtually silent on the utilitarian gray carpet.

"You hear all that?" asked Pantel.

"Yeah."

"What do you think?" Unlike with Carroway, Pantel actually cared what Blaisdell thought. Nominally she was a PR assistant with duty supporting the governor's office. In reality, she was a combination of secret police and fixer. She investigated problems, and, more important, she made them go away.

"I think she's telling the truth. She has no idea how the information got out."

"I believe her, too, but it's still out. What's your recommendation?"

"I've got somebody working on finding the real leak, which is priority one. Beyond that, we've got to mitigate the damage, and before we do *that*, we need to make sure that nobody makes it any worse."

"How do we do that?"

"Without somebody stirring the pot, the rumor becomes just that—a rumor. Some of the harm is done, but without reinforcement, it dies with the next big thing. So we find the agitators and shut them up, and then we give people something else to think about."

"You have something?" asked Pantel.

"Not yet. But I will." Blaisdell said it with confidence, and Pantel had no reason to doubt her. She'd come through dozens of times before.

"What about the other thing?"

"It goes without saying that we deny that the death is even an incident. We go public with our own account, smear the dead woman as a traitor to the ship. She caused the incident. After all, there's no damage done. She is *supposed* to be dead. All that the security officer did was change the method."

Pantel considered it. It was cold-blooded, but she wasn't wrong. The seventy-five-year age limit was a core principle of their society, and while people might grumble, they knew the importance of it. Secfor had screwed up—that was for sure—but people would forget that if they pushed the bigger issue of her crime. It meant disparaging the dead, but the good of the ship came before any one person. "Yes. That's good. Get that opinion out across the ship. Also, I want you to look into Sheila Jackson. Carroway says she can keep her under control, but something struck me about Jackson when I met her. She's very . . . earnest. She might be too unaware to consider the political ramifications of her own actions, especially if a rabble-rouser gets to her. Dig in and find a button we can push. We need her to stay in line."

"No problem." Blaisdell's expression didn't change, and he knew she had just spoken the absolute truth. She had no problem with his ruthless tactics. She never did. That was what made her good at her job. "Anything else?"

"That's it for now."

"Your plants need water," she said, and then she turned to leave the way she came. He glanced behind him, and sure enough, there were signs of wilt. He'd need to turn up the drip irrigator. There was something wrong with it, but he didn't want to call in maintenance. Technically he shouldn't have plants in his office space—they should all be down on the ag decks. But as governor, he could allow himself a *few* small privileges. Even so, he didn't want to rub anyone else's face in it.

Before the door could slide shut behind Blaisdell, Pantel's assistant, Jeremy, stepped through, waiting to be acknowledged before speaking. He was tall and thin, with slightly longer than average hair that he kept immaculately groomed. Pantel looked at him and nodded.

"The captain wants to see you. She requested that it be immediately."

"Any idea what she wants?"

"She wouldn't say, but I called her aide and he said she's pissed about the security officer incident," said Jeremy.

"Let her wait," he said, drawing a slight smile from Jeremy. The captain and the governor were coequals, according to the Charter, but much like with the directors, the relationship had changed in the 253 years since that was written. The ship—the captain's purview—mostly ran itself. It existed in the background, forgotten by most people. The day that they had started reverse thrusting to cut speed to approach the planet had been a big one for her and her team, but then they'd returned to obscurity. She had about two hundred people who reported to her. The governor had more. Many more. The last thing he needed was her getting involved in this, and making her wait—reminding her of her place in the hierarchy—would help that. "In the meantime, get me the security officer. The imbecile with the overactive stun stick."

"Right away, Governor."

Once the door closed Pantel slumped back into his chair. He

closed his eyes and did a deep breathing exercise, five seconds each, twelve repetitions. He stood and did ten air squats. When he'd taken over the job seven years back, he'd had the governor's office moved to a lower deck where the gravity registered 0.73. Partly he'd wanted to help maintain his fitness despite his sometimes-long office hours, but mostly he wanted other people to be uncomfortable when they visited him.

He settled himself back in his padded chair and drank water from a lidded cup until Jeremy buzzed that the security officer had arrived. His boss, security force director Sebastian Darvan, accompanied him.

"Send them both in," he said. Darvan entered first, then Rector; both kept their heads down. "Gentlemen. Welcome. Kill anyone today?" He let the silence linger for a few seconds. "What? Too soon?"

"We know we screwed up," said Darvan, finally meeting his eyes.

"What's your mitigation plan, Director?" asked Pantel.

Darvan frowned, glanced at Rector, then back to the governor. Pantel had no trouble reading his body language. The director wanted to sack Rector and blame everything on him, but he didn't have the guts to voice it in front of the man. For a moment, Pantel considered making Darvan say it out loud, just to torment him. It was a dick thought, but then, he was in a dick mood.

"Here's our plan," said the governor, when nobody else spoke. "This man"—he gestured to Rector—"is a hero. A bunch of troublemakers tried to interfere with justice, and he did what had to be done to uphold the law . . . to uphold the very Charter that we hold dear."

Disbelief showed plainly on Darvan's features, in his slumped shoulders, the slight shake of his head. Rector, however, stood up a little straighter and met Pantel's gaze for the first time. He was buying it. Pantel suppressed a smile. It couldn't possibly be this easy. He studied Rector for a moment. With light tan skin, he was one of the fairest people on the ship, the racial mixing over ten generations tending to make everyone some shade of brown. He had a strong jaw, and he wasn't bad looking. Yes. Pantel needed a distraction, and Rector would do.

Darvan finally found his voice. "Governor, do you think that's the best idea? People are angry."

"It will pass. They're just misinformed."

"A woman is dead," said Darvan.

"She was supposed to be dead anyway," answered Pantel. "We just need to put our own spin on the story. Get Rector over to my PR team. They'll set him up with an interview." He looked at Rector. "Keep it simple. You were a man doing your job. You love the Charter and would defend it at risk to your own life."

"Yes," said Rector. "I would!"

"Of course you would," said Pantel. "You're a hero. It's what you do."

The man smiled.

"We'll get him over to PR right away, Governor," said Darvan, as if he wanted to get the meeting over with as quickly as possible. "Officer Rector, will you excuse us." It wasn't a question. They waited for him to depart.

"Problem, Director?"

"What are you playing at?" asked Darvan. "You're going to make him out as a *hero*? Do you know how much harder it's going to be policing this ship after that?"

Pantel frowned. He was in no mood for that kind of whining. They had a ship to protect, and he didn't appreciate the man questioning how he chose to do it without offering ideas of his own. Besides, he was missing the point. The woman was dead, but that wasn't the problem. The problem came from the idea that people didn't have to follow the rules anymore. An attitude like that was contagious, and it would kill the ship. "That sounds like a problem for the director of security. Now, if you'll excuse me, the captain wants a meeting, and I'd hate to keep her waiting."

Darvan glared for a few seconds and then stormed out, and as if on cue Captain Ava Wharton stormed in. The short woman wore the same vac suit as the rest of the crew, though it had her rank on each shoulder, and she kept her gray hair back in a bun. "Glad you could make time for me," she said.

"I'm sorry, Captain. I figured you would have questions about the woman who failed to attend her appointment, so I felt it prudent to talk directly to the security officer who apprehended her."

"'Apprehended'? He killed her!"

Pantel ignored her outburst, stood, and moved over to his plants. He began at one end, pouring a little water from his cup into each of them. "I asked my assistant to make that clear . . . that I was questioning the officer . . . did he not?"

"No, he didn't." Her tone said she didn't believe him, but it took the energy out of her offensive.

"I'll speak to Jeremy about that," he said.

"How about you tell me how you're going to fix this shit show that your people created? I trust you're dealing harshly with the officer who caused the problem."

Pantel turned to face her and pasted on a fake smile. "As you know, security forces fall under the direct purview of the governor—they're a civilian asset, not a military one—so it's not really your business how I handle it."

"It's my business when the people who are protesting work on *my* ship. See how well your purview functions if the ship fails. In case you missed it, we're under reverse thrust now, which is stressing systems that haven't been used at full function in over two centuries. What I *don't* need is the population adding extra stress."

"Of course. We're absolutely agreed on that, Captain. The last thing I want is the crew causing problems." Pantel continued to smile and did his best to project a positive attitude. Ava Wharton was a hard-ass, but the woman put the ship first, and he respected that. "Please. Trust that I'm handling it."

"You're going to deal with Rector?"

"I am," said Pantel. "I'm absolutely going to make an example of him."

CHAPTER 5

GEORGE IANNOU

124 CYCLES UNTIL ARRIVAL

George Iannou sat in his morning meeting, unsure what do with his massive hands. He was in a narrow room with the subdirectors and section leads for agriculture sitting in chairs that folded out of each wall while Jaffri Anazar, the deputy director—and the boss of everyone else in the room—stood at one end. It was Anazar's daily meeting, but today he was mostly silent while the others yelled at one another.

Raised voices weren't common in George's line of work; nobody got all that excited about farming. It wasn't a profession that had a whole lot of emergencies. Sure, a broken hydroponic pump was critical, but you put in the work order and maintenance came and they fixed it. But for the last several days, daily meetings had grown louder and louder. George got it. Kind of. A woman died, and that wasn't right. But she wasn't part of their directorate, and she was scheduled to die that day anyway, so it didn't feel like the massive tragedy that people were making it out to be. Some people were just looking for something to be mad about. At least that was his considered opinion. He didn't feel the need to share it, but then, that was true about most things. All he really wanted was for people to stop talking so he could get on with his work for the day.

Koshi Tanaka, the section lead for hydroponics, had other ideas. He had damned near suggested taking up arms against the ship's government. Thankfully Sara Washburn, who worked somewhere in protein farming (George wasn't sure of her exact title), had jumped in before the man could say too much. That was important, because it wouldn't have surprised George if they were being monitored. The ship had cameras everywhere, so it wasn't that much of a stretch that someone could be watching them. It was rare for someone from security to *physically* come to the high-gravity ag decks—not unless they absolutely had to—but that didn't mean they didn't care what happened here.

And seeing what security was apparently capable of . . .

By his estimation, the fifteen people in the room were split, though it was hard to tell for sure. The same five or six people had dominated the conversations of the past few days, with the rest, like George, keeping their thoughts to themselves. Given that this was the leadership of the agricultural directorate, it stood to reason that the rest of the personnel in the department were similarly split. Not that you could completely count on leaders to reflect their subordinates in a situation like this. There was too much emotion for that.

Koshi was up and pacing now, though he barely had enough space to pass between the knees of the people seated along each wall. "We have to do *something*."

"We don't *have* to," responded Sara, but the murmurs that responded to her showed that on this, the room was decidedly not on her side. Sensing the temperature, she backtracked. "Okay, fine. We'll do something. But what are we going to do that matters?"

"We have to get their attention," said Koshi.

While the others continued to talk, George studied Anazar, who still had offered no opinion of his own despite being in charge. Even his face betrayed nothing. George would have liked to know his thoughts. Would Mr. Anazar feel obligated to pass it on to his own boss, the director of sustainment? That could be trouble because she might have to take action. Or maybe she wouldn't. She never came down to these decks except for scheduled visits. George hated those days, as they always had to clean up for them, as if somehow cleanliness meant they were doing a good job. There was nothing clean about carbohydrate farming. People should understand that. A clean farmer was somebody who didn't do any work.

By the time he faded back into the discussion, people were standing and heading for the doors at each end of the narrow room. Finally. He stood to go, but Mr. Anazar put a hand on his forearm. The man had to look up to meet George's eyes, but he didn't say anything until most everyone else had cleared out. Only two other people remained, and they were enmeshed in their own private conversation at the other end of the room.

"I want you to go with them," said Mr. Anazar.

George furrowed his brow. "Now? I have work."

Mr. Anazar looked at him, confused. "No . . . not now. After work."

"What's after work?"

"Weren't you listening?"

"Not really," admitted George.

Mr. Anazar looked at him, as if trying to determine whether he was joking or not, and then the older man laughed. "George, you're the best. That's why I need you to go with them. They're going to gather some people together to protest the continued policy of mandatory deaths."

George nodded. "Okay. Why do I need to go? Don't get me

wrong, I'm all for ending the policy. But I'm not much of a protestor, you know?"

"I know. That's why I want you there. Your presence should
keep things calm."

"How do you mean?"

Mr. Anazar patted him on the arm. "You're a giant, and you're
always calm. If you're there, people are a lot less likely to cause
trouble."

"Wait . . . you think there will be trouble? What kind of trouble?"

The boss shrugged. "I don't know. People are excited, and I
don't want to take a chance on someone doing something stupid."

"You mean Koshi."

"Among others. Yeah. You'll balance out the hotheads."

"I don't know," said George. "It's not really my thing."

"Please. Do it for me. As a favor."

George considered it, but not for long. He wasn't comfortable
saying no to his boss, and it *did* seem like a simple enough thing.
"Okay. I'll be there."

"Good. Thanks."

GEORGE'S DAUGHTER, KAYLA, LIVED IN THE APARTMENT NEXT TO HIS,
but they had a connecting door between them, so they practically
lived together, which was good. She brightened up the place with
her personality and by decorating it. She changed it every so often.
Right now the walls were white with a fat red stripe running di-
agonally from corner to corner, which Kayla said was the current
style, and he didn't care enough to argue. It looked fine and it made
her happy to do it, and that was all that mattered.

"Dinner's in the warmer," Kayla said, as George walked in.

"Thanks."

"You're late tonight."

George grabbed his plate and slumped into a chair at his small table. The protest, which was more akin to a gathering of loud people during most of it, had gone on for almost three hours. That was wasted time he'd never get back. "Didn't you get my message?"

"I did. It's right here. 'Going to be late.'"

George snorted. "Right. I was late."

"Do you maybe want to talk about why? It's not like you to put in extra hours on the farm."

"There was a protest—"

"You were *there*? The protest about changing the rules for mandatory end of life?"

"Yeah." George rubbed a bite of vat-grown turkey in some gravy and shoved it into his mouth, and then spoke with his mouth full. "You heard about it?"

"Read about it on the net. Everyone's talking about it."

George grunted. Everyone. In Kayla's parlance, that meant four young people. She was twenty-two, and sometimes she didn't realize that not everybody cared about things the way that she did. "Don't know why."

"Are you kidding me? I wanted to go, but I wasn't sure what would happen. Like . . . are those people going to get in trouble?"

George shrugged his big shoulders. His boss had told him to go, so he didn't think *he* would get in trouble. He certainly hadn't done anything illegal. He'd stood there as people milled about and made noise. Judging from what he'd seen, *nobody* had actually done anything, so any punishment should at least be light. "Don't know."

"Tell me about it. What happened?"

George looked at her and found her staring, hanging on what he said next. She didn't even have her device out, which was unprecedented. She actually wanted to hear what he had to say. "It was no big deal," he said, because while he liked having her attention, he wasn't going to embellish the truth. "Some people got together because they wanted . . . well, a bunch of things."

"This is amazing," said Kayla. "Was it mostly ag folks? The news said it was mostly ag folks." She paused, but not long enough to wait for an answer. "We didn't hear about it up in the main office until after it started." Kayla worked in sustainment, too. As his daughter, she'd been born into the division, but her aptitude for math got her assigned to forecasting and projections instead of down on the farms. George didn't really know what she did if he was being honest. Calculations. He was pretty sure about that part. She had her mother's head for that kind of thing.

"It was mostly ag people," said George. "Some others. Spouses and partners, I think, mostly. There wasn't a lot of planning."

"There will be next time," said Kayla.

George stopped his fork midair, gravy dripping from it back to his plate. "Next time?"

"Yeah. People are already talking about it. A bigger protest, though. And not just for extended-life authorizations. We're going to protest for changes to how directorates work."

He hesitated. More protests were a recipe for trouble, but he didn't want to discourage his daughter when she seemed excited about something. "Yeah? What kind of changes?"

"Directors have too much power—they pretty much control our entire lives."

He frowned. Of course they did. They always had. "Yeah. We're on a ship in the middle of an unforgiving vacuum. That kind of comes with the territory."

Kayla shook her head. "I'm not talking about ship functions. I'm talking about life! Do you know that to change directorates, you have to get approval of the directorate that you're leaving?"

"Yeah. Sure." George had heard people at the protest talking about things like that, but he hadn't paid a lot of attention.

"Do you know how many people transferred in the first fifty years of the mission?" She waited for a response, and when she didn't get one, she continued. "Three hundred and forty-seven. Do you know how many have been approved in the *last* fifty years of the mission?"

"No," George admitted. Why would he? It wasn't something he even thought about. He was a farmer. Always had been and had never considered anything else.

"Four."

"Huh. I guess that's not good."

"It's not." Kayla was resting her hands on the table now, lowering herself to where they were eye to eye. "They wrote the Charter way back then with a belief that everybody would naturally work together and do what's best for the ship, and for a while it worked. Now it doesn't. It's important for us to do something about it."

Sure, George thought. Maybe she had a point, but what could they do? It wasn't like the ship's leadership was going to suddenly change the way they did things just because some people didn't like it. He was smart enough not to say that out loud to his daughter, though. He'd made enough mistakes with her mother, which was why she didn't live with them anymore. She'd left fifteen years ago, but it still felt fresh sometimes when he looked at Kayla. They looked very similar, especially in the way that they smiled. "Just promise me you'll be careful. Today's protest was fine. Nothing happened. But when you get a bunch of riled-up people in the same place with nothing to do, bad things can happen."

"Maybe then they'll listen," said Kayla, but she was smiling as she said it.

George didn't worry too much about it. She was a smart girl—

much smarter than him—and she could look out for herself. "Okay. Well, just watch yourself. Don't go falling for some wild radical."

"Dad," she said, smiling as she turned away.

"I know, I know. You're not a little girl anymore." He sopped up the last of the gravy on his plate with some bread. "I need to get a shower—"

"—because farming's dirty work," Kayla continued, imitating his deep voice.

"What? It is."

"I know it is, Daddy." She walked around the table and hugged him.

CHAPTER 6

SHEILA JACKSON

120 CYCLES UNTIL ARRIVAL

Sheila sat at the small table in the quarters she shared with her husband. It was barely large enough to fit the half-completed, old-fashioned jigsaw puzzle that she had been working on in her free time for the last couple of days. Her husband, Alex, hated them, probably because it forced them to eat standing up or seated on their cushioned love seat in front of their entertainment suite. Sheila didn't get the problem. Three days out of four they ate at one of the communal dining facilities anyway. She wouldn't even have been home had Alex not messaged her to tell her he had important news to share. She'd have stayed at work, restrictions on the workday be damned. There was too much exciting stuff happening, and even now, at her puzzle, she found herself drifting off occasionally, her mind going back to her job. She placed another piece just as the door slid open and Alex arrived.

"Oh good, you're home."

"It sounded important." Sheila smiled. Alex was practically vibrating with excitement, and it infected her.

"How was your day?" he asked.

"Uh . . . well . . . not great. But that can wait. You've got good news?"

"The best." He came over and took the chair across from her. "They approved our application."

Sheila hesitated. He was clearly excited, and she wanted to be too, but she had absolutely no idea what he was talking about. "Our application?"

"For a child. My division got an unexpected allocation, and they gave it to us!"

"Oh . . . that's . . ." She let her voice trail off. She didn't know what to say. Their application *for a baby.* Seventy-five percent of children were raised by the early life directorate, but the Charter allowed for some couples to have one of their own. Alex had wanted it for years, and she'd supported the idea as a hypothetical. But now that it was real . . . well, the timing couldn't be worse with her work.

Alex's face fell. "What? I thought you'd be happy."

She looked at him, his sad eyes reflecting her betrayal, and she felt like crap. So she did what she had to do to make that look go away. She lied. "I am. Really. I'm sorry. It's just work stuff. It was a bad day."

Alex stood, pushing off of the table hard enough to knock one of the puzzle pieces to the floor. He paced away, but by the time he turned back to her his face had softened. "I understand. You've got a lot going on. But this!" He gestured with his hands. "It's great!"

Sheila bit her lip and nodded. "It is."

"We probably won't get a natural birth allocation. It's rare for them to give that to someone over thirty-five."

Sheila kept herself from letting out a sigh of relief. At least there was that much. Natural births were rare—maybe fifteen a year—and required a lot of specialized care. "That makes sense."

"They still want us to go for the medical tests, though."

"Sure. I'll take a look at my schedule and set that up." She had no intention of carrying a child. It would mean moving to a living space on a higher-gravity deck, along with a lot of other restrictions. But she didn't have to reject the idea outright and crush Alex's joy any more than she already had. The medical people could do that for her.

Alex studied her in that way he had. He worked as a cameraman in the news and entertainment directorate, and she often joked that it was his cameraman's look, observing things. It wasn't a joke this time. "Are you okay?" he asked.

"I told you. It's work. You know that arrival is approaching, and you know that I have a major part in that."

"Yeah, I know. But you never talk about it." His tone had changed, bitterness creeping into it. It was an old argument, and he couldn't hide his resentment.

"We've been over this." Sheila stood so she wouldn't have to look up at him. "I'm not allowed to share my work."

"Your work is all over the ship. We're supposed to be a team, and I had to hear about the atmospheric data and the lost contact with the first probe from somebody else. You know how stupid that makes me look?"

"My career could be in jeopardy because of that information getting out. I think my boss believes that I leaked it."

"I'd be happy to tell her that you didn't," said Alex. "You don't share anything."

Sheila started to snap back, to go for a soft spot, but held herself back at the last second. She was stressed about work, and she didn't need to take that frustration out on Alex. She'd been totally unprepared for his news about the baby, but that wasn't his fault. "What do you want from me?"

"I want you to be excited for this opportunity."

She nodded. "I'll try to be. It caught me a bit by surprise, and my mind has been elsewhere."

Alex's face softened. "I'm sorry I snapped at you. I know you're under a lot of pressure."

"I really am."

"You know you can share with me, right? I won't tell anybody."

Sheila considered it. She shouldn't, she knew that, but Alex wasn't a liar. He wouldn't tell. And maybe it would ease some of the drama about the baby, which she *wanted* to be excited about. Maybe with a little bit of time to process it, she would be. "We get a new dump of data every day from our orbital satellites, and I have to sit there and pretend that I'm not getting it. I'm the only one who receives it, and now my people *know it*. So we all sit there in a room and pretend that it's not happening. Makes it pretty hard to lead the team."

"Wow. Yeah. It has to. I never thought about that part of it."

"And the thing is, the information is both good and bad, but in both ways, it's *significant*. I *want* to share it."

"Like what?" asked Alex. "Tell me the good part."

She hesitated, but only for a second. "Okay. We got a satellite into orbit and it gave us an estimated gravity measurement that's more accurate than anything else we've had by an order of magnitude."

"Yeah? That's important?"

"For livability of the planet, other than the atmosphere, it's probably the most important thing."

"Didn't we have a good estimate of that because of the size of the planet?" asked Alex.

"An estimate, yes. But that couldn't account for the planet's density and uniformity of composition. Now we can."

Alex's face lit up. "And it's good. I can tell by the way you're talking about it."

Sheila smiled, as much at his excitement for her work as for the news itself. It was almost as if their disagreement from a minute ago hadn't happened. She loved that he had a short memory for things like that. "It's good. We were hoping for anything between 0.9 and 1.1, as human life can definitely adapt within that range, and it would also support, at least theoretically, most of our possible flora and fauna transplants."

"So? What is it?"

"Point nine seven."

Alex smiled. "Okay, I'm no scientist."

"A generation of teachers would attest to that," teased Sheila.

"They would," agreed Alex. "But even I know that point nine seven is good."

"So good."

"Will this speed our ability to get down to the planet?"

"Maybe a little. There's still a long way to go. We need to test for pathogens and compatibility of proteins and all kinds of other stuff. That's where the bad news comes in. We have contact with that satellite, but we lost another surface probe, which puts us behind on some things." She did her best to downplay it and not show how worried she was. Losing a second probe . . . once was random. Twice was a pattern. A pattern she couldn't share with anybody in her directorate.

He pursed his lips. "So that's two in a row you lost? You're worried about that."

She should have known he'd pick up on her discomfort. "Yeah. It's a problem."

He seemed to sense her mood shifting and brightened his tone to compensate. "But the gravity! That's good."

"It is. What the gravity means—and the atmosphere—is that when we *do* go down to the surface, there's a much better outlook for quality of life."

"When will we go down?" he asked.

It was such an abrupt shift that it took her a moment to process. "'We' as in 'you and me'? I'd love to go right away, but probably not until the second group. Our skills aren't really at the top of the priority list, but my position will give me some standing for follow-on groups after the initial—" She stopped midsentence. She'd forgotten about the baby. Thankfully, Alex brushed past her mistake.

"I meant 'we' as a civilization."

"I don't know. There are a lot of factors and it's impossible to say."

Alex smirked at her.

"What? I really can't predict."

"Yeah, but you have a guess."

She shrugged. She did have a guess, but that wasn't how science—how *she*—worked, and it frustrated her a bit that Alex didn't seem to know that. "Could be a year. Could be twenty. Probably somewhere in between those. We'll go when the science supports it, and we'll know more about that once we start getting data from the surface."

"And you'll get that once you have a successful probe landing?"

"Yeah." She bit her lip and refrained from saying *if*. "We're not sure if the problem is with the probes themselves, or if there's something on the planet interfering with communications. That's the problem with holding the data back. I'm not allowed to involve all of the people who should be working on the issue."

Alex came forward and hugged her. "That's a shitty way to have to work."

She hugged him back, and in that moment she was happy. Deep inside, however, she knew they hadn't resolved anything about the baby. She just hoped that her husband could be as supportive about that as he was about this.

EDDIE DANNIN

‖‖

117 CYCLES UNTIL ARRIVAL

Eddie made her way through the Black Cat Café, stepping aside as someone brushed by her in the small aisle between two rows of rectangular tables, before continuing to work her way to the back. The back wall had a large picture featuring a small animal from back on Earth—a black cat—which seemed like an odd choice, given that nobody had seen a real cat in more than two centuries. In theory, the café itself had no owner—it was, like all such establishments, public property, serving a selection of free meals and drinks as well as some that could be had for luxury credits. It wasn't a particularly popular place, though, with only a few of the tables presently occupied by a dozen or so total patrons.

In practice, people didn't come here for the food. The Black Cat was the de facto property and headquarters of the Organization and its leader, Cecil Sharakan. At some point, a few tables had been removed to create a space around three tables at the back of the place, and Cecil—or somebody who worked for him—could be found there at almost any hour of the day. At present, the boss was in, seated alone at one of the burnt-orange tables with built-in benches.

Eddie wiped her palms on the legs of her vac suit. If she wanted to pretend that she wasn't nervous, her hands marked that as a lie. It was only natural. Mikayla Irving, an underling of Cecil's, had told her that the boss wanted to see her, and when it came to less-than-legal activities, if Cecil called for you, you went. He didn't look like much, sitting there at his back table. A balding man of maybe fifty years, he was shorter than average and had a paunch that even a loose vac suit couldn't hide. He worked somewhere in ship administration. Everybody had a real job, after all. But that wasn't why she was there. She had no reason to deal with Cecil in his official administrative capacity and was pretty sure that he hadn't called her there to make a maintenance request.

This was almost surely about her extracurricular hacking. Maybe he wanted to hire her—he had before—but then, he'd never summoned her for that, instead passing a message through one of his couriers. Hacking wasn't exactly a we-need-to-meet-in-person kind of thing, which meant this was something else. If you did business on the dark side of the ship, Cecil was the law. Eddie had racked her brain on the walk over. It could be about the hack she'd pulled for Lila, but that shouldn't have drawn his attention. Nobody knew about that. If they did, she'd have heard about it before now. She hoped she hadn't stepped on somebody's toes without knowing it.

"Eddie!" Cecil gestured with his meaty hands, welcoming her without getting up. "Have a seat."

Eddie moved to the seat directly across from the heavyset man. As she did, Mikayla, who looked like she spent more than her share of time working out on a high-grav deck, moved away to give them some privacy. The muscular woman stopped at the edge of the main group of tables, positioning herself so that anybody who wanted to get to Eddie and Cecil would have to go through her.

Nobody would.

"Cecil," said Eddie. "Good to see you."

"Care for a drink? There's decent vodka here. That's your spirit, right?"

Eddie nodded. "It is, but I don't have the lux to afford it right now." That was a lie. The truth was that she didn't want to drink because she didn't know what kind of shit she was in, and she wanted to keep her head straight.

"It's on the house."

Eddie hesitated. "On the house" meant that Cecil was paying, or, more likely, that they had some sort of hack on the machines here. Either way, she didn't see how she could refuse Cecil's hospitality. "Sure, then. Vodka soda with lime."

Cecil gestured to a man two tables away that Eddie didn't know, and the man got up and headed for the vending area. Eddie folded her hands on the chipped surface of the table in front of her. She hadn't consciously planned to keep them visible, but when she thought about it, she decided it was a good idea.

"How are you?" asked Cecil. "Keeping busy?"

Eddie considered the question and decided it wasn't why he had called her there. He was just making small talk until the drinks came. "Keeping my head down, mostly. Small jobs. Did some work that earned me some star." It was a safe enough answer. She'd fenced the drugs through Cecil's people, and she'd paid her tithe on it as well, so he already knew about it. He knew about *most* of her illicit jobs. Sure, she skimmed once in a long while, but she hadn't recently.

"Good. Good." He waited as the man he had dispatched returned and set a vodka tonic in a plastic cup in front of her and a coffee in front of Cecil.

Eddie lifted her glass to the boss and said, "Thanks," before taking a sip. The liquid hit her throat and cooled it before a bloom of warmth seeped in.

"You're very welcome. I'm sure you're wondering why I called for you."

Eddie set the cup down on the table and forced a smile. "It *had* crossed my mind."

"It's okay. I like you, Eddie." It was a bizarre thing to say, and Eddie had to think about it. He liked her. Did that mean it was okay, he liked her, so she wasn't in trouble?

"That's good, right?"

"It's good."

"I figure if you didn't like me, I'd know about it," she offered.

"That you would."

"Okay. Thanks." She was confused, but there was nothing for it but to let him get to his point in his own time, and he didn't seem like he was in a rush.

"I want you to do something for me."

"Of course. What do you need?" It was an automatic response. She didn't have a choice, so she might as well be on board with it. Besides, Cecil paid well, and he always had the scrip. As a bonus, there was no tithe on a job he commissioned directly.

Cecil leaned his head over the table, closer, and Eddie instinctively followed suit. He spoke in a softer voice. "I heard that you were responsible for a certain piece of information that has been making the rounds for the last couple of weeks. Information that has caused . . . something of an uproar."

"No," said Eddie, and then held her hand up to indicate that there was more to her answer. If she was questioned by the authorities, she'd deny any involvement, but if Cecil was asking, he already knew, and lying to him would be worse than whatever was going to happen for the deed itself. She didn't know how he'd found out, but he had. She took a deep breath and spoke in a measured cadence. "No, I didn't leak the information. Yes, I was involved in obtaining it."

Cecil nodded and pursed his lips. "Right. Obtaining it is the important part. Leaking it? That was unfortunate."

"I'd say. It caused a protest."

Cecil snorted. "That part was fine. What was unfortunate was that somebody released the information for free when they could have charged."

Eddie took a sip of her drink to cover a grin. The pure capitalism of Cecil amused her, but it probably wouldn't be wise to show him that. "Understood. As I said, I didn't release it. You mentioned that you need me to do something?"

"Yes," said Cecil. "Get more."

Eddie was in the process of setting her drink down and stopped, frozen. "Get more?"

Cecil sat back and shrugged. "Information. You obviously know where it came from, and you obviously know how to get to it. So yes. Get more."

Eddie's mind raced. She couldn't do that, but she also couldn't sit there, face-to-face with the most powerful man in her world and tell him no. With no good option, she did the only thing she could think of. She stalled. "What specifically are you wanting?"

"I don't know." He interlocked his fingers and cracked his knuckles. It was almost a cliché. "Anything will do, as long as it goes to the habitability of Prom . . . or really anything that gives information in that general vein."

Eddie considered it, thought about why someone like Cecil would care about that. Was he trying to project his crime empire into the new reality of reaching the planet? No, probably not. It was likely simpler than that. He probably wanted to sell it. She decided to take a risk. "Can I ask why?"

"I'm not usually in the business of explaining myself." He let the statement hang out there for a few seconds before continuing, "But . . . as I said, I like you. It's business. When there's a demand for a thing and people are willing to pay for it, I provide that thing. You know?"

Eddie nodded. "I get it."

"Usually it's a physical thing, but information has value, too, to the right people."

Eddie let out a deep breath. She knew what the man wanted to hear, but she couldn't make herself say it. "Cecil, you know I'd do anything for you. I mean no disrespect by this, but I can't."

Cecil gave a performative sigh. "'Can't' is not a word I like to hear."

"I know that. I'm really sorry."

"'Can't' is not a word that I *usually* hear."

"I understand." Eddie sat back in her chair to give herself the illusion of distance. Cecil wasn't known as a violent man. He had people like Mikayla for that. But at that moment she wasn't sure he wasn't going to come across the table. "Can I explain?"

Cecil gave her an obviously fake smile. "Yes. Please. *Explain.*"

She swallowed, annoyed she hadn't asked for a water rather than the vodka. No such thing as a free drink, she thought, too late. "It's too dangerous. I did it before, but when nobody was looking. We didn't even know the information was there. But now that there's been a breach? Security will be all over it. Not only will it be harder to do, but they'll be watching for anybody trying to do it. It would be like trying to pilfer goods off of the printers when there's a patrol specifically there to watch for it."

"Oh," said Cecil. "Is that all?"

Eddie hesitated, waiting for him to smile, but he didn't. "That's a lot."

"You will be very well compensated."

"It's not about the scrip. I can't spend scrip if they arrest me."

"I'll protect you."

"I appreciate that, Cecil, I really do. But I don't think you can in this case."

Cecil stared her down. "Eddie."

"Yes?" Her voice hitched.

"Despite the appearance here, we're not having a debate." Eddie hesitated, but before she could speak, Cecil continued. "There's a war coming. Everyone is going to need protection. You want mine."

"A war?"

Cecil shrugged and smiled. "It's a metaphor."

"If I do this, I am *going* to get caught. I'm good . . . maybe the best . . . but even *I* can't do this."

"So be somebody else."

She started to respond, to tell him again that it couldn't be done, but then hesitated. "Excuse me?"

"Whoever does this is going to get caught, right?"

"Absolutely."

"So be someone else."

"You mean like log on with somebody else's credentials? It still won't work." She'd done it enough to know what she was talking about. It wasn't like she did hacks while announcing her true identity.

"More than that. I mean do it as somebody else, from their interface."

She considered it. Maybe it *was* possible. Maybe someone was watching the data in real time and would be able to physically trace her, but that she could probably handle. She'd have to be fast, and she'd have to have a plan to physically get away once she was finished. And then there were the cameras. There were cameras everywhere . . .

"You're thinking about it," said Cecil, a touch of humor creeping into his voice. "You're thinking about how to do it."

"I am," admitted Eddie. "They're going to come after whoever I pretend to be."

"That's why you're going to be someone beyond reproach."

"You have someone in mind?"

"The director of manufacturing, Elizabeth Paulsen."

Eddie bounced her head from side to side, considering it. There was a kind of beauty to the idea, she had to admit. Nobody would fuck with a director, especially not the one who ran all the matter printers on the ship. "I assume that you have a way to get me to her equipment or we wouldn't be having this conversation."

"That is correct."

"This isn't a one-person job. I need someone else to handle the cameras."

"Eddie. I said I liked you. Please don't make me have Mikayla slap the shit out of you for implying that I'm stupid. I wouldn't be in this business if I couldn't manage the cameras in manufacturing, would I?"

"No, I don't guess you would."

"So you'll do it?"

Eddie downed the rest of her drink. She didn't love being in a situation where she didn't have options, and if she had the choice, she'd have backed out just on the principle of it. But Cecil could make her life extremely difficult, and when he said it wasn't a debate, he meant it. She did this job, or she didn't work again. Or worse. "Yeah. Sure. There are a few details to plan out, but I'll do it."

"Good. You're on in two hours."

Eddie nodded, not surprised by the tight deadline. She'd known it was important when he called for her. "Please don't take this the wrong way," she said. "I mean no disrespect. But you know if we do this thing and you sell the information, there's going to be chaos, right?"

"I'm counting on it," said Cecil. "Chaos is good for business."

<CHAPTER 8>

MARK RECTOR

115 CYCLES UNTIL ARRIVAL

Mark Rector finished his protein bar lunch, drained the last of his coffee, and tried to summon the will to leave his apartment. He took out a biodegradable disinfectant wipe, cleaned his small table with it, and then tossed it in the recycle bin. He could almost make himself believe that it was a necessary thing. He lived alone, after all, and nobody else would be there to clean things. Almost. In truth, though he did keep a very neat apartment, he was stalling. He didn't want to go outside.

He'd picked up the habit of hiding in his apartment in the two weeks since the incident that flipped his life upside down. People *hated* him. Well, not everybody. Not even half of the ship, probably. Rationally, he knew that it was just a few people. But it took only a few loud ones to make things uncomfortable.

He had just about gathered the courage to push out into the corridor and make his way to his shift, which started at 1300, when his comm buzzed. "Rector," he answered.

"Get your ass in here." The gravelly and decidedly pissed-off voice of Sebastian Darvan was unmistakable.

Rector took a moment to think about what he might be in trouble for now but couldn't come up with anything. "Everything okay, boss?"

"No, everything is not fucking okay. There was another data breach last night. The governor is pissed, and he wants to talk to you and me about it."

"The governor wants to talk to me? Again?"

"Trust me, I told him you were of no use, but he insisted. Now get in here and get a briefing about last night. We've got to be down there at 1700 and I want you up to speed."

Rector hesitated for half a second, trying to figure out if his boss had intentionally insulted him. He probably had. Rector had never been Darvan's favorite, and since the incident that had only become more pronounced. That Darvan held the keys to his promotion made that a problem. You didn't make somebody your deputy director if you didn't like them. In that regard, some of those recent protestors had a point about the system. Not that he'd ever admit that publicly. "On the way."

Outside his apartment, he checked his door to make sure it was secure while saying a silent thanks that the corridor was empty. He hurried to the lift, which opened almost immediately when he hit the button. The door opened revealing one other passenger, a short, petite woman whom he recognized but couldn't recall a name for. Vincenza, maybe? She glared at him, and he hurriedly stepped through the door. She continued to stare at him once he was inside, even after the door closed and they were on their way. Three decks later they stopped, and the doors opened.

"I was just doing my job," he said, as he stepped out. He thought he heard her scoff before the door closed, but he might have imagined it.

In the office two women and a man occupied three of the ten

workstations arranged along the walls. Katrina Wu, an older woman, was the dispatcher, and the other two were officers like him.

"In here," called Darvan. His office occupied one corner of the space, separated from the rest by mostly soundproof polymer walls. Another officer, Julian Adebayo, the chief's favorite and Rector's primary competition for deputy director, was already in there standing in front of a smart board. "Listen up," said Darvan. "This was Adebayo's case, now it's yours."

Rector didn't immediately understand that. Adebayo was the boss's boy, and if he was being honest, a pretty good Secfor officer, too, even though they had different methods. Adebayo took lead on most of the important cases, which was something Rector had mixed feelings about. On the one hand, a few high-profile cases would help in his quest for the promotion. But on the other hand, screwing up a high-profile case could end him—or Adebayo—for good. He couldn't mention any of that to the director, so all he said was, "The whole thing?"

"The governor wants you, so he can fucking have you," said Darvan. Yep. Definitely pissed, which seemed unfair. Rector couldn't control the governor.

"Roger, boss." He turned to Adebayo. "What've you got?"

"Last night there was another data breach in the space exploration department. Information was stolen from the system of Dr. Sheila Jackson, who is the deputy director of science and medicine for space exploration. Our cyber-forensics team traced the source of the breach and identified the system."

"That's a good start." Rector meant it. They hadn't been able to figure out where the initial breach had come from, so this was at least a step up from that.

"Not really. The system that initiated the breach was the work terminal of Elizabeth Paulsen."

"The director of manufacturing? That can't be right," said Rector.

"Obviously," said Adebayo. "Somebody broke into her workspace and used her system."

"Did you check the cameras?"

Adebayo smacked his forehead. "Holy shit, why didn't I think of that?"

"Really—"

"Of course I checked the fucking cameras," said Adebayo, cutting him off. "Somebody got to those, too. Our team estimates three total hackers worked in concert to make this happen."

Fucking dick. Rector had initially felt a little bad for taking Adebayo's case. Not anymore. "Do we know what they got?"

"Everything on Jackson's system, which, according to the report that she submitted at 0817 this morning, included the past eleven days' worth of data sent to her from two different satellites in the Promissa system. According to her, the data, in the hands of a trained scientist, gives a very good initial picture of the possibility for colonization of the planet, and even in uneducated hands, a quick net search could give somebody a pretty good idea."

"So you flagged the keywords on the net," said Rector, careful to phrase it as a statement this time instead of a question.

"Exactly. No hits yet."

Rector considered it. Someone who was savvy enough to pull off a hack like the one last night would know how to get around that, so it seemed unlikely to pan out. "What else have you got?"

"Just one more thing. We caught a break in the first data breach."

"Yeah?"

"An hour ago, we got an anonymous tip about the source of the atmosphere information and the lost contact with the first probe."

"Any chance it's the same hacker?"

Adebayo shook his head. "Not the hacker, I don't think. What we got was a scientist. She doesn't have a record, and there's nothing to suggest that she has coding skills beyond the baseline that any scientist has. The tip said that she was the one who initially told people about the information, and it spread from there. Patient zero, if you will. So there's a chance that there wasn't a breach at all. Maybe she got the information from her own directorate and spread it."

Rector whistled. "That's big. Have you brought her in?"

"She's in the interrogation room, waiting for you. With your recent notoriety, I thought it best if you weren't seen picking her up, so I had somebody else do it."

"Thanks," said Rector. That was smart, and he probably wouldn't have thought about it. And now he felt a little bad for taking the case from Adebayo again. But it was his whether he wanted it or not, so there was nothing for it but to get started. "I guess I better get to it, then, if we have to brief the governor in three hours."

"Guess so," said Adebayo.

"Don't fuck it up," said Darvan.

RECTOR TRIED TO PUT DARVAN AND ADEBAYO OUT OF HIS MIND AS he observed Lila Jurgens via monitor as she sat in the interrogation room while simultaneously pulling up her file on his device. She was a pretty woman, tall, aged twenty-six, and with nothing but excellent evaluations. He shouldn't technically have had access to those, but somebody—probably in cyber—had included it in the packet. He didn't have a problem with that. It helped him understand her, and sometimes they danced around the rules a little for the greater good.

She was a senior space exploration technician, but he didn't know exactly what that entailed beyond the obvious. No suspicious connections; her only infraction was a warning for vandalism when she was sixteen. As Adebayo had said, nothing in her record indicated any sort of high-end computer skills, which on the surface likely meant she wasn't the hacker. Though that was exactly what a hacker would want him to think. He found the anonymous report that she was the source of the information and read it twice. The informant seemed confident enough, but you couldn't always trust the agenda of someone giving an anonymous tip.

He didn't know *anything* for sure, but he'd get it. He didn't have a choice. The boss would be watching him hard on this one, and if he screwed up even a little bit, Darvan would use it to bury him, regardless of what the governor wanted. That was fine. Adebayo had skills, but Rector had some, too, and this was his strong suit. He knew how to talk to people, to get them to talk to *him*. Having assessed both Jurgens's file and her body language as she waited, he had come up with his course of attack. He'd go in hard, scare the crap out of her, and she'd break. She'd tell him everything. He took a breath to center himself and then hit the button to open the door.

"Why'd you do it?" No greeting, no introduction. He asked it in his toughest voice and stared Lila down as he walked to the chair on the opposite side from where she sat. His shoes clacked against the hard floor of the room, a satisfying sound that emphasized his power in the situation. The door closed behind him.

Lila stared back, and for several seconds, silence blanketed the room. Then she started crying. It began as tears but quickly turned to sobs, growing in violence until her whole body shook.

Unsure what to do, Rector fidgeted, and then sat. He had wanted to break her, but he hadn't expected it to be quite that easy.

A small part of him felt like an asshole, but only a small part. That was the job. Now all he had to do was throw her a tether. "It's okay."

"I didn't. Mean. It," she wheezed between sobs. "I didn't. Want—"

"Take it easy." Rector stood and walked to a locker built into one of the walls, opened it and took out a packet of tissues, which he brought back to Lila. "Here, take these."

She took them, fishing one out and blowing her nose, and then another to wipe her eyes. "My career is over."

"Maybe not," offered Rector.

"I've been arrested," she said, looking like the sobs might come back any second.

"You're not under arrest. You're just here for questioning. And you said you didn't mean to do it. Maybe we can work something out." He couldn't believe that she was making it this easy, and for a second he considered the possibility that she was playing him. Using tears as a way to soften him. He didn't think so, but even if she was it didn't matter. He'd still turn it around and get what he needed.

She looked at him, and for the first time there was hope on her face. If she was faking, she should have been an actress instead of a scientist. "Yeah?"

"It's just you and me here. Tell me what happened."

"You, me, and that camera in the corner."

Rector shook his head. "Nope. That camera is here for your safety . . . to make sure that while you're in here, nothing happens to you. But it's video only. No sound."

"You expect me to believe that?"

"It's the truth," said Rector honestly. "You have rights. We're only allowed to record you if we specifically tell you it's being recorded, and it has to be with a recorder you can see. It's the law. I promise."

"Okay. I told two people about the information, but we were drinking, and there were a lot of people around, so I don't even know if it was them who told someone else or if somebody overheard us."

"Where were you drinking?"

"Café Regal."

Rector made a note in his device. "And why did you share the information?"

"I don't know. Because it was exciting, I guess? I really didn't see how it mattered if people knew about it. It didn't seem like something that would be secret. And I had no idea all that stuff would happen."

Rector thought about it, wondered if she knew about his role in the "stuff that happened." She didn't seem to recognize him, and he didn't mark her as a skilled pretender. He thought she was exactly what she seemed to be: a scared academic in over her head. He didn't want her to start crying again, but he did have to push her for more information. Maybe if he couched it as a way for her to get out of trouble, that would help. "I have one more thing to ask, and then I'm going to get you out of here."

She nodded. "Okay."

"Where did you get the information?"

"It was in our department files. I just opened it from my computer." She was a horrible liar. She might as well have been holding her breath as she tried to get the falsehood out, she was so uncomfortable.

"Lila." He paused until she met his eyes. "I know that's not true. We checked every computer in your department, and nobody accessed the information from there." At least he assumed they checked it. Adebayo was thorough. Having just taken over the case, Rector himself didn't have that information, but Lila didn't know that. "If you want me to help you stay out of trouble, you have to be honest with me. Where did you get the information?"

She stared down at the table. "I accessed it from my computer in my quarters."

"See? That wasn't so hard. There's nothing illegal about that."

"It's against the rules in my department," she said.

"Okay. Maybe. Sure. But it's not a crime. Now . . . how did you gain access to the specific information? You shouldn't have had rights."

"It was just there," she blurted. "I swear."

Interesting. He was as sure that she was telling the truth as he had been previously that she was lying. "I believe you."

Tension leeched from Lila's neck and shoulders. "It's the truth."

Rector nodded and pretended to make another note in his device. "Just one more thing. If it's against the rules in your department, how did you get a work order to access work files from your apartment? Your director would have had to approve it."

Lila's eyes went wide.

So that was it—the thing she did wrong. Rector would have bet anything on it. It almost seemed too simple, and for a moment, he wondered again who the anonymous tip came from. Something was still off, though. Her crime seemed too small to have her this worked up. There had to be something more to it, so he decided to take a stab at it and gauge her reaction. "Who did the hack for you?"

She met his eyes. "How did you know?"

He held back a smile. He hadn't known until she confirmed it, but it made sense. A hack like that wasn't a major crime, but to him it was another step, another person he could push on for information. If they'd been involved in the first breach, there was at least some chance they'd been part of the second as well, and that was the real prize. "It's my job to see through things like this."

She breathed audibly through her nose, nervous. "I can't tell you. I don't want her to get in trouble."

It was a woman. That in itself was helpful since it cut his possible suspects in half. "They're not in that much trouble. Sure, the result was a big deal, but that wasn't their fault. Their infraction is probably nothing more than unauthorized access. That's a fine, not brig time." That wasn't *completely* true, but it wasn't a total lie. The law technically allowed quite a bit of leeway for computer crimes, but nobody had seen the brig for committing one in as long as he could remember.

Lila looked at him with her big, brown eyes. She was so close to spilling it that he could almost taste it. Just one more push.

"Look, I hate to be a hard-ass . . . but it's her or you."

Lila stared down at her hands, folded on the gray table, considering it. For his part, Rector was willing to give her all the time she needed. It wasn't like she was going anywhere until she told him. It was probably thirty seconds before she whispered, "Eddie Dannin."

AFTER RECTOR WALKED LILA TO THE EXIT AND SAW HER OFF, HE found Darvan standing in the door of his office, looking out into the bullpen, waiting on him.

"So? How did it go? Did you find our hacker?" asked Darvan.

Adebayo was still in the office, and he was definitely paying attention. Rector wondered if Darvan had the other man shadowing the case, ready to jump back in at the first sign of Rector struggling. He couldn't get past the idea that Darvan wanted him to fail. He wasn't sure why, whether it was professional or personal, but the reason didn't matter. Rector's instinct was screaming for him to protect himself, and he always trusted his instinct. "I got nothing. It was a bullshit lead. She wasn't the source."

The lie came easy. Lila wouldn't tell them, and he could always walk it back later, once he had a better feel for where he stood. Meanwhile, he could solve the case himself without them looking over his shoulder.

"You sure she was telling the truth?"

"I'm absolutely sure she told me the truth." This time it wasn't a lie. He was sure that Lila had told him the truth. He just wasn't sharing that truth with them. Now he had to brief the governor, but later he'd find Eddie Dannin and get to the bottom of the second data theft.

If Darvan wanted to play games, okay—they could play. But Rector was going to raise the stakes. He'd get his promotion one way or another, and he'd arrest the hacker and protect the ship while he was at it. The governor had called him a hero, and while part of him knew that was bullshit propaganda, another part of him knew that he *could* be.

<CHAPTER 9>

JARRED PANTEL

115 CYCLES UNTIL ARRIVAL

The governor sat with his feet up at his desk while Marjorie Blaisdell stood at the smart board that came down from the ceiling, briefing him on the growing opposition to mandatory end of life at age seventy-five.

"It's a pretty loose group right now, with maybe a hundred people who have taken physical action against the practice in the form of protest. Some number of them have showed up at every scheduled Sleep appointment since the incident, sometimes protesting, other times just making themselves present. We've got video of them and a list of names."

"Have they stopped any of the appointments?"

"Not yet. There have only been three since the incident, and all of the people scheduled for Sleep have done their duty. The protestors haven't physically tried to stop them."

"That's good," said Pantel.

"The problem is that the idea itself is gaining momentum. It's polling at 42 percent, and that's without much more than word-of-mouth effort to raise the issue. It's only a matter of time until someone else refuses, and then we have a confrontation. The thing we've got going for us is that the movement is mostly young people, and, by definition, the people who are scheduled for Sleep are not young and therefore are more likely to do their duty."

"Okay. We can swing public opinion back, but we have to act before we have another incident. I don't trust Secfor to handle it appropriately, unfortunately. Let's focus on the leaders. Who's in charge?"

"Nobody," said Blaisdell. "That's the thing. It's organic. No announced organization at all. There might be leaders behind the scenes, but to date, nobody is talking about them. I do expect someone will come forward soon, though. Maybe more than one person. There's a lot of cachet in being at the head of something like this."

That seemed to be a hole in Blaisdell's intelligence gathering, but he decided not to mention that and instead focused on the problem at hand. If he let the movement grow organically, it would, and an organized cohort under a strong leader might not stop at just preventing end-of-life procedures. If he believed it would end there, he'd just let them have their way. They were close to their destination, and relaxing the guidelines for a short time wouldn't overly tax the ship's resources. The issue was that if he gave in on this, they'd be encouraged to demand more and more. That could threaten their entire way of life, perhaps even damage the ship itself—and later the colony. "We need to be the ones who change it," he said.

Blaisdell considered him for a moment. "You lost me."

"If we wait, someone charismatic and with a lot of drive is going to come to the fore, right?"

"Sure. Probably," said Blaisdell. "Someone ambitious at a minimum."

"So we don't wait. We pick their leader."

"Okay. I see where you're going, and I'm with you in theory. How do you want to do it?"

"Take a look at people near the front of the developing movement and pick somebody we can manipulate. Not completely incompetent—it needs to be believable—but definitely someone they wouldn't pick organically. We want someone who will see reason and not protest for the sake of protest."

"The group will just turn on them."

"Maybe. Maybe not. Whichever way it goes, we win. Either we get our person in charge, or they spend their energy bickering among themselves. We split them. A few small groups of angry people are fine. One organized group, not so much. Work fast. Pick somebody today, and I want to meet with them here tomorrow morning. We'll leak it to the news that I'm meeting with the movement leader to work out their demands, and they'll run with it. Once it's out there around the ship, it will be hard for anybody to put it back in the vacuum pack."

Blaisdell chuckled. "So we pick their leader for them and then negotiate with that leader. I like it."

"There's risk, for sure, but not as much as letting the movement go unchecked. They're blinded by what's happening in the moment and not thinking ahead. We can't afford to run a long-term mission that way." He paused, another idea forming. "We should name their movement. Something that will turn the general populace against them."

"How about Eternal Lifers?" offered Blaisdell.

"Eternal. I like it. It makes them seem unreasonable."

"Okay. I'll get to work. But . . . are you sure about this? Once we go down this corridor, we can't turn around."

"I'm sure. We've got too many variables in play, and we need to eliminate the ones we can. What if we find the planet to be uninhabitable? I know the data looks good so far, but it's not a hundred percent. Mandatory end of life is part of the Charter, and we need to stick with that foundation. We're coming into one of the most critical moments in human history, and what we need to survive it is organization and law and order. A firm hand."

"I'll have their new leader for you tomorrow." Blaisdell clicked off the smart board and it slipped back into the ceiling.

"Good. Now what do we know about the data breach?"

"Security doesn't have a suspect yet. Darvan has reassigned the case to Rector, like you asked."

"How did he take that?" asked Pantel.

"He's pissed. He sees it as you interfering in his job. He's not likely to work very hard to support Rector."

"I'm sensing a 'but' here."

"But," said Blaisdell, smiling, "that might work to our advantage. Rector isn't an idiot. He probably understands that he's out of favor with Darvan. So if we were to work *with* him . . ."

Pantel smiled. "Have I told you lately how much I appreciate your work? I'll talk to him."

"You have, but it's never a bad thing to hear." She paused. "But I get a sense there's more to this data breach than you're telling me. Something's bothering you."

Not for the first time, Pantel was glad that she was on his side. She was good. "Yeah, you're right."

"What's up?"

"Something feels off. Why haven't we seen the data yet?"

The corners of her mouth turned down as she thought. "What do you mean?"

"Someone hacked in to steal this information, but it hasn't gone public yet. So . . . why? Why put in that effort and then not do anything with it?"

Blaisdell leaned back against the table, tapping her lips with her index finger. "I don't know. Maybe they're analyzing it to figure out what it means."

"Maybe. But I looked at the information and even I could tell pretty quickly what was important. No . . . I think there's another motive."

"Like what?"

"Could it be money?" asked Pantel.

Blaisdell grunted. "Maybe. Can't ever rule it out, I guess. It's easy enough to find out if that's the case."

"Yeah?"

"Sure. If somebody's selling something dirty, there are rules."

"And you know them."

Blaisdell smirked. "Of course."

"Make a call. Let's see what we're dealing with."

"On it." With that, she departed.

Pantel took a minute to think things through. He didn't like leading by deception, but he didn't have a better option. And Blaisdell could be too agreeable sometimes—she wouldn't push back enough on his ideas even if she thought they were flawed.

He'd have to discuss it with his wife. He tried to keep her out of political things—she didn't have the taste for it—but she did have an unfailingly accurate bullshit detector. Especially when it came to *his* bullshit. He'd be a fool not to include her in something as big as this. He picked up his comm and buzzed her.

PANTEL MADE THE JOURNEY TO THE SECFOR OFFICES FOR HIS BRIEFING with Security Director Darvan and his underling, Rector. Sure, he could have summoned them to his own space, but he liked to get out and about, occasionally, to see the ship. And it never hurt to show up at your subordinates' workplace, remind them that you *could*. If Darvan was more comfortable in his own office, it didn't show. He fidgeted, glanced to a couple of the other Secfor personnel who came to the briefing, as if looking for support. Pantel couldn't tell if the director was nervous because of the visit, or because he had absolutely no useful leads on the identity of the hacker or the purpose of the data breach.

The only person in the room who looked comfortable was Rector, who didn't present anything revelatory in his part of the briefing, either, but somehow looked smug about it. Pantel had believed there might be a rift between Darvan and Rector before, but now he was sure of it. He found his mind drifting away from what they were saying and focusing on that instead. How he could exploit it. He had to treat Darvan with care. They weren't enemies, and even if they weren't completely aligned, he still needed Secfor. If nothing else, they'd make a convenient target for the protestors. If someone attacked a security officer, that would sway public opinion against the protestors in a hurry.

He met Darvan's eyes as he spoke. "I want a security presence outside of the Sleep facility for every appointment. I'm told there are protestors there every time now, and I don't want them to disrupt even one. As soon as they do that, it's going to multiply the problem."

"You know we don't have a lot of extra personnel hours," said Darvan.

Directors, Pantel thought. They never missed an opportunity to whine about personnel and how busy they were.

"And while we're at it," said Rector, "we should put some guards on the printers." The man clearly didn't see the way his boss was glaring at him. Or maybe he did and was ignoring it. Either way, it allowed Pantel to drive in a wedge to further the gap between the two.

He fought to suppress a smile as he asked, "What about the printers? Why would we need to do that?"

Rector continued while Darvan stared lasers at him. "The criminals, whoever they are, were able to break into manufacturing and use a terminal there while circumventing the cameras. If they can do that, what's to stop them from printing illegal items? When you combine that with a group of protestors, we could be talking about anything. Weapons, for example."

"We can put security drones on the printers," suggested Darvan with the enthusiasm of someone about to have a tooth filled.

Pantel considered the idea. It would probably work, but he couldn't see how it would help turn the ship against the protestors, and that was his primary purpose here, even if he couldn't say that to Darvan. "If they can hack cameras and get into the head of manufacturing's terminal, I don't think we can rule out the possibility of them hacking a drone. Or hacking the printers themselves to make them think they're printing something harmless when they're really not."

Darvan made a sour face but he couldn't argue, as all of them knew that printers had been hacked before. "I definitely don't have personnel to put a full-time guard on the printers."

"That's true," agreed Pantel.

Darvan started to speak again but stopped, perhaps not having expected Pantel to agree with him so readily.

Pantel filled the silence before the other man could recover. "What if I gave you extra people?"

"Where would you get them?" asked Darvan.

"I'm going to take them from other directorates. You'd have to train them, of course, but it shouldn't take much. They just need to watch the printers, inspect everything that comes off of them." The other directors would squeal about it, but that was the point. Directors had a lot of power, and this was a chance to make them feel the protests directly. If he hit them where it hurt, they'd be more likely to put pressure on their people not to participate.

"You know they're going to send me their worst people," said Darvan, but the argument had gone out of his voice. He just needed a little push. Of course he'd accept in the end. No director would turn down more people.

"I'll have each director submit five names, and you can go over their files and choose the candidates that you want."

Darvan considered it. "Okay. That will work."

"Good. How many can you use?"

"Twenty?"

"Twenty it is." That drew murmurs from the half dozen people watching the conversation from the walls, but Pantel kept his gaze focused on the director. "We good?"

Darvan hesitated for a couple of seconds, but then nodded.

"Good. Officer Rector, walk me back to my office? I have a couple more things I want to discuss about the data breach case."

Rector glanced at his boss, who was glaring at Pantel. What could Darvan do? He'd just agreed that they were good.

Rector waited until they were outside in the corridor before he spoke, another indication that he understood the situation the same way Pantel did. "What can I do for you, Governor?"

"I feel like you and I are on the same wavelength," said Pantel.

"I'd like to think so." It was a canny response by the Secfor man, agreeing without specifically committing to anything. It made the next step a risk for Pantel. Oh well. There was nothing to do but leap.

"I want to bring you in on something. One of my people is waiting to see me, and she might have information that helps your case." What better way to draw Rector closer to him than to trust him with some secrets?

"I'd welcome that." They walked in silence for a minute, allowing a couple of people to pass them, before Rector spoke again. "I might have a little more than I let on in the briefing."

"Might?" Pantel smiled. He liked this guy.

"I didn't want to spill everything to that audience. I don't trust everybody there."

Interesting. He wanted to ask more about that but decided to let it lie for now. He didn't need to get too far ahead of himself.

BLAISDELL WAS WAITING IN HIS OFFICE WHEN THEY GOT THERE. "I've got your answer about who has the data," she said.

"That fast?" He nodded and smiled. She'd done good work, as usual. "Nice job." He turned to Rector. "Have you met Marjorie Blaisdell? She . . . provides information."

"Mark Rector." The Secfor officer held out his hand and shook hers. "Good to meet you."

"You too," she said. "The Organization has the data."

"You're sure?" Pantel glanced to Rector to gauge his reaction, but the man had a straight face.

"As sure as I can be about something like this. Ninety-plus percent."

"You mean Sharakan?" Rector asked.

"Him, or someone close to him, yeah," said Blaisdell. "Probably him."

"What's he want with it?" asked Pantel. He knew of Shara-kan. Everybody did. But he also knew Sharakan wasn't tied to the protests—or not as far as they knew. That would have set off all kinds of alarms.

"He's selling it to the highest bidder. They're reaching out and soliciting offers, even as we speak."

"What? Why does it have value?" asked Pantel. "Who would pay for it?"

"I'm not sure," said Blaisdell. "People are interested, but I can't see a way to monetize it. Unless someone would pay for it just to further their agenda for change. One of the protestors."

Pantel sighed. "Can we stop it?"

"That's the money," interjected Rector.

"Excuse me?"

"You want to stop it. That's the value to Sharakan. He probably knows that you want it suppressed and believes that creates a market for it." He paused, assessing their reactions. "*You're* the money."

Blaisdell looked at Rector in that way that she had, perhaps seeing something she hadn't seen before. "It's funny that you mention that. My contact offered to let us buy it."

Pantel considered that. Rector was already proving his value. Knowing that was worth almost as much as the information itself. "What are our options?"

"We could pay them," said Blaisdell. "Or we could arrest some-one. Or several people."

Pantel looked to Rector. It was another opportunity to draw him in, asking for his opinion. "What do you think?"

"We could arrest people," replied the Secfor officer, though his folded arms and skeptical look said he thought it was a bad idea. "But if it's Sharakan, he's definitely got an alibi in place, and we'll never make it stick. And if we bring him in for questioning, which we can legally do if we want—or even if we bring in one of his top people—he might just release the data out of spite. A poison pill. So the best option if you want to stop it is probably to pay him."

Pantel nodded. Rector seemed sure of his assessment, and he had no reason to distrust him on this. "What's to stop them from taking our money and releasing it anyway?"

Rector shook his head. "Nope. They've got a code, and as odd as it seems, you can take them at their word on something like this. If Sharakan makes a deal, he'll stick to it."

Blaisdell nodded her agreement.

"How much?" asked Pantel

"Forty thousand lux," said Blaisdell.

Pantel snorted. "Right. Forty K. Nobody else can afford to pay that."

"But we can," said Blaisdell. "I'm sure the number is negotiable."

"This is a fucking mess." Pantel walked to his desk and sat, and the other two followed but remained on their feet. *Mess* was an understatement. The protestors weren't yet a problem on their own. They were disorganized, and he could keep them that way. But if the Organization got together with them . . . that was an entirely different matter altogether. He couldn't allow that. But he also couldn't pay forty thousand in ransom to a group of criminals without incentivizing them to commit another crime. "I need to think about it."

"We've got one full cycle," said Blaisdell.

Twenty-four hours. Great. "Got it. I'll keep the two of you informed." He looked at Rector. "If you need anything, you come directly to me. Understood?"

"Yes, sir. I appreciate it."

"And I trust that you will keep *me* informed as well."

Rector met his gaze. "Right. About that."

Pantel smiled. "You know who stole the data, don't you?"

Rector's face ran through multiple emotions in less than a second, but to his credit, he didn't hesitate much before responding. "Yes I do." He didn't elaborate, and Pantel didn't feel the need to push him. Let the man keep some of his secrets for now.

"What are you going to do about him?"

"Her," said Rector. "I'm going to bring her in and break her down. Once I do that, I'll see what charges I can make stick."

Pantel shook his head. "Don't do that."

Rector narrowed his eyes. "No?"

"The hacker is small change. What risk do they pose for now?"

"They could do it again. It's a constant threat until we eliminate it."

Something had dawned on him—an actual solution to a few of their problems. "Unless we remove that threat in another way."

Rector thought about it. "You lost me."

Pantel smiled. "I'm going to make the data that she stole public. After that, it's worth nothing, so there's no financial motivation for her—or anybody else—to do it again."

"Public?" Rector and Blaisdell said at the same time.

"Public," said Pantel. "They want to blackmail me? I'll *give* their secret away."

"It could work," allowed Blaisdell.

Rector nodded. "Interesting. That'll definitely shake things up a bit."

"I'm counting on it. And I want *you* to be ready to exploit it. Keep an eye on your hacker. Whoever used her for this will use her for something else, and next time it might be something more important."

"Even with you releasing the data, if we bring her in now, we cut it off before it happens," said Rector.

"Think bigger."

Rector considered it. "You want to nail who she works for. Sharakan."

"Exactly. If we could definitively tie something to him . . . well, we probably still couldn't arrest him. But it would give us leverage, right?"

Rector licked his lips. "Yeah. Okay. I can work with that."

"Before you go, I want to make sure that we understand each other, so let me just lay it out there. I think we can do a lot of good working together."

Rector smiled and nodded slightly. "I'm on board for that."

THE FOLLOWING MORNING, PANTEL STOOD FROM HIS SEAT AT THE conference table in his office as Jeremy escorted in the newly minted leader of the Eternal Lifers. Pantel knew everything about George Iannou, having selected him from the three options that Blaisdell had presented to him the night before. He was a couple years younger than Pantel, at fifty-three, and he had a daughter he was close with. His ex-wife and he were cordial, but rarely spoke. The man stood there, wearing worn coveralls over his vac suit, staring all around the office, clearly intimidated. His boots had flaked dirt onto the carpet.

Jeremy played his role perfectly. "Sir, this is Mr. George Iannou, the leader of the protestors."

Iannou flinched at that. "I wouldn't say I'm the leader."

Pantel walked around the table and offered his hand. Iannou's grip was crushing, and Pantel realized that as a farmer, the man spent most of his workdays in full gravity. He waited until he had his hand back before speaking. "I think you'll find that you *are* the leader. In fact, there's probably footage of you entering my office and an announcement that we're meeting running on the news feeds right now."

Iannou glared at him for several seconds. "You son of a bitch. I knew something was up with this. You screwed me."

"Only a little bit," said Pantel, keeping his voice light. "Have a seat. Hear me out, and you can call me names later."

Iannou fumed for several seconds more, unmoving, and Pantel briefly began to rethink his decision. If this giant man decided to take out his frustrations physically, there wasn't much he or Jeremy could do to stop him. Finally Iannou acquiesced and took the chair at the other end of the table.

"Coffee?" offered Pantel.

"No."

"So, Mr. Iannou, what is it that your group wants?"

"I told you, it's not my group."

Pantel held his hands out to each side, as if to say *What can you do?* "Surely you know what *you* want, then. You've been at almost every protest."

Iannou continued to glare. "You know what we want. We want an end to mandatory deaths."

"The need for mandatory end of life is firmly laid out in the Charter, signed by fifty representatives of the First Crew. There's an established way to alter the Charter, should you want to put forth a proposal to do that."

"Charter alterations are impossible. They require a 60 percent vote from 70 percent of divisions."

Pantel knew all that, though he was surprised that the farmer did. The man wasn't an idiot. That was good. His elevation to leader needed to look plausible. "I'm told it's a popular issue."

"Not *that* popular."

"Regardless, the First Crew was directed by the Founder to consider all situations when they drafted the Charter."

"The Founder was a rich asshole whose only contribution to the mission was to fund it with some of his trillions."

Pantel almost laughed. That was absolutely true, but it was a horrible political position, which made him glad to hear Iannou say it. He almost wanted to get the man his own news conference so he could trash the Founder and the First Crew publicly. The movement would be over by the end of the week. "Either way, the procedure is the procedure."

"There are other options."

"Such as?"

The big man didn't speak for several seconds, perhaps debating with himself what to share, before finally saying, "I don't know."

Pantel held back a smile. It was almost too easy. But he had to play the part, pretend to be acting in good faith. "Look, I know it's frustrating. But we have to put the ship first. I'm happy to explain that to people. I just need you to help me. Can you do that, George?"

Iannou studied him, and for a moment Pantel thought the man was going to grow a spine and tell him off. But when he finally spoke, it was barely audible. "Yeah. I can do that."

AN HOUR LATER, PANTEL STOOD BEHIND A PODIUM IN THE MEDIA room, a separate space from his office complex where ship leaders could record messages for broadcast to the entire contingent. Those messages would repeat regularly, since there wasn't enough news in a community their size to fill an entire cycle's worth of programming. Two of the ship's four news personnel were here for this, recording live, to give the proceeding a more important feel. Two cameras, one crewed and one remote, added to the production.

Pantel wanted to keep the remarks about the protests short. On the surface, he was directing his comments to the opposition group, but in reality his target was the rest of the community. If they turned on the protests, the opposition group would fade away.

"Fifteen days ago, there was an incident on this ship. I think most of you have probably heard about it by now, but I wanted to address you, the citizens of this great ship, about it directly. For the first time in memory, one of our own turned her back on her duties to the ship and refused to go to her final appointment. This man"—he indicated Rector, standing off to the side, then waited for the cameras to come back to him—"went to apprehend her, at which time she assaulted him with a deadly weapon. In the ensuing scuffle, Officer Rector followed his training and moved to disarm the woman with his standard-issue stun stick. Due to her advanced age, the shock overwhelmed the assailant's system, and she passed."

Pantel paused, keeping his eyes directly on one of the cameras. "Officer Rector is to be commended for his by-the-book actions." He paused again, for effect. "However, in response to this routine and legal action, a group has arisen calling itself the Eternal Life Coalition. This group has been protesting the necessary functions of our ship that have held for over 250 years. A necessity so important that the First Crew placed it in our Charter.

"These Eternal Lifers are a threat to our values, a threat to our ship, a threat to our very lives. Friends, we live in a resource-constrained environment. Hopefully one day we won't, but it's irrational to wish for something until we can verify it.

"Now . . . I admit, some of this is my fault." He switched his gaze to the second camera and did his best to fake a look of contrition. "There is information about the planet Promissa, and some of that information, both true and false, is making its way around the ship. I should have done a better job managing that." He could admit to that minor sin. Sometimes you had to mix in some truth to sell the rest of it. "But no more. I will not shirk my responsibilities to this ship, even if the Eternal Lifers shirk theirs. I am ordering the director of science to make all data received from the probes orbiting the planet public, no later than two cycles from now. I give her that long not to keep information from you, but to allow her to determine the best mechanism to share it."

One more pause as he let that part of the message sink in. "In addition to that, due to an increased risk to the ship from the Eternal Lifers, I am requisitioning additional security personnel from every directorate. For those of you chosen, you have my thanks. I know you'll do your duty. Thank you, and may the ship fly true."

Pantel waited for the lights on the camera to switch off, and then came out from behind the podium, shook hands with Rector for the benefit of the nine or ten onlookers in the room, and then joined his staff. "What did you think?"

"Good speech, sir," said Jeremy. The attending PR specialist nodded and smiled.

"Thanks." He walked toward the exit.

As he headed to his office, Blaisdell fell in beside him. "He's right. It was a good speech. I think you'll catch some people by surprise by releasing all the data."

"We have to keep the Organization separated from the Eternal

Lifers. What better way to do that than to make sure they don't have anything the Lifers want?"

"Good thought."

"Plus, fuck them for thinking they were going to hold me out an airlock for forty thousand lux."

Blaisdell laughed. "Indeed."

<CHAPTER 10>

GEORGE IANNOU

||||||||||||||||||||||||||||||||||||||||||||||||||||||||||||||||||||||

114 CYCLES UNTIL ARRIVAL

It had been several hours since his meeting with the governor and the governor's subsequent news conference, and as he sat at his table eating reheated noodles, he still wasn't sure what happened. It wasn't good, though. George wasn't a leader of the movement, wasn't really a leader of anything. He was a farmer. It wasn't that he was against the protestors—mandatory deaths needed to go. But he'd only gone himself because Anazar had told him to. The same reason he'd ended up talking to the governor. He didn't hold Anazar at fault. George believed that his boss had been manipulated as much as he had. But he had known it was a bad idea before he went, and he wished that he'd pushed back more.

The noodles were bland and tasteless. He hadn't planned for that to be dinner—he was supposed to be dining in the common facility with Kayla. But given the reaction of people at work when the news feed had shown him walking into the governor's office with *Eternal Life Protest Leader* under his picture, he figured it best to avoid the public eye for now. He'd told Kayla he wasn't feeling well, but he probably hadn't fooled her. She watched the news.

He was a coward. Part of him wondered if the governor chose

him because he wanted somebody he could push around. That was paranoid, though. The governor probably picked him at random. He'd been at all the rallies, and at his size, he did stand out in the crowd. Assigning more motive than that seemed a little cynical.

Kayla entered her apartment next door, and a few seconds later she came through to his. "You okay, Dad?"

George grunted. "Depends on who you ask. Koshi Tanaka says I'm a self-serving sycophant."

"I'm asking *you*. What other people think is irrelevant."

Was it, though? He'd worked with the same people for years, and as much as he wanted to believe her, Kayla had a young person's naïveté about some things. "It's going to make life difficult. I've got to go back to the governor and set the record straight."

"Absolutely not!" Kayla slid into the chair across from him, produced a fork from somewhere, and stole a bite of his noodles.

"Hey!"

"You're barely eating them," she said, talking through a mouthful.

George laughed at that, which surprised him. He hadn't thought he could do that in his current mood, but then, Kayla had always been able to break him out of any funk. "I'm not the right person. I'm no leader."

"That's what makes you perfect for it."

George looked at her, looked for the joke in it, but saw she was serious. "How do you figure?"

"Anybody who *wants* to be a leader has an agenda. They're either laser focused on a single outcome or they're out for themselves and their own ego. Probably both."

"It's impossible," said George. "The governor has everything twisted around and he's going to hold to every bullshit bureaucratic thing in the law to prevent any real change. And on the other side, everybody wants something different. You've got Tanaka, who I think wants to foment full-on anarchy, and others who want everything from the basic end to mandatory deaths to medical reform to a full-scale rewrite of the Charter. Nobody is going to listen."

"Yeah, but they all forgot one thing."

"What's that?"

"They're all counting on dealing with a politician. You're a farmer. And you know what we say about farmers."

George sighed, realizing that his daughter had led him to his own words. "They get shit done."

"Exactly. What did the governor tell you when you met with him today?"

"He said that if we want change, we can initiate a change to the Charter."

"Pfft. That's bullshit."

"That's what I told him," said George.

Kayla thought about it. "How much do you know about the Charter revision process?"

George shrugged as he downed a bite of noodles. "I don't know. Not much. The basics that everybody knows, probably."

"I guess you've got some studying to do, then." Kayla rose, smiled, stole another bite of noodles from his plate, and then danced away before he could stop her.

GEORGE DIDN'T EVEN MAKE IT TO WORK THE FOLLOWING DAY BEFORE people started accosting him. He walked to the elevator with a woman who cursed him out for, in her words, caving to the governor. On the way down to the ag levels, another man praised him and told him to fight the good fight, whatever that meant. It was at least nice to know that not everybody hated him. When it really hit him was when he walked into his morning meeting and the room went silent. There were nine people already gathered inside, and he glanced around, noting the faces, who was there and who wasn't. Most notably, Mr. Anazar, the boss, wasn't there.

"What's up?" asked George, more to break the awkward silence than anything else.

"Sit down," said Tanaka. "We need to talk."

George didn't move immediately, considering his options. "Okay. Do I get to talk, too?"

"We've been discussing our situation all night," said Sara Washburn. "We've come to some decisions—some agreements—and I think once we explain ourselves, it'll answer some of your questions. So if it's okay, we'd like to speak first, and then you can have your say afterward."

Coming from Sara, George found it easier to accept than if it had come from Tanaka, so he moved to take a seat. "Okay. Is anybody else coming?"

"They're not," said a younger man. George recognized his face but didn't know anything else about him. "There are people who aren't comfortable being part of this, and the boss was nice enough to give us the meeting to work through our . . . issues."

George nodded. "Okay."

"I'm Leonard Kaslov," the man continued. "I work in protein. For Ms. Washburn." He hesitated. "Sorry, I mean Sara."

"It's good to meet you, Leonard." Given the younger man's hesitance in addressing Sara, George assumed that the first-name basis was a new thing for him. It also highlighted something about the group overall. While it contained several section leads or their immediate assistants, at least three members besides Leonard weren't part of the traditional leadership. That was interesting, and it told him at least a little bit about this opposition group he'd found himself in charge of.

That was how he thought of them now. Opposition to the governor. Not the government. The governor.

"You too. We represent a wider group from across the ship. After a *long* discussion, we have decided to accept you as the leader of the movement."

George wanted to respond but held it back. *They'd* decided. Without consulting him as to whether he wanted to do it or not. He'd accepted that his daughter was right, that he should take charge for now, but it still rankled that they'd just assume his participation. "If I can ask," he said carefully, "what led you to that?"

"Several things," said Leonard. "First, it's been all over the news, and as much as we might try to change that narrative, it would be difficult. And we have enough challenges right now. Second, the rest of us have varying ideas, from the more radical to quite conservative." He didn't mention anybody by name, but the way he cut his eyes to Tanaka when he said *radical* and to Washburn when he said *conservative* made it pretty clear.

"I assume you, by virtue of being the spokesperson, are somewhere in the middle?" asked George.

"Exactly right," said Leonard.

"Is it just people from ag involved?"

"We're the majority right now, but we've got representation from around the ship, and it's growing. Jodi Anford is here from maintenance, which is where all of this started." He indicated a person with short-cropped hair and an ambiguously gendered face.

"Good to meet you," said George.

"There's a strong opinion in maintenance about mandatory deaths," they said. "Mrs. Applebaum was well loved."

"Got it." George made a note in his device about that align-ment but wasn't sure how much it meant. An emotional reaction to a specific incident could start something but didn't always lead to sustained action.

"And Erica Chavez is here from engineering." The other per-son George didn't recognize raised her hand in greeting. "We've also got representatives from manufacturing and entertainment, but they couldn't get away from work to be here right now. How-ever, they were okay with me speaking on their behalf."

George nodded. And when the man didn't immediately con-tinue, he said, "Can I talk now?"

"Sure," said Leonard.

"First, before I address the idea of being in charge, I'd like to tell you what really happened in the meeting with the governor. It was a setup." George looked around, saw nods, and continued. "He knew I wasn't in charge. After thinking about it for a while, I now believe that was intentional on his part. He had everything planned. He said that if we want a change to the Charter, there are established rules for how to do that."

"The rules are impossible!" interjected Tanaka.

"Which is exactly what I told him." George gave him what he hoped was a good look of annoyance, but it didn't change the other man's expression.

"What else did you tell him about that?" asked Tanaka.

George shrugged. "Nothing. What could I say?"

"You could tell him we're going to strike."

"We're going on strike?"

"We're *not* going to strike," said Washburn, speaking loudly to cut Tanaka off. George got the impression from the way they looked at each other that it wasn't the first time they'd had that argument. It gave him a flash of what he could expect from them in the future, and he wasn't looking forward to it.

"We have to do something to let them know we're serious—"

"If I may," said Leonard, cutting Tanaka off smoothly, showing why they'd made him spokesman. Tanaka and Washburn both glared but remained silent. "Thank you. We feel that it's necessary to make it clear to the governor that his proposal to alter the Charter through established methods is insufficient."

George considered that for several seconds. "Okay. I can do that."

"*How?*" asked Tanaka, his voice dripping with contempt.

George met his eyes and held them. "I'm going to walk in there and fucking tell him."

For the first time since he got there, it seemed like nobody had anything else to say.

THE SMALL MAN IN THE GOVERNOR'S OUTER OFFICE—THE PLATE ON his desk said his name was Jeremy—was standing behind his desk, glancing back and forth between George and the door that led to the governor's office, and occasionally to the main door to the corridor, as if hoping someone would enter and break the tension. They wouldn't. George had made sure of that. The six volunteers he'd brought with him weren't exactly blocking the entry, but they weren't making it easy for people to get by, either.

"Maybe check again, see if his calendar has freed up?" offered George.

"I told you, I can get you in early next week," said Jeremy, clearly annoyed. They'd had the same exchange every fifteen minutes for the last hour.

"Okay. I'll wait."

Jeremy sat back at his desk, pretended to work. After a few minutes he got up and let himself into the governor's office. Less than a minute later, the governor himself appeared in the door.

"Mr. Iannou! To what do I owe the pleasure?" The smile on his face seemed genuine. If he was as annoyed as Jeremy, he was really good at hiding it.

"We need to talk." George kept his voice flat and didn't return the smile. He'd rehearsed this with Kayla. Whatever happened today, he wasn't buying into the governor's bullshit.

"Sure. Come on in."

"It won't take long. We can talk right here."

The governor hesitated. "Okay. What's on your mind?"

"Your proposal that we address our issues through the established Charter amendment procedures is unacceptable."

The governor raised his palms on either side of his body, as if saying, *What can I do?* "I'm sorry, but that's the law."

"It takes months to file and requires six months' debate time before there can even be a vote. We'll be in orbit around Prom before we even get a chance. Dozens of people will needlessly die."

"It's the procedure that the First Crew put in place."

George felt his control slipping away and raised his voice. "The First Crew isn't here. It's a completely different situation and they didn't consider it."

"I'm sorry. You really don't have any other options."

But he wasn't sorry. Until that moment, despite rehearsing it, George hadn't been sure how he'd respond to that. He hadn't expected the governor to roll over and give in to his demand. He wasn't that naïve. Not anymore. But he wanted to see the man's attitude before he committed to his next action. What he saw made him simultaneously sure that the governor had no intention of acting in good faith and that he wanted to punch the man in the face. "We could strike."

Pantel scoffed. "You do realize that we're all together on a ship in the middle of an unforgiving void, and a strike is not only illegal, but it could also lead to all of us dying."

Iannou gave him a flat smile. "I *do* realize that. You should think about what that means." The governor still hadn't responded when George reached the door and let himself out.

<CHAPTER 11>

EDDIE DANNIN

113 CYCLES UNTIL ARRIVAL

Cecil was pissed. He hadn't said as much—hadn't said anything, really—but the signs were there. Normally his narrowed eyes and hunched shoulders would have Eddie worried, but while she wasn't exactly happy to be meeting with him late at night in an empty recreation room, she was mostly sure that his anger wasn't directed at her. The governor had given away the data that they'd stolen, and now the work they'd done was worthless. Eddie really hoped she was still getting paid, but it wasn't the right time to bring that up. She didn't always pick up social cues, but she knew that much.

Mikayla was there, but she was acting more as a DJ than anything else, standing across the room playing pop music loud enough so nobody would overhear them but not so loud as to draw complaints. Cecil was now focused on two of his other workers, Rina Fetterman and Charlie the Pick (Eddie didn't know his real name). They'd broken into manufacturing with Eddie, and she was glad they had Cecil's attention and not her. She'd have preferred not to be there at all, but the invitation hadn't been optional.

"I know you're mad, boss," said Rina.

"I'm not mad. The governor got us. Sometimes that happens. I'm just trying to think through what we could have done differently."

"Nothing," said Charlie. "We had to try to sell the data, and to do that we had to tip off the people who might pay."

"There has to be a way," said Cecil. "There's always a way. More important, though—how do we monetize this kind of thing going forward?" They looked at one another in silence. After several seconds, Cecil's gaze fixed on Eddie.

"What?" she asked.

"You're our big brain when it comes to stealing information. What are your thoughts?"

Eddie resisted the urge to take a step back. Honestly, she was glad the plan had failed because it meant she didn't have to take the risk again. "I don't see what we can do if they're making everything public. Nobody's going to pay for what they get for free."

Cecil grunted, but it wasn't clear if it was a grunt of agreement or of something else.

"It feels personal," said Rina.

Cecil turned to her. "You think?"

She met his gaze without blinking. "Absolutely. The governor knew what we'd done, and he wanted to hurt us."

Cecil considered it. "You know, I think you're right."

Rina smiled. "So. What do we do about it?"

Eddie scrunched up her face. "What do you mean 'what do we do'? He's the governor."

Cecil turned back to her, and she immediately wished she hadn't said anything. "I don't care who he is. He fucked with me. He's gotta pay."

"But how? That's the question," said Charlie.

Cecil studied his meaty hands for a second and then looked

at each of them in turn. "That's definitely the question. You three think about it. How do we make him hurt? Get back to me with ideas."

Charlie and Rina nodded, and Eddie nodded, too. "You got it, boss," said Rina.

"Soon," Cecil added.

A WEEK LATER, EDDIE STILL HADN'T COME UP WITH ANY IDEAS. WELL, she had, but none that she wanted to share. It was easy enough to make someone hurt in her line of work. Everyone had secrets, and she could find them. But hacking the governor seemed like a horrible idea from a self-preservation standpoint. The last thing she wanted was to be smashed between Cecil and the governor, so she did what she always did in this sort of situation: She avoided it. She hid out, leaving her room only when she had to for work.

Today that work saw her piloting a maintenance bot between rows of grain. She wasn't sure if it was barley or wheat, if she was being honest—just that it was one of the few grain farms on the ship. Mostly they used algae, fungus, and crickets to produce the base materials that the food printers used. She'd learned that much about agriculture in school and forgotten pretty much everything else, other than how to maintain and fix their machinery. In this case, she was doing routine work, replacing gaskets in the drip irrigation system to prevent leakage. They changed seals every ten years, but with the thousands of kilometers of piping required to water the various plants that fed the ship and provided oxygen, maintenance techs were working on the task almost constantly.

The bot was about half a meter tall and almost as wide, and it propelled itself through the dirt of the farm deck on six all-terrain tires. They had apparently tried hovering bots early in the expedition, but the heat from the engines harmed the plants, so they had reverted to an old-fashioned solution. She used her work tablet to direct the bot's limited AI functions, which never failed to strike her as ridiculous. With a little time and effort she could upgrade the bot's AI so it could do the work by itself, but the ship had strict rules on the use of AIs because of some event or other that had happened on Earth a few centuries ago. It didn't stop her from tinkering with it, but she wouldn't do that here, where somebody might see and report it.

Even with having to pilot the bot, the work was nearly mindless, but it still beat working customer service. She used it as a mini vacation, paying more attention to the audiobook she was listening to than to the bot. The bot didn't move fast, and Eddie was glad of that as she trudged along behind it. The combination of walking in dirt and the 97 percent gravity meant that while the work was mentally relaxing, it was physically exhausting. At least for her. Exercise had never really been one of her passions, and she was a good enough hacker to override the monitor that insisted she spend ninety minutes a day in heavy gravity.

She was so lost in her work and the story in her earbuds— a murder mystery set on a fictional cruise ship—that when she saw a big man watching her from maybe fifteen meters away, she couldn't be sure how long he'd been there. There was nothing ominous about him, but she still got the feeling he had something important for her. At least in *his* mind. She paused her audiobook and called out, "Can I help you?"

The man walked toward her, lifting his feet deliberately to clear the dirt, as if the gravity didn't bother him and he did this every day. Which he probably did. His coveralls were dirty, and his well-worn boots were more suited to the dirt than to the rest of the ship. But his outfit still had the required seals that would allow him to quickly attach a helmet in case of oxygen loss. Not that that had ever happened, as far as Eddie knew. What struck her the most about the man were his shoulders. He was tall, but more than that he looked like he could rip the door off an airlock.

"You're Eddie, right?" he said.

"That's right." It was odd that he knew her name since she didn't know his, but not that far from the norm. They'd have a copy of the maintenance schedule in their devices, and it wouldn't take much for him to look it up. Why he'd bother to do that . . . that was another story. Maybe he was an overzealous supervisor or something, wanting to check her work. She paused the bot so she could focus on the big farmer. "What can I do for you?"

"I've got some information for you."

"Yeah? You got a name?"

"George. George Iannou."

It struck Eddie as familiar, but she couldn't remember from where. "I've heard of you, but I can't place it."

The man grunted. "Some people are calling me the leader of the Extended Lifers."

That was it, though Eddie had heard it called Eternal Lifers. "People are calling you that, or you *are* that?"

Iannou nodded. "That's a good question. I guess to some extent I am. But what matters at the moment is that I've got some information about you that I think you're going to want to know. Because of . . . uh . . . my affiliation."

Eddie glanced around, checking her surroundings, but the grain and the low ceiling conspired to limit her vision.

"No cameras can see us here," said Iannou, correctly guessing Eddie's concern.

"Yeah? What've you got?" Eddie almost asked what it was going to cost her, as that concerned her more than the information itself.

She kept pretty aware of things, and she doubted that a farmer had anything that truly affected her.

"Secfor is watching you."

She hesitated for just a second. Maybe he *did* have something that mattered—if he was telling the truth. But why would he lie? She could check it easily enough, and he hadn't asked for payment. It made sense. They'd brought Lila in for questioning ten or fifteen cycles before, and while she said that she hadn't given Eddie up, it wouldn't take a crack investigator to draw the connection. Eddie had actually expected them to bring her in as well and had only recently come to believe that they'd missed her. But of course they hadn't. "Watching me how? Like having me followed?"

"All I can tell you for sure is that you're a person of interest and that you're flagged by Secfor's cybersecurity division."

Well, shit. That shouldn't be possible. But . . . maybe? What did *flagged* mean? But even that they were watching her was embarrassing. She knew more about cybersecurity on the ship than most, so for a farmer to know something that she didn't . . . well . . . it stung a little. More than a little, maybe, assuming he had his information right. "And you know this . . . how?"

"So, uh . . . someone gave me a list of people who are flagged for additional scrutiny. I wanted to see which of my people were on it and which weren't, for . . ." His voice trailed off.

"For reasons that I don't need to know. Right. I get it," said Eddie. "And my name was on it. And you tracked me down because . . ."

His face tightened and his voice gained intensity, if not volume. "Because they shouldn't be allowed to do that." He paused. "They shouldn't be allowed to spy on people who haven't committed crimes."

Eddie kept a straight face. The man clearly believed what he was saying, though in Eddie's case, the *haven't committed crimes* part wasn't exactly true. "So this is completely altruistic."

Iannou looked down at his feet. "Not completely."

"Of course not. Listen—don't worry about it. We've all gotta do what we've gotta do to get by. I'm a capitalist. I don't hold it against you."

"Word is that you have a set of skills."

"Word is probably right," admitted Eddie, without giving anything extra away. The man seemed to be on her side, but a lot of people pretended to be a lot of things.

"Our group of . . . mutually aligned folks . . . could probably use your services."

Eddie wasn't sure what he was angling at, but she didn't do work for free. "I'm not hard to find. If you've got a contact feeding you insider information on Secfor, you've surely got somebody who knows how to go about employing me."

Iannou shifted his weight from one foot to the other. "We do."

"Okay then. I look forward to hearing from you." She paused, but he didn't take the hint and leave. "You do understand that I'm not going to accept a job right here, right now. I vet my customers." She paused again, before adding, "I understand your position within your faction, but . . . you're not vetted."

The man fidgeted, uncomfortable, despite being in his natural environment. "I appreciate your caution."

"But?" prompted Eddie, when he paused.

"But," he continued, "I was thinking more of you coming on as a partner in the cause than as a contractor."

Eddie half snorted before she got herself under control and schooled her face to neutral. The man in front of her was serious, and he hadn't meant it as a joke. She wasn't joining any cause, but she didn't need to embarrass him and make a potential enemy. Probably shouldn't, given that he might have enough sway with his group to make her life difficult. "I'm more of a 'what's in it for me' kind of person than a joiner, if you get my meaning. I'm sorry. I don't mean any offense."

Iannou nodded. "Totally okay. But can I *tell* you what's in it for you?"

Eddie glanced over her shoulder to her bot, still paused. She did need to get back to it, but it was an easy day and she had extra time. She couldn't say why, but Iannou seemed more confident all of a sudden. She had to admit, he intrigued her. "Sure."

"You're probably thinking to yourself, 'I'm twenty-one'—or whatever you are—'and I don't need extended life.'"

"That's a fair read," she allowed.

"I'm fifty-three. I don't need it, either. We'll be in orbit around Prom way before it affects me directly, and contrary to what the news feed is saying, I'm not just in this to save some old people. Sure, they deserve our help, but as you said . . . as *most* people say . . . what's in it for me?" He became more animated as he spoke, his voice rising. "It's not just about mandatory death. That's part of it. But there are a lot of things that the First Crew put into our Charter that we just accept as the way of things, and a lot of them don't apply anymore."

Eddie found herself nodding automatically. "Like what?"

"Like people being stuck in a directorate and not having any way to change it, even if they'd be happier doing something else."

A chill washed over Eddie despite the warmth of the farm deck. She couldn't tell if the man had been talking about himself or about her. She hadn't exactly made a secret of her desire to leave maintenance, but if he meant her, that still implied that someone was paying attention. "You're talking about large-scale change."

"Maybe not at first. Maybe one thing at a time. But . . . yeah."

Eddie considered it. She wanted out of maintenance and into engineering, but that wasn't actually going to happen. Maybe George believed it would, or maybe he was manipulating her to secure her help. He didn't *seem* like the sneaky type, but people could fool you. Regardless, something about him made her want to protect him. "They're going to come for you," she said. "You know that, right? The people in charge are going to do everything in their power to make sure things *don't* change."

"You're right." Iannou sighed. "I didn't know that thirty cycles ago, but I know it now. You're absolutely right." He paused and then smiled. "And that's why we could use someone like you."

This time Eddie did let herself laugh. "You. You, George Iannou, are good. I can see why they picked you as a leader."

"I don't think that's why they picked me, but maybe I've got some surprises for them. Look, I'm going to let you get back to work on the wheat field. We've all got schedules to keep. Just think about it, okay?" He extended a massive forearm, dwarfing Eddie's as she bumped it with hers.

"I will," said Eddie. Unlike when she'd told Cecil the same thing, she found that this time she meant it.

BACK IN HER ROOM, EDDIE STEPPED OUT OF THE SHOWER. SHE'D broken down and spent some lux for an extra twenty seconds of water. She was used to being filthy—it came with the territory when you worked maintenance—but having been on the farm deck all day, somehow dirt got everywhere. Dirt should *not* be able to find its way into a suit that would protect her for a period of time in a hard vacuum. She put on a sweatshirt and some soft pants. Inside her own room was the only place on the ship where she didn't have to wear a vac suit. The living quarters sealed themselves in case of an emergency, allowing time for people there to get into the proper gear before exiting into the ship to crew their emergency stations. Nobody wanted to sleep in a vac suit.

She put on socks—the deck was always cold, and rough enough where it irritated her skin. She kept meaning to buy herself a carpet, but she never got around to it. She didn't get around to much when it came to her living quarters. The only nonstandard thing in the room sat on her desk amid plastic containers of tools, circuit boards, and random parts that fit anything from bots to computers to entertainment centers. Her tools of the trade—and not her official one. Her computer *looked* like every other standard room model, but looks could be deceiving. She updated it regularly with the best processors the ship had to offer. The trickiest part had been adding liquid cooling, since the base room-model shell wasn't built for it. Now, she'd put it up against any rig on the ship, personal or otherwise.

She slipped into her haptic gloves and used them to call up a virtual keyboard, after which she began the complicated process of entering the net anonymously. Because as much as Iannou's words had struck her when he was talking about changing the Charter, something else he said hit her more. Cyber had her flagged. If true, *that* was a problem.

On the surface, her virtual environment looked unaltered, spartan, and sleek, much neater than her physical room but with the same level of practicality. This wasn't a place of relaxation; this was a place of work. She checked her alarms and triggers—all three layers of them—and when she found them undisturbed, she breathed a little easier. She wasn't defenseless. Then she shunted aside the virtual environment and flowed into the code itself, immersing herself in an almost subconscious way. If something was off, she'd feel it before she saw it.

There.

Just a tickle in the back of her brain, so subtle that she didn't know at first where it came from. But something felt wrong, so she grabbed the end of the thread and started pulling.

It was subtle, hidden, innovative. An active tracker would have tipped her immediately, but this was something different. A single line that wouldn't interact with her environment at all, hidden in a subroutine that she used to erase her own actions. Kind of brilliant, really, because it would act *almost* like it was supposed to. But if she'd been unaware of it, someone could use it to find her, if not in real time, then after the fact. A tag. The virtual equivalent of dipping her hand in red paint. They wouldn't necessarily know what she did, but they'd know where she went. Her heart rate spiked. How long had it been here?

She scrambled through her mind, half in the virtual world, half in the real, trying to remember where she'd been, how she might have incriminated herself. Thankfully, Lila's brush with security and the job she did for Cecil had caused Eddie to lie low. Once she tamped down the panic, her rational brain took over. She was nothing if not a problem solver, and she sat back and analyzed the situation. After looking at things from every angle, she came to the only logical conclusion.

She was fucked.

If she left the tag in place, someone could follow her, and it would be a matter of time until she went somewhere she shouldn't. Once that happened, she couldn't predict what they'd do with that information. Unacceptable. On the other hand, if she took it out, she might as well announce to whoever placed the tag that she'd discovered it. She couldn't get in trouble for that—it was her environment, after all, and she was allowed to secure it—but it wouldn't solve anything. Someone capable of doing this once could do it again, and as many times as Eddie searched it out, they could just keep placing them. It would never end. Slightly more acceptable, but not good.

She backed away from the code for a moment. She had to admit, the whole thing made her curious. On one level, she was impressed with the work. Someone who could do this was good. *Really* good. She could think of two people other than herself who could pull it off, but she couldn't come up with a reason either one of them would. They were competitors, sure, but like her, they didn't do things without a reason. Usually a financial one. And she could come up with only two options for who might have paid for it: Cecil or Secfor's cybersecurity.

Then the anger hit. This was fucking illegal. More than illegal—illegal on its own wasn't a deal-breaker—this was *wrong*. Now she understood a little better why Cecil wanted the governor to pay. She felt the same way. Someone needed to pay for this. The only question was who.

She really didn't think it was Cecil, because if he wanted to get at her he had more direct methods. Why challenge her in her world, where she was strong, when he could have Mikayla bounce her head off the wall? That left cybersecurity—the ship's government.

This is bullshit!

Because if they would do that, maybe George had been right. Maybe somebody needed to stand up to them.

But then a third thought crept in: Iannou wanted her on his side. What better way to do that than to turn her against the government? He had known that she'd been tagged, and maybe that was because he'd paid somebody to put the tracker in her system. That seemed a bit paranoid—he didn't seem like the type—but maybe somebody who worked with him had come up with the plan. There *was* a tracker in her system, so maybe a little paranoia wasn't unwarranted.

One thing was for sure: she couldn't trust anybody but herself, and that was fine. She didn't need help dealing with this hacker. No, she did not. You don't touch a hot wire, and whoever had done this . . . they'd touched the hottest fucking wire on the ship.

Now they were going to get shocked.

They wanted to come after her? That was like the cricket coming for the protein blender. She dove back into the code, not absorbing the whole of it this time, but instead as focused as a cutting laser. She whipped together her own construct, not benign like the tag they'd put on her, but malicious and ugly and exploitative. She didn't delete theirs—didn't even touch it. Instead, she locked it inside of another of her own constructs so it would keep broadcasting, send proof of life. Except instead of telling them what she was doing, it would send them a false version depicting whatever she wanted them to see. That was her *defense*. Offensively, she ensconced the malicious code in the intruder's bubble. When they searched for it to track her, they'd bring her worm right back to their own system, opening a portal for her to follow. See how they liked that.

She sat back and looked at the code with a grim little smile. Whatever she chose to do with it in the future, it gave her options. She could track it and still remain on the outside, find out who they were and reevaluate. As a bonus, she could use this to tell Cecil she was looking for a way to make someone pay. It might be related to the governor. Probably not, but it should at least buy her some goodwill with the crime boss.

And later, should she choose, she could exploit the hacker's system for her own purposes.

Sure, maybe they'd catch it. Maybe they'd beat her at her own game. But in here, in the code?

Eddie was willing to take that chance.

CHAPTER 12

SHEILA JACKSON

101 CYCLES UNTIL ARRIVAL

The release of all the data from Prom almost a week prior created a mixed blessing for Sheila and the space exploration subdirectorate. On the positive side, she could bring all her people together and openly discuss what continued to arrive daily from the orbital satellites. On the negative side, it brought the additional burden of outside pressure. For the first time ever, everyone on the ship was paying attention to what she did, and she found herself bombarded with interview requests, consults from other science directorates, and attention from her boss. She couldn't even get through a meal at a common facility without people she'd barely said ten words to in her life stopping by her table *just to chat*. Stars, she had to send a one-screen summary of each day's new data to the governor himself.

Worse, she wasn't even sure what to say, because while they'd learned a lot from satellites in orbit, so much more was missing because of the continuing problems with landing probes on the planet's surface. They'd established connections with each newly arriving probe only to lose it again sometime after it entered the atmosphere, and it had happened enough times now that it had

Sheila worried. Their current hypotheses included everything from natural interference to a failure in the communications relays to anomalies with the planet's magnetosphere. But from this distance, the time lag played havoc with their ability to fix anything. If they were in real time, they could have adjusted the plan for the probes, moved them in slowly, and figured out exactly where in the process they were going offline. Instead, with signals still taking days to traverse the distance, all they could do was watch it happen.

That meant she couldn't meet the voracious appetite for information that had developed across the ship—and more, she couldn't explain *why*. Because openness only went so far. The governor had ordered them to release all their data as it came in, yet he didn't want to alarm the crew with news of the communications problems.

She couldn't say she disagreed. The last thing she wanted was to speculate to a crowd, and she didn't *know* anything. She and her team needed time to figure out the problem with their probes, and every minute she spent having to answer questions was one she couldn't spend on that work. If she was being honest, part of that was personal preference, too. She loved the work and would always choose it over communicating with others. But even dismissing her bias, she thought it was objectively the right decision.

It didn't make her day-to-day any easier, though.

"What's on the agenda for today?" she asked Lila Jurgens, who had early duty for the current ten cycles. Lila had come in two hours early to go through any data that had come in overnight and prepare for the rest of the team. That way, Sheila could assign work priorities and they could get to them faster. They rotated early duty among the team members, and whoever pulled early duty would leave work two hours early to compensate. Sheila had put this technique in place on her second day, and the team liked it. It saved crew hours.

"Exciting news. We lost connection with another surface probe—"

"That's not that exciting," someone—probably Marcus—offered from the back.

"*But,*" Lila said louder, "before we lost connectivity we received some still photos. The computers are still working on enhancing them, but we should have them any minute now."

"That *is* exciting." Sheila wasn't alone in that—the entire team was buzzing. "What else?"

"Xenobiology wants a meeting to discuss tasking priorities for the drones."

"All right. Set it up, but make sure they know about our communications failures," said Sheila. It made sense. XB was a small section—just six scientists—but along with space exploration, they had the most important job on the ship at the moment. Sheila's section had to determine what was on the planet. XB had to determine if they could *live* with it. If Sheila were in charge, she'd have combined the two departments, but there was no way Lavonia would go for that. It would put too much authority under one person that *wasn't* her, and that wouldn't do. Thankfully Sheila got along well enough with Dr. David Zimdal, her XB counterpart. "Did they send anything over to set the agenda?"

"They did, and it's interesting. They want to dial back on the compatibility studies at the microbial level beyond the basics that we're already scheduled to receive—pathogens and the like—and add some additional scans for intelligent life."

"Intelligent? They said intelligent, and not complex?"

"In writing," said Lila.

Sheila considered it while looking around, meeting the eyes of each of her team in turn, trying to read the reaction, but deciphering personal cues wasn't her strong suit. Facts. That she could do. And the data didn't yet suggest anything that would indicate cause to accelerate those studies ahead of other priorities. Not that they could accelerate anything until they figured out why they kept losing the ability to talk to whatever they tried to land on the surface.

She addressed the entire team. "I'm going to propose a thesis, and I want all of you to brainstorm ways that I could be wrong. Right now, we have no indications that would lead us to believe there's intelligent life on the planet. From our space-based assets, we can already definitively rule out artificial lights, air travel, space travel, and radio waves of any kind. We are already doing the work to detect artificial pollutants in the air, and while we don't have definitive results, our initial indications make it seem unlikely." She paused, letting her argument sink in. "So. Tell me why I'm wrong. Why should we consider changing our well-thought-out priorities of collection and slant them toward detecting intelligent life?"

The room stayed silent except for the air circulator for at least half a minute before Marcus Bhatt spoke up. "Maybe it's not a matter of strict scientific priority. What if instead we considered the most significant impacts to the mission and prioritized our collection on that?"

Of course he spoke first. He insisted on playing the devil's advocate, thinking it made him a valuable part of the team. In reality, nobody liked him. But this time, Sheila *wanted* someone to challenge her thinking on the matter, so she welcomed his input. "Interesting," she said. Despite her mild dislike of Marcus, she found that she meant it. "Expound."

Marcus stood. "Well, if there's intelligent life, or even sufficiently complex life, it may not be a science issue at all. It may be a moral one."

Sheila knew that argument well. She didn't buy it, but it was significant enough where she'd considered the question of whether they had the right to colonize a planet that already harbored life. "But we have the indicators I mentioned."

"But those indicators may not be universal." Yanai Parkinson was *not* one to make an argument just for the sake of arguing. She rarely took an alternate opinion, which sometimes weighed against her as a scientist.

"Continue," said Sheila, leaving her two subordinates to decide which of them she was talking to.

Yanai took the lead. "There are multiple possible technology trees, so the lack of evidence of traditional Earth indicators, while it does give some credence to a lack of development, can't be established as definitive."

Sheila nodded. "That's an astute point. Be sure to bring it up in our meeting with XB, if they don't."

"And we can't deny the almost perfect conditions for life," added Yanai.

"Which comes back to my point," said Marcus. "We need to know the level of life so that we can best advise decision makers, so they can determine whether to pursue colonization or not."

"*Of course* we're going to colonize," said Utan Vespa, his voice a little too loud for the setting. "We're not going to pass up the only habitable planet in this part of the galaxy for another hundred or more years in space just because we find some ants on the surface."

"What's an ant?" asked Marcus.

"It's a species of small bug from Earth that lived in colonies, usually in the ground," said Yanai. It became hard to follow the arguments after that, with everybody talking to each other at once, ignoring the group format.

"Okay, let's focus," said Sheila. Even after that, it took several long seconds for everyone to settle down. "We're in the business of science. It's not our job to set the political guidelines for the ship."

Yanai raised her hand.

"Go ahead."

"Then whose job is it? We're the best people to interpret the data and what it means."

Sheila nodded. "We are. But we have to work at presenting it in a neutral manner and avoid politicizing it."

A few of her subordinates glanced at one another, as if each was hoping someone else might say something, but nobody contradicted her. It was times like this that Sheila wished she was better at reading people. She considered pushing them, making one of them spell out what they were thinking, but ultimately she let the moment pass.

THE FOLLOWING DAY, SHEILA SAT ACROSS FROM KAREN NEWBOTTOM, one of the ship's news reporters, squinting, unused to the bright lights. The producer of the ship's main news show had asked for her to appear in their studio. She'd rejected them, following her own directive to her team about not politicizing science. Lavonia, however, insisted she do the interview, so here she was, about to go live. They said it had to be live, though she couldn't imagine why. It was a five-minute segment, so she wouldn't have to go into too much detail, but her words would be replayed and scrutinized endlessly, so why not just record it whenever?

She glanced at the notes on her device that she had made and remade, studied and restudied. She hadn't slept more than two hours, and she wasn't exactly happy with what that had done to her face for her first-ever appearance on a ship-wide broadcast, though a cheerful technician had applied enough makeup to her that probably nobody would know.

Alex was out there in the studio watching, though the lights obscured him. He was part of news and entertainment, and he wouldn't miss the opportunity to see her in action, despite the unspoken tension between them that still lingered from their different perspectives on having a child. He had nothing to be upset about. She'd given in, agreed to have their genetic material harvested and to move forward with the process, but things between them were still off.

From behind the wall of cameras and lights and crew, a voice counted them down. "We're live in five, four, three . . ." The rest of the count was silent.

"Hello! I'm Karen Newbottom, and I'm here today with the deputy director for space exploration, Dr. Sheila Jackson. Dr. Jackson has agreed to answer some questions that I know are on all our minds about our destination planet, Promissa. Dr. Jackson, welcome!"

"Thank you for having me, Karen. Please, call me Sheila."

"Let's jump right into it. Sheila . . . can we live on this planet or not?"

She was ready for this obvious opener, so she launched into her preplanned speech. "Based on our initial research, we can almost certainly live on Promissa at some point in the future. What we don't know is when we'll be able to do that." She paused and was about to discuss a fifteen- to twenty-year timeline for responsible discovery when Newbottom cut her off.

"Let's talk about that. What are some of the things that make this planet habitable or not?"

Sheila hesitated, wanting to get back to her previous answer to clarify, but not wanting to ignore this one. "There are a lot of factors, Karen. Chemically, we've already seen that the atmosphere is compatible, the planet has plate tectonics, and the composition of the planet itself is relatively stable and agreeable."

"Those are the most important factors, correct?"

Sheila hesitated again, unused to being interrupted. "They are. But they aren't the only important factors."

"Interesting," said Newbottom. "What are some of the other factors?"

"Something we don't have yet is good data at the microscopic level." She had to be careful here, as she wasn't allowed to talk about the communication problems. "Our probes are good, but we had to build them with the ability to survive automated atmospheric entry, so they're limited." It wasn't a total lie—it *was* difficult—though it certainly left some things unsaid. She paused to let the interviewer interject. She was getting the hang of it.

Newbottom didn't miss her cue. "That has got to be tough!"

"It is," said Sheila. "We don't have all the data we need right now from the surface to calculate the effects the environment might have on humans."

"You need to dig deeper, then?"

"We do. Regardless of our preventative measures, eventual microbial introduction and transmission is inevitable. Proteins could, at a minimum, be incompatible and, at the worst, be toxic."

"Whoa, whoa, Doctor." Karen smiled and gave a rehearsed laugh. "You're talking over most of our heads. What's that mean in English?"

"It means that things that we can't see can, and probably will, kill us."

That wiped the false happiness from Newbottom's face, and Sheila realized that she might have messed up. Maybe she could have worded that in a better way. A way that wouldn't cause the entire ship to panic.

"It's not all bad," she offered. "We're as dangerous to the ecosystem as it is to us."

For the first time, Karen Newbottom was speechless, and there were a couple of seconds of silence. They felt like a minute, and Sheila wondered if she should say something else. She had wanted to stay neutral, but perhaps in trying to tamp down the irrational exuberance of discovery, she had strayed too far to the negative.

"So tell us, Dr. Jackson," said Newbottom, recomposing herself and speaking deliberately. "Will we be able to go down to the planet at all?"

"Oh. Oh yes," said Sheila. "With the proper quarantine and containment protocols in place, I expect that we'll send people to the surface to gather further information within a week or two of arriving in orbit."

"That's great news!" said Newbottom, smiling her newscaster smile again, and immediately Sheila wanted to follow up, talk about the protocols and that they'd be in biohazard suits, if not full spacesuits, but Newbottom didn't give her a chance. "And that's all the time we have for today. Dr. Jackson, thank you so much for joining us. We hope you can come back soon."

Sheila looked at the other woman, and then made the mistake of looking out toward the crew, and the lights dazzled her. "Of course. Thanks for having me."

AS THE TECH DISCONNECTED SHEILA'S MICROPHONE, THE ROOM cleared quickly. Sheila and Alex were alone now, except for two crew members who were reconfiguring the set for whatever was coming up next.

"How did I do?" Sheila asked.

"You did good. Very smart sounding. It's kind of sexy."

"She kept cutting me off. I had so much more I wanted to say about some of those things." She hadn't ever gotten back to her fifteen- to twenty-year timeline talking point. She'd have to do better with that. Maybe she could release a written statement and make that evident.

"It's okay." Alex put his arm around her, pulling her in, and she rested her head on his shoulder. "They'll cut this whole thing down to one sound bite by next cycle, anyway."

Sheila smiled and squeezed Alex around his waist. "Okay. I've got to get back to my office and see what new data the probes have sent us. We're expecting pictures today."

"And I've got to go shoot the next episode of *Bottom Deckers*."

"Aw. I love that show!"

"I've invited you to the set," said Alex.

"I know, I know. And I'm going to come, I promise."

Alex kissed her chastely. "Okay. I'm going to hold you to it."

WHEN SHE ARRIVED BACK AT SPACE EXPLORATION, NOBODY MET HER at the door, which surprised her. They'd surely have watched her performance, and she didn't know what it meant that nobody wanted to talk to her about it. Instead, the entire shift was gathered around one monitor, staring and taking turns pointing at it.

"What's going on?"

"We got the photos from the surface," said Marcus.

"Oh good. How many did we get?"

"We got five images before we lost the connection, but there's one that you're definitely going to want to see." Marcus spun the monitor.

Sheila wound her way through the workstations until she could see it. It was a picture of a thinly vegetated bush with narrow branches and small, greenish leaves with a sepia hue cast over the entire picture. But that wasn't what everyone had been looking at. They were looking at the blurry thing behind the bush. More specifically, they had been looking at what resembled a pair of eyes, staring through the leaves. "Holy shit."

Marcus nodded without taking his eyes off of the image. "Right?"

"Just . . ." Sheila couldn't speak for a few seconds. "Wow." It hit her hard, and it was almost difficult to catch her breath. This changed . . . everything. The problem with communication had been significant, but mostly theoretical. Now it presented a specific question—one they needed an answer to. An answer they couldn't get. "Who else has seen this?"

"Nobody outside the department," said Lila, coming up behind her. "We wanted you to see it before anybody else."

"Thanks for that."

"So what do we do?"

Her first thought was *I don't know,* but that wasn't acceptable. Like it or not, she was the boss and she had to make a decision. Word would get out even if she tried to hide it—this was too big— and when it did . . . no. She couldn't think like that. *Stop. Think about what you can control.* She took two deep breaths to calm herself. She couldn't control what happened in the end—there were going to be some extreme reactions—but she could decide who saw it first.

"Yanai, you interface with xeno. Alana Wilson is their point on this right now, so link up with her. I want them to see this before anybody else does. They need to start working theories about what we're looking at."

"Can do."

"Marcus, I know engineering is already working on the communication issues with the probes and there's probably nothing new to report, but I want you to go down there and check personally with everybody involved. I'm going to have to talk about this and I want to make sure my information is up-to-the-minute."

"I'm on it, boss."

She took a few more seconds to think but couldn't come up with any other specific tasks to hand out at the moment. She needed time alone to sit and contemplate.

"Okay. If that's all we've got, the rest of you break down into teams and pull apart everything you can glean from each picture. I want preliminary assessments by end of shift." It was all she could do—focusing her people. She really wished she had someone who could focus her.

CHAPTER 13

MARK RECTOR

98 CYCLES UNTIL ARRIVAL

Mark Rector paced in front of the five trainees—that was what they were calling them—as they stood in a mostly straight line in a large room full of exercise equipment. A gravity display on the wall read 0.95. They wore workout suits, and two of the trainees were sweating already, though they hadn't even started moving. The directorates had coughed up their required people, but their fitness for service as Secfor remained to be seen. Rector wasn't expecting much. There was a big man named Danielson and a fit looking nonbinary person named Mwangi who looked like they might have what it took. The rest of their little group was filled out by a nondescript woman of about forty, an older woman who looked like she might be her mother but wasn't, and a thirty- or fortysomething-year-old man named Jesse Sierks whose file was incomplete and might be okay but might not.

At least they'd finally gotten them. Some of the directorates had taken multiple promptings and threats from Rector's boss to make the transfers happen. For his part, Darvan hadn't assigned them to guard the printers as they'd promised the governor, so nobody was actually doing what they should. It didn't take a genius to see Darvan's plan. He wasn't going to give the people back—he was going to make them permanent Secfor.

And that was where it became Rector's problem. He had to train them, and this group looked as if any serious physical exertion might kill them. Darvan had probably assigned him the dregs on purpose, but he could work with that. He just couldn't rush it. They did come with one benefit, though. Since they were all from different directorates, they were a great source of information, and he could take advantage of that while delaying the workout.

"So what's happening around the ship?"

They glanced at each other, nobody wanting to speak right away, until finally Mwangi spoke up. "Everyone is talking about what the scientist said. About us going to the planet in the first week we're in orbit."

"Yeah," said Sierks. "Hey . . . how do you think that's going to affect *us*?"

"What do you mean?" asked Rector.

"Like, if we're going down to colonize the planet, they'll need security, right?"

Rector hadn't really thought about that. "I guess they would. Yeah."

"Do you think we'll go?" asked Sierks.

"I don't know. But that's a good question." It really was. *Somebody* would have to go. The real question was whether it was a good thing or a bad thing. It might be an opportunity to advance, but it also might be a dead end—maybe literally. Either way, he definitely needed to think about it. In the meantime . . .

"Okay, everybody. Ninety minutes of exercise at your own pace. Make sure to mix in both cardio and strength training."

TWO HOURS LATER RECTOR WAS STARING AT THE DOOR TO HIS quarters. He pushed his thumb against the pad for the third time, this time keying his security override code at the same time, but still nothing. He pulled out his device to call maintenance, but after a second, he slammed it back into its holder. He'd had enough of this. It was bad enough when his entertainment wouldn't connect, and then when his shower went hot and cold. He'd suspected foul play each time, but this was the final step. He stalked off down the narrow corridor to the elevator. Two people approached from the opposite direction, but Rector held his line, forcing one of the two to slow and slide partially behind the other.

"Asshole," muttered one of them once he'd passed. Not to his face, of course. Never to his face. He took the elevator to the maintenance level and stomped toward the main office.

Two workers were talking in front of a row of lockers as he entered. "Where's your boss?" barked Rector.

One of the men jerked his thumb toward the far side of the room without bothering to look, and Rector followed the gesture to a portal. He slammed the button above the biometric pad and the door opened, apparently unlocked. The door slid open slowly, unmoved by his emotion.

"I'm looking for the director of maintenance," he barked as he entered the room.

The man looked away from his screen, which was mounted to a cluttered desk. "You found him. Name's Walter. Security? What did one of my people do now?"

"They locked me out of my room."

The man grunted. "Did you fill out an emergency work order?"

"No—"

"You've got to fill out an emergency work order. It will send a priority alert to the on-call customer service tech. Goal for an emergency is service in fifteen minutes. Regulations allow for an hour if there are exacerbating conditions." Walter turned back to his screen.

"They broke it on purpose."

Walter made an exaggerated show of turning back to him. "You think somebody broke your door *on purpose.*"

Coming down here had seemed like a good idea at the time, but now that he was here, Rector had no idea what he was going to do. His complaint sounded stupid, even to himself. It didn't change the fact that it was true, though. "Things have been happening to me lately."

"Yeah? What kind of things?"

"My entertainment system went out two days ago, and my shower three days ago."

"That does seem like a lot," allowed Walter. "But you gotta remember, this ship is old. Stuff breaks."

"Everything at once?"

"Might be something bad in the control board for your room. I can send somebody by to give the entire thing a once-over, see if it needs replacing."

"Wouldn't that give whoever that was access to my entire place?"

Walter shrugged. "Yeah. So? You want it fixed or not?"

"Look. People have been giving Secfor trouble lately, and I believe this is part of that."

Walter pursed his lips and tapped absently at his chin. "Well, we did all have to give people up to your directorate recently, and that makes more work for everyone here. But listen, I don't think anybody's going to blame you, or any individual, for that specifically."

"It's more than that," said Rector, and when Walter didn't react, he continued, "I had an incident where somebody died."

"Oh. Right. That was you? Applebaum, right? Everybody liked her."

"Yeah. Right."

"And you think that somebody thinks that breaking your door is payback for that."

Rector hesitated. "Yes."

Walter sighed. "Look. I support Secfor. I didn't even complain when they told me to give somebody up. You can ask your boss. But what do you want me to do here?"

Rector considered it. "Just fix my door. Room K0866."

Walter took his pad off of his desk and keyed some commands into it and waited for a response. "Someone will be there in under ten minutes."

"Thanks." With that, Rector turned and left.

Outside, there were five people where there had been two before, and Rector stopped. He recognized one of them, though he couldn't place where he recognized her from. A young woman, short but not small, with cropped hair. And then it hit him. Eddie Dannin, the woman that Lila Jurgens mentioned as her accomplice. Dannin had seen him, too, and was staring.

Rector broke eye contact and made a point of keeping his pace steady on the way to the door. He had a good feeling he knew who had been messing with his room.

RECTOR BLEW INTO THE OFFICE THE NEXT DAY ON A MISSION AND made a beeline for the portal that led down a short corridor to where cyber worked. Six people occupied workstations that ran down each wall of the rectangular space, which reflected the fact that computers played a role in more than 75 percent of all crime. Something had everybody agitated, but Rector didn't have time for that. He approached Jan Koenig and waited for them to drop their lenses and acknowledge him, fidgeting when it took longer than a minute.

"Little busy here," they said, without stopping work.

"I need whatever you found on Eddie Dannin."

"Can't help you right now," said Koenig. Their tone wasn't rude—more distracted.

"This is a priority!" Rector raised his voice, and for a brief moment, all sound in the room vanished before the low hums and clicks started up again a couple seconds later.

Koenig made a dramatic show of slowly removing their haptic gloves, one finger at a time, and then removing their lenses. When they spoke, it was a voice one might use to explain something to a petulant child, slow and measured. "I understand that it's a priority. I said I can't help you. Would you like to know why?"

Rector fidgeted. "Yes, please."

"I can't give you anything because something has infiltrated all of our systems and is busy scrambling our brains. And while I can't guarantee it, I kind of have a feeling that whatever"—they gestured to the rest of the room—"*this* is, it rode in on the tracking tag that I had on Ms. Dannin."

"That . . ." Rector hesitated, unsure. "That's illegal, right? We've got her!"

Koenig rolled their eyes. "I told you I couldn't guarantee it. I *certainly* can't prove it. And even if I could, what are we going to do? Go to the magistrate and say, 'Yes, Your Honor. They sent an attack into our system via the very illegal tag that I put in theirs.' Because I don't think that's going to end well for us."

Rector considered it. "How sure are you that it's her? Give me a percentage. Off the record."

Koenig bounced their head from side to side, debating. "We'll know more once we isolate whatever caused this. Which we *will* do, because whatever it is, it's acting passively. Someone fired it and forgot it rather than actively controlling it, which . . . thank the stars for that. I'd say maybe 80 percent chance that's what happened, just based on the timing, and if something rode in on that tag . . . I don't know, 95 percent chance it was her who put it there?"

"Who else would have done it? It would have had to be her, right?"

"I mean . . . there are five, maybe six people on the ship who could even contemplate trying something like that. Two of them are in this room. So yeah, it was probably her, but you never want to rule anything out until you're *sure* in my line of work."

"I'm going to bring her in. I'll get her to confess to it."

"You can't bring her in on something that we can't acknowledge exists," said Koenig.

"I'm not. I'm bringing her in based on the testimony of a witness with direct knowledge of her doing an illegal hack to move work files onto a personal system."

Koenig snorted. "That's a slap on the wrist. You can't hold her an hour on that, and you'll screw up anything you want to do to her in the future."

Rector gave a thin smile. "She doesn't need to know why I brought her in. If she did *this*, and she thinks I know it, well . . . that's on her."

Koenig shrugged. "Okay. You're the one who works the corridors. Good luck."

"MWANGI, DANIELSON, YOU'RE WITH ME." RECTOR DIDN'T STOP AS HE walked back through the main office. The two trainees scrambled to get themselves together and catch up to him. He'd checked maintenance's schedule, and she was off duty, so there was no better time than the present to bring her in.

"Where are we going, boss?" asked Danielson, who stood almost two and a half meters and massed a hundred kilos.

"Making an arrest."

"All three of us?" asked Mwangi, who was also above average height, though they had narrow shoulders and didn't weigh nearly as much as their counterpart. It was a fair question. It shouldn't take three people to pick up one small maintenance worker, but if she bolted, he'd appreciate having the help boxing her in. Maybe it would save him a run. Not that one could run very far on a ship in space.

"It's a good chance for you to learn," he said. "Normally we'd just put out an all-ship message for her to turn herself in, but I'm not sure she'd do it. Danielson, I want you to circle around and come from the other direction."

"Aww, you're giving me spin-side?" By going around to the other elevator, he'd have to walk significantly farther to reach their destination.

Rector glared at him, and the big man shrank a bit. "You don't have to get all the way to her room. Just block the corridor in case she runs that way."

"On it."

Rector slowed his pace, giving the man time to make up some of the longer distance.

"You expecting trouble?" asked Mwangi.

"I don't know. I've just got a feeling."

Rector liked them. They asked a lot of questions, but they were *smart* questions. They were young but had good instincts, might actually make a good security officer.

They reached the corridor that contained Dannin's unit a

couple minutes later. Rector had let his mind drift, rehearsing his words, preparing for the verbal confrontation to come.

"Boss?"

"Yeah?"

"I've got a feeling, too."

Rector looked up, hearing the edge in their voice. About fifteen people stood in the corridor, blocking the way to Dannin's room. Most of them were men, but there were three or four women among them as well. Rector set his face into a grim look and marched forward. He projected his voice, speaking with his practiced authoritative tone. "What's going on?"

"Corridor's closed," said a short, stocky man with gravel in his voice.

"Clear the way," said Rector. "Secfor business."

"Can't," said the man.

"Why *can't* you?"

"We're stuck." The man smirked, as if he though he were being clever.

"Stuck?" asked Rector.

"Yep."

"Listen, just walk away, and I'll pretend like none of this happened."

"None of what?" asked the man.

The man was stalling, which meant that Dannin was on the run. He almost smiled. Sending Danielson around the other way had been a good decision, but he couldn't let that on, had to keep their attention focused on him. "I said clear the way!" he shouted.

The group reacted to that, fidgeting and looking at each other. But not leaving.

"The man said clear the way!" bellowed a voice from the other side of the crowd.

Somebody went down—Rector couldn't see who, through the press of bodies, but a person definitely hit the deck. A woman cried in pain, then a man. Suddenly the crowd was surging toward him, and he slammed himself to one side and hugged the wall, trying to avoid the mass of flesh and limbs, and he couldn't make out anything as everyone was shouting at the same time and someone was screaming.

After a few seconds, he gathered his bearings, tried to get to his comm, but somebody hit him as they pushed by and it spun out of his hand. He tried to chase after it, ran into somebody, spun, and hit the wall, banging his shoulder for his efforts. The scream had turned into a sob, and with the crowd past him now, he spotted Mwangi, sitting on the floor, cradling their arm. A bone in their forearm jutted through the skin, all white and jagged and . . . *wrong*. Danielson stood a few meters away, three bodies at his feet. Two were unconscious—at least Rector hoped they were just unconscious—and the third cowered back from the big man, who had his stun stick held in the air, looking like he was about to use it as a club to strike the woman beneath him.

"Danielson, stand down!"

The big man's head snapped toward Rector, and for a second, with that look in his eyes, Rector wasn't sure he'd comply. But he lowered his weapon to his side, stood there, breathing hard, his weight evenly balanced on both feet, like even then he was ready for a fight. He didn't speak.

"Holster your weapon," said Rector, his tone flat and even, demanding compliance. "Help Mwangi up. Be careful, they've got a broken arm."

The big man hesitated for a moment, and then nodded. "Roger, boss."

"What were you thinking?" asked Rector.

The man stopped, looked at him blankly. "They weren't complying."

"That doesn't mean you wade into them with your *weapon*."

Danielson looked at his feet. "Sorry, boss."

Rector glanced down the hall, first the way the crowd had gone, and then toward their target room. He could still go after Dannin, and he considered it for several seconds before finally rejecting the idea. That crowd could come back, maybe with reinforcements, and there were injured people to tend to. Not to mention his career problems. One incident? That had been bad. Two was unheard of. Danielson had caused this one, but Rector had led the mission. He'd have to suspend the rookie immediately to have any chance of avoiding consequence himself. On the other hand, Darvan had brought in the new people . . . maybe there was an opportunity there. First he had to deal with the immediate problems. "Get Mwangi to the infirmary. I'm going to call in help to get these three to medical as well."

"Aren't we going to take them in, boss?"

"On what charge? Failure to comply? We'll be laughed out of the magistrate's office. Besides, don't you think they've suffered enough?"

"You warned them."

Rector nodded. "I did. But still." He glanced to the downed protestors again. The woman met his stare, which was kind of badass, given the unnatural lump where her collarbone should have been. "Let's go."

As he walked back to the Secfor office, he kept turning the situation over in his mind, looking for a way out. They had to have known where he was going to be. How else could fifteen people have gotten there before him? Figuring that out took precedence over Dannin. Either someone was using the hack of their system to spy on them, or there was a leak in the department. Either possibility presented a problem. One that was maybe even big enough to draw attention away from his mistake.

IT WAS ELEVEN HOURS BEFORE RECTOR LEFT WORK. HIS SHIFT HAD run long with reports to file, an incident report to write, and not one, but two exceptional ass chewings from Darvan, sandwiched around a weird video call from the governor himself who asked what happened, took notes, and nodded to himself, but didn't seem all that upset. Rector respected the man. He never lost his cool and always seemed to have a plan. Most important, he didn't fire Rector, which meant that Darvan couldn't, either. Somehow the growing tension between the two leaders had saved his ass.

Despite that good news, by the time he finally staggered to his room, all he wanted was a hot shower and a beer. He pressed his thumb to the pad, but the door didn't open.

Because of fucking course it didn't.

CHAPTER 14

JARRED PANTEL

||||||||||||||||||||||||||||||||||||||||||||||||||||||||||||||

95 CYCLES UNTIL ARRIVAL

"Fucking find her! A person cannot just disappear on a closed spaceship."

Jarred Pantel jumped to his feet behind his desk and glared at Rector, his throat raw from yelling so much in the past few hours, first at Darvan, then venting to Blaisdell, and now here, alone in his office with the Secfor officer. He'd taken it calmly when the incident had first happened, figuring that while Dannin had escaped them, they'd quickly find her and pick her up. If he was honest with himself, he'd overlooked her importance, but once Blaisdell had explained the risk of having her at large and potentially aligning with the Eternal Lifers, he'd changed his attitude. Dannin had done a number on the Secfor computers, and that made her too important an asset to let fall into the hands of protestors. He'd originally used the idea of someone hacking manufacturing as an artificial way to put pressure on directors, but now it didn't seem so hypothetical.

"Yes, sir, but . . . she has. We've put out a ship-wide message that anybody who sees her should report her whereabouts to Secfor, but the results have been . . . less than helpful." Rector stood in front of the desk, stiff and uncomfortable. At least he had the decency to look embarrassed.

"What's that mean, exactly?"

"We've received multiple reports about her location, all of them false."

"So they're hiding her."

"It seems likely."

Pantel took a deep breath and tried to relax. Rector had made mistakes, but even that was better than having Darvan fight him on every last thing. At least he could trust that Rector was working toward the same goals as he was.

"It's been two days. You can't even *eat* without logging in to the system. There are cameras everywhere. You're telling me she's not eating?"

"Not in any facility, no. Someone's obviously bringing her food."

"And you know *who*?"

"My belief is that it's the same people who prevented us from detaining her. There are a lot of suspects, but we're working to narrow it down."

"Work faster. The longer this goes on, the more risk there is that they'll use her to do something big."

"Yes, sir. Sorry, sir. There are . . . some . . . challenges. I think somebody tipped them off. They were waiting for us, and I'm concerned that the leak might have come from inside."

"Not just the problem with your computers? Somebody in your office?" That caused Pantel pause. It could be anybody, but if they'd infiltrated even Secfor, then it was spreading more than he previously understood.

"I can't rule it out," said Rector. "There are other issues as well.

We're working to integrate new personnel, but Director Darvan didn't really have a cohesive plan for training them, and they're holding us back."

Pantel nodded. Of course Rector would cast the blame on Darvan. That didn't necessarily mean it was his fault, but it also didn't mean it *wasn't*. He made a mental note of that in case he needed to use it to push on the director later. It didn't help with his current problem, though. He couldn't go after Secfor as a whole without alienating the entire directorate against him. Better to let Rector do that. "Any ideas on who the leak might be?"

Rector thought about it—or he pretended to think about it to make it seem as if he didn't already have an answer in mind. He had to have expected the question. The man had made mistakes, but he was impulsive, not an idiot. "Nothing I can prove. But I'm running some tests, limiting who I tell certain things to. It's almost more important than finding the hacker."

"Almost, but not quite," said Pantel. "If somebody is hiding her, there's information somewhere. We need to find it. Put all our cyber people on it."

"Sir, that's a violation of—"

"It's not a violation if I invoke the Safety of the Ship statute."

"Sir . . ." Rector hesitated, and when Pantel didn't cut him off, continued, "Invoking Safety of the Ship requires the governor *and* the captain."

"That's a technicality," said Pantel, but he dropped his voice back to a conversational level.

"I'll still do it if you tell me to," offered Rector. "I just wanted to be clear that you knew the law."

Pantel sighed. Rector was right. Safety of the Ship, which suspended all crew rights to privacy, was designed to be invoked when crew members were acting in a way that would harm the ship. Which they were, in his opinion. But others wouldn't see it that way, and taking unilateral action came with significant risks. Majority opinion was still on his side, but nothing would change that faster than getting caught violating the Charter himself. That meant he had to go to the captain for her concurrence, and while much of the way the ship ran had evolved to give the governor power while diminishing hers, in this she was a true equal. "No. Not yet. Just fucking find her and find the leak. We need to ensure the reliability of Secfor, and we need to get her out of the hands of the Lifers. Give me even the slightest evidence, and I'll authorize a search of whatever area you need."

"Yes, sir."

Rector left, and when the door closed behind him, Blaisdell reappeared.

"Tell me *you* have some good news." Pantel sat and gestured her to a chair, which she took.

"Of course. I've got the video of the incident ready to release."

"The video that shows a Secfor officer leaping into an unarmed crowd?"

Blaisdell chuckled. "Obviously not that part. I should have said the *edited* video. The one that shows the crowd plowing into two Secfor who had no weapons drawn and were doing their job, seriously injuring one of them."

Pantel considered it. "You think we should release that? It's risky."

"Us? No. We already got lucky that nobody on the scene got their own personal video. I guess the big man with a stun stick charging into their midst caught them by surprise. We can't let ourselves be tied to a video release, and especially not to a doctored one, but should an anonymous user leak it on the net and let people share it organically . . . ? I don't see the downside."

"The downside is blowing it up into a bigger deal than it is. If we let it die, it dies."

Blaisdell shook her head. "If we try to let it die, then they get to use the incident to recruit at their leisure. Need I remind you that the Secfor officer incited this? That they *do* have the truth on their side? This video throws doubt on that truth."

"And if it's exposed as an edit?"

"We obfuscate. If there are multiple versions, there's always going to be doubt. In this case, doubt is better for us than the truth."

Pantel considered it, tried to envision all the ways it could go, but his mind was still stuck back on having a leak inside Secfor. He felt he needed to act on *something* or he was going to burst. "Okay. Launch it. What else have you got?"

"Are you familiar with the term Panem et Circenses?"

"Sounds Latin. I was never very good in the sciences, so I never had much use for it."

"It *is* Latin," said Blaisdell. "But it's not science. It's psychology. It stands for 'bread and circuses.'"

It seemed like a familiar phrase to Pantel, but he couldn't place it. "You lost me."

"It means if you give the people something shiny to focus on, they won't pay attention to the stuff you'd rather keep quiet."

"So a distraction."

"Yes," said Blaisdell.

Pantel nodded. "That makes sense. A revolution can only prosper if people care, so I need to give them something else to care about. But what?"

"The obvious answer is right in front of us."

"The planet," he said.

"Give them that, and nothing else matters."

He took some time mulling it over. "Yes. I'll set a news conference for tomorrow. Start making a big deal about it today. Get it out there that we're going to make a major announcement, so that we've got as many eyes and ears on us as possible. Get that scientist, Jackson. I want her there."

Blaisdell gave him a quizzical look. "You think it's a good idea to have *her* talk?"

"*She's* not going to talk. *I'm* going to talk. She's going to stand there beside me and give me credibility." Pantel spoke quickly now, warming to the plan.

Blaisdell thought about it. "I've looked into her. She's not going to like that. She's very apolitical, focused on her work. Really kind of the perfect crew member, if a little boring. She might refuse to show up."

Rector sighed. "So lie to her. Tell her that she's there in case I get a technical question I can't answer. She's there so that I can turn and ask her for clarification."

"Which you won't do."

"Exactly."

"She's going to be pissed," said Blaisdell.

"She can get in line. Now if you'll excuse me, I have to go talk the captain into letting me catch an invisible criminal."

THE COMMAND DECK WAS NOMINALLY TOWARD THE FRONT OF THE ship, though not at the *actual* front. The actual front of the ship was a conical section made up of a combination of armor, absorptive material, and an ion shield generator. Nobody went there beyond the occasional excursion by engineering to fix or maintain something. The section didn't spin, so it didn't have gravity. It served to protect the rest of the ship and nothing more. So the bridge, as they called the command deck, being near the front of the habitable part of the ship was nothing more than an illusion of an era when captains actually piloted. The *Voyager* flew itself.

Pantel fixed that in his mind as he approached, the propensity of the captain and her people to cling to nostalgia and outdated ideas in case he could use that to manipulate her. He had a nauseous feeling in his stomach, but he attributed that to the low gravity. It was below 39 percent, making it the lowest on the ship for an area that had a constant crew. He wondered briefly how that affected the health of those working and living there, but the military had its own rules and procedures, and he figured that it would have some method of accounting for it.

Inside, even the layout of the bridge gave a picture of an earlier time, with only the grated floor sloping gently up to each wall, as it did in any large room on the ship, giving lie to the illusion. At the front of the room, one could almost believe they could see out into space through three giant windows. In truth, they were large LED screens projecting a picture from outside the ship, but given that the ship was surrounded by empty space, it hardly mattered. It would present a nice view—and make a good location for a speech—as they got closer to the planet. That would be quite a spectacle: him in the foreground, Promissa behind him.

Eight technicians sat at stations around the outside of the room, doing what, he couldn't even speculate. An officer occupied the center of the room, his own displays in front of him. The raised dais on which he sat in a swiveling chair gave him sight lines to all his subordinates. When he noticed the governor, he stood and came toward him.

"Governor. Welcome to the bridge." If the man—his name tag said *Banerjee*—thought it odd that the governor had shown up for the first time since the first week after he'd been elected to his eight-year term three years before, he didn't let it show. "What can I do for you?"

"I need to talk to the captain."

"Is she expecting you?"

"She is not. But I needed a walk and I needed to talk to her, so I decided that I'd accomplish two tasks with one mission."

"You're in luck. She's in her office. Let me call her and see if she's accepting visitors."

Pantel wanted to push past the man, go knock on her door. He didn't want to give her time to prepare or to reach out to others to potentially ascertain why he was there. But he couldn't come up with a reason to insist on that, and more practically, he didn't actually know where her office was. She had always come to him. "Thanks."

Banerjee walked back to the command station, spoke quietly into some sort of comm, and then gestured for Pantel, and when he saw that he was looking, gestured to a portal on the far side from where he'd entered. "Through that portal there, then it's your second portal on the right. First one is the XO."

Pantel nodded and headed for the portal, which opened for him; he suspected Banerjee had triggered it from his station. It wouldn't make sense that anyone could just access the leadership corridor at will. Through the portal the grated metal floor shifted to thin red-and-black carpet.

Captain Wharton was waiting outside her office, looking like she did any other time in her ship-regulation vac suit with four bars on each shoulder, her gray hair tied back in a bun. No slacking off on uniform standards for this woman just because she was alone in her own domain.

"You must really want something to find your way up here," she said, but she was almost laughing, softening the quip.

"How do you live in this low g?" he asked, half seriously. "I feel like I'm almost floating."

She shrugged and leaned against the bulkhead. "When they designed the ship, they were worried about losing spin gravity, and they thought the transition to zero g would be less of a strain if you were in low g to begin with."

"Has the ship actually ever lost spin?"

"Once. Mission year fifty-seven. I forget what happened. It's been a long time since I went to school."

"You look like it could have been just yesterday," joked Pantel.

Wharton laughed fully this time. "Okay. You're *always* full of shit, but now I *know* you want something. This about your Secfor fucking up again and you losing control of the population?"

Her remark bit at Pantel, but he did his best to keep it from showing. The tone had been congenial so far, and he didn't want to lose that, because he *did* want something. "Can we talk?"

She studied him for a moment and then pushed herself to full standing. "Come on in." As they walked in, she couldn't resist another dig. "You know you could give Secfor to me, let me handle this kind of thing."

"And be the man responsible for blurring the lines between military and civilian authority? Never."

Inside, her office wasn't the spartan space he expected, though he hadn't actually thought about it before embarking on this visit. The walls were painted in pastels, and a shelf behind her desk had a variety of knickknacks on it, though it also had an acrylic plastic facing that would prevent them from floating free in the event of some kind of ship failure, and the floor was covered in the same thin, slip-resistant carpet as the corridor. He took one of two seats bolted to the floor in front of her desk at her silent offer. "You're not far off, though," he added. "About losing control of the population."

She sat behind her desk and gave him a flat look. "I hear things. What can I do to help?"

Pantel felt that being straight gave him his best chance. Wharton was nothing if not direct. "I want to invoke Safety of the Ship."

Wharton's face didn't move at the request. "I'm listening."

"We've identified the person behind the hack of Dr. Jackson's system. The same person launched a cyberattack on Secfor systems. In trying to apprehend that person—Eddie Dannin—you might have seen her name on the ship-wide bulletin—"

"I did."

"She's gone off the net. We can't find her anywhere."

"I assume you checked her quarters." Wharton smiled.

Pantel smiled back, despite not feeling it. "This is serious. How does a person just disappear?"

"One would expect that if she was behind the incursion into a protected system in space exploration and also Secfor, she might also have ways to fool the ship into believing that she's not somewhere that she actually is. So, let me repeat my question in a different way. Have you had somebody physically look in her room?"

"Of course we have," said Pantel, though in truth he had no idea if Rector had thought to do that. "Someone is hiding her."

"And this presents a threat to ship safety . . . how? For all we know she could have fallen through an access panel and died somewhere with no sensors."

"Can we take that risk?"

"*What* risk?"

"This woman—Dannin—if she did what we think, then that means she not only broke into the space exploration system, she did it from the terminal of the director of manufacturing."

"That *is* concerning, though I'm not sure whether I should be worried about the hacker or the director who has such poor security that someone can enter her system."

"That's the point, right? If she can enter *that*, she can enter anything."

"She hasn't entered mine," said Wharton, smirking. "Has she entered yours?"

"She hasn't entered yours *yet*," countered Pantel.

"She hasn't *tried* to enter mine. Which makes me question if she's a danger to the ship or just a pain in your ass. Because if 'pain in the ass' was the standard, I'd be very supportive of your request."

"It's not like I'm asking to execute her on sight."

"Though the Safety of the Ship Act *does* allow for that," said Wharton.

"You have my word. We're not going there."

"You probably didn't intend for there to be a brawl in the corridor outside her quarters, either. But that happened. Have you seen the footage of that? Ugly business."

Pantel tightened at that. Wharton had seen the real video . . . was she bringing it up now because she knew about the edited version and his plan for it? Or had she just thrown it out there as a casual jab? Either way, she was getting to him, and she might be doing it intentionally, so he took a second and calmed himself. "We need to find her to protect the ship."

Wharton smiled, her eyes crinkling as it engulfed her entire face. "This is fun. We should do it more often."

"So that's a no?"

She leaned back in her chair, thinking. "You say you're not

going to kill her on sight. So what *do* you want the SOTS invoked for? What powers are you planning to use?"

"We want to digitally surveil the people we expect are hiding her and use that information to locate her."

The captain nodded. "So you want to spy on the people who are protesting about how you run the ship."

Pantel flinched at that. As soon as she said it, he knew her answer wouldn't change, but he didn't have much choice but to play out the loss. "That's not it at all."

"Isn't it? Or, isn't it at least the same thing? Let's say you're being genuine, and your true goal is to find Ms. Dannin. Now let's suppose that in the course of that surveillance you mentioned, you learn of the activities of those who are . . . let's call it 'not politically aligned with you.' You're telling me that you wouldn't use that information to thwart them?"

"Yes, that's what I'm saying."

She paused for a moment. "Okay, Governor, well . . . I'm sorry. I don't believe you. No offense, because I wouldn't believe anybody who told me that. Human nature and such. But I *especially* don't believe *you*."

Pantel stared at her, mouth slightly agape, before composing himself. It wasn't the no itself; it was the personal shot. He wanted to react, to lash out. Insults ran through his head, the foremost of which involved the fact that her job was pointless, but instead he just said, "I really wish you would support me on this."

"I'm sorry. I can't."

Pantel nodded. He'd deal with this, but in his own time. He had things that Wharton needed, too, and those situations would arise. But he didn't have to commit himself to open hostility now. He had enough enemies where he didn't need to make another. He could wait.

"WHAT'S WRONG? YOU LOOK DOWN," SAID CAMINA, PANTEL'S WIFE OF almost thirty years. They'd married young, which was uncommon on the ship, but it worked. She always understood him, so he wasn't surprised that she could read his mood. Though to be fair, him moping at the table, pushing his food around his plate without eating anything, probably wasn't all that hard to read.

"Rough day."

"You want to tell me about it, or do you want to just sit there and stew?" She walked across their larger-than-standard apartment slowly, swaying her hips a little more than necessary. By the time she reached him, he was laughing despite himself.

"Well if you want to cheer me up, you know I'd never turn that down."

It was her turn to laugh. She moved behind him and started massaging his shoulders. "Maybe later. Now go ahead. Spill it. What's on your mind?"

"I just can't get anybody to do what we need to do for the ship. I've got all these people pushing for change right at the worst possible time to make changes. We're almost *there*."

"Mmm." Camina didn't say anything more for a good while, continuing to work the knots out of his neck and shoulders. "You know that nobody cares, right?"

That caught him off guard. "What?"

"On the ship. Nobody cares about the protests. Not really. I mean . . . the people who go to them probably care. Maybe. But everybody else? Eh."

"Really? Because the opinion polls say that there's some real support for a couple of the issues."

"Sure, if you *ask* people. But nobody's talking about it. You're locked away in that office of yours all day, so you don't experience it the same way I do."

He considered that. She did have a point about him being isolated, and he was definitely focused on the issues for a large part of every day. She worked in administration, far from the politics. Maybe she was right. He leaned his head back into her chest and looked up at her. "You really think that's it?"

She kissed him on the forehead. "I know it is. Now eat your food before it gets cold."

CHAPTER 15

SHEILA JACKSON

94 CYCLES UNTIL ARRIVAL

Sheila stood on the side of the raised platform, letting her eyes adjust to the lights and generally trying to stay out of everyone's way. The makeup people were preparing the governor. His hair was perfect, neatly trimmed, with just a hint of gray at the temples that gave him a distinguished look. She wasn't sure why she was really there. They told her she was needed to answer any technical questions, but she didn't see that as likely. Her daily briefings had been thorough, so she didn't suspect that the journalists would ask the governor anything he couldn't handle. She had asked permission to skip the event, claiming—truthfully—that she had more important things to do, but Lavonia wasn't having it, as usual.

Governor Pantel turned to her and waved her closer. She moved a couple of steps before he held up his hand to hold her in position, as if he was framing a shot or something. Alex would know, but he wasn't there.

This nagged at her because they had fought again about the baby. She'd done her part, gone to the fertility clinic to have her eggs harvested, but he could see she wasn't excited about it, and that bothered him. It was a silly reason to be mad, but at the same time, she felt guilty. She *should* be excited about it. She wanted to be. But she wasn't, and she wasn't a good liar. She was still thinking about that when the governor's spokesperson came to the microphone and made an announcement.

"The governor will make a short statement, and then he will take questions." She walked off, and the governor took his spot behind the podium.

"By now you've all seen the video going around of the vicious attack perpetrated by members of the Eternal Life Coalition in which Secfor officer Mwangi was injured. I'm happy to report that Mwangi is recovering and will regain full use of their arm, and that we are pursuing those responsible to the fullest extent of the law." He paused, letting that sink in. "Those people—those criminals responsible—don't care about the ship. They only care about their own personal desires. We . . . we will not stoop to that level. On the contrary, my office is even now putting together efforts not to divide us, but to bring our ship together in our common cause— *the* common cause.

"To colonize the planet of Promissa."

There was audible applause from the small audience. Sheila shifted from one foot to the other, uncomfortable under the lights, but also with the idea of colonizing the planet without fully understanding it first. They still hadn't solved their communications issues, there were too many holes in their knowledge, and the recent photos only made it more irresponsible for him to be making pronouncements like that. The science didn't support a landing yet, so why were they talking about it now?

"To that end," continued the governor, "in the next few weeks, we will be taking volunteers to train for early missions to the planet's surface. In addition to that, we will, at the advice of the ship's psychologists, be scheduling *all* personnel for virtual reality training to help them cope with the open spaces we will face down on the surface. It's important that we all be ready to do our part for the greater mission if we are to succeed. Thank you."

Volunteers? That was ridiculous. Sheila wanted to say something, started to speak, but she didn't have a microphone, and the woman running things had come back to the front.

"The governor will now take questions," she said.

"Governor." A man waited for the governor to turn his way, and then asked, "Is there any further thought about ending mandatory end-of-life dates?"

"That's an issue that is enshrined in our Charter, and we would be happy to consider it if the extremists who are pushing that agenda want to begin the procedures to alter the Charter. Any questions about our mission to the planet?" He was dodging the question. With her limited interest in politics and lack of ability to read people, she didn't always trust her own judgment on such things, but this was obvious.

"Governor," asked a woman whom Sheila recognized but couldn't name, "how quickly do you envision sending teams down to the planet?"

"As soon as we're in orbit and it's safe to do so."

"That's vague, sir. Can you be a little more specific?"

The governor gave a rehearsed laugh. "Always pushing. Let's just say that I think we're talking about a matter of weeks, not a matter of months."

Sheila's heart raced at that answer, and she was sure her eyes went wide. Again she wanted to step in, to clarify, to let everybody know that it would only be safe for specialized teams to go planetside that quickly and only with very limited missions—and that was still only after they confirmed certain things, which they hadn't been able to do yet. But she couldn't interrupt the governor in this environment without the very likely chance of it ending badly. So why did he have her there? He was speaking again, and she'd missed part of it, so she tuned back in.

"—I don't think the initial VR training will be that much of a burden, but we do want to get an idea of who is suited for immediate planetside life and who isn't. After all, we wouldn't want our first mission to the surface to be derailed by a bunch of people suffering from agoraphobia." He paused. "That's fear of open spaces, and I'm told it can be debilitating, if we're not prepared. But I assure you, our medical team is working on that."

"Last question," announced the woman.

Last question? But there was so much more to talk about. Yet everyone seemed okay with the speed of this conference—if one person speaking could even be called a conference. For the fiftieth time, Sheila wondered what the point of her presence was.

"Governor." It was the same man as before. "Tell us: will you yourself go to the planet's surface?"

The governor pretended to consider the question, drawing it out, though Sheila expected he'd been absolutely prepared for it. "That's a good question. It's the job of a leader to do what's right for the ship—that's all our jobs, really. If it were up to me? I'd be the first one down. But I'm going to confer with my experts, such as Dr. Jackson here, and I'm going to consider their input before I make that decision. Thank you."

The lights dimmed and the crowd buzzed, and Sheila wanted to scream. She'd been set up. She hadn't even suspected it, which was embarrassing. She'd been stupid not to see through the news conference from the start. As much as she wanted to focus on the science—her actual job—she should have thought through it to the real purpose: the governor had used her as a prop. In five minutes, he'd totally cemented the ship's outlook for the upcoming mission and created impossible expectations, and she'd had to stand there doing nothing while he did it. She hated confrontation, found that her hands were shaking, but she couldn't keep quiet about it any longer. She took a deep breath and then pushed her way past the governor's handler to get to him.

"You set me up."

He smiled at her, as if he couldn't recognize her tone, or, more likely, like he didn't want to acknowledge it. "Come with me. We'll talk about it." He grabbed her by the upper arm and steered her toward the back of the dais, his grip not quite painful, but a little harder than it needed to be.

Sheila started talking the moment he stopped, not wanting to give him the chance to make excuses. "You had no intention of having me speak here. You wanted me here so you could make your point and make it look like I was backing you up."

"That's absolutely correct."

Sheila stopped, unsure what to say. She'd been ready for him to give an excuse, not to simply admit it. "I'm going to clear the record; I'm going to make the science known. People need to know that it's not going to be safe for any but the most well-trained missions to descend the surface for the first few *years*, and those only under the strictest safety protocols."

"The people *don't* need to know that," said the governor. "As leaders, it's our job to make the right decisions so that the people don't have to worry about it, and the right course of action for us is to get to the surface."

"That's *not* the right decision. It's rash."

"I'm sorry you disagree. Regardless, you're not going to say a word about it."

"Why not? You can't put a gag order on me." Sheila had to concentrate to keep from raising her hand to the man. He was the governor, but he didn't have that authority.

"I don't have to. You're going to keep quiet on your own."

"Why would I do that?" Sheila asked, more curious than angry now. He seemed so confident, as if he actually believed his own words.

The governor lowered his voice. "Because if you cross me, that allocation for a child that magically showed up from your husband's directorate is going to just as magically disappear."

Sheila's lips moved, but she couldn't speak, caught between surprise and rage and . . . what? She couldn't even process it. Part of her thought that he wouldn't dare, that if she exposed the threat people would see him for the monster that he was. But a bigger part of her was scared. She'd just watched him manipulate the entire ship's worth of news coverage, which was something she didn't have the skill to do. More worrying was the thing that he couldn't know: he had her. It wasn't about the child—she might even have welcomed the news that she wouldn't be allowed to have it—it was what it would do to her marriage if she did something to lose the allocation. Alex wouldn't forgive her. He might even think that she'd done something to scuttle the opportunity on purpose. She couldn't help but resent Alex for that—that he put her into that situation—but it wasn't his fault any more than it was hers. The governor had used it intentionally to manipulate them, and he was the one to blame.

When she didn't respond, the governor filled the void in the conversation himself. "What I want you to do is to go back to work and get behind this plan. You're the scientist. Figure out how to make it work."

Sheila wanted to speak, wanted to cry, wanted to scream. That wasn't how science worked at all. But she couldn't challenge this. At least not here, not now. The governor had been setting this up for a long time, and she was behind. There might be something she could do, someone she could tell, but she wasn't good on her feet in the best of circumstances, and this was far from the best. She needed time to think, to plan. That was what she did. She was a scientist, and she was thorough. Face-to-face confrontation was an entirely different equation. She wanted to tell the man in front of her—that pompous, overconfident ass—that he wouldn't get away with it. But she wasn't sure that was true.

He walked off and left her standing there.

SHE REPLAYED THE SCENE IN HER HEAD REPEATEDLY AS SHE MADE her way back to her office, thinking up multiple good retorts that she wished she'd thought of in the moment but didn't. Her brain was good for that. When she wasn't winning the argument over and over in her imagination, she started planning the actual discussion she was going to have with her husband. Because as much as she needed to focus on the science and showing the governor exactly why he was wrong, she couldn't get past the need to tell Alex everything . . . if she could summon the nerve. The trouble was, she wasn't sure she could. Caught between the science and the emotion, she found herself somewhere between regret and rage when she entered her section, only to find everyone clustered around a screen again.

"Tell me we found another example of something that might

be a complex life form." If they couldn't tell her that, at least maybe they had some good news about the communications problems. She could really use a win. But everyone slowly scattered back to their own workstations, and she deflated. It wasn't good news, then. "Okay. What's up?"

"It's . . . not work," offered Marcus, who couldn't get away because it was his screen.

Sheila rolled her eyes. Of all the things she cared about right then, her underlings screwing off at work wasn't one of them. She *should* have cared, but given everything else, she just couldn't make herself. They were probably watching her performance—or lack of performance—at the news conference. "Just show me."

Marcus flipped his screen as Sheila approached. "Someone posted the unedited video from the altercation between the protestors and Secfor."

"The governor was just talking about that in our news conference."

"I know. We saw. This hit the net immediately after. The footage starts earlier than what the news had before, and from multiple angles."

Sheila wasn't sure why any of this mattered. But she watched as a burly Secfor officer pushed into the crowd, laying about with his stun stick. This caused the crowd to panic and bolt, running over the other two officers. "This *is* different. Is it real?"

"I think so. There's a whole thread talking about the process that the leadership used to edit the first one and how you can dig into the metadata and tell that it was altered. I'm not a codehead, but enough people are confirming it that it seems legit."

Sheila looked around and found others nodding. This certainly put the governor in a difficult spot, and Sheila had to work hard not to smile. "Any progress on the communication issue?"

"We lost another one."

Sheila's momentary elation left her with a sigh and she nodded. "Great."

THAT NIGHT, SHE SAT BY HERSELF IN ONE OF THE CAFETERIAS, AWAY from the three couples they often sat with. If anybody wondered why, they didn't ask. It happened from time to time on the ship, people needing a break from their small group of friends. These things came and went. Alex noticed immediately when he walked in and slid into the seat across from her.

"What's wrong?"

"What do you mean?" asked Sheila.

"Come on. You think I can't tell when something's bothering you?"

Sheila shook her head. "You're not going to like it."

"I'll like it less if you sulk about it for five days." He smiled, and it was clear that he was trying to cheer her up, but she didn't appreciate the implication. She wasn't sulking. She had a real problem, and to belittle it like that didn't help. It didn't matter that he meant well. "You'll feel better if you talk about it," he added.

Sheila sighed. "Work sucked today."

"I figured *that* much."

"The governor used me as a prop. He announced some ridiculous plans for our arrival in orbit—stuff that has no basis in science—and all I could do was stand there in the background, silent."

"I saw the recording. The governor's an asshole. That's nothing new."

Sheila snorted despite herself. "He really is. But in this case, it's worse than that: he's going to get people killed." She whispered the last bit, so as not to be overheard.

"Is there a chance you're exaggerating?" he asked.

"*No!* I'm the expert on this, and I know what I'm talking about."

The smile drained off of his face. "Okay. I'm sorry. Do you want to tell me about it?"

Sheila glanced around, and then spoke in a low voice. "I can't tell you here. I can't be heard contradicting the governor."

"Why? That's never been a problem for anybody before. Like I said, the guy's an asshole. What's he going to do to you?"

Sheila glared at him, but after a second realized there was no malice in what he said. How could he know? "Like I said, you're not going to like it."

His eyes narrowed, seeming to grasp the seriousness finally. After a second, he nodded, his lips drawn tight. "Tell me."

"After he put that nonsense plan out to the ship, I confronted him."

"Confronted him how?"

"I pulled him aside after the news conference and told him that I was going to release the truth. That I was going to counter the lies he was telling about the planet with the real science."

"And he didn't take it well."

"He did not. But it was more than that. He said that if I did, he was going to pull our authorization to have a child. He implied that the only reason we got it was because he made it happen—as if he specifically got it for us in order to control me."

Alex's face went cold and hard in a way that Sheila had only seen a couple of times before. It was just like she feared. He was mad at her.

After a bit, she couldn't take the silence anymore. "I need you to believe that this was nothing to do with me. It was all him."

A dozen emotions seemed to pass across his face, but despite knowing him as well as she did, Sheila couldn't figure his mindset.

Finally, he spoke. "That motherfucker."

"Excuse me?" said Sheila.

Alex pressed his fists into the table. "I'm going to kill him."

"The governor?"

"Yes, the governor! He thinks he can do that to us? I don't care who he is—I'm going to find him and I'm going to beat the shit out of him."

Sheila felt tears welling up in her eyes. That was the last thing she needed, people seeing her cry in the cafeteria. He said he was mad at the governor, but she couldn't help thinking he was mad at *her* for causing the confrontation in the first place. She knew she should trust that he had her back in this. She almost did. "You can't fight the governor."

"Can't I?"

"He'll know I told you and carry out his threat. He's not bluffing."

Alex seethed for a few more seconds. "We can't just do nothing."

"What *can* we do?"

Alex took a deep breath and considered it. "I don't know. Half of me wants to go announce what he did on the news right now and screw the consequences."

Sheila thought about it. They could do that. Alex certainly had the connections for it, if they were truly willing to accept the consequences. If *he* was. But him saying he wanted to do that was an emotional response in the moment. He might mean it, but later it would eat at him, and he'd resent her. For her part, she wasn't even sure that *she* could deal with the conflict. It would mean going head-to-head with the most powerful man on the ship, and it didn't take a space scientist to know that he wouldn't just sit there and take it. If they exposed his plan and he removed the allocation for the child, it would remove his leverage over them. But he'd just find something else. And she certainly couldn't count on her director to have her back if it came to that. She needed allies. She needed . . .

"I've got an idea."

"Yeah?"

"I'm going to go talk to the captain."

STANDING OUTSIDE THE DOOR TO THE COMMAND DECK, SHEILA reconsidered her plan. She was a scientist, not a politician, and this was *way* outside of her comfort zone. But she was here now, and there was nothing for it but to push forward. She had only rumors to go on, but on the ship rumors almost always had some truth to them, and the word was that the captain and the governor didn't get along. Sheila hoped that was true. Even if it wasn't, she could at least express her concern to another authority. More, she didn't have to talk rumors: she could talk science.

That the captain had agreed to see her seemed to be a good sign.

She put her thumb to the pad and the door opened for her. The command deck looked like something out of the entertainment vids. She wondered if they'd created the vids based on the actual command deck or if someone way back when had built the command deck based on a vid. She wouldn't have bet against that. Regardless, the display windows up front simulating a view of space were pointless, a needless expense that served no purpose. She could stream the same thing from the monitor in her office. It had a floor of metal grating, and her feet sounded on it despite the low gravity.

She recognized the captain immediately. Ava Wharton was an intimidating woman with graying hair in a bun and four bars on each shoulder, and again Sheila wished she could reconsider her plan. But the captain had seen her, so it was too late now.

"Dr. Jackson, it's good to see you," called Captain Wharton.

Sheila approached the military woman, bouncing a bit in the low g. "Good to meet you as well, Captain. Call me Sheila."

"Shall we talk in my office?"

"That would be good."

"First time on the bridge?" asked Wharton as they walked.

"It is. I never really thought about people flying the ship. From inside, it's easy to forget sometimes that we're moving at all."

"I know it. Tens of thousands of kilometers per second and it feels like we're standing still."

"That's actually what I'm here to talk to you about," said Sheila, as they reached the door to the captain's office.

"The velocity of the ship? That seems like a pretty unusual topic."

"Yes, well . . ." She hesitated, changing her mind. She had an elaborate story in her head about needing to slow the ship for scientific reasons, delay their arrival, but the way the captain looked at her made her discard that. "Actually no."

"So . . . not about the velocity?" The captain smiled, a natural thing, a woman comfortable in her own skin.

"It's not. I want to talk about the governor."

Wharton nodded. "I saw your news conference. Have a seat. Can I get you anything?"

Sheila took the offered chair while the captain moved behind her desk. She couldn't believe she had planned to lie to this woman who seemed to see right through her. "I'm fine, thank you."

"You sure? Tea, maybe?"

"Actually, tea would be nice."

"Great. You talk while I make it." Wharton moved to a water heater, pushed a button, and busied herself pulling things from a small cabinet. It surprised Sheila to see her doing that herself. She always assumed that the ship's captain would have somebody to serve her or something.

Realizing Wharton was waiting for her to start talking, she let out a deep breath. She was here. There was nothing to do but spit it out. "His plan won't work."

"Mmmm," said the captain.

"The science for a general landing isn't there yet. There's too much that we don't know."

The stocky woman poured water into two mugs. "Is there a cause for that?"

"For starters, it was always going to be that way. We need time in orbit with specialized teams on the ground to fully analyze our best options. But a lack of communication with all of our surface probes so far is exacerbating it exponentially."

She nodded. "I've read about that. Since my briefings on that are duplicates of the governor's, I have to assume that he's aware as well. Milk or sugar?"

"Yes, please. Both. And yes, he's definitely aware."

Wharton carried two mugs over, handed one to Sheila, and then retreated behind her desk. "And you're here because you don't like his decision to expedite the missions to the surface."

"Honestly? I'm here because I didn't have anywhere else to go. He's not listening, and the course he's charting for us is going to put people needlessly at risk. We'd need *years* to ensure a safe colony, and he's talking about weeks."

"You have to know you're on record and widely quoted as supporting an immediate move to the planet." Wharton had a calm way of speaking that relaxed Sheila, even as she called out her own role in the problem.

"I am. But that was taken out of context. Yes, we can send people to the planet. We *should*. A small team of trained scientists and technicians observing strict contamination protocols who can do the research we need to discover what's there—especially on the microscopic level—and give us time to develop protections. But not colonize it—not yet."

The captain considered it. "I hear what you're saying, and I believe you, but the governor has to have his reasons."

"Science doesn't much care about his reasons. The planet won't care if it kills everyone."

"That's a lot to put on Promissa." The captain chuckled. "You're right, though—it surely doesn't. But have you considered his side of things? I'm no fan of Governor Pantel, but I've never found him to be irrational."

Sheila took a sip of tea as she considered that. She *had* dismissed his plan outright, but now that the captain said it, she saw the error. She'd made the same mistake before. She was smart, so sometimes it was easy for her to just dismiss other people as being stupid instead of considering that they might have their own valid ideas—or maybe invalid. That didn't mean he didn't have his own reasons. "So . . . what's his motivation?"

"Let me think." With that, Wharton fell silent, sipping at her tea and appearing to do exactly that. It was over a minute before she spoke again. "If we give him the purest possible motive, we could attribute it to morale."

"Morale?"

"People need to see the potential for the future. The idea of getting to our destination and spending . . . what, ten years? Twenty . . . ?"

"Something like that."

"Spending twenty years in orbit, not able to touch the prize . . . that's depressing, even to me."

"That was *always* the plan, though."

Wharton barked a laugh. "And the plan was always unrealistic, at least in regard to expectations."

"None of this changes the facts."

"I think you've got a very narrow view of what *facts* are." She paused to sip at her tea.

Sheila's discomfort grew. The captain's remark hit a lot harder than she'd have thought it would.

"There are other forces at play beyond science. Sociological factors, political ones. You can't ignore those."

"But *he* can ignore the science?"

"He shouldn't, but yes, he can. So lay out your case. What are the facts bearing on the situation from your perspective?" asked the captain.

"First, we've got no sense of the microbial environment on the planet, but contamination—in both directions—is not just likely, it's inevitable. And the larger the group we send, the more we exacerbate that."

"If it's inevitable, then why not get it over with?"

Sheila wanted to scream. She was losing control of this the same way she'd lost control of the news.

Perhaps sensing that, Wharton didn't wait for her response. "You have to be able to answer that question. If contamination is inevitable, why not accept it and move on? I'm not going to be the only one who asks."

Sheila responded with a raised voice. "Because there's inevitable where we have a small contamination and we study it, and there's inevitable where we wipe out a third of the ship's population or we destroy the planet's ecosystem before we can figure out what's happened."

"Calm down," said Wharton. Just from her tone, Sheila felt the fight going out of her. That was an impressive skill the captain had. "Maybe think about how you're going to answer it scientifically, not emotionally. You've got a case to make. Back it up."

"That's the problem. I need more time and more information before I even *know* the case. We don't have as much as a soil sample yet."

"How much time do you need?"

"I can't even tell you *that* without more information."

Wharton nodded. "Do you see why that's a problem? I hear you. You need more time. But the idea that you're going to get an unlimited amount until you reach some arbitrary—"

"It's not arbitrary," Sheila interrupted, and immediately stopped speaking when the captain glared at her.

Wharton sipped her tea, letting the silence linger for a few seconds. "Asking for an undefined amount of time is going to get you nowhere. The governor—the crew—needs specifics. If you want to make a case, that's how you do it."

Sheila hesitated. The woman had essentially just told her to do her job, and somehow all she wanted to do was exactly that. "Okay. I hear what you're saying and I'll work on laying out a . . . potential . . . timeline." She couldn't bring herself to say that she'd come up with a definite one because there was no way she could promise that. As soon as they got real data from the surface, it would change any hypothesis she could craft now. "But I'll need at least *some* time when we reach orbit. Will you talk to him?"

Wharton thought about that for a little bit. "I don't think I can. I'm sorry."

"What? Of course you can. You're the captain."

She shook her head. "I make it a point not to get involved in politics. I can't. My role is to stay above that, and it's important that I'm seen to be doing that."

"This isn't politics! It's science."

"You still don't get it. Of *course* it's politics. It's both. Yes, the science is the science. But the presentation of that science and the decisions stemming from it—"

"—are politics," finished Sheila. "So . . . what? I just give up? Do my job and shut up while he flies us down a path—and this is not hyperbole—a path to possible extinction?"

"Of course not. I'm not getting involved, but you should talk to him. Control it. Find an acceptable course based on the information you have—or don't have. One that you can convince him to support. And then put in the control measures to mitigate things and get the best outcome that you can."

"Like more training for people going down."

"Sure. Among other things. Use your imagination. If I told you I wanted three hundred people living on the planet in two months, what's the best possible way to do that?"

"Multiple settlements, separated by enough distance so they didn't interact with each other to avoid cross-contamination."

"There you go."

"And with a bias toward colder climates."

"That works, too," said Wharton. "None of that interferes with anything I heard the governor say."

"Fully contained habitats with airlocks and decontamination."

"Which is even better because we'd need to start manufacturing those things early, right? Which fits with the governor's possible desire to give people something to look forward to: hope."

For the first time in a while, Sheila could see that herself. Hope. "I'm really sorry I bothered you with this."

Wharton laughed. "Don't be. If it's like you say and the survival of our species depends on it? I think I can spare you whatever time you need. Even if it means listening to you work the problem out loud."

"But not talk to the governor." Sheila faked a smile, trying to take the bite out of the shot, but probably failed.

Wharton turned her palms up. "My role is my role. We all have them. Try to figure out how yours fits with the governor's."

Sheila laughed. "I'd rather not."

"We'd *all* rather not."

<CHAPTER 16>

GEORGE IANNOU

|||||||||||||||||||||||||||||||||||||||||||||||||||||||||||||||||||||||||||

92 CYCLES UNTIL ARRIVAL

George walked down the center of the long, narrow oxygenation chamber—almost more a corridor than a room, crowded as it was on both sides by polymer trellises roped with walls of English ivy and floor bins of some sort of philodendrons—the ones with the broad leaves named after some animal or something. Oxygenation plants weren't his specialty. The thick green foliage dampened the sound, and the continuous drip irrigation made the air heavy with moisture, giving the whole place a peaceful feel. It made George feel comfortable despite the 92 percent gravity.

He pushed some ivy aside and shone his flashlight through, but he found only the metal wall of the compartment and some pipes. That didn't stop him from repeating the process a half dozen times on each side. He'd chosen this location for the meeting because it was an unlikely spot for Secfor to monitor, but he still had to check for recording devices. He wasn't a good leader, hadn't wanted to be one at all, but he knew enough not to cut corners.

There was a single camera in the compartment, and the oxygenation chamber was one of hundreds of nearly identical ones. Despite the video hardware being in place, nobody had time to watch them all. It was one place where the restrictions on AIs helped them, as those rules were strictly enforced when it came to cameras. Nobody wanted computers watching them full-time. Ironically, turning it off or blocking it would be more likely to draw attention than simply meeting in front of it. It didn't record sound, and even if it did, they'd be using a baffle to disrupt that as a second line of security and in case any of their own people decided to bring in their own recorder. If he thought he could get away with it, he'd have searched everybody, but he didn't dare test the bounds of his authority. So he did what he could. If he had to have a meeting, he'd have a safe one.

And as tired as he was of meetings, he did have to do it. For ship's sake, all he ever did these days was talk. He started the day talking at his morning meeting, which inevitably spilled over into several after-meetings, and then throughout the day, as he tried to get his work done, people found him and wanted to talk even more. He did what he could to make himself scarce, but he couldn't ignore the three people who wanted to meet now. They represented different factions of the opposition to the government, though each of those factions had their own internal divisions as well. Despite the varied politics, they still looked to him, at least on the surface, as the overall leader. Not that that meant they'd do what he said or anything useful like that. But they'd listen when he talked.

Koshi Tanaka and Sara Washburn entered at the same time, comfortable together even though their politics weren't. They'd spent enough time with each other to reach an uneasy understanding. Sara generally supported change, would even discuss specific changes, such as extended life. She'd call herself antiestablishment if pushed, but she'd be among the first to fall in line if things got hard. But as the leader of the moderates, she represented the most people, even though they were the least likely to actually do anything. Still, there was benefit in numbers alone, especially when it came to protests.

Koshi wanted action, and he wanted it now. He treated Sara as an honored peer, but if you put a lie detector on him, he'd probably admit that he detested her and saw her as a bigger problem than the establishment itself. He wanted things she'd never support, and he was willing to take risks and push boundaries to get those things. He'd have probably been detained already if he hadn't done such a good job rotating his two dozen or so followers on the most visible tasks. And he wasn't even the most radical. That role belonged to a short woman who entered a moment later.

Delta Acevedo. Oddly, she was probably the least known of the four of them, despite having a much more militant ideology. Because of the nature of what they did, her people had to be more secretive. If not, they'd be in the brig and likely heading to execution. Rumors were circulating, albeit quietly, that she had bigger plans in mind, and that worried George more than anything else.

"Can we make this quick?" asked Delta as she sauntered up, dragging her feet a bit. Unlike the rest of them, she didn't regularly work on the farm decks—though she'd been spending more time there lately, as most of the semi-illegal things happened in the lower levels where there was a smaller risk of Secfor interference.

As usual, Koshi responded first. George was convinced that half the reason he was involved in the opposition at all was because he liked to hear himself speak. "We all know that the governor isn't taking us seriously." The man couldn't even come up with a new line, repeating his refrain from previous days.

"You're right." George wouldn't have argued even if he disagreed. He'd learned that the fastest way to end a conversation was to agree with everything. Tanaka wasn't going to be happy regardless, so why not humor him?

"You saw the news conference. He's accelerating the timeline and he's asking for volunteers. It's a pure distraction."

"You're right," George said again.

"That's all you ever say."

He didn't bother pointing out the hypocrisy of Tanaka saying that. "What else do you want me to say? I agree with you. I really do." And that was the truth. The governor had put out a call for volunteers to go to the planet, and people were signing up. Not the core of the movement. They'd reject anything the governor asked as a matter of principle. But the people in the middle, the ones they needed to convince if they wanted to effect change . . . *they'd* bought into the plan. And that was a problem.

"I don't want you to *say* anything. I want you to *do* something."

"So give me some ideas. What should I do?"

Tanaka paced as he spoke. "You've got that woman—the computer genius. Have her do something." He kept saying *something* like it was actually constructive.

"She did something: she released the unedited video of the Secfor incident. Unless you forgot about that." George said the last bit with sarcasm. The man hadn't forgotten. The video had been released two days before, and it had made a big impression on people. It wasn't even what Secfor did—it was that the government had lied about it and tried to cover it up.

"And what did that change?"

George sighed. Anything short of armed rebellion would always fall short in some people's eyes, and Tanaka seemed to be moving in that direction. "It changed people's minds. It showed the governor's lies."

"Not enough."

"These things take time."

"Time." Delta spit on the deck. "We'll be sitting on the planet, wondering how we got there, destroying dozens of species of intelligent life, and you'll still be saying that it takes time."

"We don't even know that there's going to *be* intelligent life."

"There's evidence. You've seen the photo."

"The photo with a grainy something in it that might be eyes or might just be distorted light? Yes. I've seen it. And I haven't seen anything else. Have you? Is there something new?"

"Something is jamming the transmissions," said Tanaka.

"Yes, there are problems with the transmissions," said George. "We all have the same source inside space ex. But 'jamming' implies active intent."

"How do you know there isn't? If there was intelligent life, the first thing they'd do would be to stop our communications."

"Are we just going to rehash the same crap?" asked Sara. "I don't even know why I need to be here. This is a 'you guys' problem."

"To you, everything's a 'you guys' problem." Delta wasn't nearly as circumspect in dealing with Sara as Koshi, which made sense, since she didn't need her except on the periphery. Delta wasn't much for protests, so a mass of people wasn't the resource it was for Koshi. If Delta needed something, it was access to a location or a special skill, and she'd never pass that through more than one person. To her, Sara's was a needless role. In George's mind it was a short-sighted view, as today's sometimes activist became tomorrow's radical, but then, Delta's strength wasn't really in thinking long-term.

He wasn't sure that was a strength of any in this little group.

"Hey, we're out there in the corridors making our voices heard," said Sara.

"Yeah," said Delta. "So helpful."

"We're on the same side," said George.

"*Are* we?" asked Delta. "Koshi said it. You've got the hacker girl. She can get into the cameras. Why not the engines?"

"Because they're the engines," Sara said as if that was the most obvious answer.

"Exactly."

"So she hacks them and we just drift out here in space and die," said Sara.

Tanaka gave an exaggerated sigh. "You don't even know how things work."

"You really don't," said Delta. "We don't shut them down forever. Just a couple of days would be long enough to cause us to miss our entry window into the system."

"Right," said Tanaka. "We fly right by. By the time we get turned around, we've got an extra three or four years to study the planet. To see what's down there. To follow the science."

Delta scowled at him. "We've got three or four years to bend the leadership to our will."

"Four years for us to all be executed," George said. "We're not stopping the ship."

Everyone went silent at that, staring at him. In Delta's case, it was more of a glare, and she was the first to break the silence. "If you're not going to take action, I will."

"And what does that mean?" asked Sara before George could.

"Nothing. Just go back to your protests."

"Don't do anything stupid," said Koshi, suddenly worried enough to change sides.

"Then make the girl stop the ship," said Delta.

"That's not how we operate," said George.

"It seems like we don't operate at all."

"We have to preserve our options," said George.

Delta shook her head. "You want to preserve options. I want to effect change. And if you won't act . . ."

"What? If I won't act, what?" George was sick of it. The complaints. Everyone had the right answer in their own mind. Nobody wanted to compromise, to find an actual workable solution.

Delta hesitated. Maybe she realized she had overstepped, but probably not. "If you won't act, maybe someone else will."

George wanted to question that, but before he could, Delta stormed off. Tanaka hesitated for a second, and then hurried to join her, leaving Sara and George by themselves.

"What are you going to do about that?" she asked.

"Do about what?"

Sarah glared at him, and then she turned and stormed off as well.

"LET ME ASK YOU SOMETHING," SAID GEORGE. KAYLA SAT ACROSS THE dinner table from him eating vat-grown pork in barbecue sauce with a side of garlic rice noodles, which seemed like an odd combination. She set her fork down and looked at him, ready as always to act as his sounding board. "What would you think if somebody did something to cause us to miss the planet and delay our arrival by a few years?"

She picked up her fork again and shrugged. "It's a start."

George narrowed his eyes, confused. "I don't understand. What do you mean, 'a start'?"

"A lot of people are talking about not colonizing the planet at all."

"They're *what*? Why would anybody think that? Of *course* we're going to colonize the planet. That's the whole purpose of the mission. Who's saying that?"

"Everyone."

George took a bite of mashed potatoes. *Everyone* was a nebulous term with Kayla, because she meant everyone she talked to, which was not everyone at all, but a small group of like-minded young people. It had taken him a while to figure that out. But the fact that *anybody* was talking about forgoing colonization was baffling. "What's driving that discussion?"

"That picture. The one with the eyes. What right do we have to take a planet away from a species that's already there?"

"We don't know that they're intelligent," said George.

"Does it matter?"

George took another bite to give himself a few seconds to think. "You really mean this? You really think we should pass up the planet after all these years?"

Kayla finished chewing before she responded. "I don't know. Probably. We should at least be planning other options. Maybe it would be okay if we got their consent. There are a lot of things to think about."

George nodded. She had that right. There were a lot of things to think about, but right then, the only ones on his mind were the numerous, conflicting ideas held by the people he was supposed to be leading, and how much trouble this one was going to cause.

<CHAPTER 17>

MARK RECTOR

‖‖

89 CYCLES UNTIL ARRIVAL

Another day, another anonymous tip, and Rector was over it. This one *had* felt different, with some specific information instead of just another ghost sighting of Eddie Dannin, but he'd felt that way before only to have the rug pulled out from under him. He'd dragged Sierks with him, all the same. Mwangi still wasn't cleared for duty, and he sure as shit wasn't taking Danielson on anything again anytime soon. The man was a walking bulkhead, in both size and intelligence. Sierks was fine, average-size, and quiet. Quiet was good, given Rector's headache. He'd been drinking too much. He needed to stop doing that.

He probably wouldn't.

They stepped off of the elevator on one of the manufacturing levels, 0.72 gravity with superhigh ceilings to accommodate some of the machinery housed there. The tip that had led them there said there was a threat to one of the big printers, but not what the threat was. They had to check it out—the printers were too vulnerable not to, and opposition groups had already shown that they could and would target manufacturing. Dannin had done her last known hack from there, and even if she hadn't, the value in controlling a printer, altering its output even in small ways, was too important to take lightly. He'd proposed putting guards there for that reason, but Darvan had never followed through.

So here he was.

They made their way down the wide corridor to where doors to the two large-printer bays stood on either side. He paused, and Sierks dutifully stopped with him. Shit. Which one had the tip mentioned? Had it been J7307A or J7307B? He pulled it up on his device. It was B. He decided to test Sierks, see if the rookie had his head in the game. "Which door?"

"B," said Sierks.

"Right. Good man." Rector moved to the door and put his hand on the pad. The large door zipped open. A flash blinded Rector and something punched him in the chest. He was on the ground, tangled with Sierks, his ears ringing . . . no, more than ringing. His shoulder ached . . . it had slammed into the far wall. *How the fuck did I get here?* His lungs burned and the acrid smell of burning plastic and electronics singed his nostrils.

"Rector!" The sound came from a long way away, muted.

He put his hand on the ground, tried to push himself up, fell back to the deck, pain lancing through his hand. Blood streaked the flooring, and he turned his palm to find a centimeter-long piece of metal protruding from it.

"Rector!" Sierks was in his face, yelling, though it didn't sound like a yell. Rector could barely hear him, as if he was speaking through water.

"What happened?"

"Bomb, I think."

Fuck. Guess it wasn't another fake tip. Which was a sick way to think about it, but his brain wasn't working right. Vaguely, he thought that he probably had a concussion. Had he lost consciousness? He didn't have time to worry about that. He rolled to his hands and knees, being careful of the injured palm, got a foot under him, staggered to his feet. "We've got to get in there!"

Sierks didn't respond, or if he did, Rector didn't hear him. He was already moving. His eyes stung from the smoke pouring from the door, which was jammed open now. If he was this bad off, he didn't want to see anybody who had been in the room. Hopefully it had been unoccupied.

A form materialized, tripped, fell into him, and Rector stumbled, trying to keep his own balance while keeping the man—no, woman—from falling. He got her to her feet, pulled her back from the entry. "Is anybody else inside?" He couldn't hear her response, so he took her face in his hands, turned it toward him. "Is anybody else in there?" he yelled this time.

She nodded, her face covered in ash, her nose bleeding.

"How many?"

She held up one finger. "Halon," she said, though he more read it from her lips than heard it.

Shit.

Halon. Of course. That was the ship's automatic fire suppression system, which would suck the oxygen out of the room to smother the fire. It would also asphyxiate any survivors. He grabbed a metal rod and jammed it into the door to physically keep it from shutting—that would help at least a little—and then he looked around for a mask station. He spotted one down the hall and started running, swaying as he went, bouncing off of the wall and righting himself. Yep. Definitely a concussion. He hit the auto release, grabbed a helmet, steadied himself, and put it over his head, and then waited impatiently for the two and a half seconds it took to form a seal with his suit. Fresh air hit his lungs, and he coughed. He looked to the small external O_2 cartridges, considered hooking one up, but that took time he didn't have if he hoped to find any-body alive in the printer room. The helmet itself had ten minutes of air. That would have to be enough. Others would respond to the alarm. He hoped. If the elevators still worked. He had no idea how extensive the damage was. An explosion. On a ship in space. The hull.

Shit.

No. He couldn't worry about that. He ran back toward the room, steadier now, didn't stop for Sierks or the woman. He en-tered the bay and stopped, tried to get his bearings. The filtration systems were fighting the smoke as it swirled around him, first revealing a large swath of the huge room then masking it again just as quickly. Machinery was still humming, though he couldn't process how loud it was. A flash of color caught his attention through the gray, and he headed toward it.

He reached it—a body, a man, lying on his side against one of the giant printers. Not the one that had blown up—this one was still running, vibrating, shaking the man's limp form. *How?* Rector reached out and put his hand on the man's neck. He had a pulse! Shit. You weren't supposed to move an injured person, but he had to get the guy out of there. He should have thought to grab a second helmet, but there was no sense dwelling on that mistake now.

Okay. Think. He had to move the man to safety. He considered a shoulder carry, but didn't trust his balance, so he wrestled the man into a sitting position, got himself under the man's arm and shoulder, and pushed them both up, pressing his back against the printer for leverage. He could do this.

They stumbled—or rather he did. The other man was limp, deadweight with dragging feet. Rector righted himself and took another step, dragging the body—the man, not a body—with him. Another step, a stop, rest. He found the door through the haze, reoriented. Took another step. How long had he been in there with his helmet? How much O2 did he have left? Didn't matter. Another step.

And then Sierks was there, helmet on, tank fastened to his hip, and supporting the limp man under his other shoulder. Together they made better speed as they moved forward, closing the distance to the exit. And then they were through the door into the corridor, away from the smoke. People were arriving, helmets on, emergency gear in hand. Someone took the man away from him, and then Rector was sitting on the floor. A tall woman fastened a canister to his hip, connected it to his helmet.

"You're okay. I've got you." Her words came through, still distant, but better. His hearing was coming back. More people had arrived, and they were taking over. He started to fade.

"Hey!" The woman shook him. "No going to sleep!"

That's right. Concussion. He nodded, but it hurt. His hand stung. His shoulder ached. If he and Sierks had arrived a few seconds earlier . . . if he hadn't stopped to quiz the rookie in the hallway . . . The tip had been right. Or . . . it was a setup, and the tip was meant to lure him there. He couldn't prove it, but once the idea took root, he couldn't shake it. He needed to think that through, but it could wait until his mind cleared. He wasn't going anywhere fast.

CHAPTER 18

EDDIE DANNIN

89 CYCLES UNTIL ARRIVAL

Something had made a noise. Eddie didn't immediately know where she was when she woke up, but she knew that.

"Come on."

She flinched and her heart slammed in her chest at the words. It was dark, the only light coming in from an open door. The lights came on and she squinted.

"Come on. We've got to go," the man repeated.

"What's going on?" asked Eddie.

"We have to move you."

"We just moved," she whined. She remembered that now. Her fourth new room. She'd gotten there, set up her stuff, and finally fallen asleep in her suit.

"There's been an emergency. Hurry."

She sat up. "What time is it?"

"Fifteenth hour."

Eddie nodded and rose from the mattress which was lying loosely on the floor of what looked to be a maintenance room. "Okay. Help me get my stuff."

"Someone else will bring it. There's no time. Secfor are searching some of the ship and they're coming here."

If they found her stuff, they'd know she'd been there. She wanted to say that to the man—she'd forgotten his name, though she'd seen his face a couple of times—but he wouldn't care. He wasn't a decision maker. Might as well argue with a bot.

They snaked through several chambers full of various green plants, the heavy gravity pulling at her, making her breathe hard. Sweat started to bead on her forehead.

"Through here," said the man, opening an access hatch. A ladder led upward, and for the first time since she woke, Eddie felt comfortable. A maintenance passage. These she knew.

"You coming?" she asked him.

"No. Go up two levels and exit. Someone will meet you there."

"Okay. Uh . . . thanks."

"Go."

Her arms and legs were heavy, so it took her a couple minutes to reach the second portal up, even though she covered only twenty or thirty meters. The metal ladder was cold against her skin, the tube lit only by a series of evenly spaced LED bulbs. She hesitated before opening the door and looked up. The passage went on as far as she could see, heading for the center of the ship. She could keep going, come out anywhere. She knew the maintenance passages, and with a little time, she'd gain her bearings, figure out where she was. If she caught a side passage, they'd never be able to track her. But eventually she'd have to come out, and if she did, she'd have to hope that she'd find a better situation than her current one. No. That was too much left to chance. She needed more information first. She opened the hatch.

A woman hurried over from where she'd been waiting down

the corridor. "I'm Anura. Hurry. We've only got a few seconds with the camera off."

"If we're killing a camera, they'll know right where we are," said Eddie.

"We're killing twelve in a bunch of different places on the ship. Besides, they have other things to worry about right now. Move."

They half walked, half jogged through little-used narrow corridors until they came out into a grain farm. Eddie did her best to commit the path to memory as they moved through the dirt.

"In here," said Anura.

Eddie poked her head through the hatch into a small room with a mattress on the floor with several blankets and a pillow. A polymer folding chair was her only other furniture, but on the far wall, there was a sink, and she almost jumped for joy seeing it. Running water. She headed to it and turned it on. Sure enough, running water, via a pipe someone had probably diverted years ago from one of the agriculture rooms. "I need my stuff. I need to get on the net."

"It's on the way. Someone's bringing it via a different route."

"The guy below mentioned an emergency. What happened?"

"Bomb," said Anura.

"Really?"

"That's what people are saying, but the news is still fuzzy."

"Thanks." Now she really needed to be on the net. Her saviors-slash-captors kept her from it at first, thinking she'd bring down security on them as soon as she logged on. That would have been true if they'd been talking to anybody else. But she was a ghost, entering at will with barely a trace, and that a fleeting one. It wasn't until she'd offered to do work for them that they'd finally relented. They'd brought her a terminal, and she was able to scrounge a few parts to increase its performance. It was nowhere close to her normal setup, but the equipment mattered less than the operator. She'd been careful at first, but as she went, she learned new tricks to move through the net without detection. Ironically, by forcing her into hiding, they'd actually made her stronger.

Her first day back on she hacked into the original video of the kerfuffle outside her room. She'd initially done it to show off some of her skills, to demonstrate her worth to the people who were keeping her hidden. That she discovered the video had been altered was mostly a lucky coincidence. Her jailors had definitely seen the value after that, so . . . mission accomplished in that regard. And when she got out of here, she could use it to show Cecil that she was doing what he said and making the governor pay.

If she got out of here. That wasn't a given. They'd kept her undetected, and while they didn't know how to use her, they *did* see her as an asset. They wanted her to turn off a camera here or there. Meanwhile, Governor Pantel was destroying the antigovernment group in the news feeds, and they weren't doing anything to counter it. But she couldn't do it on her own. Well, she could do *anything* on the technical side. The political side was their business, and from what she could see, they were thinking too small.

They'd had her for a while now—about ten cycles—and she'd started to see things in a different light. She wasn't always quick to see when people were using her—never had been—but she always did figure it out eventually. She'd first thought of them as friends, and she'd tried to do things to help their cause since they were hiding her. But in truth, they'd screwed her. If they'd just let her get caught, the most Secfor could have done was thrown her in the brig for a bit. Sure, she'd done illegal stuff, but they probably couldn't prove it. Now? By her not showing up for work, they had an open-and-shut case, and it might be enough to send her to the recycler. It *shouldn't* be. People had missed work for stretches of time before, usually when they'd been on some kind of bender. But work was enshrined in the Charter as one of the core tenets of the ship, and in theory failure to work could warrant the death penalty. In practice, if it was a first offense, it was usually forgiven. But Secfor wanted her for other crimes—the hack of the science information that they didn't want to talk about—so the absent-without-leave charge might be a convenient excuse to eliminate her.

Which all meant she was stuck. She'd simply traded one set of captors for another.

She hadn't seen George since the first day in hiding, despite her demanding a meeting. He was supposed to see her today, but now? Who knew. Did he even know where she was? They could be lying to her, and she wouldn't know it. She needed to change that.

A HALF HOUR PASSED BEFORE SOMEONE SHOWED UP—A YOUNG GUY, her age, leading what she thought might be a harvesting cart that he parked in the door. "Hey," he said.

"Hi."

"I'm Ryan."

"Eddie."

"I brought your stuff." He turned to the cart and retracted the lid. He had to bend over to reach it, then came back up with her deck. She hurried over and took it from him. After a couple more trips, she had her computer rig on the floor by her mattress and a sack with her other meager possessions beside her.

"Thanks," she said.

"Yeah." Ryan turned and left, and Eddie couldn't help but wonder if he knew why she was there or if he was just doing what he was told.

She took her time connecting to the net, hiding her presence.

Once there, she found it afire with conflicting rumors, all of them having one thing in common: there had been an explosion. Stories didn't agree on much else. Even the location was under debate, with at least three different people in three different places claiming to have seen it with their own eyes. One theory held that there had been multiple explosions. And that didn't even begin to explain the confusion about how it happened. It was simultaneously a grossly malfunctioning printer, a problem with one of the engines, a cooking accident, and a bomb. Eddie didn't believe the part about the engine, as that would have shown up immediately in engineering spaces, and it hadn't—she'd checked there first. Besides, if something had gone boom in the engines, well . . . they wouldn't still be here. There was no such thing as a *small* problem with a fusion reactor.

Not that any explosion inside a sealed ship was a good thing.

She was still sifting through information an hour later when George Iannou knocked on the frame of her makeshift door—the door itself being a canvas tarp. His face was drawn and sallow, with dark circles under both eyes. He looked like he'd been awake for two days.

"You look like shit."

Iannou's expression didn't change, his mouth stuck in a half frown. "It's been a bit of a day. Sorry I'm late."

"This about what people are talking about on the net?"

"Yeah."

"What actually happened? Do you know?" asked Eddie. She had other questions for him, but she was curious enough that she couldn't help it.

Iannou walked over and took a seat in her only chair. "They bombed one of the big printers."

"Bombed . . . who's 'they'?"

"I'm not completely sure. I've got some ideas, but . . ." He shrugged. "I couldn't prove them. I'm not sure I want to."

"So . . . your people? The Eternal Lifers?" If they'd set off a bomb, they'd just moved higher up her shit list. She needed to get out of there, and soon.

Iannou snorted. "My people? I don't even know if I have any people."

Eddie leaned back against the wall. "What do you mean?"

"This whole thing has gotten out of control. It started as a bunch of folks protesting mandatory end of life—a simple cause, and a pretty popular one—and then some people joined on because they want job mobility across directorates. A little more complicated, but pretty rational, right?"

"Sure," said Eddie. "I'm *definitely* for that one."

"Now? Every group that has a beef with the ship's leadership for any reason is making noise. And some of them have some ideas that are *way* out there."

"Yeah? Like what?"

"Like bombs."

"Hmph."

"Yeah. And then there's a group that wants to save the planet. They claim there's evidence of intelligent life down there—secret pictures that the scientists aren't releasing, or something like that—and that we should bypass the planet altogether. That we don't have a right to it."

"That's . . ." Eddie let her voice trail off. She didn't know what it was, or what she thought about it. She'd never even considered the idea, and immediately it struck her as incredibly complicated. Intelligent life? Would that life welcome their arrival? Did they have a right to impinge upon the ecosystem if that was the case? It was too much to process in a short span, so she gave it up and turned to the practical. "Was it them who planted the bomb?"

"I think so. It fits their mindset. They're by far the most radical subgroup in the protest movement. Whether they have the capability or the will to do something this drastic? I don't know."

"A freakin' bomb," Eddie muttered. "Don't they realize that we're on a ship traveling through a vacuum? They could have killed us all."

"I don't think it was initially that big of an explosion. From what I'm hearing, it may have set off some kind of secondary reaction in the printer itself."

"Which is why you don't set off *bombs* on a ship!"

Iannou put his hands up to calm her. "I hear you. We didn't exactly have a committee meeting about it."

"Sorry," said Eddie. And she was. It wasn't his fault. Well, maybe it was. Either way, she just hadn't had a lot of contact with people recently, and as much as she liked to think of herself as an introvert, now she had someone to listen, and she wanted to air her feelings.

"Don't worry about it. Now . . . you asked for me before the bomb ever happened, so clearly that's not what you wanted to talk about. I've only got a couple of minutes. What can I do for you?"

"You've got to get me out of here."

"We'll move you to another safe space in a couple of days—"

"That's not what I mean," said Eddie. "I mean you have to get me back to my real life."

Iannou furrowed his full brow, confused. "How are we supposed to do that?"

"I don't know. You're the strategist. Figure something out. Your people got me into this situation. What am I supposed to do? Hide for the rest of my life?"

"I kind of figured that something would present itself somewhere down the line."

"Not good enough," said Eddie. She kept her voice calm, but inside she was seething. *Something would present itself* . . . he might as well have said that he had no clue, and they had no plan for her at all. And if that was his thought, what recourse did she have? She could threaten him, but if she did, she might find herself in an even worse situation. It wouldn't take much for them to physically cut her off from net access, and without that, she was powerless.

"I'm not sure what to tell you. If we return you to normal life, they're going to arrest you immediately. You know that."

Unless I cut a deal to turn in other people. "Then you've got to negotiate something to get me immunity."

Iannou stayed silent for several seconds. "That's a possibility. I'll need to think on it."

"*Think* on it? What's to think about?"

"How about what I could offer in trade? Or do you want me to go into a negotiation with Secfor—or the governor—and say, 'Well, I think she's learned her lesson. How about we all agree to just let this go, m'kay?' Be realistic. I've got to have some sort of leverage."

"What about the bomber?"

"What do you mean?"

Eddie thought about it. What *did* she mean? "I mean, maybe you can solve two problems at once. You've got a radical group that's subverting your purpose, right?"

"Sure, but I don't see how—"

Eddie cut him off. "And it stands to reason that Secfor is going to *really* want this bomber, right?"

"Sure. Yeah. I'd assume so."

"Maybe more than they want me."

Iannou's face lit up. "So you're saying I should go to the authorities and offer to trade the bomber in exchange for immunity for you."

"You do it, or someone else does. As long as I can stop hiding."

He thought about it. "That could work, but there are a couple of problems with it."

"Such as?" asked Eddie.

"Such as we don't know who the bomber is."

"Don't you?"

"Seriously—I don't have any definitive proof."

"Fine—leave that to me."

Iannou studied her, and then nodded. "You'd have to figure it out before Secfor does, or we'd lose our leverage."

"Yep. So consider me a *very motivated* participant in this little endeavor. If that's what I've got to do to get my life back, I'm on it." Eddie paused. "You said 'a couple of problems.' What's the other one?"

"These people—the ones you want to turn in—they're not playing around, Eddie. These folks are dangerous. If they find out that you turned them in, I don't know what they'd do."

"You think they'd come after me?"

"I couldn't rule it out."

Eddie thought about it, and then shrugged. "I'll solder that circuit when I get to it." She tried to keep her voice light, as if it didn't matter, but she kept her hands clasped together so Iannou wouldn't see them shaking. People who would set off a bomb on a ship were not a threat to ignore. But if that was the risk she had to take in order to get her life back, what choice did she have?

"You sure?"

"I'm sure. I'll find the asshole. You just figure out how you're going to trade the information for my freedom."

Iannou stood and held out a meaty hand, engulfing Eddie's. "Deal. What do you need?"

"Give me some names you *think* are associated with the save-the-planet group. I'll take it from there." *Where* she would take it, she didn't say, but it probably wouldn't be to Iannou. It wasn't that she didn't trust him. Okay, it was a *little bit* that she didn't trust him. But more than that, he cared too much. If it came to his cause or her well-being, he'd choose the cause every time. Some people would find that admirable. Eddie found it inconvenient. But they could work together for a time. After all, they both wanted to find the same information.

"Names?"

"You said you had some ideas. Give me one."

Iannou thought about it. "Koshi Tanaka and Delta Acevedo. Neither of them did it, but odds are pretty good that one of them knows who did."

EDDIE WASN'T SURE WHEN SHE'D LAST SLEPT. MORE THAN A CYCLE ago, for sure, if she didn't count the catnaps she stole in front of her terminal while she waited for one of her processes to finish. Without her powerful system, she'd had to be inventive with the code. She'd embedded some weak AIs in the system to parse information for her and allow her to watch more of the same things at the same time. Those were illegal, of course, but at this point so was everything she was doing. It wasn't like they could throw her in the brig twice. But even with the AIs working, she couldn't afford to turn away from it herself for long—there were too many moving elements.

Among other things, she was watching Secfor, who weren't

afraid to talk about their entire investigation over the net, which, well . . . that was not bright. They probably thought nobody was stupid enough to hack into them and read their conversations. *Surprise, assholes.* Someone *was* that stupid. It was delicate work, monitoring their leads but simultaneously having to avoid their cyber people, who were looking for her. One benefit to the bomb was that they were spending a lot less time trying to find *her.*

Nothing like a major terrorist incident to move you down the most-wanted list.

She learned right away the major advantage of spying on Secfor: When they had a suspect, they couldn't invade the person's privacy without going through a magistrate. Eddie could. That Secfor seemed to actually follow that law surprised her a little. She had always thought that they secretly sifted through people's personal data, but if they were doing it, they were being super cautious, like they'd been when they started trying to spy on her. Or maybe they'd stopped *because* of her. Because of what she'd done to them when she found them out. Regardless of the reason, it gave her a head start looking into their suspects. More, she was careful not to limit herself to Secfor's list of potential culprits. She had her digital tentacles in the information of *everybody* associated with the initial contact circles of Tanaka and Acevedo.

She could have felt bad about it, invading the privacy of innocent people, but she didn't. Somebody set off a *bomb,* and if they'd go after a printer, who was to say they wouldn't go after one of the cricket-processing plants and cripple the ship's protein supply? Or the water? Or breach the hull? She didn't like the ship's government, but she liked the *ship,* and she didn't think it was in anyone's interest to have people start blowing up parts of it. If she could prevent that, she'd sleep with a clear conscience. And then there was that whole part where it was them or her. If she wanted to get back to her life, she had to find the bomber, and Eddie had never had much of a moral problem with putting her own needs first.

That was easier said than done, though. She'd had to learn some new skills. She'd hacked cameras before, but never with a lot of thought and never for a long period of time. A camera provided an overwhelming amount of data. That was where AIs came in. She could even move the cameras to focus on things other than their original intent, but when she did, she couldn't hide her tracks. Since moving them was too risky, she stuck to the natural observation pattern. That they covered about 90 percent of the ship, not counting living quarters, made things a little easier. It also gave her a strong appreciation of what *wasn't* covered. She'd never considered it before, as her kind of crime didn't involve a lot of physical movement around the ship. Others seemed to know a lot more about it, however—including, unfortunately, many of the people who might have been involved in the bombing.

There were a *lot* of blind spots for them to exploit.

The second obstacle was that the cameras didn't record sound, so while she could follow the actions of her targets, she couldn't do much more than that. At least not until she discovered a lip-reading algorithm. It was too tedious and clunky to put every observed conversation through the software, but it seemed worth the effort when someone Eddie didn't recognize at all met with Secfor's top suspect in a busy cafeteria.

And it was.

Reviewing the transcript of the conversation showed that Secfor was wrong, but not by much. Their suspect, Adrian Abenafor, was not the bomber. His associate, Teresa Fleming, was. That Teresa seemed to be nowhere on Secfor's suspect list told Eddie a lot about their process. She openly met with Abenafor yet wasn't added to their list of suspects; therefore, Secfor wasn't watching Abenafor on camera—or at least not constantly. And if they weren't constantly watching him, they probably weren't watching for her. Which meant that she could move around, too. At least a little bit. Interesting.

Knowing the name of the bomber was one thing, but she needed evidence. Sure, she had a lip-read confession, but that wasn't enough. Secfor wouldn't cut her even a tiny break. She had to have an airtight case, or they'd owe her nothing. That meant she needed to find bomb-making material. Sadly, Fleming wasn't going to put that in front of a camera for her with a big sign that said *Evidence*. But if Eddie planted her own camera? Iannou wouldn't like it, but he didn't need to know. And hey, Iannou's people hadn't put guards on her door or specifically told her *not* to leave . . .

She had to hurry. Secfor were nowhere close to solving the case, but they could have a breakthrough at any moment, and the more they found on their own, the less they needed her. But she couldn't rush to failure, either. She needed to prepare, and she needed rest, because maybe all her thoughts at that moment were born of sleep-deprived dementia.

Eddie set an alarm for four hours and lay down on her pallet, concerned that with everything swirling in her mind she might not be able to sleep at all.

She needn't have worried.

EDDIE AWOKE SEVEN HOURS LATER AND WONDERED WHAT HAPPENED to her alarm. It turned out that in her exhaustion, she'd set the time but not turned it on. *Shit.* Hopefully she hadn't blown her chance by a stupid oversight. She rushed to her makeshift terminal in a panic, and calmed down once she found that Secfor hadn't made any progress while she'd slept. *Woo-hoo for the incompetence of others.* A cricket chirped from somewhere outside her room, which was out of place but not uncommon. As the primary protein source for the ship's food printers, there were entire swaths of ship space reserved for crickets, and sometimes they got out. She heard them in the maintenance crawl spaces all the time. Crickets were resourceful like that. That gave her an idea.

Two hours later, she had cricket cam. She'd created a reasonable facsimile of a cricket soldered together from spare parts and wire, complete with a tiny camera that she'd cannibalized out of an inactive maintenance bot. The cricket wouldn't move—she didn't have the time to make something that sophisticated—but if somebody saw it, they might not immediately investigate, either. She'd improve the model later, as she could see all kinds of new uses for a camera that could fly around on its own, but for now, somebody was going to have to place it. And her labor pool was pretty limited at the moment.

She pushed through the canvas privacy screen and stretched, trying to give the impression that she was just out getting some air. Her room opened onto a supply area attached to the grain farm. Nobody appeared. When she was sure she was alone, she hurried around a corner and wound her way back to the maintenance access hatch. As much as she now believed that Secfor wasn't monitoring cameras effectively, one thing she *couldn't* do was get on an elevator—not even with her fake credentials. That meant she had a lot of climbing to do. At least the gravity would get lower as she progressed toward the interior of the ship.

She started her climb upward—inward—stopping every minute or so to rest and to listen for any sound outside of the familiar hum and creak of the ship's innards. If somebody found her missing from her room, it wouldn't take them long to figure out that she'd headed for the access passage. But she had very few visitors—usually only to bring food or a clean jumpsuit—so she might be back before they missed her. If they did come after her, she'd have to hope her superior knowledge of the shaft schematic would save her. She'd worked in the tunnels since her first day in maintenance, but there weren't a lot of places to hide when what she needed was straight up.

By the time she reached the top, she was spent. Climbing in high g was a lot of work. Eighty meters? Forget it. She'd sweated through her suit. And to add to it, the passage didn't go far enough. To reach the level she wanted, she needed a different shaft, which meant leaving the safety of the ship's guts and heading into the real world. She'd have to travel through two public passages covering about sixty meters of corridor to get to her next maintenance-shaft entry point. One camera along the way would see her face straight on, but she knew where it was and could probably keep from giving it a good picture. What she couldn't account for was random people walking by. With her luck, she could walk right into a Secfor patrol. She wanted to kick herself for not figuring out their schedule before she left her room. But she couldn't go back now, because no way was she making that climb again.

Instead, she listened at the hatch, and when she didn't hear anybody, she swung herself out into the corridor. It took her a second to orient, and by the time she had, she heard voices through the next bulkhead. She panicked for a split second and almost dove back through the maintenance hatch but caught herself. If they got to her before she made it in, that might appear even more suspicious. Instead, she headed right at them, keeping her head down as much as she could. She wanted to see if she recognized them. But if she could see their faces, they could see hers, and while most people on the ship wouldn't report anybody to Secfor, there were always a few assholes. And that number might have gone up, given the bombing and how it had probably scared people.

The two lowered their voices as they approached her, but that seemed natural, not wanting to share your conversation with a stranger. She held her breath, but then they were past her, and if they'd recognized her they'd have probably reacted. Still, one of them could have sent a silent message to Secfor. *Stop being paranoid.* As she crossed through the bulkhead, she kept her face down and to the right to avoid the camera, high on the left side of the passage, and then she was past that, too. That started the timer. Even if nobody picked up on it right away, the camera had her image, and as soon as somebody IDed her, Secfor would be on the way. She didn't intend to be there.

She reached another maintenance-access hatch, keyed in a dummy code, and entered. The passage was narrower, but it led directly to an air-recycling duct. This duct serviced the area she strongly suspected the bomber was using for storage, based on her pattern of movement over the previous two cycles. Eddie shimmied on her belly, unable to quite crawl, until she reached her target outtake. Footsteps sounded below her, and she froze. She waited two minutes for the person to disappear and until she was sure there was nobody else moving in the corridor below. In the back of her mind, the Secfor timer kept blinking forward.

She took out her camera and moved quickly to put it in place.

The cricket didn't fit.

She'd thought that she could set it up so that it would sit naturally in the grate and observe her suspected storage. But of course it didn't. She wedged it in, ripping the legs off of it in the process and hoping that at least she didn't damage the camera. She pulled up the display on her device and let out the breath she'd been holding. Boom. Video. She adjusted the view until it showed the door. Nobody would mistake her spy cam for a cricket anymore, so she'd have to hope that nobody looked up into the air circulator.

She couldn't turn around because the smaller access tunnel didn't leave room for maneuver, so she did the only thing she could and headed forward. The clock in her head also kept blinking forward. She hit an intersection and backed herself into a side tunnel before reversing direction. And then finally she was on her way. She had to pause twice as people walked below her. By the time she reached the access hatch again, too much time had passed. Instead of hesitating, she ran. Luckily, she didn't pass anybody in the corridor between the two maintenance hatches. The camera probably caught her, but once she hit the second hatch, she was gone.

She scrambled down the ladder, finding it almost as exhausting as climbing up it. After checking for sounds, she opened the hatch that led back to her room.

Iannou was waiting at the door.

Guess the big guy wasn't so busy after all. She wondered if he'd personally discovered her missing or someone else reported it. It didn't matter. What was he going to do? Turn her in?

"Where'd you go?"

"I got a little room crazy. I needed to get out and stretch. Don't worry, nobody saw me."

"We'd rather you didn't do that. A lot of people are taking a lot of risk trying to hide you."

"Right. Sorry. It won't happen again." But she wasn't sorry, and if necessary, it *would* happen again, though they'd be keeping a closer eye on her now. Whatever. She hadn't been sure before, but Iannou confronting her made it clear. When she found the bomber—and she would—she wasn't telling him. Their goals didn't line up, and she had her own methods.

Cecil would do it. Him, she trusted. At least, she trusted him to do what she paid for, and she could pay. With the new net skills she'd learned, she could take on new clients and make up the scrip in a hurry.

"Did you need something?" she asked.

Iannou continued to stare her down for several seconds before saying, "No. Just be careful." Then he turned and walked away.

CHAPTER 19

MARK RECTOR

||||||||||||||||||||||||||||||||||||||||||||||||||||||||||||||||

84 CYCLES UNTIL ARRIVAL

It took multiple cycles for Rector to be cleared for duty—the docs didn't mess around when it came to concussions. Now he walked through a corridor on one of the manufacturing levels—the same one where the bombing happened—and he couldn't help but replay the events in his mind. On his right, Mwangi was back, their arm not fully healed but good enough where they could walk a patrol. He didn't want to be here, but he didn't have any leads on the bomber, and Darvan was pressuring him. He had to do *something*. Unlike in the office, at least here he wasn't being constantly watched.

Darvan had assigned him the case without the governor's intervention this time, which might have been a sign of respect. He did get blown up and save somebody's life, after all. But probably not. As far as he could tell, Darvan hated him more than ever and saw his relationship with the governor as a threat. Giving him the case was win-win for the boss. Either Rector would solve it and Darvan could claim credit on behalf of Secfor, or Rector would fail and make himself look bad.

The latter seemed like a very real possibility, because cyber was still drawing blanks on the bomber's identity. The magistrate had denied all their privacy violation requests, so he was left with chasing down anonymous tips that led to nothing. Nobody could solve a case under these conditions. He was so preoccupied with the thought that he jumped when Mwangi nudged him.

"Hey, boss."

A woman stood a dozen meters down the passage, clearly waiting for them. How she knew they'd be there, he couldn't say. But he knew her. Not exactly an upstanding citizen of the ship.

"Mikayla," he said, as they continued to approach her. "To what do we owe the pleasure?"

"Someone wants to see you." She didn't bother to hide the fact that she'd been waiting for them. He liked that. No bullshit.

"You know where our office is," he said.

"It's not that kind of talk. Let's go."

"I don't take orders from thugs."

Mikayla put her hand over her heart and pursed her lips at him. "I'm hurt. And you do take orders. You've got no clue about your bomber and our friend does. If you want the information, meet in the Black Cat in twenty-eight minutes. If not, I'm sure Director Darvan would be interested in it."

He wanted to tell her off. Like, really bad. But he couldn't. She'd hit the mark with her threat, and she'd absolutely make good on it. Darvan wouldn't hesitate to use the information to solve the case himself and make Rector look like an idiot.

"We going?" asked Mwangi.

"Yep. Do you know Mikayla?"

"Vaguely. She's dirty."

"Yep," said Rector. "You know who she works for?"

"I don't."

"You will," said Rector. "Cecil Sharakan."

"Ah. Got it. So . . . why are we going to see him?"

"Because she was telling the truth. They've got information, and if we don't go, we don't get it."

THEY GOT TO THE BLACK CAT FOUR MINUTES EARLY, BUT CECIL WAS already there, seated at a back table.

"Wait by the door and keep an eye on the room," Rector told Mwangi. Their keeping watch probably wouldn't change anything, but he trusted them not to overreact. More important, he didn't want them at the table when he heard whatever Cecil had to say. He *thought* they were on his side, but he couldn't rule out them reporting to Darvan as well.

He didn't bother to look if Mwangi complied; instead he went directly to the table where the heavyset man waited. "Cecil. It's been a while."

"Why is that? We should get together more often. As the resident hero, have you become too big for me?" He laughed. "Anyway, welcome. Coffee? Two sugars, right?" Sharakan himself had a cocktail with some sort of amber liquid in a clear polymer cup.

"Yes. Please. You actually pay for that?" Rector nodded to the other man's drink, but he kept his tone light so he could play it off as a joke.

"Of course. One hundred percent legit, all the time." Cecil smiled, choosing not to take offense at the insult.

"How's business?"

"Not great. The loss of the big printer has caused problems across the ship."

"I'd have thought that shortages would help you. Supply and demand, and all that," said Rector.

"Eh. We work with what we've got. But me? I'm a man who appreciates routine."

"How long do you figure until we're back to normal?"

"Well, I'm no engineer." He smiled.

Rector chuckled. "Right. But your estimate is probably at least as good as theirs."

"Months. They need the other printers to print repair parts, but they're all maxed out trying to make up for the bombed printer. Add to that all the extra equipment needed for the governor's colonization push and . . . well . . ." He shrugged.

"So you're not happy with the bomber, and so you want to help me out. Is that it?"

"Let's just say I've got my own reasons."

Rector sighed. He'd have liked the crime boss to share his motive so he could better judge the information, but he wasn't really in a spot to be making demands. "What have you got for me?"

"What I've got . . . isn't free. No offense. I just want us to be clear."

"If I don't know what you've got, how can I decide how much it's worth?"

"Given that the price is nonnegotiable, I'm not sure it matters. But what I have is simple enough: I have your bomber."

Rector hesitated. He'd been prepared for information—maybe even valuable information, given Cecil's resourcefulness—but he hadn't expected that. He took a sip of coffee to give himself a second to process the news. "What do you mean by *have*? You mean you know who it is, or you physically have them?"

"She's in a secure place. Let's just say she won't be leaving that place until you—or someone else—pick her up."

Interesting. It was a woman. That ruled out his top suspect, assuming Cecil was correct, and for all that he didn't trust the man in most things, they wouldn't be sitting there if he didn't have the goods. But it wouldn't hurt to suss it out a bit more. They also wouldn't be there unless Cecil really wanted something—something more than just money—so they could dance a little longer. "How sure are you that you have the right person?"

"She confessed."

"She *confessed*. That easy."

"We might have encouraged her a bit."

Rector snorted. "You mean you tortured her."

Cecil shrugged. "Eh."

"So she'd have said anything and we can't trust it. And even if it's true, I can't use it as evidence."

Cecil smiled the kind of smile that said he knew more than Rector. He seemed even more confident than usual. "Well, then it's a good thing that I also have the location of materials used in the construction of the bomb, which I think you'll find have her fingerprints and DNA all over them."

Rector sat up a little straighter. "That would help."

"And video of her accessing that area, on her own, under no duress."

Rector sat his cup back on the table and met the other man's eyes. "No shit. So this is legit."

"As legit as anything I've ever told you."

"Hopefully it's more than that," said Rector, allowing himself to smile. If the man had what he said, Rector could solve this case and take a dangerous person out of circulation. Let Darvan try to fuck with him after that.

"Let's not play games. You want what I have. We both know that."

Rector nodded. "What do you want?"

"Full immunity."

Rector considered it, but he couldn't authorize that. Not for Sharakan, not without specifying charges and time frames. As important as the bomber was, nobody would sign off on that kind of blanket indemnity. "That might be tough, unless you can give me specifics."

"I'll be very specific," said Cecil. "And as I said, this is not negotiable. It's also not for me."

That caught Rector's attention. "Really? Okay. For who?"

"Eddie Dannin. You know her."

"I do." Dannin and Cecil together. Well, *shit*. That was new information. How had he not seen that before?

"Full immunity for her for anything she might have done . . . not that she's done anything illegal, of course. So . . . call it a clearing up of poor information on your part."

Rector genuinely chuckled at that. "Not sure we have the same definitions of 'illegal' there. Dannin has caused a lot of problems."

"Misunderstandings," said Cecil. "And . . . again . . . non-negotiable."

Shit. To solve one case, he'd have to give up another, but any way he looked at it, the decision was easy. Some mostly harmless hacks versus someone who set off a literal bomb. "To be clear, we're talking immunity for Dannin for everything before right now. Anything that she does in the future will still be fair game."

"Of course."

Rector considered it. He could still watch her in the future. He'd have to sell this, and the governor might buy that . . . after all, the governor had told him not to bring her in previously. He needed time to think it through, so he stalled. "What's in this for you?"

"I think you can rest assured that I have my own interests covered," said Cecil without hesitation or expression. The man was locked into negotiation mode and not giving anything away. "These questions are really a waste of time, yes? Do you really have a choice here?"

It pissed Rector off a little that the man across the table from him had such a good read on the situation. He'd have to watch that going forward—it made him vulnerable. But for now, what could he do? There was always a chance that they didn't have the real bomber, that Cecil had planted the evidence. But even that didn't matter. The person he had detained was going down either way, and Rector could either take the credit or cede it, and that was no decision at all. Darvan wouldn't even think twice about using it. He sighed. He really hoped they had the right person. "Okay," he said finally.

"We have a deal?"

Rector reached across the table and shook the other man's chubby hand. "We have a deal. I need a little time to get the immunity lined up, but I can make it happen." He'd go directly to the governor. Darvan would be pissed, but he wouldn't be able to stop it. Getting the bomber was too important. "How's this going to work?"

"You'll get an anonymous tip in the next two hours with everything you need to know. Make sure you're in your office, so you're the first one to get it and that it's officially recorded."

"Two hours? I'm not sure I can get immunity for Dannin that fast."

"Tomorrow, Ms. Dannin will return to her normal work. I trust that you'll sort everything out by then."

"You're just going to trust me to hold up my side of things, even after you give me the information?"

Sharakan shrugged. "You're not going to go back on our deal."

And once again the man was right. Rector was in it deep now. He'd worry about that later. For now, he needed a story, and it was starting to form in his head. He'd lie and say that he and Dannin were working together all along, and no, of course he didn't tell Darvan. After all, there was a leak in the department, and he didn't want to let information out that might interfere with the arrest. People would believe it—some of them, anyway—and those who didn't still wouldn't be able to openly challenge it. He was on a roll. First saving someone's life, now apprehending the bomber. Maybe that promotion wasn't out of reach after all.

<CHAPTER 20>

GEORGE IANNOU

||||||||||||||||||||||||||||||||||||||||||||||||||||||||||||||||||

79 CYCLES UNTIL ARRIVAL

"I didn't expect to see you here," said George.

Eddie stood a few paces away, hands on her hips. "Yeah. I drew drip irrigation maintenance today, so I was in the area. Asked around and somebody told me where to find you."

"I'd have thought you'd be busy, what with the missing printer."

"We are. Irrigation work can't stop, but they're giving me less time to do the same amount. Without the printer, a bunch of other stuff on the ship has to work harder to make up for it, and things are always breaking."

George nodded. "We going to be okay?"

"Oh sure. Just more work."

He didn't want to point out the obvious, but he was curious. "But you're here talking to me."

"The bot's working. I automated it."

He thought about that for a second. "Is that legal?"

"Not exactly. But I don't figure you're going to rat me out."

"No. I don't suppose I would. What can I do for you?"

Eddie looked down at her feet, shifted her weight from one to the other. "I just wanted to apologize."

"For what? We should be apologizing to you." He had a good idea what she was talking about, but it was clear that she had something on her mind, and it seemed best to let her unburden.

She nodded but kept staring at her feet. "Yeah. That too. But I meant to you directly. I told you I'd find the bomber for you."

"It's—"

"Hold on, let me finish," she said. "I told you I'd get you the information—and I did get it—but once I did . . . well . . . I had to look out for myself."

"I understand." He didn't, really. Or maybe he did. What did he know about negotiating amnesty? What was important was that it worked out for her. "Is anybody giving you trouble?"

"Not yet. I'm kind of keeping my head down, though. Anyway, if there's ever something I can do—"

"There is one thing," said George. She looked receptive, so he continued, "We need a way to counter all the misinformation coming out of the governor's office."

"People just get on the net," she said.

"Yeah, I know it. But there's so much conflicting stuff going around, and he's got the news. We need something more . . . official. Something that people will hear and believe."

"Like your own news." She thought about it. "How often would you need it?"

"Not often. Just to counter when he does something big that's not accurate and to put out information when he's suppressing it. Like back at the start of this whole thing when he said I was in charge when I wasn't. If I had a way to counter that, well . . ." He let his words trail off. He was going to say that he wouldn't be stuck where he is now, but he didn't need to share that.

"Yeah, okay. I'll see what I can come up with."

"I know you can't do it for free, but I don't have much to work with."

"Get me some apples?"

"Apples?"

"Yeah. You're a farmer. You grow stuff, right?"

"Yeah. Sure. But why apples? What are you going to do with them?"

Eddie looked at him like he was an idiot. "Eat them? I like apples. We'll call it a trade. Just don't tell anybody I'm doing a job for fruit. It'll ruin my reputation."

"Your secret is safe with me."

GEORGE SAT ACROSS FROM KOSHI TANAKA AND SARA WASHBURN, poking at a vat-grown pork tenderloin. The three of them had taken to meeting for dinner every other night and rotating through different dining facilities. It helped the cause to let people see them together, and since they were in public, it forced them to keep things cordial. Delta hadn't joined them since the bombing, and George wasn't holding his breath waiting for her to return. She was lying low. Instead, Kayla sat next to him. She'd been joining them more and more for these sorts of things, and nobody seemed to mind. She rarely said anything, and when she did it was always insightful.

"So what's the news on the ship?" he asked.

"Not much change on my end," said Sara. "Having trouble getting people to come out for anything. Nobody wants to be associated with the bombing."

"Protests aren't tied to the bombing," said Koshi. "I keep telling you that."

"What do you want me to do about it? Public sentiment is public sentiment."

"Not everybody feels that way," said Koshi.

"Yeah. Sure. A lot of people are pro bombing."

Okay, thought George. *Mostly* cordial.

"Don't be an ass," said Koshi. "I'm saying that I've seen gains since it happened. Nobody is *happy* there was a bomb. But at the same time . . . at least someone did *something*. There's almost certainly life on the planet, and people are mad that nobody in power is addressing that."

Sara shook her head. "This again."

"Yep. This again. Imagine that. The governor is thwarting change and pushing us to potentially destroy a native climate that we don't know enough about, and people want to do something about it."

"Do what?"

Koshi smiled. "I'm glad you asked. We need to stage a work slowdown in agriculture. Make the supply system feel it."

"That won't work," said Sara.

"Why not?"

She hesitated. "I can't get the support."

"That's fine. I'll get it started and your people will jump on. They don't have to *do* anything. That's the beauty of it. They come to work just like any other day, and all they do is a little less than usual. It shouldn't be hard to convince people to do less work."

George wasn't so sure about that. The logic was sound, but people were hard to predict, and the ship's culture valued work.

"You're okay with this?" Sara glared at George, and he didn't answer right away.

"We should do it," said Kayla.

George turned to her. "You think so?"

"Yeah. It's easy to execute, hard to stop, and it makes the leadership pay attention. It's a way to get them to the table, and at the same time, people will see it and know that you're doing something. If they see that, maybe they won't rush to do their own thing."

"You're saying that we're preventing another bomber." Sara's voice said she didn't buy it.

"I'm saying it accomplishes the same thing as the bombing—stopping production—with the benefit that it doesn't put all our lives in danger."

"Let's do it," said George. He wasn't sold on the strategy, but they could try. If it didn't work out, they could always change course. "What do you need to make it happen?"

"Leave it to me," said Koshi. "I've got this."

George pushed away his plate at that, dread more than filling his stomach.

<CHAPTER 21>

JARRED PANTEL

|||||||||||||||||||||||||||||||||||||||||||||||||||||||||||||||

72 CYCLES UNTIL ARRIVAL

Jarred Pantel wanted to bang his head against the desk. Today's crisis stood in front of him in the form of Maritza Kowalski, the director of subsistence. She had a lot of responsibilities, but in Pantel's mind, she was the person who made sure that everybody got to eat.

"I've got the report," said Pantel. "But run through it for me from your point of view. How much trouble are we in?"

Kowalski referred to her tablet. "Protein deliveries are at 87 percent of quota. Carbohydrates are at 86. Those directly impact food printing, and while we haven't felt the bite from it yet because we're pulling from surplus, we need about 96 percent production to maintain the status quo."

"How long can we hold out?"

"I don't have the exact calculations," said Kowalski, "but it's measured in cycles. Maybe a week. Production numbers continue to drop, and that's only the staples. If we look at fresh fruits and vegetables from hydroponics and other lux items, production there is barely at 80 percent. Those have fallen off faster because of the shorter life cycle involved in production."

Pantel leaned back in his chair. "I'm not as worried about lux items."

"You should be. Fresh food not from printers is the number two luxury purchase on the ship, right behind alcohol. Lose that, and you're going to see a huge drop in morale." She didn't have to say the next part.

"And if we're forced to cut rations because we can't even *print* enough food? You don't think that will be worse?"

Horror flashed on the deputy director's face. Apparently she hadn't considered that. "That's not an option."

Wasn't it? She was half right—it wasn't a *good* option. But if they didn't find another solution, it might be a reality. "What can we do? We can't print from material we don't have."

"You can do something about the worker slowdown."

"I could say the same about you," snapped Pantel. "Last I checked, farmers fall under one of your subdirectorates."

Kowalski clenched her fists by her sides and took a small step toward Pantel's desk, and for a minute, he thought she might come after him physically. For all that she was a director now, she'd been a farmer before and still had the calluses and muscles that came with it. "What would you have me do?"

"Make an example of the people who are missing work."

"That's just it. *Nobody* is missing work. Not even the normal percentage who would miss for legitimate reasons. They're all showing up, almost as if to make sure there's no way to blame them. The issue is that they're getting less done while they're there. Things that are broken are taking longer to fix. Bots are malfunctioning. Systems that require routine cleaning are spending more time offline."

"Okay. So what's your recommendation?"

"Give them what they want."

"As soon as I do that, every time they want something else, they'll go right back to the same action."

"I figured you'd say that." Her voice didn't let on her feelings about his response. "If you won't give them what they want, then release the emergency nutrition stores."

Pantel remembered something about that vaguely, some briefing he got the first week he took office, but he'd gotten a *lot* of information that week. Something about basic nutritional building blocks stored in tanks. "How long would that last us?"

"There are enough stores to feed the entire crew on 80 percent rations for two hundred cycles. It's designed as a fail-safe in case of a total production failure. We rotate 10 percent of the stock into utilization each year and replace it with fresh stores."

"So it's two hundred cycles if we're at zero percent production."

"Correct," said Kowalski. "Right now, we'd need only a fraction of that. If you authorize us to use 10 percent of the emergency stores without replacing it, given our current rate of production, we could maintain normal rations for at least fifty cycles. Maybe longer."

"What do you need for the authorization? Is that my authority?"

Kowalski nodded. "Joint authority between the governor and the captain."

Pantel sighed. Of course it was. He'd have to go back to the captain again trying to claim they had an emergency and he'd get to listen to her berate him for allowing the work slowdown in the first place. Then again, maybe she'd agree to this one. After all, it was that or cut rations, and even she should want to avoid that. But he couldn't guarantee her response, and he couldn't tell a subordinate that he and the captain had differences—especially since he wasn't sure of Kowalski's exact allegiances. He was stuck, so he did what he always did in that situation: he stalled. "What do we do about the fresh foods? We can't make that up from storage."

Kowalski's lips quirked up at one corner. "I have an idea for that, but I'm not sure you're going to like it."

"Hit me."

"We raise prices," she said.

"So—more lux to get the same product. That seems . . . reasonable. Lower supply, same demand, price goes up. I don't remember much from economics class, but I do remember that."

"More than that, it lets the population feel the pinch and shows them there's a consequence to not meeting quota. Maybe if people are pissed off enough, that will put some pressure on my workers."

Pantel smiled. He couldn't help himself. He hadn't wanted to go to the captain with this problem, and Kowalski had given him a perfect solution. "I like it. But let's take it one step further."

"How do we do that?"

"We announce a cut to basic subsistence rations. If we provide at 90 percent, how long can we hold out?"

Kowalski considered it for several seconds, and Pantel wasn't sure if she was trying to figure out the math or thinking through his idea as a whole. "I'd have to do more calculations, and it would depend on how far the production rates fall. But at least thirty cycles. Probably forty. Maybe even more than that."

"What are your thoughts on that as a solution?" asked Pantel. He didn't need her on board to do it, but it would help. Regardless, he wanted her to commit, so he wasn't on the line by himself for all the blame if it went poorly.

"It's risky," she said. "If we're simultaneously raising lux prices on supplemental food, people are definitely going to be angry."

Pantel nodded. He was counting on it. What he had to do was make sure that they were angry at the right people. "That *is* a risk."

"But it might be worth it," she said. "We can always go back and release emergency stores later, so it's not an irreversible decision. And maybe it will be enough to jump-start production again."

"My thoughts exactly," lied Pantel. He was much more interested at the moment in throwing the blame on the opposition, but he paused to give the illusion that he was thinking. "Director, how well do you know your people?"

"I've been part of the department since I was born. My parents were sustainers. I'm sixty now. Pretty well, I'd say."

"Give me the names of some people who you think are most influencing the slowdown."

She hesitated at that, for which Pantel didn't blame her. They were, after all, still her people, even if they were being recalcitrant.

"I'm not going to harm them," he said. "No legal action or anything. But if we're going to ramp up the pressure, I want to make sure we're putting it on the right people."

"If you announce their names in the news feeds, you could put them in danger."

"I won't do that. You have my word." He met her eyes evenly, his best politician's face plastered on.

She thought about it for several seconds. "Okay. Give me two hours. I'll message you with the names."

THREE CYCLES LATER, PANTEL SAT IN HIS OFFICE AGAIN, WATCHING and rewatching the news. The official feeds had done as they were told and put out the story that the work slowdown had caused the ration cut. On a separate screen ran a recording from a pirate feed that had appeared within six hours of the official version, specifically detailing the stored rations that he'd chosen not to use.

"How did this happen?"

Marjorie Blaisdell sat in a chair across from him, one foot resting on the other knee. That she appeared relaxed bothered him more than it should have. "Which part?"

"Which one do you think? The fucking pirate feed! How does that happen on a closed ship? Why can't we find it and shut it down?"

"It's a big ship. And they're not broadcasting live, or from the same place."

"Do you know who's behind it?"

"I have some ideas. Nothing I can prove."

"Do I care about proof right now? Is it that hacker that I gave immunity to? Because I'll end her." He still wasn't sure about that decision that Rector talked him into, even though it did net them the bomber.

"I don't have anything that points to her. Making a quality recording is the hardest part, and even that's not difficult. Nothing that would require someone like Dannin."

"Whoever it is, they're blaming me for not releasing emergency stocks. They don't even mention that I have to get the captain's approval."

"Of course they don't. She's not the target. You are."

Pantel considered that. Normally he might take it as a compliment. If they cared enough to challenge him, it meant they saw him as important. Normally, but not now. Now it was just a pain in the ass. "If they'd just listen, everyone would be better off." He sounded whiny, even to himself, and he hated it. At least Marjorie had the grace not to respond. He needed to get his feelings out of the way and move forward. Kowalski had sent him some names, just as she promised, but *someone* had leaked the information about the emergency nutrition storage and he wasn't sure how much he could trust her. "What's your take on Kowalski?"

"In what way?"

"Can we trust her? How many people know about the emergency rations? Could she have been the one to leak that?"

"A lot of people in ag know about that, but you know her better than I do. What do you think?"

He shook his head. "I don't know. I don't really trust anybody at this point." It was true. Nobody outside of his personal staff and his wife. Even those who mostly followed his instructions—people like Rector and the news and entertainment director—still gave him occasional doubts.

"Never a bad policy," she said.

"Yeah. But we need *somebody* on our side."

"I can look into it if you want. Ag is a hard place to break right now—they're pretty tight—but there's always a way."

"Nah. You've got other priorities. If she's against us, we'll figure it out soon enough. I'll come up with something."

"Roger. Anything else?"

"No. Thanks." As she left, he reopened the message from Kowalski—the one with the names and nothing in the subject header. He had options. He wasn't sure yet if he was going to implement them, but they were there, forming. Bread and circuses. He'd taken away the bread because he thought it would help him against his enemies, but it had blown back on him. He could give it back, restore the rations, but it would show weakness, and he'd only do that if he had absolutely no other option. That left him with the other side: more circus.

Thankfully he had just the thing. He was going to announce the initial landing parties, and he was going to pick people for them based on his own criteria—mainly, how much it helped him regain control of the ship. He had volunteers—some people saw it as an opportunity—and he'd choose some of those people, both for appearance's sake and because he wanted the colony to succeed. But he could make a good argument that farmers should be some of the first people planetside. They'd be best able to handle the high gravity, and to survive long-term on the planet, they'd have to establish a way to sustain themselves organically.

He didn't know if that was exactly accurate, but it *seemed* true, and people would believe it. He needed a distraction *and* he needed to send a message. That message was to get your asses back to work or find yourself exiled to the unknown. In the short term, assigning them to the planet would pull them away from their primary job for training, in theory exacerbating the food production slowdown. In practice, removing the agitators should weaken the will of the opposition and motivate others who wanted to avoid the same fate.

He picked two names he recognized as being opposition leaders, but he left George Iannou alone. Selecting him would be too obvious, and besides, exempting Iannou should stir up some resentment and paint a target on him for his own followers. That done, he started working through lists other departments had submitted as well. There were no specifics on individuals from the other directors, but he had some ideas from Blaisdell. Removing the most vocal advocates for Eternal Life from across the ship would rip the heart out of the movement, and then the rest of them could get back to normal business.

That was all he wanted.

THE FOLLOWING NIGHT, CAMINA SAT QUIETLY ACROSS FROM HIM as he ate his dinner. She'd been sullen for a couple of days, but he'd been too preoccupied with his own problems to give her the attention she deserved. He needed to fix that, and he would, just as soon as things got back to normal. But in the meantime, he could still make an effort. "What's bothering you?"

She glanced up at him. "It's nothing."

"It's *not* nothing. How long have I known you?"

She studied him now, and then sighed. "Fine. You remember when I told you that nobody was talking about the things that were bothering you?"

"Yeah. Sure."

"Well, now they are."

"Okay. What are they saying?"

"Jarred . . ." But then she stopped.

"Go ahead," he said. "You can tell me."

"It's not so much what they're saying specifically . . . just that everybody is talking about politics all the time now. The bombing. The crews assigned to go to the planet. The ration shortage. Every day, it's the same stuff."

"The bombing was a huge event. I think it's natural that people are worried about it."

"That's just it . . . not everybody is against it."

"*What?* How can somebody be pro-bomber?"

Camina shook her head. "It's not that anybody is *pro-bomber*. It's more like . . . some people understand the sentiment even if they don't approve of the method. If that makes sense."

Pantel bit his lip as he thought about it. He wanted to dismiss it as something that would pass, but he couldn't help worrying about it. If there was any sympathy at all for the bomber, he couldn't help but see that as a referendum on himself. "Are people talking about . . . me?"

Camina hesitated. "What they're . . . what *some people* . . . are saying is that you aren't trying to fix problems. Especially the ration shortage. That all you cared about was assigning the blame for it. But that's not really the point; people are all over the place with what they think, and some people change from day to day."

"If they're just talking about it . . ."

"The point is that people who never cared about this kind of stuff now do."

He needed to consider that. In trying to shift the balance of opinion in his favor, had he simply brought more people into the discourse? That was what she was saying, and she was too smart to dismiss.

Well . . . shit.

He'd been worried about others not listening to him, causing him trouble, but here he might be the source of his own problem. "Yeah. I probably screwed that up."

The tension came out of Camina's face. "I'm so glad you can see that. What are you going to do about it?"

He considered it and found that harder. He could admit it here, with Camina. That he'd mistakenly overstepped and led them in the wrong direction. But he couldn't admit that in public, and he didn't see a great way to walk back his actions.

"I'm honestly not sure."

The two of them sat there for a long time, not saying anything.

<CHAPTER 22>

GEORGE IANNOU

||||||||||||||||||||||||||||||||||||||||||||||||||||||||||||||

65 CYCLES UNTIL ARRIVAL·

George rode the elevator back down to the ag decks after completing his VR training for the new planet. Even though he wasn't scheduled to go to the surface, everyone had to attend two one-hour sessions a week, just in case. He didn't struggle with agoraphobia the way that half the people in his session had—some of them had panicked, and more than one had vomited. For him it was usually just a chance to get away.

Not today.

Koshi Tanaka and Sara Washburn had met him outside the VR room and walked back with him, each of them talking into a different ear as they went. He tried to ignore them, but they wouldn't quit.

They'd had a couple of good moments when Eddie had built them a pirate feed to counter the governor's propaganda. When the governor had raised prices and cut rations, George had been ready. People craved information, and now they could deliver it, and for a day or two it really seemed to be turning sentiment against the governor. They'd seen a couple of new recruits to the cause, but more important, people now knew and were pissed that Pantel was lying.

But even with the truth out there, a lot of people still blamed the workers. One man had put it succinctly when he'd said, "Yes, it's the governor's doing, but if you just go back to work, you'd end it."

And there was something to that, maybe, but at this point George couldn't gain enough consensus to get people back to full production even if he wanted to. Everyone had their own agenda, and nobody—not him, not the governor—had control. And that was the real problem. They couldn't get together and compromise because nobody listened to either of them. Within his own camp, there were simultaneous calls for a return to full capacity, a complete shutdown, and a hybrid where they went to work but gave the food directly to the people instead of via institutions. The last option was ridiculous because the government controlled the food synthesizers, and what were people going to do with raw grains and crickets? Yet to understand that, people would have to listen to experts who actually understood how stuff worked, and people were listening only within their own echo chambers.

Then the governor announced crews for initial landing parties, further inflaming the rhetoric. That killed any chance George had of his people coming to a rational agreement, which was abundantly clear based on the two people shouting at him in an elevator.

"I can't focus with both of you yelling at me at the same time," he said, finally giving in.

"This has gone too far," said Sara. "We need to get back to work and put an end to it."

Tanaka moved so George couldn't look at Sarah without also seeing him. "If we cave now, we're showing the governor that he can beat us. If anything, we should slow down even further. It's the only way to win."

"There's no winning!" Sara's voice turned shrill as she increased the volume.

"I hate to say it, but I agree with Koshi," said George. He wished that he didn't, but the man was right. If they gave in the minute the governor made things difficult, they might as well give up on ever accomplishing anything. He wasn't willing to do that, and he knew that the zealots like Tanaka were *definitely* not willing to. Even with the current slowdown, they ran the risk that someone like Acevedo would take things into their own hands again.

Sara put a fist on each hip and glared. "Easy for you to say. *You're* not on the list to go down to the planet in the first wave."

"*I* am," said Koshi.

"Maybe they just want to keep you from blowing up the ship," offered Sara.

"Hey," said George, stopping Koshi before he could respond. "Enough of that. That wasn't him. And we're doing the governor's work for him if we split ourselves. This is exactly what he was trying to accomplish when he put your names on the list." The elevator reached their destination, and the door opened on two people waiting to enter. "Let's find somewhere private and discuss things we can actually do."

They walked quietly after that, heading to one of the farms, and George was thankful for the respite. He had some ideas—he wasn't sure they were good ones, but as they'd said, he had to show that he was doing *something*—and he used the time to rehearse them in his head again. By the time they reached the center of a grain field, he was ready. "We need to take concrete action, and here's what I've got. First, we have people fail to show up for planetary training—"

"They'll arrest us," said Sara. "It's exactly the excuse that they want."

"If you'll let me finish?" George waited to see if she was going to continue, and when she didn't, he said, "We can only do that if we get a good percentage of the people scheduled to go along with it. It needs to be a number big enough where they *can't* just arrest people."

Koshi nodded, as if he'd get behind it, but Sara glared at him. "What else have you got?" she asked, almost spitting the words.

"We increase food production—"

"I already said that was untenable," interrupted Koshi.

"Again," George sighed, "if you'd let me finish." It was like herding crickets. "We increase production, but we don't deliver it."

"So we steal it?" asked Koshi.

"From ourselves. Yes. Or we allow someone else to steal it. Either way, we release it onto the black market."

"We've talked about this," said Sara. "We need the synthesizers and we don't have them."

"We need them if we were trying to give *everything* away. But people can make use of *some* things in raw form. Obviously we don't steal crickets, and we rely on the ingenuity of the people profiting off of the sale to improvise."

"People would still be short rations," said Koshi.

"But added supply on the black market would drive prices down there, making it easier for people to get food that way."

Koshi considered it, and that fact alone gave George hope. Every other thing he said, the two immediately questioned, but now they were at least listening. That was a step in the right direction. "Can we pull it off?"

George wasn't sure. They'd need help, specifically from those who ran the black market, and they might not be happy about losing their profit margin. "Absolutely," he said. "The question is, can we get Delta to buy into it for long enough that we can make it work? If there's another bombing—"

"Let me talk to her," said Koshi. "I can get her to give us some time."

George studied the other man for a couple of seconds and then nodded. "Okay. I'll get it started." Now he'd just have to get the black market distributors to buy into it.

"I HEARD ABOUT THE FOOD HEADING TO THE BLACK MARKET." Kayla slid into the seat across from him at their table, reached over to his plate, and swiped a tater tot.

"Hey!"

"There's a food shortage," she said around her tot. "You gotta be quick. Ow. That's hot!"

"Serves you right. Where'd you hear about the black market thing?" He tried to say it casually so as not to make her suspicious, but he really wanted to know where that info was leaking. They hadn't even started yet.

"You know. Here and there." She reached for his plate again and he swatted her away.

"Make your own plate," he said.

"I will. I just wanted to talk about what's going on."

"With the black market?"

"With everything. The planet. They've got six hundred people lined up to go. *Six hundred.*"

"I'm aware. Trust me."

"I do. But we've gotta stop it."

He wanted to shake his head, to stop the conversation or turn it to something else, but it was the first time they'd sat down and talked in a while, and he wasn't willing to let that go. "It's not that easy. Everybody in our movement has different ideas about almost every single thing. I'm trying to build a coalition to at least get the little stuff done."

"The little stuff doesn't matter, though."

"Little stuff leads to big stuff."

"Yeah? When? Because in two months or so, we'll have invaded the planet's ecosystem and it'll be too late to do anything about it."

"So what should I do? I can't *make* people agree."

"Find the people who already do." She got up, went to the cabinet, took out a meal. "Look outside of the people who regularly show up to things for people who have the same opinions."

"Clearly you have something in mind. Want to skip ahead to where you just tell me?"

Kayla popped her meal tray into the heater. "The scientists."

"The scientists? You think they're worried about preserving the planet?"

Kayla shrugged. "What's pretty clear is that a lot of them—including the big one, Jackson—don't want us going to the planet right now. *Why* doesn't matter. We want the same things, and we're both running out of time."

George swallowed a tater tot as he thought. "I suppose you're right. It's at least worth a shot."

THE FOLLOWING DAY, HE WENT TO IMPLEMENT KAYLA'S IDEA. "Dr. Jackson?"

She eyed him warily, looking up to his face and then all the way down to take in his boots, which made him glad he'd changed out of his farm gear for this. She probably recognized him—he'd been on video enough in the past weeks where people did that now. Hopefully that didn't color her opinion of him so much that his chances with her were over before they started. "You look bigger in real life."

George snorted. Whatever he'd expected her to say, it hadn't been that. "I get that a lot."

"I bet. Can I help you?"

"Can we walk together?"

Jackson considered it. "It depends. What do you want?"

George hesitated for only a second. "I want to ask you something: are you happy with the governor's plan to send people to the planet?"

She studied him for several seconds before speaking. "Walk with me."

George kept his face neutral, but on the inside, he was pumping his fists. Kayla had guessed right—Dr. Jackson was *not* happy with the governor's plan. But now that he had her, or at least had her interest, he thought it best to let her make the next move. So he fell in beside her, matched his pace to her shorter stride, and said nothing.

They put some distance between themselves and others leaving the same training session. "I'm absolutely not happy with it," she finally said.

"Well, then—"

"But I'm not happy with you, either," she said, cutting George off before he could continue his pitch.

"Because we disrupt the ship?" he asked.

"Because you don't follow the science any more than the governor does."

George thought about it but wasn't sure what specifically she was talking about. "So in your mind, *we're* the same as the governor?"

She sighed as they reached the elevator, but she didn't push the call button, instead moving away from three people who were waiting there already. "Not the same, but similar. His decision to push people to the surface of the planet before we do further study is reckless to the point of negligence."

"And you blame us for him taking that action."

"No. Yes. Maybe. Gah! No. I don't blame you for that. Or I shouldn't. He chose that action to punish you, and that's on him. What I'm mad at you about is your push for extended life and half a dozen other things that don't fit the science, either."

"Extended life doesn't . . . I'm not sure I follow."

"You don't follow? Seriously?"

"Ma'am, I'm a farmer. I don't understand things at the same level that you do." He wasn't placating her. She clearly believed what she was saying, but he really didn't know why she felt that way.

She considered it, perhaps trying to gauge his sincerity. "Okay. I'll explain, but if you call yourself a leader, you should take the time to learn stuff like this on your own. All the information is out there."

George looked at his feet and mumbled, "I'll try to do better."

"When we arrive in orbit, we should be doing research for somewhere between one and twenty years. Statistically most likely, we should end up somewhere in the middle of that range, but it depends on what we find."

"I thought we were getting data back from advanced probes. Is this about the problems?"

"Yes and no." She hesitated again. "You've heard the rumors that we're not getting everything we're supposed to be."

"Sure."

"Those rumors are true. But even if everything was going perfectly and we were getting all the scheduled data, it was never going to be enough."

"And if it takes twenty years to gather the correct data—"

"—or to prepare the potential landing sites via terraforming processes," interjected Jackson. "To alter bacteria or proteins or—"

"I get it," said George, though he didn't necessarily get it. The people like Kayla who wanted to protect the planet would not be on board with terraforming. If they were really going to work together, he'd need to tamp down that part of it. For now, he thought it best to pivot back to extended life and avoid challenging Jackson. "If science takes twenty years in orbit, then extending life for those on the ship puts us in resource constraint. I get it."

"Yes."

"One question," said George.

"What's that?"

"If we were looking at a twenty-year timeline, why didn't you say that from the start?"

She winced at that. "I should have. I got flustered when I went on to talk about it, and after that I never got the same chance to correct the record."

"*That* I understand." And he really did. He'd been pushed into a lot of spots he didn't want to be in.

"The governor wasn't exactly going to let me fix it once he got what he wanted, you know?"

"I definitely do." It was interesting to learn that the governor was manipulating things with scientists, too, not just the workers. He should have talked to her sooner. "So then, in theory, we have a common enemy."

She thought for a moment. "I don't know if I'd use the word 'enemy.' But we have some common *challenges*."

George didn't really see the difference, but he didn't care what they called it. Not as long as she was willing to join forces. "What if I could help you with your challenge?"

She stood silent for several seconds. "How would you do that?"

"We could get you access to alternate means of communications."

"The pirate news feed."

"My official response to that is 'What pirate news feed?' But yes."

She tapped her chin. "I don't know."

"Can I ask what the issue is?"

"You can ask whatever you want," said Jackson. "It doesn't mean I have to answer."

"You've got an information problem. We have a solution. I don't see the issue."

"The problem is, the minute I do that, everyone is going to know it was me, including the governor."

"And you think that puts you at risk," said George.

"Doesn't it?"

"Aren't some things worth risking? Let me ask you this: do you believe that there's intelligent life on Prom? Because a lot of people do."

"And that's the problem. Anybody who believes that there's intelligent life on the planet is wrong—"

"So there isn't—" George started to say.

"Anybody who believes that there's *not* intelligent life on the planet is wrong," said Sheila, talking over him. "I've looked at *all* the data, and there's not enough to provide even a reasonably conclusive determination either way. So do you see why I'm not excited about joining forces? You're not even asking the right questions."

He did see her point, but he also saw her fatal flaw. By not taking a side, she was committing to failure. She thought she needed more information, but that wasn't what she needed at all. "You need more time. *We*—the ship and all the people here—need more time. So why not work with us to get it? What are your other options?"

"I develop a better plan, present it to the powers that be, and hope that they listen."

He wanted to yell at her, shake her. She was so smart, yet somehow couldn't see the obvious fact that the governor would *never* listen. But he forced himself to reply calmly. "And if they don't?"

"If they don't . . . well . . . I know where to find you."

<CHAPTER 23>

SHEILA JACKSON

|||||||||||||||||||||||||||||||||||||||||||||||||||||||||||||||||||||||||

61 CYCLES UNTIL ARRIVAL

Sheila stood in the baby development room with her husband, Alex, holding hands as he watched the whirring artificial wombs, enraptured. He was almost glowing. There were two walls full of machines, and while one of them was *theirs*, it looked like all the others, and if she was honest, she wasn't 100 percent sure which one it was. It was on the left, near the middle. She knew that much. Regardless, they couldn't see inside of it or any of the others, and even if they could, the three-week-old embryo was so small that it was invisible to the naked eye. But Alex had wanted to see it, and while she felt nothing for it at this point, she felt *bad* that she felt nothing. That was why she came. Maybe if she spent time here, she'd start to feel it. The level's 81 percent gravity pulled at her, reminded her that she needed to use the toilet. She also needed to get back to work. But Alex was so happy, and she could give him another few minutes.

Three days after meeting with George Iannou, Sheila was still fuming about her inability to sway the governor on key issues. The captain had suggested working solutions within the set parameters that he'd provided, and she'd done that, but the governor kept ignoring even her most basic recommendations. His personnel list for the first missions to the planet made no sense, as he'd failed to include some of the most important specialties while including people who had no reason at all to be there. It was as if he'd just made the entire thing up at random.

She'd gone through the qualifications of dozens of potential candidates, organized her data in such a way that even someone like the governor could understand it, made her arguments. Part of her felt stupid for trying to convince someone who had, to date, shown no interest in reason. Still, she'd spent a lot of time preparing to brief him on potential personnel changes, which was time she could have been using to focus on her work.

And there was a lot of work to do. They had a new satellite in orbit around Prom—one with a mapping mission—and every day it delivered gigabytes of useful data. It wasn't surface data—they still didn't have that, and that lack loomed larger every day—but they now at least had excellent maps of the land masses on the planet—the massive supercontinent and the two smaller continents. A fourth continent existed at the northern pole of the planet, but that was ice covered and assumed to be uninhabitable. But what was more exciting were the nine in-atmosphere flying drones that the satellite supported. If everything worked right, those drones, which had been released into the atmosphere more than a week before, would soon deliver more detailed pictures taken from eleven thousand meters' altitude at nine different potential landing sites.

The flying drones couldn't replace the surface probes, but they'd do things that the orbital satellites couldn't and would provide critical information that they'd been missing to this point. And they needed it. If the governor persisted with his plan to launch early missions to the surface, they had to start picking out landing sites, and potential conditions—including wind speeds, humidity, and weather—factored heavily into that.

They had a lot of what they needed from orbit, identifying areas with water that supported vegetation that was not so dense they would have to clear huge swaths in order to support their mission. But as with everything she did, having a big-picture solution was a long, long way from having the details required for a truly intelligent plan. Along with the potential for new data, in the back of her mind, she hoped that the in-atmosphere flying drones would help her better understand the communications issues they'd been having, too. If they solved that, maybe it would tip the balance with the governor and buy her more time.

Maybe not.

Maybe he'd just stick his finger on a screen and pick a landing site at random. She couldn't rule it out. The asshole.

Alex tilted his head and rested it against hers while still staring at the artificial wombs. "Isn't this amazing?"

"Yeah. It's great."

LATER THAT DAY, SHEILA WAS IN HER OFFICE WHEN A CHEER WENT up outside, which could only mean the arrival of the pictures. She headed out to the main work area to see for herself.

"What've we got?"

"The first pictures, ma'am," said Utan. "I'm putting them up on the big screen now."

"What are we looking at?"

"First images from drone nine. It's the southern island continent."

"Let's see it," said Sheila. Given the latitude and axial tilt of the planet along with scans from orbit, the southern island seemed the least likely to provide what they needed, but it was new information, and that had been a scarce thing.

The picture lit the screen on the big wall at the front of the room, and everybody went quiet for several seconds, absorbing it. The color hit first, all black and dark brown, and then the angles, which seemed almost unnatural in their sharpness. A second picture cycled up onto the screen, more of the same. A third showed flatter land, but the same texture and colors.

"That's it," said Utan. "Just the three images so far. We'll hopefully get more once the satellite relay rounds the planet in about ninety minutes."

Nobody else spoke until Marcus broke the tension. "Well, that sucks."

People laughed, but there was no joy in the room. Sheila wanted to reprimand him, but he was right. *Sucks* summed it up.

"Okay. It looks like it's mostly volcanic, though different in composition from what they had back on Earth. Based on that, we could live there if we had to. People back on Earth lived in Iceland," she said.

"Water would be a problem," said Yanai. "I don't see any, and there's no major internal body shown on the satellite photos."

"Just the one river, and that might be seasonal," added Utan. "But we have desalinization. Assuming the oceans are salt water, which we can't confirm until we get a probe into one of them."

"We'll probably want to avoid a coastal settlement until we have more time to observe seasonal weather patterns and storms," said Sheila.

"It *could* solve our potential conflict with indigenous life," offered Yanai. "It doesn't look like there would be much living there above the microbial level."

"If we could grow anything ourselves," said Marcus.

"Ma'am," said Karen Moriarty. Something in her tone made

Sheila turn toward her immediately. Karen wasn't looking at the big screen but at her own, which wasn't unusual. Her role focused more on equipment and processes than data analysis, but still, most people would have stopped work for *this* data.

"What is it?"

"You're going to want to see this." This time others caught her tone as well, and everyone started moving toward her.

"Tell me what you've got," said Sheila. If there was bad news, waiting wouldn't make it better.

"Function report from the main mapping satellite. It's still active—or it was when it went around to the other side of the planet—but it's lost contact with some of its in-atmosphere drones."

Sheila held back an epithet, but just barely. "That's . . . unfortunate."

"Shit!" said Marcus, voicing it for her. They'd put a lot of hope into the flying drones, and losing them hit hard, even though it wasn't completely unexpected given their previous issues.

"How many have we lost?"

"Seven," said Karen, and the room went silent again, as if the entire facility had stopped breathing. "Specifically, numbers one through seven. Only eight and nine are functioning."

"Eight is the one . . ." started Sheila.

"Eight is the other island," said Karen. "We've apparently lost contact with all seven on the supercontinent."

"Pictures from eight are here," said Utan.

"Stand by," said Sheila, more focused on what she didn't have than what she did. Those drones were solar powered and supposed to fly for five to seven cycles, each providing hundreds, if not thousands, of images along with atmospheric data readings. "Karen, can you glean anything new on what might be causing the communications problems from this?"

"Nothing initially, but engineering may be able to figure something out from the metadata. Hold on, I may be able to get some of it." She moved her fingers across an interface only she could see, and figures changed on her screen. "Okay. It established initial contact with . . . five of them. Which means two of them it never even touched."

All from one continent. Was that somehow the cause of the problems? It was too early to say, but Sheila wasn't a fan of coincidence. "But the five are gone now. Work the data with engineering and get us any details you can."

"Yes, ma'am. The contact times ranged from a few seconds to a little over a minute."

"I've got a picture from drone five!" announced Utan.

"Makes sense—five had contact longest before it was lost," said Karen.

Nothing about this made sense, but Sheila kept that to herself and took a deep breath. She let it out, trying to clear her head, her heart pounding as a bit of panic set in. *Focus. Everything is not lost.* That was especially true if this could help them figure out what was blocking their communications. Solving that would more than make up for the current loss of data, so there was still a chance that they could turn this into a success. At least some of these had established initial contact, which was a step beyond what many of the ground probes had managed. This new data poked a small hole in their leading theory that the problem stemmed from some sort of electromagnetic issue on the surface, but that was good. The more they ruled out—even if it was their best hypothesis—the closer they got to the answer. It also added weight to a problem they would face on the planet's surface: whether they'd be able to communicate with the ship in orbit. Without knowing that, a landing should be completely out of the question.

Should be.

She wanted to go to the governor and tell him exactly that, but ethically she couldn't, because while they currently couldn't communicate with the surface, she couldn't say with confidence that they *wouldn't* be able to once they put people on the ground. Engineers on the surface would have access to higher-powered systems to burn through potential interference and could work the problem in real time instead of on a multiday delay.

"Another picture from five," said Utan.

"How long before download?"

"A minute or so. The connection is slow."

"Let's put up the pictures from eight, then," said Sheila. They might as well focus on what they *did* have. They could do the autopsy on the rest later. The island that eight surveyed was almost six hundred thousand square kilometers—almost twice the size of the volcanic island, making it plenty big enough to host an initial landing and many years of development if conditions were right.

"On the way," said Utan. An image appeared, lighting the room. It was almost a uniform color, much brighter than the pictures from the other island.

"Is that blurry?" asked Marcus. "Something wrong with the lens, maybe?"

"I'm not sure," said Utan. He flipped to the next image, which didn't change much, despite being taken a hundred kilometers west of the first. It had the same problem with definition.

"Blowing sand?" asked Yanai, and once she said it, Sheila couldn't unsee it. That was exactly what it was: a desert. They could live with that. This was only a portion of the island, and they only needed a small parcel of it to support life. The third photo cycled onto the screen, and it was the same as the other two. Sensing the tension in the room, Sheila felt like she had to say something.

"It's a big island. We'll see more as we go. It won't *all* be lifeless desert." It was something like five hundred kilometers east to west and twelve hundred north to south, and assuming they didn't lose contact with this drone, too, they'd get to see all of it. The images they were seeing were sent more than a dozen cycles ago, and all they could do was parse the information they had and hope that it got better. "What else have we got?"

"The two pictures from five and one picture from drone three, ma'am," said Utan. "Looks like maybe that's all we're going to get."

"Put them up."

"Yes, ma'am. Here's the first one from five."

The image appeared on the screen and drew a round of *ooh*s. Sheila felt herself relax, almost allowing a smile, and the tension in the room eased right along with the tension in her shoulders. The image was all green and blue and brown, an inland lake surrounded by what appeared to be forest, with a few clearings and a wide river that either fed or flowed from the lake. It appeared to be a somewhat uniform elevation; they could match it to the satellite data to confirm that, though they wouldn't get exact elevations until more mapping satellites entered orbit. "I wonder if that's salt water or fresh," she said, more to say something than anything else. The lake *looked* like water, dark blue with hints of green and brown, but for all they knew it could have been something altogether different. Earth had salt water, but there was nothing to say for sure that other planets had it. They could have other compounds more or less hazardous than sodium chloride.

"Should I put up the next?"

"Do it," said Sheila. The next image appeared, the lake no longer in the frame, though it still showed the river.

"I think the river flows toward the lake," said Yanai. "Look, you can see from that large rock and how it divides the current. We'll be able to tell for sure once we get down into the image and blow it up."

"Good catch," said Sheila, even if it didn't matter much. It was interesting, and it added to the bigger picture. The vegetation was thickest right around the river, thinning on both sides as it moved away. They could follow up on that as well. They'd be interpreting a *lot* from these two images and what they could get from satellites if they didn't get more pictures. "Show us the image from drone three."

A new image flashed, and another round of *oohs*, though to Sheila, this one showed a little less promise. Light green grassland dotted with what looked like small clumps of trees or other vegetation. There was no visible water, but the vegetation suggested that at least some fell there or there were underground sources. After looking at it for another minute, she addressed the group.

"Today's job, before you go . . . I want a new round of brainstorming on the loss of connection to those drones, given the new information. Karen, you collate it along with what you get from engineering. Get me an updated take on what's causing the issues, ranked from most likely to least likely. Lila, you and Yanai lead the analysis of the new images. Questions?"

"No, ma'am," the room chorused.

She debated telling them not to share the pictures outside of the subdirectorate, but that was pointless. It was going to get out. She had to show her boss and probably the governor and they wouldn't keep them quiet unless it suited their purposes. Maybe she'd share them with Iannou, too. He'd probably get them anyway, but she could make sure that he had the accurate information and not what got filtered through the news feeds or rumor. "I'm going to finish my presentation to the governor. Let me know if we get more data in." Regardless of what the pictures showed, she still had to talk to him about personnel.

SHEILA WAITED TWENTY MINUTES PAST HER MEETING TIME THE following day before the governor's aide finally let her in to see his boss. She launched into her pitch, but the governor barely looked at her. She delivered her information flawlessly, having rehearsed it to a tight twelve minutes. She tried not to let it bother her as he checked his screen again, but even she could hear her tone gaining an edge.

"Questions?" she asked, when she'd finished.

"To sum up," said the governor, "what I'm hearing you say is that you support going to the planet early, but with much smaller teams and only with people assigned specific missions. I hear you."

Sheila did her best not to react. He *had* been listening, or at least he'd looked over the read-ahead material. He didn't have the details that she'd provided on individuals and why they were a good fit, but he had the basics. Yet he missed the point, and his tone didn't indicate support. But she was prepared this time and wasn't leaving without clarifying. "Almost, sir. I *don't* support going to the planet early. That hasn't changed, and it won't change. But if that decision is made—if we *have* to do that—then my recommendations give us the best chance of success."

He nodded. "I'll take it under consideration."

And with that, his assistant appeared in the door and motioned her out. What had just happened? He'll take it under *consideration?* Was he actually going to consider it, or was that a polite blow-off? She couldn't tell. It would have been easier if he'd just said that he wasn't going to do what she asked. In that case, she could justify further action on her own. But this? It made her decision tougher.

If she went public with her opposition, she might push him into a conflict and cause him to ignore her—or worse. If she didn't oppose him openly, maybe he'd end up supporting her in some limited way that might be better than nothing. Somehow, she was even less sure of her situation coming out than she had been going in.

She was still thinking it through as she arrived back at the office, which was abuzz. She headed into the hub of activity. Forget the politics for a bit. She needed to dive into the science. "What've we got? Did we reestablish communication with the in-atmosphere drones?"

"No, ma'am," said Karen.

"It's the pictures that we do have," said Lila, who cast her screen image up to the front wall. "Drone eight. The one that's showing only desert."

Sheila studied the picture, which had been resolved and zoomed in so they were looking at just a small section. She felt chills that had nothing to do with the air circulator. "What am I seeing?"

"These lines here." Lila indicated the center of the image with a laser pointer. "They don't look natural."

"No, they don't," said Sheila. They were too straight, too angular. "What do we think we're looking at?"

Lila paused, as if waiting for someone else to speak up, but continued when nobody did. "We think it's the ruins of a building."

She stood there, stunned. A building meant . . . well, it meant . . . so much. Intelligent life. A *civilization*. This changed everything. It could mean first contact. The greatest discovery in the history of the human species. With all that, Sheila almost hated herself for her primary thought.

Here was another opportunity for her to influence the governor.

<CHAPTER 24>

EDDIE DANNIN

||||||||||||||||||||||||||||||||||||||||||||||||||||||||||||||||

57 CYCLES UNTIL ARRIVAL

Work sucked. Well, not the work itself—okay, that sucked too. But no more than it ever had. She continued to get shitty assignments, but if they were any worse than what she'd had before her little hiatus, she couldn't tell the difference. No, the thing that sucked was how everybody treated her. Or, more accurate, didn't treat her. They ignored her, sometimes even when she spoke to people directly. At the same time, she caught people looking at her when they thought she couldn't see them like she was some sort of display in a virtual reality zoo. Everybody seemed to have heard of her—which was unavoidable. She'd missed work for cycles on end, and that just didn't happen enough *not* to cause talk. There were so many rumors, and very few of them were true, but it wasn't like she could come out and defend herself.

Her only safe space was her room, so she spent as much time there as she could. Eddie was deep in the net, working on the development of her new neural relay, when she distantly realized that something in the outside world was buzzing. It annoyed her because she was making progress. Her time in hiding had made her better and faster on the net, and she'd only continued to improve since she'd returned to civilization. The more she pulled back from people, the more she integrated herself with the ship's network. Reluctantly, she pulled herself out and shut down her links.

Her door buzzed again. A visitor. She wasn't expecting any-body, half thought that it might be Secfor, there to renege on their deal and finally take her to the brig. They were watching her, she was sure of it, but they hadn't resorted to face-to-face harassment. Nobody else would visit her, pariah that she was. Whatever. She didn't need people anyway.

She did still owe Cecil quite a bit, but she was good for it and he knew it. He wouldn't bother her here, so she was at a loss when she sighed and triggered the door to open. Lila stood framed in the opening, tall and beautiful as ever, even in her somewhat formless vac suit. Eddie stood. Of all the people who had avoided her, she hadn't even seen Lila in passing. She had no clue if that was on purpose or just chance—it wasn't like they normally occupied the same spaces. "Hey."

"Hey. I came to apologize."

Eddie moved toward the door, closer to her visitor. "You don't have to—"

"I really do," said Lila. "Can I come in?"

Eddie hesitated, nervous. "Yeah. Sure. Of course."

Lila moved past her and into the small room. She gestured to the pile of circuits and soldering tools. "What are you working on?"

"I'm trying to create ways to access and process information faster. Build a better hack, for lack of a better term."

Lila smiled. "Very cool. I should get you to look at image pro-cessing for us. We're getting some exciting stuff lately, but it feels like we're spending an eternity going through every pixel of every picture."

"I saw the rumors going around the net about pieces of

buildings . . . that's pretty wild. But I don't think any directors are going to willingly me let me anywhere near their data."

Lila's smile faded. "Yeah. I guess not. Which brings me back to why I came. I'm really sorry that I got you mixed up in this."

Eddie shook her head. "Nah, don't be. I did it willingly."

"I know. But I also know that you had a bit of a crush on me—"

"Nah." Eddie felt her face heating, though. Lila knew. Some part of Eddie had known that she did, but that wasn't the same as hearing it out loud.

"You did. And I used that to manipulate you—"

"It's okay—" Eddie tried to interject, to make the awkward stop.

"Just let me get this out," said Lila, cutting her off. "I used your feelings to manipulate you, even though I don't feel that way about you. That was wrong, and I'm sorry."

It should have hurt, having someone expose her heart and then stomp on it, but for whatever reason, it didn't. Maybe because she never really felt like she had a chance with Lila anyway. Maybe it was just better to know. But at the same time, she couldn't just leave it. "You're not into girls, or . . ."

"I'm really not into . . . well . . . girls, guys, or anybody."

"But I always see you with people," said Eddie.

"Yeah . . . it's weird like that, you know? I genuinely like people and being around them. I just don't *like* them like them."

"I get it," said Eddie, though she wasn't 100 percent sure that she did. She was the opposite. She didn't care to be around people much at all, but she'd really like to have *one* person. But Lila was being honest and open, even if Eddie herself couldn't relate. "Could we maybe still be friends?"

"I'd like that a lot," said Lila.

"Okay, cool." Eddie didn't know what else to say, and lapsed into an awkward silence, hating herself a bit for it.

"Do you want to go get some food? When was the last time you ate?"

"Uh . . .." Eddie checked her device for the time. "I don't know . . . I mean, yes, I'd like to get some food. I don't know when I ate last."

"You've got to take better care of yourself," chided Lila.

"I'll try."

"I'll help."

And Eddie had to admit: if this was what it meant to actually have a friend, she kind of liked it.

THE FOLLOWING DAY AT WORK, EDDIE FELT BETTER DESPITE THE fact that after she and Lila got food, she had worked in the net well into the night. Today, she didn't automatically hate everyone, and she engaged with Niko when they got their job assignments. "Want to trade?" she asked.

"What, you get customer service again?" Everyone else had changed how they thought about her, but Niko was the same as he ever was.

"Nah. I've got repairs to a hydroponics pump to start, and then duct cleaning after that if there's time. The pump job is to assess and fix, so there's no set hourly on it yet."

"That's not bad work," he said.

"I know it. I'm just trying to avoid the farms for . . . reasons."

"Ah," said Niko. "I get it. But I'm afraid I can't help you. I've got system repair in food production, smack dab on a 0.51-grav floor. You can keep your heavy-gravity morning." That he said it with a smile softened the refusal.

She thought about asking someone else, but while she wanted out of the job, she didn't want it bad enough to ask anybody other than Niko for a trade. A girl had her lines.

When she arrived at the assigned ag level, she wasn't super surprised to find Big George waiting for her. "Is the pump in hydroponics even broken?" asked Eddie.

He laughed. "Of course. We had to generate a fault code. But I think if you look at one of the circuit boards—oh, maybe D7—you'll find that it's come loose and has a broken connector. Fix that and I bet the whole thing will be good as new."

Eddie gave him a fake smile. "As much as I appreciate you helping me get in my high-grav time for the day, as soon as I plug in my tablet the diagnostic software is going to tell me to replace the card and give me about fifteen minutes to do the job. *Maybe* I can stretch it to twenty if I do a manual override and say that I can solder the connector to save material."

"That's okay," said George. "I only need ten."

Eddie sighed and started walking toward the pump room. She really didn't want to talk to him, but she also wanted to keep a clean worksheet and get back in at least some semblance of good grace with her boss. "I'm going to work. You talk. Because I'm sure I can't stop you."

"We need your help again." George easily matched her stride as he launched into his pitch.

"Sorry, but no. I've got all of security watching me. My hacking days are through." That wasn't true, of course, but he didn't need to know that. The more people that thought she was out of business right now, the better.

"You're not the only one they're pressuring."

"I'm sure I'm not," said Eddie. "But I'm the only one that I care about."

"You don't mean that," said George.

"But I do." He was right to a degree. It wasn't the entire truth, but it was *mostly* truth. She'd still take risks for the right reasons.

But those reasons were hers, not George's. She was done being used.

"The governor is targeting leaders of the movement, assigning them to dangerous early missions to the planet."

Eddie reached the pump and went immediately to the card that George said was damaged. She didn't even bother to plug in her diagnostic. Sure enough, it had a broken connector. "Look, I feel bad for them, okay? I really do. I just don't want to end up joining them on those missions."

"But you do want things," offered George.

"Sure. Everybody wants things." Eddie extracted the cable from her tablet and plugged it into the diagnostic socket on the pump. She knew what it would tell her, but she had to go through the motions in order to get the job on the record.

"What do you want?"

"Right now?" She looked at the display on her tablet. "I want to fix this pump and get out of here. Huh, look at that. You've actually got a real issue here. Leaky seal. This thing's only running at 97 percent water efficiency. You should have reported that."

"Ninety-five percent is the tolerance. We'd have caught it on our next routine survey."

"Probably. But since I'm here, I can fix it." She fished in her tool belt to see if she had the correct seal, but she didn't. She hit the part request tab and keyed in what she needed with practiced fingers. "It'll take the delivery bot eight minutes to get here, so it looks like you've got bonus time. But can we get to the point?"

"I've got you an interview with the director of engineering."

She almost looked up at that, and just barely continued to study her tablet, pretending it didn't interest her. "Yeah? What good will that do?"

"I told you before that we want to enable movement between

directorates, right? Well, somebody has to be the test case. Why not you?"

Why not her? She could think of a ton of reasons, starting with the fact that he was clearly manipulating her, but even being aware of that, the offer was seductive. But she wasn't giving in so easily. The governor had already showed what he would do to people who opposed him, and the smart thing, especially for her, was to keep her head down and hope people forgot about her. But she couldn't lie well enough to say she wasn't interested. *Engineering. Important stuff. Outside the ship.*

"What do I have to do?"

"Go to the interview; impress the director. If you do, he'll make the case to bring you over to his department and force the system. We'll help."

"Why would he do that?"

"I'm not going to guess at other people's reasons. But he'll do it."

Eddie had been around Cecil's people enough to know that meant either the director of engineering was on their side, or they had something on him. Either way, her fingerprints weren't on it, which was at least something, and she'd be a hypocrite if she started worrying about other people's methods. "Okay. And what do I have to *do?* You said it yourself: everybody wants something. You're not doing this for free, so what's the catch?"

"I think that Secfor is illegally surveilling some of us."

"Yeah? What makes you say that?" Given what she'd seen from Secfor, she could believe it, but she wasn't sharing that just yet.

"Too many coincidences. We plan something, and Secfor just happens to be there. If it was once, I'd write it off to chance, but it's happening too often."

"They might have a spy in your organization."

"Maybe. But that's hard to find, and questioning people creates conflict. If you rule out the net, that gives us more reason to look for a human cause."

"So you want me to . . . what? Find out if they're watching you and stop them?"

"No. Don't stop them. Just figure out exactly what they're doing and tell me. We'll take it from there."

"So I just have to look," said Eddie. "I don't even have to touch the code."

"Exactly. Is that within your skill set?"

It was *well* within her skill set—and more than that, it was practically risk-free. She'd barely be doing anything illegal. And if Secfor *was* doing that, well, fuck them. She'd have taken this job on gratis, but she didn't need to tell George that. "Yeah. I can do that. Give me the names of the people you think are being watched."

"Will do."

She expected that to be the end of it, but he stood there. "Anything else?"

"Have you noticed anything unusual with other people watching you?"

"You mean like the whole ship looking at me like I'm some sort of entertainment vid?"

"I was talking more about friends of Fleming."

Ah. Right. She'd kept an eye out for the first couple days, but she'd mostly put the bomber out of her mind. But now that he mentioned it, she felt her heart rate pick up. "Nope. Nothing out of the ordinary. Why? Have you heard anything?"

"I haven't. And honestly, that surprises me. But I'll keep my ear out for anything. You should too."

"Sure," said Eddie.

George stood there awkwardly for a few more seconds before finally turning and departing.

That had certainly been a mixed bag of emotions. On the one hand, she was cautiously excited about the opportunity with engineering. She wasn't going to get the job, but at least she'd have her shot. But on the other hand, now Fleming was back in her head, and she couldn't help but look around to make sure nobody was watching her.

<CHAPTER 25>

MARK RECTOR

||||||||||||||||||||||||||||||||||||||||||||||||||||||||||||||||

51 CYCLES UNTIL ARRIVAL

Mark Rector sat still, trying not to squirm as a young man—probably a student training for his future job—clipped a wireless microphone to his patrol vac suit. He'd put on a clean one for the occasion. He glanced toward the door for the fifth or sixth time, expecting Darvan or one of his lackeys to storm through at any minute and put an end to his plan. That he hadn't told anybody about his interview—that he'd set it up himself—was a complete breach of directorate protocol, and he'd be reprimanded for it. He could accept that, but he wanted to make sure it was *after* the fact, not before it. Better to ask forgiveness than seek permission. Fortune favored the bold, and even if Darvan came after him later, it was time to take things to the next level. This would help cement Rector's position with the governor.

The news reporter had been only too happy to comply. For the past two cycles, they'd been running a report with evidence about Secfor illegally surveilling people, and Darvan's failure to address it head-on wasn't helping. The director thought that by letting it go, people would forget about it, and he was probably right. Rector might not have liked Darvan, but the man wasn't stupid.

They were just on different sides when it came to methods. Darvan wanted people to forget. Rector didn't. He wanted to turn their blunder into an advantage.

Karen Newbottom approached him, the look on her face short of her normally friendly countenance, drawing up about a meter from him, right on her mark. "I'm not going to go easy on you."

"Okay," said Rector, as if he wasn't a trained interrogator.

She studied him for a couple seconds, as if looking for a weakness. "I mean it. I'm going to come right at you."

"I wouldn't have it any other way."

Newbottom's face relaxed visibly at that, as if she'd been worried. What she didn't know was that it played right into Rector's plan. Having someone opposing him would only help him get his point across.

A production tech began a countdown, and when it reached time, Newbottom turned her smile on and addressed the camera. "I'm Karen Newbottom, and we're here live with Secfor officer Mark Rector." She changed her head position so that she was addressing him but still at a good angle to the camera. "Officer Rector, your department has been accused of illegally tapping into the private net presences of multiple citizens. What can you tell us about that?"

"Thanks for having me, Karen. What I can tell you is that the directorate is conducting an internal investigation into the matter, and that if there was wrongdoing, whoever is responsible will be punished accordingly."

"Hmm. And what do you say to the many people out there who suggest that an *external* investigation is warranted?"

"Unfortunately that's impossible due to the sensitive nature of the material that Secfor has on our systems. It would be like giving free access to the worst elements on our ship—the 1 percent of people who think they are above the rules."

"Wasn't the directorate itself acting as if you're above the rules?"

Rector looked directly at the camera. "The enemies of our ship—those who would bomb it or do *who knows what else* to harm all of us—don't play by the rules. Yet *we're* supposed to? I think we owe it to the people of this ship—the ones who do the right thing for our community every day—to protect them from these fringe elements who mean them harm."

If Newbottom realized that the interview was getting away from her, she didn't show it, keeping the same perfect smile plastered to her face. Rector wasn't completely sure she was even listening to his answers.

"I was under the impression that you had already captured the bomber."

"The *alleged* bomber. She still has to face trial, but yes, we have her in custody," said Rector. "But she didn't do it alone. There are bad actors still out there in our community, so we have to keep vigilant."

"Officer Rector . . . the people you were spying on have rights. All of us do. What about those of us who aren't doing anything wrong? Are we subject to the same kind of violation? Certainly not everybody you put surveillance on was a bad actor."

Rector nodded solemnly. "It's true. People do have rights, and where innocent people get caught up"—he paused for effect—"that's unfortunate. And I promise, we will do everything we can to make sure we protect those who are doing the right thing. Yes, there will be mistakes. But people who aren't doing anything wrong don't have anything to worry about. And when people mean to do harm, we can't be tied up in bureaucracy while they destroy our way of life. While they threaten our lives. People almost died in that bombing. *I* almost died in that bombing."

Newbottom nodded subtly, as if she might be buying what he

said. "Do you have any idea of the scope of this? How many people were affected?"

"Just a handful," said Rector, though he didn't have a complete list from cyber. "I don't have the exact number, but trust me, we're only after the bad actors. Somebody in the security directorate may have simply gotten overzealous in that pursuit."

"That's certainly reassuring," said Newbottom, though Rector couldn't tell if she meant it or not. "Is there anything else you want to tell the people?"

Rector looked directly at the camera again. "There is. We've stopped surveilling people in their personal net spaces without the approval of a magistrate, but we haven't stopped looking for the perpetrators of crimes. If you have ill intentions toward the people of this ship, we're coming for you."

Newbottom continued to smile as he delivered his line, and then turned to the camera herself. "Thank you very much for your time, Officer. We look forward to an update after the investigation into the violation is complete."

The light on the camera blinked out and the room came to life, the dozen or so people there all talking at once, responding to what he'd said. For his part, he didn't have time to engage. "Do you need anything else from me?"

"We're good," said the producer.

"Thanks." Rector unclipped his microphone, tossed it to the student, and headed for the door. He had to get back to the directorate and get in front of things with his boss.

"WHAT THE FUCK WERE YOU THINKING?" ASKED DARVAN, AS SOON AS the door to his office slid closed. Yep. He was pissed. His raised voice meant the door was only an illusion of privacy. Everybody in the outer office would be able to hear, and they'd all be listening. Rector was counting on it. It was time for people to take sides.

"No—never mind. You clearly *weren't* thinking!"

"I wanted to get in front of things," said Rector.

"In front of things? I specifically told you to let this die. Do you recall that?"

"I do. But I'm tired of hiding. We face an unprecedented threat, and we need to take it on."

"And by take it on, you mean *violate the fucking ship's Charter*! Need I remind you that the rules have stood for two and a half centuries?"

Rector raised his own voice in response. "And how many times in those two and a half centuries has someone set off a bomb on the ship? There was a fucking *bomb*."

"You weren't the one standing in front of the magistrate, getting his ass reamed for the violation."

"And you weren't the one who had a bomb blow up in your face."

Darvan clenched his jaw, but Rector didn't care. The more he tried to take the side of the opposition, the stronger he made Rector's case to the rest of the force. "You know how hard it's going to be to get a *legal* tap approved now?"

"It doesn't matter," said Rector. "They've got somebody who can find even our best technology. Anything we put out there they'll know about, so there's no point until we can develop something new."

"That's not the point," said Darvan.

"What *is* the point, Director?"

Darvan studied him for a moment. "You're walking a narrow line. I could suspend you right now for insubordination."

Could he, though? Rector didn't think so—not with the governor on his side after he brought in the bomber. And while normally that was a thought he would have kept to himself, it served him more here to bring it out in the open for everybody listening. "I think you're forgetting that *I'm* the one who captured the bomber in the first place. I'm not sure that questioning my methods—"

"I'll question whatever the fuck I want to question! This is *my* directorate. And about you capturing the bomber—you still owe me your source."

Rector smiled thinly. "That's right, sir. It's *your* directorate. And I have no idea. It was an anonymous tip."

"Bullshit."

"You can check the recording that came in," said Rector. He could afford to be confident, because it was true. Even though he did know, the official record showed it as anonymous.

"We'll see what voice analysis says," said Darvan, but he was bluffing. Rector was sure of it. "I know that you had a meeting with Cecil Sharakan the same day you got that tip."

Rector didn't react, even though that caught him a bit by surprise.

"That's right," continued Darvan. "I have my own sources, too."

"I meet with lots of people," said Rector, thinking through what sources might have spilled that. "As it turns out, knowing what's going on is a pretty effective way of securing the ship."

Darvan glared at him. He definitely understood that Rector was taking a shot at him with his quip. "Sharakan has been known to pay people off from time to time. As someone who *knows what's going on,* I'm sure you're aware of that."

"I am." Rector met his boss's gaze without wavering.

"And I'm sure that if I got a warrant and dug through your accounts, I wouldn't find anything there that shouldn't be there."

Rector spread his hands wide, away from his sides. Darvan was making a threat, but a useless one. He hadn't taken a bribe in his life. Not a financial one, anyway. Sure, he took the occasional upgrade in services as a favor, but even if Darvan could trace that, nobody would hold it against him. "I'm an open-source program. You can check anything you want. You don't even need a warrant. I'll give you permission. Want me to log in at your terminal?" He made as if to move toward the other side of Darvan's desk.

Darvan moved to block his way and stared him down for several seconds. "Get the fuck out of my office."

"Roger that, boss."

Outside of Darvan's office, Rector rolled his eyes dramatically. Several people in the office chuckled, though Rector noted that Julian Adebayo wasn't one of them. No surprise there. He and Darvan had the same sticks up their asses, but Rector was done competing for a job he couldn't win while Darvan was in charge. He'd drawn the lines of battle, and now he needed to get over to cyber and make sure that they had their stories straight. While he was prepared to stand up and defend himself for authorizing the tap, he would prefer if it didn't happen *immediately*, so he needed his coconspirator to keep quiet a little longer.

And he needed to confirm a suspicion. He had a good feeling that he knew who found the trackers and tipped the news feeds off, and he needed to test that hypothesis. If it was her—Dannin—and she was that good, he might not be able to challenge her. But maybe he could co-opt her.

RECTOR POPPED HIS NECK AS HE HEADED FOR THE ELEVATOR. HE'D controlled most of the backblast, and so far cyber was keeping his secrets from Darvan. All in all, a good day's work. There was one other guy waiting for the elevator, which arrived a few seconds later. Cecil Sharakan was inside. The big man pushed himself up from a leaning position on the back wall and addressed the man at the elevator door. "Maybe you wait for the next one, yeah?"

"Uh . . . sure thing."

"Thanks," said Cecil. "Officer Rector. What a coincidence. Come on in."

Caught completely off guard, Rector entered, unsure what else to do. He definitely didn't want a confrontation right here in the corridor that led to Secfor's offices.

They waited for the door to close, and Cecil hit the button for Rector's level. "Your boss called me today."

"Yeah? What'd Darvan want?" He'd regained a bit of his composure. Cecil was here to push on him, and he was ready to push back if he needed to.

"Information. He thinks you had help in solving that one case."

Rector stayed silent. What could he say to that? Cecil wanted him to ask what he told him, but that was playing into his hands by showing that it mattered. Of course it *did* matter, but best to hide how much.

"I didn't tell him anything, of course."

"Of course not," said Rector. "Neither did I."

"How could I? What would I know about a bombing?"

"Right."

"He *really* wanted to know, though."

"I'm sure he did."

"And so *I* need to know."

"Know what?"

"I need to know if you're going to be easier to work with than Darvan. Because I can take or leave either of you. No offense."

"None taken." The elevator came to a stop and the door opened to an empty corridor.

"So. Are you?"

Rector walked out and got about five steps before speaking without turning back. "Yes."

After all, what choice did he have?

"Good," Cecil said.

HE WAS HALFWAY TO HIS QUARTERS WHEN HIS DEVICE BUZZED WITH a message from the governor. Shit. If that wasn't just a trifecta: him and Darvan and Cecil.

You should have talked to me before you went on
the news.

That was it. He waited to see if something else came through, some guidance or something to clarify, but nothing did. He wanted to respond but couldn't think of anything that would help. He needed time to think. To bolster himself, he flipped over to see what people were saying about his news conference on the net, and for the first time that day he smiled.

<CHAPTER 26>

JARRED PANTEL

46 CYCLES UNTIL ARRIVAL

Pantel finished his breakfast wrap, cleaned up his spot at the table, and kissed Camina goodbye on the cheek. "Wish me luck. I've got to decide the fate of the bomber today."

She hugged him. "What are you going to do?"

"Still not sure." That he wasn't confident about it troubled him. He'd been putting it off, and he hadn't ever had this kind of indecision in the past.

"People are going to be angry whichever way you decide. You can't change that. Do what's right."

He squeezed her back before releasing her and heading to the door. She was correct. Now he just had to figure out what *right* meant. But a lot of his recent decisions had blown back in his face, and he couldn't get past Camina's earlier words about the people of the ship saying he wasn't focusing on actually solving problems. He was. They just didn't understand the problems the same way he did.

But this one . . . it *should* be easy. Fleming was guilty. There had been executions in the history of the ship—eighteen of them—but sixteen of them involved crimes that also took a life. On the surface, the bombing was every bit as serious as those, but nobody had died. What hazed the decision was that opposition factions would use an execution as a rallying event, turning even more people to their side. Before, he'd have thought that supporting keeping a terrorist alive would hurt their cause, but he'd misjudged public reaction enough lately where he wasn't sure. The vocal opposition were still a small group—barely 10 percent of the population— but the number of people who at least sympathized with them was three or four times greater than that, and together they were approaching a majority.

He'd have pawned off the decision if he could, avoided responsibility altogether, but he didn't have a good candidate for that. Rector had been grabbing headlines lately for his hard-line stance— he'd make the decision. He wouldn't hesitate. But he'd probably try to stage the execution with news coverage in an attempt to further bolster his own standing. A couple weeks ago, Pantel would have done the same thing. He'd learned better. Rector's stunt with the news had brought out people who supported law and order, but it had also motivated the opposition. If he had just let it go, nobody would be talking about Secfor's indiscretions anymore, but now the illegal surveillance story wouldn't die. Rector was quickly becoming another problem that he needed to find a solution for.

He cleared that from his mind as he reached his office, where he found Jeremy waiting along with his first appointment. Another problem, undoubtedly. Yannick Ferentz, the head of engineering, was young for a director, thin and wiry. He carried two tablets with him—one for routine use, and one that monitored all the systems on the ship in real time. It would have been easier to incorporate everything into one, and Pantel felt like the engineer used two as an affectation, to try to seem like he had more going on than he actually did.

"I read your proposal. Come on in." They made their way into the inner office, the lights came on automatically, and Pantel gestured to a chair in front of his desk.

The skinny man took it and deliberately placed one tablet on each leg. "And?"

"Why now? Why this?"

"Eddie Dannin is a generational talent, and she would best serve the ship in engineering," said Ferentz.

"And you know this how?"

"I had her tested as part of our interview process."

"Your interview process that you conducted without the release of her current directorate, which is very much against the rules," said Pantel. The last thing he needed was a rogue director. Especially one who was usually so by the book.

If it bothered Ferentz, he didn't show it. He was pretty much untouchable, and he knew it. He, too, was a generational talent, and arguably the most important person on the ship, even if not everybody knew that. "I gave her a bunch of code for the power plant. Code that *I* personally revised."

"Let me guess. She made it better."

"She made it *a lot* better. She tuned the P.I.D. loop and brought the system closer to—"

"I have no idea what that means," interrupted Pantel.

"What it *means* is that she's brilliant, with an organized mind that can see things that other people don't see. It took me two days to understand what she did and how she made it work. And she did it in twelve hours."

"But you understand it now."

"That's not the point."

"So what *is* the point? Was the power plant not running properly? That would seem to be the type of thing you'd want to inform me about." If he couldn't argue with the man on the merits, perhaps he could get him off track by distracting him.

"It was—it *is*—running just fine."

"So why do you need her?"

"It's not about the reactor. It's what she can do and how we can apply that in other places."

"I don't see the need." It wasn't about Dannin. It was bigger than one person.

"Let me put it this way. Do you know what keeps me awake at night?" asked Ferentz.

"Your husband?"

Ferentz didn't crack a smile. "What keeps me awake is all the things that could go wrong. We're in the middle of twenty weeks of straight propulsion, something this ship hasn't done in 250 years. Two hundred and fifty years! Sometimes things go wrong for no reason. Seals wear out, lubrication leaks, parts just break. There are thousands of things that could go wrong, and I stay awake thinking about all of them."

"She's a coder. She's not going to keep things from breaking."

"You're right. Nobody can do that. What they *can* do is create workarounds for things when they do inevitably break, and she can do it faster than anybody I've got. More than that, the people that I *do* have can learn from her. She'll make us all better. And let me remind you of the fact that you're sending a dozen of my engineers—in a couple cases some of my *best* engineers—to the planet. I haven't pushed back on that at all. So you can give me this one."

He had a point there. Several directors had given him trouble or at least tried to influence his list of names. Ferentz had accepted it without comment.

"She's a troublemaker. She didn't show up to work for something like ten cycles."

"She's the best chance we have of keeping the ship running and on time. Do you know what happens if we miss two days of burn?"

"We miss our system."

"Yep. Shoot right by it. That'll add months, maybe even years, to our trip. Or we'll have to over-decelerate to compensate, which will strain the very old ship even more. Given all the promises you've made, do you really want to spend an additional year or more on this ship?"

Pantel smiled in spite of himself. The prospect of missing the system wasn't funny, but it amused him to see Ferentz in a different light. Pantel wouldn't have marked him as somebody who understood the political situation, but here he was, trying to use it to his own advantage. Any other time, Pantel would have said, *Good for him*. At the moment, though, it was inconvenient. "Yes, I'm in a bind either way."

"You're worried that if you make this one move, it will fuel the argument building against you that all positions should be competitive."

"It's bigger than that."

"The Charter," said Ferentz.

"Exactly. Do away with one part and we create questions about the entire thing. The structural reorganization required to change even that one part would be massive."

Ferentz considered it. "If we made free movement the norm, you'd have to change the way we do education, build a testing system at different checkpoints."

Pantel picked up the list when the other man paused. "Change the way we allocate births. Change the way we select directors. There are impacts across more than where somebody works. It changes everything."

"And it's the worst possible time to be making a change."

"Exactly."

Ferentz smiled. "But changing directorates doesn't violate the Charter."

Pantel stopped short at that, and then he chuckled. The engineer had set him up. He'd walked him down the corridor he wanted him to follow, right to the door that led to his own desired outcome. He almost didn't push back, almost let him have his way right there, but the discussion had triggered something else in his mind. The timing. He pressed on with the argument as he thought it through. "The Charter states that the losing director has to give approval."

"So? Get the losing director to approve. We both know that's not an issue for you."

Pantel smiled, and Ferentz returned it, probably thinking he'd won. And he had. But he'd given Pantel an even bigger win with the idea about timing. Those who wanted change were pushing for it at the absolute worst time, a time when all sorts of *unavoidable* changes were coming. Maybe they'd picked that time deliberately, knowing the governor was weaker. Maybe it was coincidence. It didn't really matter *why* they were doing it, just that they were. This wasn't the *time* to take on change. They already had enough to deal with. But by saying it that way—that this wasn't the time—he left open the implication that there would be a time in the future. They'd be colonizing a planet, and once they did that, they would *have* to change. But that was a problem for another day, and any problem for another day beat any problem today.

"So I can have the young woman?"

"Yes you can."

"Great—"

"*But.*"

"I'm listening," said Ferentz.

"This is a one-time thing."

"Of course."

"And you have to *sell* it as a one-time thing."

"I'm open to that. How would you like me to sell it?"

"I want you to put out a release hyping up her talent—one of my people will craft it for you and send it over. Generational, blah blah blah. It will lay out the time of unprecedented change that we're entering, and how this move is a direct response to all that change."

Ferentz considered it. "Okay. That doesn't seem too onerous."

"If you're questioned about the statement, I want you to say that you believe I will be open to more changes in the future, but only once we've established ourselves on Prom."

"Is that true?"

"It is. You have my word."

Ferentz only hesitated a second before nodding. "Okay. I'll hold you to it."

"And I expect your very, very vocal support that this is not the time to make wholesale changes to the system, specifically because of those challenges that we're facing."

Ferentz's face twisted a bit at that. "What you really mean is vocal support of you."

"If that's how you see it, I'm not going to try to convince you otherwise. It's what's best for the ship, regardless."

"It might be. But how many prodigies like Dannin do you think we've missed in the last couple of decades?"

"And yet here we are, on the brink of success," said Pantel. "For all the complaints, the Charter has—and continues—to work."

Ferentz took a deep breath and blew it out audibly, as if coming to a distasteful decision. "I will support you fully on that right up until we reach orbit around the planet."

"Sixty days beyond that," countered Pantel.

Ferentz closed his eyes for a second, thinking. "Sixty days beyond that, but you inform maintenance that Dannin is moving as if it's your idea, and she reports to me tomorrow."

Pantel hesitated intentionally. He was going to accept the counter, but he didn't want to make it seem easy. "Fine. I'll make the call immediately following this meeting."

"Okay. Deal." Ferentz glanced around. "Are we done?"

"I think we are. Pleasure doing business with you."

Ferentz nodded, tucked a tablet under each arm, and departed.

AFTER A FIFTEEN-MINUTE CALL WITH WALTER KRASNOV IN MAINTE-nance, Pantel had a new view on how to deal with his problems. He'd been holding on too tight instead of letting his directors handle things. He could keep making certain decisions when he had to, but he didn't *have to* as often as he was. He'd had to promise maintenance two birth allocations and an extra budget of printer time, which was hard with one of them out of commission, plus the resources to replace four air-handler units ahead of schedule. All for Dannin, a woman that maintenance was probably happy to see the back of. But Pantel didn't let it bother him. The director was doing his job. If their positions had been reversed, Pantel would have done the same thing.

Buoyed by his success, he picked up his comm again and connected to the Secfor director.

He answered almost immediately. "Darvan here."

"Rector is a problem."

"Governor. Good to talk to you, too. I agree. We probably don't agree on who caused it, though."

"You think *I* did," said Pantel.

"You think you *didn't*?"

Pantel sighed. "I can accept a lot of the responsibility, but it doesn't change the fact that *we* have a problem. What do *you* want to do about it?"

"Funny that you asked. I was just thinking about exactly that."

"Really." Pantel wasn't sure he believed that, but he could play along.

"My first thought is to suspend him, but that won't work."

"Right. If you do that, he'll play it up to the people who support him, and they'll just love him more."

"Exactly," said Darvan. "That got me thinking . . . we should have a security presence with our landing missions."

"Of course. I've got security assigned to each team."

"I think they need a leader," said Darvan.

"Ah." Pantel smiled. "You think he'll buy it? He's been pretty active with the news feeds. He might try to make trouble."

"If *I* tell him, he'll definitely make trouble. But if *you* tell him? Better yet, if you sell it like it's a promotion—that you need his leadership—"

"He'll buy that?"

"He'll absolutely buy that."

"Consider it done." Pantel cut the connection.

Once finished, he couldn't sit still. He needed to get up and move, so he headed out into the corridors with a bounce to his step despite the relatively high gravity. He'd spent too much time in his office lately, and while he had more people he had to meet—that wouldn't end—he could do some of it on the go. One of his operatives told him that George Iannou had met with Sheila Jackson, and that seemed ominous. This one he couldn't pass off to the director. Dr. Carroway was good enough at her job, but he'd come to see that she couldn't handle Jackson. He needed to do that himself.

He stepped off the elevator on the science level and headed to space exploration. Obviously he couldn't come right out and announce why he was really there, but he had an excuse ready. "Everybody is talking about pictures of the planet," he announced from the entryway. "I figured it was time I saw it directly from the source." Without waiting, he moved over to the workstation closest to him, where a tall woman with excellent posture sat analyzing a screen. "Is this it? What are we looking at?"

The woman responded without introducing herself. "Look at this, sir, here in frames two and twenty-one. What does that look like?"

He examined two pictures of sandscapes, one with almost white sand, the other with more of an orange-tan tint. "There are rocks in the sand."

"Not rocks, sir. You see how straight those lines are?"

"Yes."

"That's not natural."

Looking at the pictures, he didn't see the fuss. The rumors going around the ship made it sound like there were full-blown buildings . . . these were . . . well, if the scientists said they were buildings, he couldn't argue. "You think something made those?"

"Yes, sir. Again, note the straight line, here, and this." She highlighted part of one of the pictures, the orange one, and blew it up. "You can clearly see formed metal here."

"Huh." Once she blew it up, it became clear that, whatever it was, it was man-made—or, no . . . not man . . . but . . . something. "Yeah. I see it now. Holy shit. How do you think it got there?"

"We have several theories, sir—"

The governor tuned out as the woman launched into an explanation—he could catch up on the theories later. Right now, he thought about how he'd address it with Jackson. She was going to tell him that this changed everything, and it was impossible to deny that it was a big deal. But they needed to put a settlement on the surface, and this was going to provide fuel to the people who were against that. When he brought his attention back to the scientist, she had finished and was waiting for him to speak . . . whoops. "Have we seen evidence of . . . manufactured construction . . . elsewhere, or only in the desert?"

"We have, at one other location, but we have fewer pictures elsewhere and haven't been able to draw the same level of conclusions."

"Thanks." He wanted to change the subject and didn't have a good transition, so he played the dumb politician and just pivoted. "And which of the sites do you think is best for colonization?"

"Over here, sir." A man addressed him from the next desk. "This is from a different drone."

He moved to stand behind the man. "Ooh, water. Nice. It's just the one picture?"

"Yes, sir," said Dr. Jackson, loudly from the other side of the room. Her tone told Pantel that she wasn't happy to see him there, and he turned to face her. "As I noted in my report, we lost the feed to seven of our nine in-atmosphere drones."

Pantel had read that in her report, but the implications of it hadn't fully hit him until he was standing here looking at it. He read a lot of reports. "Right. I remember now."

Jackson's glare said that she didn't believe him, and she almost seemed to stomp as she came across the room. "I'd be happy to update you now. We've received only three total images from the group we lost."

"Yeah. That's bad."

"It's very bad. What's worse is that we still don't know why we lost them or our surface probes, and we can't immediately replace them. Anything we launch at this point will only beat us there by a few days. We're still doing it, of course, but that doesn't help us much in terms of advance preparation. We're lacking a lot of necessary data, but as you can see, we're not prepared for a landing."

"I see," said Pantel. "What about the two drones that you do still have?"

"They're localized to two islands, leaving us unable to survey the main continent."

"You couldn't move them?"

"No, sir. They had a five- to seven-cycle fuel capacity, and by the time we could have gotten a message to them they would have already been down."

"So all we have is the desert?"

"Right. The other observed what's essentially a semi-active volcano."

"We can't live there," said Pantel.

"Probably not ideal, no. Though as you saw, some of what we're finding on the desert island bears a lot of further scrutiny."

"It does deserve study, but it's not our priority. It's a desert."

"It's a desert where we think something—or someone—used to live. We've got multiple pictures of what looks like ruined buildings covered and uncovered by continually shifting sand. We have to follow up on that."

"And we will," he said. "But not at the expense of preparing for our landing, which is not going to be in the desert."

She glared at him again. "Sir, could I speak to you in my office?"

"Sure." He followed her to what was little more than a closet.

It seemed like an important deputy director should have more room than that. It wouldn't be difficult to shift walls and carve some extra space from the larger communal work area. He thought about mentioning that but decided against it, given her rigid shoulders and hostile tone. "What's bothering you?"

"What's *bothering* me?" She nearly spit the words, but stopped to close the door, locking them into the confined space. Pantel took a step back until he bumped into the desk, trying to keep a reasonable distance between them. "What's bothering me is that you've formed work parties and demanded that they train to go to the surface way before we're ready for that. Who do you think has to do all the work to provide training guidance?"

"That certainly shouldn't fall to you."

"It didn't, at first. But unless you want a mass casualty event on your hands by the end of the first cycle, *somebody* has to prepare them. That's a process that should happen over *years,* so now I'm rushing to get that done when what I *should* be doing is spending every waking hour working on what is going wrong with all of our exploration equipment."

"Do you have theories on that?" Pantel thought that maybe shifting the discussion to science would deflect some of her anger.

And maybe it had, since she paused before speaking. "That's all we have. Theories. But with no way to corroborate them and no time for me to work on them, thanks to your political stunts."

Pantel studied her long enough so that the silence became awkward. He didn't believe her about the time. Yes, she was probably overworked, but she'd said herself that she couldn't contact the surface probes, and no amount of extra time was going to change that right now. They'd get there and they'd figure it out. Part of him wanted to put her in her place, but a slightly larger part of him knew that would risk pushing her into Iannou's arms. It was better to mollify her. "How can I help?"

She hesitated, as if she hadn't expected that response. "You can stand down the training for landing parties and announce that we intend to study the planet before committing to a course of action."

"I can't do that," he said, almost reflexively, and then immediately wished he could pull it back. He spoke again before she could launch into another tirade. "What I mean is, we *are* studying, and you should continue to do that. And I can provide you resources to help with the training of the planet-bound personnel."

"What *resources*? The only resource I need is time. Nothing else you give me is of any use, because we don't have enough information and we can't get it from here."

This was going nowhere good. She wanted more time, which he couldn't give her. Unless one of them gave in, further discussion was pointless. But the last thing he needed was her directly opposing him. He sighed, let his shoulders sag, tried to look like he was giving in. "How much time do you need? I can't give you ten years."

"Can you give me one?" she asked. When he didn't immediately respond, she said, "Can you give me six months?"

She was a terrible negotiator, that was for sure.

"Six months I can do," he allowed, meeting her eyes to hide the lie. It had an immediate effect: her face lit up and her body relaxed. If she believed she had more time, at least for now, it gave him more time to figure out how he was going to handle her. She'd be even madder when she learned the truth, but at least he'd be better prepared for it.

"Thank you. I promise you that every month we have in orbit adds greatly to our overall chances of success. There are so many things that we don't know. You saw the remains of the buildings . . . I think it's important that we figure out why they're *remains*."

He sensed an opportunity to draw her in and lowered his voice a bit as he said, "Tell me . . . and I won't hold you to this . . . what do you think the ruins mean?"

Jackson studied him, shifted her weight to one side, probably deciding if she could trust him, which, of course, she couldn't. But hopefully she still *thought* she could. "It almost certainly indicates that there was intelligent life on the planet at some point."

"Is it still there?"

"That's the question, right? That's why we need time."

"But if there's life now, you'd have found it," protested Pantel.

Jackson warmed to the discussion now, in her element. "Not necessarily. We *should* have detected it, yes. We've seen none of the signs that we associate with advanced life forms such as flight, objects in orbit, lights, or any sort of radio waves."

"I understand."

"But timelines could be different. And on Earth, there were buildings over a hundred meters tall as early as the thirteenth century, when we wouldn't have seen any of the markers that we've ruled out on Prom."

"But you haven't seen any standing buildings."

"We haven't."

"So if there were buildings . . . in the desert . . . what happened to them? Where are the—" Pantel paused. He almost said *people*. But that wouldn't be right. "Where are the intelligent life forms?"

"We don't know. They're definitely not on that island—or if they are, they can't be seen from the air. We have enough coverage of that region now to be pretty sure of that. But think about this." She fixed him with an intense look. "If there *was* intelligent life there but it's not there now, don't we want to know *why*?"

She had a point. That *would* be good to know, though he wasn't sure she'd agree with him on the reasons for that. "What about on the supercontinent where we found the water? Do you think we'll find the same signs of life there?"

She considered his question, but Pantel got the feeling that she already had an opinion, which made him suspicious. Why hadn't she just answered? "I think that's possible."

For the first time since the conversation started, he was pretty sure *she* was lying to *him*. Not a total lie, probably. She probably did think it was *possible*. But that didn't mean she gave it a high probability. Maybe she was lying to try to give weight to her argument for more time. But he'd already given her that, at least in her mind. He considered confronting her about it but decided against it. Nothing she told him was going to change his mind, anyway. They had to go to the planet. "Okay. Let's talk about what's important. I need you to prioritize our landing sites. We'll research the building remains, but if it comes down to choosing where you put limited resources, it's to our short-term priority."

She glared at him again, but there wasn't as much heat behind it as there had been. "There's only so much we can do from here with regards to landing sites. We have to wait for additional assets to arrive. In the interim, we can try to program current orbital assets to focus on a narrower scope to replace the data we don't have, but it takes time to reprogram them and more time to transmit it across the required distance. And regardless, they can't replicate some of the most important data we needed from surface assets."

"When do we get more systems to the surface?" he asked.

"We're getting to the point where we've got something arriving at the planet almost every day now, but there's still nothing that suggests we'll have any better results communicating with the surface than we've already had."

Pantel paused, thinking about how to word the next part without angering her further. "I know you've mentioned this in your reports—and I've read them—but I can't remember right now. How many systems have we lost contact with?"

"Fourteen."

"Fourteen?" It didn't take a scientist to know that was not good.

"That's not including the seven air assets we already talked about."

He nodded. "I can see why you're worried."

She remained silent for several seconds before saying, "Thank you."

"Dr. Jackson . . . Sheila . . . I appreciate your work. I know it's hard and there are a ton of challenges. But we've got to get to the surface, and we've got to establish a colony on the supercontinent, so please . . . do everything you can."

"Six months, right?"

"Excuse me?"

"You promised me six months in orbit."

"Right. Six months."

As he walked back to his office, he wasn't sure that he'd swayed her to his side. Maybe she was more agreeable now than before, but she definitely wasn't under control. He would need to find a different solution for Jackson—and sooner rather than later.

<CHAPTER 27>

SHEILA JACKSON

46 CYCLES UNTIL ARRIVAL

Sheila stood there in her office after Governor Pantel left, unable to stop shaking. It wasn't from rage—not exactly. It was more the adrenaline flooding her body from the confrontation. He'd listened to her, but he hadn't *heard* her, and he was wedded to a rash course of action. She had dedicated her life to this, and yet he'd told her to prioritize getting the colony to the planet. In return, he'd given her six months. Which was something. Or, rather, it would have been something if she believed him.

She didn't.

Sheila wasn't great at reading people, but the governor made it easy—you could tell he was lying any time you saw his lips moving. Even if he truly intended to give her six months, he would almost surely change his mind the second it became politically expedient. As she thought back through their interaction, she wished she'd asked what was now the obvious question: *Why* was the governor so adamant about establishing the colony? It was their purpose in coming, sure, but why rush? He had to have a reason, and it wasn't a scientific one. He wasn't irrational, he was just wrong. If she knew why he was so attached to the idea, maybe she'd better know how to deal with it.

But for now, she could only act on what she knew.

She'd follow his priorities, but in order to not self-combust at the stupidity of it all, she needed to switch her approach to things. If he was going to lie to her, she could lie, too. Or at least she could withhold some of the truth. To do that, however, she needed to control the information. As long as the governor had access to everything she did, he'd continue to dominate the news and distort the facts. Iannou and his band of protestors were the obvious other option, but they'd use her for their own purposes, just like the governor, with no promise of a better outcome. No, the only person she could trust was herself.

She took three deep breaths to center herself and tried to remember why she did this. She'd loved science from an early age. When she was seven, she already knew everything there was to know at the time about Promissa, and now there was so much more knowledge waiting just outside her grasp. She should be reaching for it, but politics and family and everything else were in the way. She clenched her fists until her nails bit into her palms.

No more.

She was going to take charge of her life. Of the science. She was going to do what was right and to the stars with the governor, the protestors, and anybody else who didn't follow the facts and logic of it all. They'd do what they would, but she was done being used.

Still, for all that this sudden streak of independence buoyed her, she needed help. Her initial thought was that she couldn't trust anybody, but there *had* to be *someone*. She thought about it for a minute, and then used her terminal to summon Lila to her office.

The tall woman was in her doorway less than a minute later. "You wanted to see me?"

"Close the door."

Lila complied, and when she turned back she was looking at her hands, at the floor, anywhere but at Sheila. "Is . . . uh, everything okay?"

Sheila was confused. The younger woman was acting nervous, as if she'd done something wrong. "You're not in trouble."

"Okay. I didn't think I was." Lila didn't seem confident in that, though, her voice soft and tentative.

Sheila shook it off. If Lila thought herself guilty of something, it didn't interfere with what she wanted. If things went well, they'd both be guilty together soon enough. "You're friends with the maintenance worker who . . . takes care of computer issues, aren't you? Eddie, I think her name is? The one who broke into my computer?"

"Engineer."

"Excuse me?"

"Eddie is an engineer," said Lila. "She used to be in maintenance, but she moved. And yeah. We're friends."

"She changed directorates? That's big news."

"It just happened—actually it hasn't technically happened yet—she starts tomorrow. You didn't say why . . ."

"Right." Sheila took a deep breath and blew it out. "I need to hire her."

Lila stood, staring, for several seconds, and then she burst out laughing. "I'm . . ." She couldn't catch her breath. "I'm sorry. Whew. You. You want to hire Eddie."

Sheila wasn't sure if she was being insulted, but she couldn't help but take it that way, and this from the woman who had hired the hacker herself not so long ago. When she spoke, it came out a little harshly. "Yes. What's wrong with that?"

Lila's eyes widened. "I'm sorry. Nothing. It's just that . . . well . . ."

"Speak freely. Just say what you have to say." She wanted to get started and wasn't in the mood for this.

"Ma'am," Lila began. "Forgive me, but you're not really the type."

"Okay. I understand that. But I need something done, and I can pay."

"You can pay? You have scrip?"

"Scrip?" She hesitated. "No. But I'm a deputy director. I have plenty of lux."

Lila shook her head. "You can't use lux for something like that. Lux is tracked. Work like what Eddie might do . . . that's off the record." At least the humor had gone out of her tone as she relayed the information.

"Right. I knew that." And she had, at some point. But it had been years since she'd used the black market, and it wasn't something she thought about. "So . . . uh . . ."

"You want to know how you get scrip?"

"Yes."

"I'm not an expert," said Lila defensively enough to make Sheila question the veracity of it.

"Of course not."

"Okay. Well if you want scrip and you have lux, there are a few people who will make the trade for you. For a cut, of course."

"Of course. But if lux is all on the record, how—"

"You buy something legal with the lux. They take it and give you scrip."

"And people do this regularly?" asked Sheila.

"All the time. I could set it up for you if you wanted."

"People don't get caught?"

Lila smiled. "Nobody cares about scrip. Besides, everybody does it. If they wanted to stop it, they'd have to arrest half the ship."

Sheila considered it. If they didn't prosecute it, maybe she was being paranoid. But she was about to potentially defy the governor *and* some powerful people opposed to him, so maybe paranoia was just good business. "I don't know."

"I could do it for you," offered Lila.

"How would that work?"

"You transfer lux to me. If anybody asks, I'll say that I was going by the commissary anyway and you asked me to pick you up some good wine. Instead, I'll bring you the scrip."

Sheila cringed inwardly at the thought. She wasn't comfortable asking a subordinate to do a personal errand that was legal for her, let alone an illegal one. "That would be enough?"

Lila shrugged. "Depends on what you needed done. But that's only if Eddie will do it. She's been keeping a low profile lately, not taking on a lot of jobs."

"Would she do it if you asked her?"

"She would. But I'm not going to take advantage of a friend." The set of her shoulders said that Sheila had crossed a line, and while Sheila didn't understand why, she respected that.

"Right. I understand."

The silence grew awkward after that, until Lila broke it. "Do you want to tell me what this is about?" She paused, and when Sheila didn't respond, she continued, "We're going to have to tell Eddie what we want her to do. I'm guessing it has something to do with that visit the governor just paid you."

Sheila's mind raced. Of course she'd figured it out. It was obvious if you thought about it, and Lila was a borderline genius. She took a deep breath and let it out. She had to trust someone. It might as well be Lila. "The governor wants to manipulate our information that we provide for political purposes."

"Well . . . yeah. That's been obvious."

"I want to stop him."

Lila thought about it. "You want Eddie to alter the data . . . no, wait, not that. You'd want the real information. You want her to *hide* the data."

"Something like that," admitted Sheila. "I'm not actually sure *what* I want. I just know I have to do *something* or he's going to take us down a path to catastrophe."

Lila nodded. "Okay. I trust you. I'm in."

Sheila hesitated, unsure. Lila was a good team member and did a lot of work for her directly, but this put her at risk. And Lila had already been brought in once by Secfor, which could mean that they were watching her. There had been that thing in the news where they'd been conducting illegal surveillance. In the end, though, need won out. She couldn't do this herself, and she didn't have anybody else. Lila was good with people, a skill that Sheila herself didn't always have. "I know you said you didn't want to push your friend into this, but I really need her. You think she'll do it?"

"To thwart the governor? I don't think convincing her will be a problem. But you'll still have to meet her price."

"Of course," Sheila said quickly. She fished out her device and flicked lux toward Lila. "Use as much of that as you need."

Lila glanced to her own device, her eyes going wide at the number. "This will be more than enough. I'll talk to her and see the best way to accomplish your goal."

"We can't hide everything."

"Right." Lila stopped to think. "That would be suspicious. But unless we can tell Eddie what we want and don't want, we can't do it."

"Is there a way where I can see things first, and then release most of it and have it look like it came direct from the orbital satellites?"

"I can ask. She's pretty good. If anybody can make it work, she can."

Sheila nodded. "Okay. Whatever you can work out. I trust you."

Lila smiled. "Thanks!"

<CHAPTER 28>

EDDIE DANNIN

||||||||||||||||||||||||||||||||||||||||||||||||||||||||

40 CYCLES UNTIL ARRIVAL

Eddie was up early, despite lying in bed without sleeping for a long time the night before. She couldn't remember the last time she had been this excited about something, and it had only grown over the five days since she first saw the schedule. She'd done the required certifications in the simulator, she'd practiced on her own in the zero g of the reactor compartment, but none of that compared to the idea of actually going outside the ship. The captain had paused their deceleration for a day as part of a planned course adjustment, which made a good opportunity to take care of routine repairs outside. A short-range sensor array was glitching, and as part of her training on all aspects of the engineering department, she'd been tagged to assist the two primary engineers on the mission.

That they were Jenkins and Capurna—well, that sucked. They were two of her least favorite people, which was saying something, since she didn't have any friends in engineering. She was new, and she was different, and people had their cliques already. It didn't help that engineering seemed to have a distaste for maintenance personnel in general, seeing them as lesser versions of themselves. That one had dared jump ranks and join their own? Pfft. Unheard-of, and to hear them talk when they thought she wasn't listening, she was unwanted. But she'd take all their crap if it meant she got to do important work outside the ship.

Stars—if it just meant *going* outside the ship.

After coffee—she skipped a shower, as she'd be in an EVA suit and want one after—she headed to the ready room early, arriving fifteen minutes before the start of her shift. A few people from the smaller overnight shift were finishing up reports or stowing gear, but Eddie noticed only one person from her own shift. One of the senior engineers—a woman named Karstaad, if she remembered correctly. She wasn't Jenkins or Capurna, so Eddie ignored her in favor of preparing her own kit for the day. Her EVA suit was right where it was supposed to be, having appeared overnight with two others on separate hooks. It wasn't hard to tell which was hers, as it was the smallest by at least ten centimeters.

She began the process of suiting up as the new shift of people straggled in around her. They were complaining about food short-ages, which didn't really concern her that much. It took her a minute to figure out one of the suit's connectors, and she was glad that she had shown up early. The others would probably be a lot faster, and the last thing she wanted was to hold up the mission. She had everything on but her helmet and gloves, which she wouldn't don until they were at the airlock, when Jenkins arrived. Though he and Capurna were equals, he had the lead on the mission today. Eddie didn't know if that was by random assignment or some sort of protocol nobody had told her about. She had a lot to learn, and it was hard when nobody wanted to share with you.

"What are you doing?" Jenkins stood, staring, his hands on his hips.

"I wanted to get an early start so I wouldn't hold you up," said Eddie.

"No, I mean why are you in a suit?"

Eddie hesitated, wondering if it was a prank. Despite the general dislike for her in the department, those had been mercifully few and mild, and Jenkins seemed serious. "We have an EVA this morning."

"*We* have an EVA this morning. You're assisting."

"Right," said Eddie, still unsure what the older man was getting at.

"Assist. You'll be at the airlock. Transport the tools."

"But the schedule said—"

"I don't care what the schedule said. It's my mission, and it's a two-person job. You can wear the suit if you want to. I *guess*. But it's just going to be uncomfortable for no reason."

Eddie froze, unsure what to say. Confrontation had never been her forte, especially not when she didn't have time to prepare, and now it was worse since she felt self-conscious in the new department all the time, anyway. But she couldn't let this go. Not this— her one chance to go outside. If she just accepted the lesser role, who knew when—or *if*—she'd get another chance? And if she let Jenkins shove her aside, that would only make it easier for others to do the same thing. No. She had to take a stand.

"I'm doing my learning tour," she said.

"What's that?" Jenkins had turned to inspect his own suit but turned back to her.

"I'm doing my learning tour," she said, softer this time.

"I understand that. Thanks for that very obvious piece of information, though." He focused on his EVA suit for a moment, before speaking again. "We're doing an important repair outside the ship. *No* EVA is safe, and this one is more dangerous than most. The last thing we need is someone out there who doesn't know what they're doing."

"If I don't go, then I'll *never* know what I'm doing." The logic seemed obvious; they did training rotations for a reason. To train. They'd done them since the beginning of the mission. "Everyone was new at some point."

"Yeah. I get it. Not my problem. If you've got an issue with it, take it up with my boss."

She wanted to. She really did. But as much as she wanted to go on the EVA, and as much as she wanted to put this asshole in his place, she needed to fit in, and running to the boss because she didn't like a decision would absolutely *not* help her do that. Besides, she wasn't sure the boss would change anything. She started to strip out of her EVA suit. She expected to see Jenkins smirking. He didn't. He was focused on his own suit and didn't even look at her.

EDDIE CUPPED HER COFFEE BETWEEN HER HANDS, LETTING IT REST on the table, sitting across from Lila as they both got in their high-grav time. Eddie wasn't a fan of the requirement, but getting to spend time with Lila made the chore worth it.

"How's the new job? Are you learning a lot?" asked Lila.

"Truthfully? I don't know . . . it kind of sucks."

"Really? I thought you were excited about it."

"I was. But I've been there a week, and, well . . . I don't do anything."

"But the director wanted you," said Lila.

"He did. He does. But he doesn't do the assignments. His deputy does."

"And he's not giving you anything interesting?"

"She. And it's not that," said Eddie. "She gives me something different every day, but then I get there with the team and they just do it without me."

"That's odd."

"I'm supposed to be learning, but nobody wants to teach me anything. I don't know . . . it feels intentional. Like they want to shut me out."

"Give me an example," said Lila.

"Really? You want to hear about it?"

"Sure. I mean, if you're okay with sharing."

Eddie hesitated for a breath. "Yeah, okay." And she told Lila the story about the aborted EVA.

"Those assholes. That *does* suck."

"I don't know what to do about it. It feels like I'm stuck."

Lila took a sip of her tea. "You need to show them what you can do."

"Yeah, but how when I can't even get on a job that means anything?"

"So? You're the woman who can break into any system on the ship. Do you really need permission?"

Eddie sipped her coffee, set it down, and met Lila's eyes. "Hack my own department?"

"Why not?"

"It's risky," said Eddie.

"Only if you don't succeed." Lila smirked.

Eddie nodded, warming to the idea. "Yeah. It'll have to be something big, though. Something nobody can ignore."

"I have confidence in you."

Eddie wasn't as sure as Lila seemed to be, but if she believed, maybe Eddie could, too. "How's that thing I did for your boss going?"

"Perfect. It's working just like you said it would. The data detours to a dummy location that only she can access, and when she releases it, it goes back into the main pipeline."

"Yeah? How much data is she keeping to herself?"

"I don't know," admitted Lila. "I don't think she fully trusts me."

"Should she?" It was a mean question, and Eddie immediately regretted it, but she relaxed when Lila seemed to take it seriously without getting angry.

"Yeah, I think so. Like, I wouldn't tell anybody. I *haven't* told anybody she's doing it except you, and you had to know since you were the one who set it up."

"This ship is so fucked," said Eddie.

"How so?"

"That she feels the need to do that. That nobody's listening to her. My job *sucks* right now, but I'm not a deputy director. For people to not listen to *her?*"

"Yeah. It's stupid, because she's brilliant."

"You saying that I'm not?" Eddie forced a smile as she said it so that Lila would know she was joking.

"Pfft. You're the most brilliant of them all. Those engineers don't even know what they've got. We need to do something to get your mind off of it. What do you think?"

Eddie thought about it. "I've got the perfect thing."

EDDIE PUT HER HAND ON THE SCAN PAD AND WAITED FOR THE DOOR to zip open so she could enter the airlock. She had her feet tucked under a support pole to keep herself anchored in the 3 percent gravity.

"Are you sure we're supposed to be here?" Lila looked around, as if afraid that somebody might see them.

"It's fine. I came here all the time back before we were under thrust and just on spin gravity. With a maintenance code, pretty much any door on the ship opens."

"Why? My stomach is rolling already, and we've only been in this low gravity a few minutes."

"Really? I don't get that." Eddie had heard that some people had an aversion to low gravity and that it sometimes manifested almost like motion sickness, but she'd never experienced it herself. "Put your oxygen on. I'm going to open the inner door."

On the other side of the airlock, they'd enter the reactor room, which had about 40 percent of normal oxygen to conserve resources, since people rarely entered and it took up so much space at the center of the ship.

Lila put her mask over her face, and it muffled her voice slightly. "So you like it here?"

Eddie grabbed a handhold and propelled herself through the inner door, then soared along for fifteen meters before she touched down and hooked her foot under another hold to arrest her motion in the big room. "I love it," she called back. "It's so free. If they're going to keep me from going outside, this is the next best thing!"

Lila moved with tentative steps from one hold to the next, afraid to let herself bounce too much. It was a natural reaction for someone new to the area, but not Eddie. From the first time she got an assignment to work at the center of the ship, she'd taken to it like walking. "What do you do here?"

"Well, the closer you get to the actual center of the ship, the lower the gravity gets."

"It feels like there's none."

Eddie did a somersault in the air and reached out to the floor with her foot to halt her rotation. "Almost none. But if you find the right spot in the center of the room, you can get to absolutely nothing and just float."

"You do that?"

"Yeah. At first I did it to practice for when I get a chance to go outside the ship on an EVA. Not that I ever expected to get the chance, since I worked in maintenance. But, you know . . . I always dreamed."

"I'm sorry," said Lila.

Eddie cleared her throat. "It's peaceful. Nobody comes here, and there's all this open space." She left unsaid that it was her own space, that she usually came here to be by herself. Lila was the first person she'd shared it with, her only real friend, but she felt saying that out loud would be awkward. Lila might read too much into it. She had said that she wasn't interested romantically, and Eddie respected that. She'd altered her own feelings to accept it. Somehow being friends meant even more than that, and she was terrified that she would mess it up.

"Yeah. Not going to lie, it's freaking me out a bit." Lila's voice quavered.

"What, the space?"

"Yeah. I think. It's so . . . big."

"Can you imagine what it's going to be like on the planet?" Eddie asked.

"I'm not going to find out. My reaction to the simulation all but disqualified me. They put me in that VR with all that open space and I just lost it." Lila released her foothold and took a step, but she miscalculated and started to drift upward. "Ah! Help!" She flailed her arms, which started her spinning.

"Make yourself big. Arms and legs out."

Lila did it, not so far gone in panic as to not listen, and it slowed her spin a bit, but she was about ten meters up and rising. "What now?"

"You've got enough momentum to make it to the ceiling. When you get there, grab on, and you'll be able to push yourself back down."

"Okay. Gah, I'm going to puke."

"Slow, deep breaths. Clench your jaw," said Eddie.

Lila remained silent, probably following instructions. She was nearing the ceiling now, some twenty-five meters overhead, and she reached her hand up and grabbed a hold. She spun a bit more until she figured out how to control herself from the single point of contact, grabbed it with her other hand as well. "Ha ha! Look at me, I'm on the ceiling!"

"In zero g, there is no ceiling. You can flip over and that's your floor."

Lila contorted herself, tried to reorient. She looked like a toddler taking her first steps. Eddie smiled. She always saw the tall woman as graceful, moving through the world with poise and confidence, utter assurance with every step. But here, in near-zero g, the tables were turned.

"Let me help you." Eddie launched herself toward a spot near Lila, a few meters away to account for the spin.

"Look out, you're going too fast!"

Eddie flipped in the air, absorbed the impact against the ceiling-cum-floor with her feet and knees, and hooked a foot under a hold to keep herself from rebounding. She reached her hand out to her friend, who took it and used it to reorient herself in the same direction.

"Ah. I get it now. The ceiling is the floor."

"Exactly." It wasn't quite true. There was about 1 percent gravity here, which made things both easier and harder, but it seemed too complicated to explain at the moment. It would ruin the mood. They stood there for another minute or so, just taking in the different perspective. No matter that there really wasn't an up or a down here; even Eddie's brain had a tough time getting past that, and the time to stand and reflect helped.

"So what now?" asked Lila.

"You want to find the exact center?" Eddie liked to do that, to find that perfect spot where she could float. As long as she was careful and had something with her that she could throw to start her moving again, just in case she really did find the spot. In theory, a person with no propulsion could get stuck there forever, though probably not.

Lila was taking deep breaths. "I think I need to go now."

"Okay." Eddie's worry for her friend immediately took over and pushed away thoughts of herself. "We're going to push off, but not too hard. We don't want to slam into the floor. Even at low gravity, that hurts. Halfway down I'll help you rotate. Got it?"

Lila nodded but didn't speak. Her face looked pale, and Eddie really hoped that she didn't puke into her mask. She *really* hoped that she didn't puke into her mask and then rip it off. Friendship was great but cleaning up floating puke was taking it a bit far.

"One, two, three, go." They pushed off together, got the speed right. "Ready, rotate."

Lila didn't do it—she didn't know how, and Eddie hadn't told her—so Eddie stiffened her grip on the other woman and tried to rotate enough to carry both of them. She overcorrected and watched as her feet passed the right orientation, unable to do anything about it. A second later they hit the floor facedown, but not hard enough to hurt. The two of them were an embarrassing jumble of arms and legs for a minute before they sorted themselves out. Lila's body shook, and for a second Eddie thought she was sobbing. She started to say something but realized her friend was laughing, which started her laughing, too.

They got straightened out, then held hands as Eddie led them through a low jump that took them to the exit. She palmed their way back into the airlock, out, and down the corridor into the elevator.

Lila seemed content to let her lead. Though she still looked pale, she didn't mention being sick again. They rode the elevator up in silence, feeling gravity start to pull at them. Eddie liked that feeling, coming back from the nothingness to the . . . something. She wondered if Lila did, too, or if that was another way in which they were different. She didn't ask. She missed that she hadn't had her time alone, floating in the large space just thinking. But this had been good, too, in a different way, and she was glad they'd done it.

IT TOOK TWO DAYS BEFORE EDDIE FOUND HER OPPORTUNITY TO show what she could do. She overheard two engineers discussing an issue with the rotation mechanism for the ship. She hadn't learned everybody's name in the department yet—machines had always come easier than humans to her—but she was pretty sure that people called the man Brew, which was short for something, but she didn't know what. The stocky woman was Karstaad, a senior engineer. They were talking in the ready room, where they kept their tools and specialized equipment.

"Can I help you?" asked Brew.

Eddie's face heated, as she realized she was staring. "Uh . . . sorry. It's just, I overheard you talking about an issue with relays in the rotation mechanism."

"And?"

"And . . . I thought maybe I could help?"

Brew—his name tag said *Brewster*—asked, "You *want* to crawl around in tiny spaces all over the ship and help us manually inspect over fourteen hundred parts to find out which *one* is causing the problem? Because sure. I'll see about getting you transferred to our team for a few cycles."

"No . . ." Eddie paused and gathered herself. "That is, what I meant was, I could take a look at the diagnostic program, see if I could fix it."

Brewster glared at her, and while Eddie wasn't always great at reading body language, she was pretty sure that she'd misstepped.

"Sure," he said. "Because we didn't think of that. We jumped immediately to the solution that would take dozens of crew-hours of labor. In fact, Senior Engineer Karstaad here was just telling me that we don't have people wasting enough time, so she just wasn't going to try to find the issue with the diagnostics program and jump right to a manual workaround."

"I'm . . . I'm sorry," said Eddie.

"Don't be such a dick, Brew," said Karstaad.

"Sorry, boss, but I don't need a jumped-up refrigerator technician to tell us how to do our job."

"She's got higher initial qualification scores than you, Brew."

That shut him up. Eddie's face heated again, partly at her proficiency being made public, but mostly in surprise that Karstaad knew anything about her.

Karstaad met Eddie's eyes. "In truth, I've been working on the diagnostics program for two cycles, and there's nothing for it. And the potential risk of losing spin gravity is bad enough that we can't wait any longer. A loss of spin could cause a cascading failure that could lead to a catastrophic event."

Eddie's breath caught. "Is that likely?"

"Not too likely. But even a fraction of a percent chance is too high when it comes to something like this."

Eddie shuddered at the thought. She didn't know what effect loss of spin would have on the overall ship, but the farms at least would have a huge problem, and without those . . . it didn't bear thinking about. She wanted to see the program, check Karstaad's work, but there was no way she could say that. Not with Brewster still glaring at her. Not with Karstaad being the only person in the entire directorate who had actually treated her like a human. "I'll help check the relays. I'm not really busy, and I don't mind getting dirty."

Brewster snorted. "I bet you—"

Karstaad cut him off. "Sure. I'll get you transferred to our team. We can use the help."

THE WATER FROM HER SHOWER STUNG THE SCRAPES ON HER ELBOWS after a long day of checking relays. She'd done sixteen, and three other people had done just about as many. Even with night shift working, too, it would take more than a week. The water cut off, and for a moment, Eddie considered spending some lux for thirty more seconds, but ultimately she stepped out and toweled off. There had to be a better way to locate that damaged relay, and she intended to find it.

Two hours later, staring at her terminal and rubbing her eyes, she realized why Senior Engineer Karstaad had said it was impossible. The code was ancient, and while it had done the job, now that there was a problem it presented such a jumbled mess that she couldn't follow it. What she *did* know was that the problem shouldn't have happened. It took two simultaneous errors—one in the diagnostics and one in a random unknown relay switch. If it had been either one of them, they'd have found it quickly and repaired it, but with both at once, as Karstaad had said, there was nothing for it. There were two options from a software perspective: brute-force it through gigabytes of data or rewrite the entire system. But even for Eddie, recoding it would take cycles, and that was if she didn't discover any incompatibility issues with all the other systems that this touched. And she *would* find those.

That left brute force, and nobody could process information fast enough. She could build an AI to do it, maybe, but coding that and doing the machine learning it would require would take longer than physically checking the relays, and time mattered. What she needed was a faster way to get through the data—something that already existed.

She sat back and blinked away the blue light of the screen, hoping for a new perspective. She glanced to the prototype of her neural interface project and had an idea. It wasn't ready yet—certainly not perfect—but it might let her process this kind of data faster. It couldn't hurt to try. Well, it *could*. It did interface directly with her brain, and that had risk. But once she started thinking about it, she couldn't *stop* thinking about it. She was going to have to try it at some point, if only to see what did and didn't work so that she could improve upon it, so why not start with this?

She picked up the neural helmet, turned it in her hands. It was ugly, still a prototype, all exposed wires and sensors and connectors. She debated with herself about getting someone else to be here with her, just in case, to disconnect her if things went horribly wrong. Maybe Lila. But that would mean explaining abort criteria to her, and it was already getting late. Besides, she wasn't sure that Lila wouldn't try to talk her out of it, and if she did, Eddie wasn't sure she'd be strong enough to do it anyway.

She started fitting the harness to her head, using a mirror to help her line everything up. Thankfully she'd trimmed her hair nearly to the scalp recently, which would create better contact with the sensors and keep them from tangling and pulling when she had to detach. Once she was satisfied that everything was in place, she took the ocular devices and swiveled them down over each eye. She sat there, rigged up, for several minutes, before finally reaching up and flipping the switch to the on position.

A rush of data slammed into her like a physical wall, passed through her, and she floundered, drowning. Vaguely she heard someone yelling, almost screaming, and it was some time before she realized it was her. There was too much. It *hurt,* though not in a physical way, but rather the impression of pain dusting through her like the afterimage of a bright light once a room was plunged into darkness.

She needed to breathe, had to specifically think about that, control it, in and out. Once she got that sorted, she reached out into the data tentatively, probing, as if sticking her finger into a cup of coffee to see if it was too hot. She pulled back quickly, scalded, but it gave her perspective. She shunted the data around her instead of straight into her, and after a time she could focus, see it, even though she wasn't experiencing it, couldn't *do anything* with it. But she had balance, equilibrium. She was there, inside the system, and she could survive. It accepted her, as it would accept a compatible program.

But she had to interact, parse the data, or there was no point. She reached back out with her mind, shunted a small fraction of the data stream into herself, just a few bits at first, but quickly she got a grasp on scale and the fidelity needed to manipulate it, and she had as much data coming in as she had been processing manually earlier. Slowly she increased it, double, and then five times, and then ten. With nothing between her brain and the information, she cut out conscious thought and sped up her internal processes. She wasn't trying to fix the code. Not yet. She was changing some of it, more subconsciously than anything else, but really she just needed to find the thing that was *different.* She stayed at that rate for some time. Time. That was a funny concept in here, where everything was measured in electric impulses and data rates and ones and zeroes. She sped it up again, twenty times, and then fifty. She validated a relay and then moved on to another, parsing thousands of things about each of them until she was sure of their proper function.

From here, she could see . . . no, she could *sense* . . . the weakness in the code. So inelegant, so crass. She wanted to rip it apart, reshape it, make it beautiful, but there was no time for that, just the data. But she would—yes, she'd come back, and she'd make it all better, make it all hers. She could see it, how it connected to other things, where it interfaced and where it passed by without touching.

Even the idea of fixing it made her giddy.

Another deep breath, another focusing moment, and then she had it. She didn't know how many relays she had been through . . . six hundred? Seven? When she reached the malfunction, by that point it was more of a feeling, a sensation of wrongness, than any specific piece of data. She slowed everything, almost stopped the flow, shunting things around her and zooming in on the infection. Closer. Until she could pick out each individual packet of information, making sure this was, in fact, the malfunctioning relay. The feeling grew stronger, and then she had the specifics: the relay number, the location. She fought with her brain to move that information away from the interface to somewhere that she would remember it. She thought of it as long-term storage, and that thought made her giggle in some place of which she was only loosely aware.

She had her answer but realized she didn't want to leave. Here, one with the system, she was warm and safe and away from . . . from . . . what? Did she ever need to leave? It took her time—there was that nebulous concept again—but slowly she detached herself, pulled back, out of the data until it was there, and she was there but outside of it. She fumbled for the switch, found it, hit it.

The loss hit her like someone had punched her in the gut. No, not the gut. The heart. She fumbled for the ocular lenses, pushed them away from her eyes, tried to focus but couldn't. Pain built in her head, behind her eyes; it kept pushing, growing more intense, escalating for several minutes until she was consumed by the pain and her entire skull throbbed. She closed her eyes, and tears seeped through her eyelids. Water. She needed water. How long . . . she searched for her device with her hand, found it there on the desk, forced herself to open her eyes just enough to see—0457.

Shit.

When had she gone in? Twenty hundred?

She'd been in the system for *nine* hours.

No wonder she was thirsty; no wonder her head throbbed. Water. She pushed herself up from her chair, wobbled, couldn't support herself on rubbery legs, tried to sit back down but misjudged and fell to the floor, jarring her tailbone. The pain barely registered, except in her head, which throbbed even harder. She crawled, stopped to rest, crawled some more, finally reached the low shelf where she kept individual boxes of drinking water. She sucked one down, and then another. That done, she lay flat on her back on the cool floor, glad for once that she didn't have a carpet, letting it soothe her until things went away.

She woke, her head still pounding, though the pain was duller. Something buzzed, and it took her a moment to clear her head and realize it was the door. Someone pounded on it.

"Dannin!" A feminine voice.

Eddie pushed herself up to a sitting position. "Hold on. Coming!" Her voice came out raw and raspy. She used the shelf built into the wall to push herself to her feet, held on, making sure she didn't fall again. She stumbled as she moved to the door, caught herself on the wall next to it, and pressed the manual release.

"You're late for work." Senior Engineer Karstaad stood there, hands on her hips. "I didn't want to call it in, because I know you've had trouble. But you can't—"

"What time is it?"

"Eight thirty-five."

"Shit. Sorry."

Karstaad peered around her. "Rough night?"

Eddie tried to nod, but that hurt. "You could say that. Come in. C6774."

Karstaad accepted the invitation and entered the small space, looked at the bed, undisturbed from the previous night. "Excuse me?"

"The bad relay." Eddie made her way to grab another box of drinking water and took a long pull from it. "C6774."

"What are you talking about?"

"I found it."

Karstaad stared at her for several seconds. "You're serious?"

Eddie nodded. It didn't hurt as much this time. "Yeah."

Karstaad hesitated, thought about it, and then punched something into her device. "I'm having someone check that one next. We've got to check them all, so there's no harm if you're wrong."

"I'm not." Eddie steadied herself, met the older woman's eyes, didn't waver.

"How do you know?"

"I found it in the software."

"You . . . that's not possible. You shouldn't even have had access to the data." She looked at Eddie, seemed to realize who she was talking to, but didn't seem upset. "Right. Of course you did. But still, there was too much . . ." Her voice trailed off.

Eddie shrugged.

"Were you up all night?"

"Most of it. Yeah."

"If I mark you as sick, you're going to have to go to med bay for a confirmation."

"I can come to work," said Eddie. "Give me a few minutes to change. Maybe get a protein bar. I'll be okay."

"You don't *look* okay."

"I don't *feel* okay, either. But I'm young. I'll recover."

Karstaad considered it. "Okay. Take your time. But not *too* much time. I'll see you by 0900."

"Count on it, boss."

EDDIE HURRIED, AS MUCH AS HER WORN BODY AND MIND WOULD LET her. The protein bar and some pain relievers washed down with coffee helped, relegating the pain in her head to a dull ache. She fought her way into a vac suit, got her boots on, and spent a minute stowing her neural rig in a locked container. Her mind was functioning now, thinking clearly, and when they found what she knew they'd find with relay C6774—that she was right, and that it was the problem—they were going to want to know how. Karstaad seemed reasonable, but would she be able to let something like this go? Probably not. She was nice, but she didn't seem like the type to pass up an explanation if it could improve performance. Eddie didn't know the senior engineer well enough to know if she would want the information for the good of the ship or for her own advancement, but it didn't matter. The result was the same for Eddie either way.

Questions.

But she wasn't ready to share her rig yet. She told herself that it was because it wasn't finished, and that she didn't know how much of an effect it had had on her and how harmful it might be, but she couldn't lie to herself. Part of it was that, sure. But another part, a bigger part, was that she wanted it for herself. Pure selfishness. She wasn't sure where that came from. It wasn't about getting ahead, though she did want to be included in more things in engineering. But no, it wasn't that.

Deep down, it wasn't about the rig at all. She simply didn't want to share the ship.

WHEN EDDIE OPENED THE DOOR AT 0856, KARSTAAD WAS STANDING there, reaching for the buzzer, apparently having just arrived. "You were right. C6774."

Eddie nodded. She didn't know what to say. She wasn't surprised.

"How?"

"Brute force. I went through the data."

Karstaad studied her, unbelieving. "We both know there was too much there for you to get through it. I don't care if you *did* work on it all night."

"I could have gotten lucky," offered Eddie, but even her tone said it wasn't true.

"Right. Sure."

"But that's not true," said Eddie. Even though she didn't want to tell the whole truth, she didn't want to lie to the one person in the engineering directorate who had treated her like a person.

"But you don't want to share the truth," said Karstaad.

Eddie shook her head. "Not really. Not now."

Karstaad thought about it. "So what do we do?"

"You're the boss."

Karstaad moved inside, closed the door. "Well, given that you saved the department somewhere north of seventy-five crew-hours of work, I'm inclined to say whatever you want." She paused. "For now."

"Right. For now. We need a story."

"I think we go with the one that the director already gave us. You're a coding savant. You used a combination of code and brute force to find the problem, and you got lucky."

"Someone might check. If they do, they'll see that I didn't alter the code all that much."

"Well, then I guess you better do that. It's a good thing you've got the rest of the day off." Karstaad smiled. "Can you make the code cleaner, so if we have a similar problem we can find it faster?"

Eddie smiled back at her. "I can do that. That code . . . it's so . . ."

"I know it." Karstaad turned to go but stopped. "And one other thing."

"What's that?"

Now it was the older woman's turn to hesitate. "After this, I think people are going to want to work with you more."

"Not all of them," said Eddie.

Karstaad snorted. "No, not all of them. But . . . I'd love for you to join my team permanently. You can take some time, think about—"

"Yes. I'll do it. I'd like that a lot."

And Eddie couldn't help but wonder if she had a second friend.

<CHAPTER 29>

MARK RECTOR

||||||||||||||||||||||||||||||||||||||||||||||||||||||||||

35 CYCLES UNTIL ARRIVAL

Mark Rector was sitting at his desk, trying to focus on the report from engineering. If he was being honest, it was a little over his head, explaining in technical detail why they suspected that some recent problems with the ship were perhaps intentional sabotage and not routine failures. It didn't help that he kept feeling like someone was watching him. Which they were. He'd made his play in the media, put himself in the spotlight, and as he'd predicted, Darvan hadn't appreciated it. Of course he hadn't. But what Rector hadn't anticipated was the governor's reaction. He'd thought they were on the same screen, but somehow Darvan got to the governor and got him on his side.

They'd assigned him to go to the fucking planet.

He could give up, he supposed. Accept it.

Fuck that.

No, Darvan had made his move, but the game wasn't over. The governor had made a decision, and he could change it—Rector just had to do enough to convince him, and that meant humbling himself. He needed to dial back the *look at me* stuff and focus on the real work. Remind them all that he was, in fact, getting results.

He'd been trying to get a meeting with Dannin for a week, but she'd been dodging him. Today he finally had his chance. The problems in engineering—the potential sabotage—had started right after she started working there, and that hardly seemed like a coincidence. But if it *was* her, he probably didn't have the technical smarts to prove it. That was why he hadn't brought her in. He needed to talk to her, read her, figure out what she knew. She was arrogant about her abilities—others who knew her said so—so if he could meet her where she felt comfortable, maybe he could trip her up. He couldn't set that up on his own, but he knew somebody who could.

He'd called Cecil, who readily agreed to get him a meeting.

The man didn't say so—not straight out—but there'd be a price for that help later. But Rector was desperate. If he didn't flip things soon, momentum would carry him right onto a shuttle and down to Prom.

He checked his notes one more time before he left for the meeting. He was going to get one shot at this, and he needed to either catch Dannin out as the saboteur or convince her to work with him to find them. He wouldn't know which until he was with her face-to-face, but at least he had a path forward.

HE ARRIVED A BIT EARLY TO THE BLACK CAT ONLY TO FIND A MAN pounding on the side of a food dispenser, which wasn't what he was here to deal with, but he couldn't very well ignore it. He approached the man slowly, hand sliding down to touch his stun stick. "Hey. What's going on?"

"This fucking thing shorted me," said the man without turning to see who was asking.

"Prices have gone up. Let it go."

"Who the fuck . . ." The man's voice trailed off as he turned and recognized Rector. "This isn't any of your business."

"Look, I get it. You're pissed. Just don't mess up the machine, okay?" Rector really hoped the man would take the hint and leave. He had more important things to get to.

It took the man a few seconds to calculate his options and respond. "Yeah. Sure."

"Have a nice day."

The man walked away silently.

Mikayla Irving was leaning against the serving counter, smiling at the encounter. Whether she was there for Eddie's protection or just to monitor their conversation for Cecil, he didn't know. Stars, for all he knew, maybe Cecil had sent her to make sure that Eddie showed up. Either way, he didn't approach her and instead used the free coffee dispenser. He couldn't see paying good lux for premium when the free stuff was perfectly adequate. Coffee acquired, he took a seat facing the entrance.

He was halfway finished with his cup before Eddie finally arrived, dragging her feet and looking like she wanted to be anywhere but there. She glanced around, and her eyes stopped on Mikayla. From her look, she clearly understood the woman's role here, perhaps better than he did. She found him soon after, and he stood as she approached.

"Can I get you anything? Coffee?"

She glared at him. "I'm good."

He gestured to the seat across from him, waited for her to sit before taking his own. "Thanks for coming."

"Yeah. Whatever."

"I know you probably didn't have a choice," he said, trying to lighten the mood a little. He needed her to talk to get a read on her, and single-word responses weren't going to cut it. But his deal with Cecil had been to get the meeting, not guarantee a result.

"Can we just get this over with? I've got work to do."

"I thought your shift was over for today. In fact, I specifically verified that with your supervisor, Senior Engineer Karstaad."

"You've been checking up on me?" He would have thought her body language couldn't get more hostile. He would have been wrong.

"No," he said quickly. "She contacted me. There have been some problems with some of the systems."

"Yeah. No shit. But why do you care?"

"Senior Engineer Karstaad thinks there's a possibility that those things were done intentionally."

"And you think that because I'm new, because you think you've got stuff on me, that *I'm* responsible?" She spoke loudly, had her palms pressed into the table as if she was ready to get up and leave. Rector didn't know what Mikayla would do in that situation, whether she'd force her to stay or not, and he didn't want to find out. But there was a fine line of balance between letting Eddie act out to figure out what she was thinking and screwing the entire endeavor.

"Not at all," he said, trying to put on a disarming smile. "The senior engineer actually told me that it was you who solved the problem with the relay in the rotation system and that you found another problem in the fusion drive code a few days later. I just wanted to get your opinion on those things."

Eddie stared at him a second longer but relaxed a little and sat fully back in her chair. "What do you mean? What do you want to know?"

There it was. Maybe it was from Karstaad's praise or from someone actually wanting her opinion, but it was her first hint of openness. Just a crack. Rector just needed to jam his foot into it and wedge it open fully.

"Could these two problems have been the work of a saboteur?"

"Who would do that?" She said it forcefully, but it seemed a genuine question, one without the anger that she'd had just a moment before. "That relay, if it had blown, could have put all of us at risk. I looked into it. A short-term loss of spin would be messy, but we could survive. Longer-term? It's not good."

"What about the code fault in the engine? Wouldn't that be even more catastrophic?" He found in this short amount of time that he'd almost dismissed the idea of her being the saboteur herself. It seemed rash to judge so quickly, but he trusted his gut, and she was too passionate about her work, too much of an emotional open book to hide it.

Eddie shook her head. "No. The fusion drive has ridiculous levels of built-in safety systems. Its redundancies have redundancies. If anything happened, it would have defaulted to taking itself offline, which would be a giant pain in the ass but wouldn't kill us."

Rector nodded. He didn't know the details, but he didn't need to. What was important was that *she* did, and she believed what she was saying. More, that *he* believed she knew what she was saying. Even better, her answer gave him a suspect. "You asked who would do that . . . I think maybe you've actually answered the question. There's a group on the ship that wants us to stay away from the planet. I talked to one of the navigators, and they said if the drives went offline for an appreciable period of time, it would force us to compensate with a higher burn or miss our destination completely."

"A higher burn?" Eddie considered it, appearing to take it seriously. It seemed like new information to her. "The senior engineer really thinks it was sabotage?"

"She thinks it's *possible*. But I want to know what *you* think."

"Why me?"

"You found both problems. She says that you're the best they've got."

Eddie's face lit up at that, though after a second she schooled it back to neutral. Karstaad's praise *definitely* meant something to her. "Maybe I put them there, so I knew where to look. Maybe I wanted to make myself look good to the boss."

Now she was reaching, trying to throw him off the truth. She hadn't done it. "Did you?"

"No."

"I didn't think so."

Eddie stared him down for a few seconds. "Why not?"

Rector considered his answer carefully before speaking. They'd reached the important moment of the interaction, the one that would determine where they ended up. He decided to go with the truth. "Because I think you care about your work, and I think you care about the ship. Just a gut feeling, but all I've got is my gut."

Eddie snorted. "You say that now, but you've been on me for weeks. Secfor tried to monitor me illegally."

Rector shrugged. "Yep. We fucked up. I'm sorry and I wish we'd handled it better. But let's not pretend you were completely innocent."

Eddie let a smile slip again, and this time it took a little longer for it to dissipate. "SE Karstaad is a smart woman. If she thinks it's sabotage, who am I to argue?"

"You're the person she said I should talk to. The person who would know best." *That* was a lie, but one that he thought he could get away with. Dannin wanted to believe it, and it might even be true. It was at least *near* the truth.

"Can I get that coffee?" Eddie asked.

"Uh, yeah. Sure." Rector got up, afraid now that he'd misjudged and that he would turn his back only to find that she'd disappeared. He even glanced over his shoulder to check that she hadn't. She was staring off into nothing, as if deep in thought. Hopefully about the potential sabotage. If she determined that it really *was* sabotage, then it was a short step to getting her to help him. Her still sitting there was a win. Her helping him: that would be total victory. It would protect the ship and allow him to remove another dangerous actor—or actors—from circulation. As a bonus, it would get him back in the governor's good graces. But he couldn't get ahead of himself. "Cream or sugar?"

"Yes please. Light on both."

Rector fixed her beverage and brought it back to her. "So what do you think?"

Eddie sipped her coffee before answering. "Yeah. Maybe it's sabotage. I didn't think about it until now because I was focused on solving the problem, not how the problem got there. But as I go back through it in my mind, it's definitely possible."

"Possible, or probable?"

Eddie slowly moved her head from side to side as she thought. "I don't want to say 'probable' at this point. Not without the code right here in front of me."

"Can you go back and look?" Rector didn't really care. *He* believed it was sabotage, would treat it like it was. That was just good business, because if he was wrong, it didn't matter. But if he ignored it and it actually was criminal action . . . well . . . that would be bad. But asking her to go back and look was another small step toward her working with him.

She shook her head. "Nope. The code isn't there anymore. I fixed it."

"There's not . . . I don't know . . . a record? A backup version?"

"Sure there is. There's always a backup. But we're not reverting back to it. What I did is better, and anyone who looks at it can see that. It gives us additional power *and* additional safety, and to revert we'd be giving that up. Uh-uh. Not happening."

"But you could go look at the backup still. The original code?"

For the first time, she looked guilty. "Well . . . about that. I didn't clone the code before I worked on it. Technically we're supposed to, but in this case, the thing is so massive, and . . . why? We don't use it anywhere else and won't use it again."

He got the feeling that she wasn't being completely honest about that, and he wanted to press her, but he didn't understand how these kinds of things worked enough to do that. Plus, he couldn't risk pissing her off—she was his key to solving the case. Better to let that slide and change the subject. "So you're the expert. Tell me how we find the asshole who did this."

"If someone altered the code, the change is tagged. One hundred percent they erased what they did, but they can't erase that they did something."

"And you can find that."

She bobbed her head back and forth again, a sign that Rector now read as her considering something. "Yeah. Probably. Now that I know to look for it. Not on this one . . . again—no more code to look at. But if they do it again? Yeah. I'll probably find it."

"Probably like 51 percent?" asked Rector.

"Probably like 99 percent."

Rector sat up a little straighter. "So when they try again—because I think they *will* try again—you'll be able to figure out who did it."

She hesitated for just a split second. "Yeah. But now that I'm looking for it, it might never get that far."

"What do you mean?"

"There are only so many systems that you can attack on the ship that will have a significant effect but not instantly kill us all, right?"

"Sure. I guess."

"So I'll stop them from attacking them."

"You can do that?"

"On this ship? I can do anything."

Rector considered the implication of that statement, which, again, he believed. Or at least he believed that she believed it, and he had no evidence to the contrary. "Would it be possible to still find out who did it? Because I'd like to see them punished."

"Punished how?" She was wary again, and he had to be careful. Just because she was aligned with him somewhat in protecting the ship didn't mean she wanted to be partners, or even to be seen cooperating. "You think you could do something worse to them than I can?"

"I mean, I could arrest them."

"You think that's worse than being locked out of all your accounts, to the point where you can't even swipe for free food?"

"You could do that?"

She smirked. "Of course not. That would be illegal."

"Like when you messed up all the Secfor systems?"

"Can you prove that?" But again, Dannin smiled as she said it. She might as well have held up a flashing *guilty* sign. She wasn't even trying to hide it.

"No. No, I cannot." And even if he could, he didn't want to. The woman sitting in front of him was a demon, but he was the one who summoned her this time. He'd fallen into that a lot lately—

needing the help of someone on the wrong side of things—and he didn't love it. He'd still use it, though. Besides, Karstaad *had* said she was the best. If she wanted to screw with the ship, what could he do to stop her? If he pushed too hard, she'd run away. Or worse, she'd run at him. He needed her to feel like she was in control. "I'll tell you what . . . let's leave it open as an option. I'm here. So if you run across someone doing something to the ship and you want to let me know, I promise I'll take action."

"I'll keep it in mind," she said, and she might have actually meant it, which was the best he could hope for.

"Let me give you my contact info—"

"I can get ahold of you if I need to," she said.

Rector laughed. "Yeah, I guess you probably could."

"We good?" Dannin made to stand.

"Yeah. Oh, one more thing." Rector lowered his voice, and Dannin leaned closer. "Don't leave a message with anybody else in Secfor."

Her eyes went wide at that. "Why not? Something wrong there?"

"Yeah. We've definitely got a spy. I'm working on it, but until I lock it down, only contact me. I don't even trust the director."

Dannin nodded. "Okay. Got it."

Rector waited at the table as she left, proud of himself. He didn't really suspect that Darvan was a threat to the ship. They had their issues, sure, but he wasn't a terrorist. But if Dannin was as good as she thought she was, that made her an asset that *he* wanted to control. What better way to do that than by making her suspicious of the rest of the directorate? That she was naturally wary of Secfor made it that much easier. If things worked out, maybe he could even talk her into identifying the leak in his own department. Now that was a thought. He didn't want her poking around Secfor systems, of course, but for that? Maybe it would be worth it.

Darvan had won the previous round. But the fight wasn't over yet, and Rector still had a few punches left to throw.

<CHAPTER 30>

JARRED PANTEL

||||||||||||||||||||||||||||||||||||||||||||||||||||||||||||||||||

32 CYCLES UNTIL ARRIVAL

Jarred Pantel sat across from Camina, both of their dinners sitting untouched on the table. She had just finished telling him about her day, but he'd sensed that there was something she wasn't telling him.

"What's wrong?" he asked.

"People are . . . acting different."

"What? Did someone do something to you? Who was it?"

"No, no. Nothing like that. Nothing so blatant. It's like . . . at work, people who would normally be pleasant are kind of avoiding me. And I've caught a couple of people whispering and looking at me when they thought I wasn't paying attention."

He consciously unclenched his jaw and tried to smile. Getting mad about it wouldn't help Camina. She'd just feel worse for bringing it to him. "Just at work?"

"It's different other places. People turn to look at me in the corridor. They say stuff. Never to my face, but sometimes loud enough that I can hear it."

He wanted to punch something, but instead he sat there, frustrated. He couldn't help feeling responsible, but what could he do?

People were mad with him and were taking it out on her. He was the most powerful man on the ship, but lately he felt completely powerless, and this seemed to confirm that. It wasn't a good feeling. Part of him knew he wasn't really powerless, that he was feeling only a fraction of what someone at the bottom of the ship's hierarchy felt. But at the same time, those people could do anything they wanted, *say* anything they wanted about him, and he couldn't do a thing about it. Which . . . okay, it came with the job. But it had never come with so much rancor. And even if it had, he could have handled it if they focused only on him.

At least that was what he told himself.

But when they came for his wife . . .

He hadn't always been a great husband, but he wasn't a bad one. He was faithful. He'd never involved his wife in his job, never used her as a political tool or forced her into anything that she didn't want to be involved in. Sure, he was somewhat of a workaholic, could spend too many hours invested in the job, but who was truly innocent of that? Now she was involved whether he liked it or not. And he really, really didn't like it.

Then the anger came.

Real tough guys, attacking a woman for things she hadn't even had a say in. He wanted to call for the camera recording, find out who was responsible, and make them pay. But he knew better than that. He'd only make things worse. All he could do was apologize to Camina for getting her caught up in something that wasn't her making. "I'm sorry. This is my fault."

"No!" said Camina, all of a sudden her voice stronger. "This is *not* your fault. You're doing what's right for the ship."

He started to talk, but realized that if he did, he was going to cry. "I . . . I . . . uh. I need to go to work."

His wife nodded, a tear winding its way down one cheek. She wiped it away, trying to look strong, which just made him feel worse.

"We're going to handle this."

She nodded again. "I trust you."

MARJORIE BLAISDELL WAS WAITING FOR HIM AT HIS OFFICE WHEN HE got there. He'd passed several people along the way, and while people looked at him, nobody said anything—which was just as well, because he was pretty sure he would have hit the first one to even cough at him. He quickly filled Blaisdell in on the situation with his wife, doing his best to keep the emotion out of his voice but probably failing.

She didn't speak right away as she considered his words. "Tell me this, Governor: what is it that you want? In basic terms."

"I want them to feel the pain of what they're doing. I'm tired of protestors, of work slowdowns, of . . . everything. Everything where someone is failing to put the ship first, thinking only of themselves. I want them to feel consequences for their actions."

"We did cut rations," she said.

"Until the black market adjusted and compensated."

"So then something more than that. Okay."

"You have thoughts?"

"I do. Do you want to know them, or do you want me to just make them happen?"

Pantel considered it. She was giving him plausible deniability, which was a coward's way to handle things. But it wasn't necessarily a dumb one. "Give me a hint."

"Schedule Teresa Fleming's execution. Make it public. I'll take care of the rest."

Pantel considered it. He could do that. He probably *should* do it—should have done it a while ago, regardless of whatever his operative had planned—but he'd been avoiding that decision. She'd been found guilty, and the magistrate had sentenced her, but he had the final say on the death penalty. "You don't think that will give them an event to further rally around?"

"I'm not going to lie. Things are going to get worse before they get better. But if you want them to feel it, we've got to bring it to a head."

"What's the outcome?"

"It's best if you don't know the specifics. You want them to feel pain, right? They'll feel it, and you'll gain public support and leverage over the leadership of the opposition at the same time."

That seemed like too much to pass up, like he was overthinking things. He knew that he should make her spell it out, that he owned it regardless. But in the moment, he didn't care. They'd gone after his wife. "Make it happen. I'll schedule the execution as soon as possible."

"Got it," said Blaisdell. "While we're here, we should talk about the scientist."

"Jackson? You want to execute her, too?" Blaisdell chuckled, and for the first time all day, Pantel felt something like relief. "What's she up to?" he asked seriously.

"Word from within her section is that she's holding back information. That she knows stuff that they're not getting."

"I don't understand. She's the boss, so . . . what's the problem? I'd expect her to know more than everybody else."

Blaisdell shook her head. "They have access to the same feeds . . . at least they always have. I'm not sure what's changed. All I know is that my contact thinks it's off. Thinks she's hiding stuff. And if she's holding it back from them—"

"—then she's holding it back from us." Pantel paced, scuffing his feet on the carpet. "What's her game?"

"I don't know. But do we want to wait and find out?"

"What can we do to her?" asked Pantel.

"That's where it gets hard. Their baby is already developing in an artificial womb, so pulling back that authorization would be pretty gross."

"Right. No way do we do that." He was mad, and he was willing to use whatever leverage he could, but there were lines he wouldn't cross. "Shit. I thought I had her under control by promising her extra time, but now I'm not so sure. Is there a chance that she could be funneling information to the other side?"

"I can't rule it out. The tough thing is, if you confront her directly, it's likely to burn my source inside of her directorate."

Pantel nodded. Blaisdell had a lot of assets that he didn't know about, and that presented its own sort of danger. If someone ever got her to turn on him . . . no, he couldn't think like that. He had to trust *someone*, and she'd never given him reason to doubt her. "There have been leaks in that department all along."

"There have. But things haven't been as tense as they are now. Some key facts released at just the right time could swing public opinion against us. There's really *a lot* we don't know about the planet, and while people kind of understand that, so far they don't really believe it's as bad as it actually is. It's just scientists talking. But can we chance that changing?"

Pantel wasn't sure he agreed, but he wasn't thinking clearly, so he gave extra weight to Blaisdell's thoughts. She didn't have emotional investment like he did. "Again: what do I do?"

"Send her to the planet."

"Excuse me?" He'd heard her, but it took him a moment to process it. "What would that do?"

"You can't take the baby away from her, but with this, you take her away from the baby."

"You think the threat of that will keep her in line?"

"I'm not sure if that alone would do it, but there's more to it. She believes that we should take our time getting down there, right? That there's risk?"

"Yes."

"So put the risk on her. It makes it a lot harder to be a maverick if you think it might put your life in danger."

"Wouldn't that just exacerbate the problem? Send her running to the other side?"

"I don't think so. She's a theorist who works in a lab. If she is faced with the threat of traveling to a harsh environment, my strong belief is that it forces her back into your arms. After all, if you make the announcement, it's only you who can rescind it, right?"

"She could run to the captain."

Blaisdell considered it. "True. She has before. But what would the captain do? What *can* she do?"

"The Charter says she has input on certain aspects of going to the surface—she owns the shuttles and the pilots, for starters." He thought about it for a few seconds. "I don't know that she'd withhold those assets—that would be a huge step, and she hasn't ever challenged me like that. Of course, a lot of unprecedented things are happening, so we can't rule it out. I guess she could ask me to change the decision . . . but she probably won't. Jackson is just one person, and her going to the surface doesn't affect the ship. The captain has fought me on some of my requests because she has some oversight authority on ship-wide decisions, but personnel decisions are solely mine, and I don't think this is a battle she'll choose to fight."

"It's a no-risk situation," said Blaisdell. "If it gets too hot, you can always back off of it later."

His gut told him that she was right, but he stopped and considered it for a bit before making a final decision. He knew he was mad about how people were treating his wife. While part of him wanted to destroy everyone involved in that, he couldn't lose sight of what was best for the ship. That had to come first, and he had to be sure he wasn't making a purely emotional decision. Scheduling Jackson to go to the planet gave him some leverage over her, and he could use that to make her focus on the key priorities. And if she ran to the captain, he could always back off as a sign of goodwill, which might make it easier to negotiate with the captain on future issues. He and the captain would need to work together more often now, and having the quid pro quo in place would make that easier, which in turn would benefit everybody.

He nodded absently, his decision made. "It's a good idea. I'll announce that we're putting scientists on each of the early landing expeditions so it's not just her. I'm not sure if we'll keep them on the list or not, but for now I think there are advantages."

"I'll work on the statement as soon as we're done here."

With that settled, they moved on to the more mundane things on their never-ending list of ship business.

<CHAPTER 31>

GEORGE IANNOU

27 CYCLES UNTIL ARRIVAL

Something didn't feel right to George, and it wasn't just the press of bodies around him. He hadn't wanted to be there at all, saw no point in it, so maybe that was it. Four days before, the governor had announced the execution of Teresa Fleming for setting off a bomb in the manufacturing directorate, and now here they were, outside the place where it was about to happen, staging the biggest protest the ship had seen in his lifetime. He didn't have the exact numbers, but he could tell that much just from looking at four or five hundred people gathered here, crowding the corridor in both directions. The news publicizing the event for the past three days had kept it at the front of every conversation.

It was kind of a stupid thing to protest. If anything, he agreed with the governor on this one. The woman had set off a *bomb* on a *spaceship,* and while he was generally against the death penalty, if anybody deserved it, she did. He was only there because Kayla had guilted him into it. She hadn't done it intentionally, and it probably wasn't fair to blame her for his own feelings, but she'd made it sound like such a big deal. To her, Fleming was a martyr, dying for trying to stop the colonization of the planet.

Not someone who almost killed them all to try to stop them from colonizing the planet. He loved his daughter, but she was wrong on this one. Still, here he was.

Either way, the energy was wrong. He couldn't explain it, but it was like when he knew that some rot or disease had taken hold in a plant. He'd hoped that by coming, maybe he could help control things, keep them from getting out of hand. But he couldn't even control the crowd jostling him this way and that, maybe twelve or fifteen meters from the double line of Secfor officers blocking their way to the actual execution site.

Fleming's execution was supposed to be done publicly, but it was actually done in a closed room by medical personnel and broadcast to the public through a live video feed. They wouldn't see anything in person. Just another reason they should have stayed home. They weren't going to stop it—only the governor could do that, and that wasn't happening. A mass rally wouldn't change that man's mind.

A couple of chants had broken out, but they lacked organization and leadership, and so they'd quickly died or gotten out of sync as the sound traveled from one end of the crowd to the other. Again, it didn't matter. As long as the day ended without arrest or injury, that would be a success as far as George was concerned.

But even that wasn't guaranteed, he thought. The tone of the gathering was changing; a hush fell in fits and starts, and that could only mean one thing. George got out his device and clicked on the same feed everyone else on the ship was watching.

There wasn't much to see. Two medical personnel wheeled Fleming in on a gurney. Strapped down and already sedated, she looked small and harmless. She had no makeup on, her face was blotchy, and her hair was stringy and greasy. For the first person to be executed in as long as anybody could remember, she looked exactly the opposite of dangerous. If George had to describe it with a single word, it would have been *sad*.

Fleming didn't move when they transferred her from the gurney to the table on which she would die. There would be no last words, no speech, no defiant gesture. Just a couple of needles into a couple of different ports, and then a trip to the recycler. George wondered about her family and other people who cared about her. Were they here in the crowd or somewhere else? Were they watching at all? He should have sought them out. He didn't support her or those like her, but still, he had an obligation as the closest thing to a leader that these people had. Maybe he'd look for them after. Maybe not, though. He assumed most of his movements were watched, and that might give ammunition to his detractors, which included . . . well . . . just about everybody, lately. It hardly seemed worth it, given how little they were accomplishing—

A loud bang sounded in front of him, ripping him from his thoughts. He looked over the crowd toward the source of the sound, and a second bang—he recognized it this time as an explosion—came from behind him. Time seemed to slow for a heartbeat, and then the crowd erupted into motion and screaming. Smoke roiled in the corridor, and it burned his nostrils, acrid, like an electric fire, but heavier. Bodies pressed into him, first trying to shove him toward the Secfor, then away. More screams, shouts, panic. The smoke grew thicker, and his eyes watered. People pushed, elbowed, anything to get away.

But where was *away*?

One thought pushed through the chaos: Kayla was in this. He needed to get to her. *Where was she?* Even if he knew, there was nothing for it. His leg buckled under him, but he caught his balance and braced himself against a body that disappeared as fast as it had been there. He'd stepped on something.

George instinctively looked down to find a man struggling to get up. He yelled for space and, using his bulk as a shield, reached down to grasp the man by the wrist and pulled him to his feet. "Can you stand?"

"Y-Yeah." The man winced. "My ankle. It's bad."

"You've got to stay on your feet," said George. It was obvious, and he felt stupid even as he said it, but he couldn't offer the man anything else. He was gone in the next moment anyway, carried away by the seething mass. George tried to stay calm, to assess, despite everyone else losing their heads around him. The air was clearing, probably filtered by the emergency ventilation system. He took a breath and it burned less. With his height, he could see over the top of the frenzied crowd. The flow was definitely more backward than forward, and it took only a second to figure out why. The Secfor were enmeshed with the crowd, their batons flailing violently, bodies falling around them.

They were attacking the protestors.

Or maybe the protestors had attacked them. He couldn't say, but the result was clear enough: the protestors were bearing the brunt. Part of him wanted to run, to follow the crowd and get away from the carnage happening just fifteen meters away, but he resisted that. He planted his feet, used his size to force the crowd to flow around him. He couldn't move forward at first, not with so many working against him, but after a time, he moved a step, and then another, until he was a couple of arm's lengths from a large Secfor man who was on his knees, swinging his baton at a fallen body in front of him.

"Stop!" George bellowed.

Around him, people hesitated. He paused, too—he hadn't expected it to work. People stared, both Secfor and protestor alike. *Thud.* The big Secfor goon struck the downed body, raised his arm to strike again. "Stop!" yelled George again, moving quickly at the same time to catch the man's wrist. The man looked up at him, his face streaked with sweat and dirt and maybe blood, his eyes feral. He started to pull away.

"Stop," said George, softer this time, directly to the man, who glanced around, took in the dozen or more fallen bodies around him, the fact that everyone else had ceased fighting. He nodded his head, and after a few seconds to be sure, George released the kneeling man's wrist, and the officer got to his feet, let his hands fall to his sides, breathing heavily from his exertion.

"You!" another man called, another Secfor.

George met his eyes, assuming that it was him that the man addressed. "Yes?"

"You're in charge? You need to come with me."

George recognized the man from the news. Rector. He gestured to the bodies around him. He wasn't against going along with Secfor if it helped calm things down, but the man clearly had his priorities wrong. "I'll come with you, but we should help the injured first."

The Secfor man hesitated, looked around as if assessing the situation, first to his own personnel, of which there were ten or so standing, and then to the injured on the ground, more than a dozen, at least two of whom were also Secfor. George glanced behind him at the protestors still hanging around. There were a few, but none were making any move to come back toward them.

"It's over," offered George. "We need to help these people."

"Let's go!" said Rector, loud and authoritative, addressing his own people. "Set up triage for the casualties, get them to the infirmary." He paused, then added, "Make sure to record their information before they go."

Of course. He'd want to make sure Secfor could arrest them later.

George wondered if Rector knew what had happened, if he'd seen who had set off the initial explosions that caused the gathering to turn violent. *He* certainly didn't know, but he very much wanted to. Maybe if he went along with Secfor, he could find out what happened. He assumed protestors did it, but specifics mattered. In fact, he was all for people being arrested if they caused the riot and weren't just caught up in it. But whatever had happened, he didn't trust Secfor to get it right without his help.

Without asking permission, he moved to a moaning woman curled up on the floor. He knelt beside her, took her head gently in both his hands, checked for bleeding, and didn't find any. Her eyes darted around, awake and alert. "Are you okay? What hurts?" he asked.

"Ribs," she gasped. "Stomach. Someone kicked me, I think."

He released her, resting her head back on the floor gently. "Any pain in your back?"

She shook her head.

George wasn't sure if he should move her. She could be bleeding internally, could have a broken rib that might puncture a lung. He looked around for someone who might know more than he did about first aid but found only Secfor and two other protestors who had come forward to help. "Can we get somebody from medical?"

"I've called them. They're on their way," said Rector.

George wasn't sure what to do. He wished he'd paid better attention in medical training, vowed to give it more attention in the future, but for now he felt helpless. He put a big hand lightly on the woman's shoulder and sat with her until someone arrived with a bot stretcher to take her away. He looked up to find Rector standing above him, waiting.

"You ready?"

"Sure."

"Do I need to cuff you, or are you going to come along peace-fully?"

George looked at him, surprised at the question but also be-cause he was being given a choice. "I'll come along. I didn't have anything to do with this, but we should talk."

Rector studied him. "We'll see how it goes."

THEY DIDN'T TALK. NOT INITIALLY, ANYWAY. INSTEAD, GEORGE SAT in a crowded cell with five men and three women from the protest. They were sitting hip to hip on the small benches. He stood leaning against the wall, away from the others. He could have been pissed that Rector stashed him in a cell—it wasn't what he'd signed up for—but at least he was here to see the treatment of the detainees. As a leader, he could at least do that much. Besides, there was no point in getting mad when you couldn't do anything about it. Not now, anyway. They could deal with Secfor overreach another day. He wondered where the others had been taken from—they hadn't been among the wounded—but he didn't want to ask because he was quite sure they were under surveillance. He didn't want to give Secfor anything more than they already had until he better under-stood the situation.

Outside the cell, Secfor personnel scurried like crickets caught under a heat lamp, gathering first around a terminal, then at a desk, receiving instructions. George didn't know how many people worked in the directorate, but he assumed that all hands had been called in response to the event. That's what he was calling it in his mind, now. *The event.* Not the protest, not the riot. Though he was sure the news feeds would have their own name for it soon enough.

Secfor had confiscated his device before putting him in the cell. He didn't even know what time it was, but by the time Rector came for him, he estimated he'd been in there about two hours.

Several of the detainees stood as he approached, but Rector gestured to George with his chin. George moved to the door, which Rector opened.

"Let's go." Rector turned and moved through the room to a door on the other side. He put his palm to the entry pad and the door zipped open, revealing a narrow corridor with a door on either side. Rector opened the one on the left and gestured for George to enter.

The room was small, with a table and three chairs; cameras in two of the upper corners could observe everything. It looked a lot like an interrogation room from a video, which was George's only reference for such things. He took a seat without being told, folded his hands on the table, and waited for Rector to take a seat across from him.

"So," said Rector.

"So."

"What happened?"

"I was going to ask you the same thing," said George.

"I don't think you get how this works."

"Maybe not. But I don't know anything and I was kind of hoping you did."

Rector dry-washed his hands. "Surely you know *something*."

"You've seen the camera feeds by now, so you probably know more than me." But as he said that, George thought about it. Did he? And even if Rector knew more than he did, it wouldn't hurt to share what little he *did* know. Maybe the other man would see it as a sign of good faith and be more open to sharing his own info. Before the Secfor officer could press, George said, "We were there, and they'd just brought out the woman—Fleming. Most of us were watching it on our devices . . . and something happened. Two pops—small explosions—like a firecracker from one of those old vids, and then a lot of smoke. One right after the other, maybe a second or two apart. The first was close to your people, the other was farther back in the crowd."

Rector nodded. "Did you see what caused them?"

"I didn't see anything."

"Do you *know* what caused them?"

"How would I know?" asked George.

"They came from your people."

George snorted. "Do you actually believe that?"

"What? That protestors set off some sort of explosives?"

"No. That seems pretty likely. Do you actually believe that all those people there were *mine*? That I have any sort of control over them?"

"Don't you?" asked Rector.

Something in his look, the set of his lips, made George think that Rector knew more than he was sharing. "I think you know that I don't. At least, I hope you know that, because if you don't, you're not very good at your job."

Rector chuckled. "I had to ask."

George relaxed, but just a little. "I get it." And he did. Just because George didn't control the protest didn't mean he *didn't* know who was responsible for the chaos. "Anything I told you would be a guess."

"So guess."

George shook his head. "No point in it. You probably already have the same guesses."

"Tanaka?" asked Rector.

"Probably not. But he might know who."

"We're looking for him now. Just to talk."

George nodded. *Sure—just to talk.* "It's been a couple hours. You haven't found him?"

"Doesn't look like he wants to be found. We think he's hiding out down on the ag decks."

"Possible," said George. *Probably more than possible.* But he wasn't sharing that with Rector. They were talking, but they weren't friends. Weren't on the same side—not by a long shot. Rector would use him as long as he could, but that's where their relationship ended. If George wanted anything, he'd have to bargain for it. He *did* want something, and that something aligned with Rector's wants more than he cared to admit:

He wanted to know who set off the bombs.

To get that out of Rector, he had to have something the man wanted, which meant he couldn't give anything away for free.

"If I let you go, can you find him?"

"Maybe." *Probably.*

"Will you bring him in?"

He absolutely would *not.* Even if he wasn't opposed to the idea, which he was, all his support—what little he had—would dry up in an instant if he turned on Tanaka openly. But instead of telling Rector that, he just said, "I don't have any authority to do that, and I'm just guessing here, but I don't think he's going to volunteer."

Rector paused for a couple seconds. "Probably not. What if you located him and called us in? We could take him."

George thought about how that might go. He could find Tanaka; he was pretty sure of that. He could probably even talk to him, for all the good that would do. But the man wouldn't be alone, and introducing Secfor on the ag levels . . . no. "That would be a bad idea, I think."

"It would be a bad idea for Secfor to do its job?"

"Down there? Yeah, probably. And with me involved, definitely."

"We could keep you safe," offered Rector.

George snorted. "It's not me I'm worried about."

"You're worried about *us*? I can assure you, we'll be—"

"I'm worried about the situation on the ship if a bunch of undisciplined clowns with weapons try to apprehend—"

"Hey," said Rector, cutting him off. "We didn't start the altercation. That was the protestors."

"And I suppose next you're going to tell me that you didn't beat unarmed people," snapped George. "That your well-trained officers de-escalated the situation rather than made it worse."

Rector started to respond, but apparently thought better of it. After a pause where they both stared each other down, he said, "Some of my people probably overreacted."

"You *think*? Now . . . how do you think the people who were at the event—"

"'The event'?" interrupted Rector.

"How do you think the people at *the event*"—George emphasized the term this time—"feel about your *overreaction*?"

Rector thought about it for a few seconds. "Okay, yeah. I get it. Not good."

"And what happens when your same overreacting people go to the ag decks, where people are still amped up and aren't all crowded in, and there are tools and shovels and any other number of dangerous things? How do you think that ends?"

Rector sighed. "Right. Okay. I hear you. So what do we do?"

"We figure out who set off the explosives. What did you see on the cameras?"

"The cameras went out for ten seconds, just before *the event* happened."

"Who did that? Who *could* do that?"

Rector shrugged. "It's like you said: I could guess, but there's no point in it. I certainly can't prove it. And it's not like there's only one possibility."

"I can ask around," George offered.

Now it was Rector that snorted. "You think anybody is going to tell you?"

"About the explosives? No. About the cameras? Maybe. If they weren't tied together."

"They had to be," said Rector. "The timing was too perfect."

"Probably. But I can still ask. You never know where something like that might lead once somebody starts talking."

"So . . . you're proposing that we work together?"

That was a loaded question. He could lie and say that he would, but he didn't know if Rector would even believe him—and besides, he didn't really feel like wasting time with a deception. "I can't be seen working with you."

"You're still going to continue your operations after what's happened today?"

"What operations? You admitted that you know I don't have control over what people do."

Rector thought for a few seconds. "Look, I think we both can agree that what happened today was bad. Either you're going to help me figure this out or you're not."

George had done a good job of not getting mad, but Rector continuing to move past his own culpability was pushing that to its limit, and he was sick of it. "You asked me if I'm still going to continue. Let me ask you the same thing: are *you* still going to be a Secfor officer after one of your guys slammed a stick into the ribs of a defenseless person?"

"That was one guy overreacting."

There was that word again, as if it exoncratcd Rector and Secfor of any responsibility.

"So was the bomber."

Rector shook his head violently. "No. Not the same."

"It's *exactly* the same. You want credit for one guy screwing things up for the whole, but you don't want to extend the same credit to anybody else."

"We were doing our *jobs*."

"Your *job* is to protect the ship. It's not to beat people. Your *job* props up a ridiculous system." George stared the other man down.

To his credit, Rector didn't waver. But he didn't say anything else, either. Maybe, just maybe, he'd gotten the point. Then he said, "So . . . what? I just let you walk out of here like nothing happened?"

Maybe not. "No—you let me walk out of here because I'm innocent. You know I didn't do anything wrong."

"And *you* know that it doesn't matter. Somebody has to pay for this. I'd prefer that we got the people actually responsible, but . . ."

George smiled as he considered the other man's words. His anger had passed. Rector had nothing, and it was all just a game to get him to cooperate. An empty threat. He was desperate, needed help, and that was George's opportunity to dictate their relationship. "Here's what I can do: I can work with you on this one specific thing."

"What thing?"

"Finding who set off the explosives at the protest." Rector started to interject, but George held up his hand to forestall it. "I'm not going to tell you how I'm going to do that, but I promise, I absolutely want to get to the bottom of it as much as you do, and I'm going to do my best. When I find something, I'll get it to you. My way."

Rector considered it. "I need more than that."

"You've got my offer."

"Yeah? Well, make a new one. Because otherwise, I'll let everyone know you *are* working with Secfor."

And there it was: a threat that actually held weight. Knowing what he did of Rector, George had no doubt he'd do it. It wouldn't even matter if it was true. Enough people would believe it. Rector might do it even if he *did* give him more, or keep holding it over his head, but he'd plow that dirt when he got to it.

"What else do you want?"

"Tanaka," said Rector without hesitating.

George started to respond, to say that was impossible, but stopped himself. It *wasn't* impossible. Finally, he said, "You want Tanaka, here's how you do it. You go nowhere near him for at least a couple of days. You don't mention him, you don't look for him, you don't even acknowledge that he exists. Not even in your own directorate, because it will leak."

If that surprised Rector, it didn't show. He knew, and that was both edifying and frustrating.

Again: for another time. "After a couple of days, he'll figure there's no heat on him and he'll come out on his own."

"And then we grab him," finished Rector.

"If that's what you want, yes. But you can't hold him. Not for long, anyway. Because the minute you take him, you start a timer."

"A timer?"

"Somebody is going to react, and I can't say what that reaction will be. I just know it'll happen, and there's a good chance that it'll make today look like a minor disturbance."

"You think it'll be something big," said Rector.

"Could be. Like I said, I don't know, and I don't have control over it. So you question him, learn what you can, and you let him go."

"What if he confesses to a serious crime?"

George just looked at the Secfor officer.

"Right. He probably won't. Got it. Okay. We'll do that."

"Good. And to be clear: I *don't* think he set off the explosions. So I don't want to hear later that he confessed after a long interrogation. If I *do* hear that, you and I are going to have a problem, and I don't give a fuck what leverage you think you have over me." He gave Rector a pointed look, but the man didn't even flinch. George thought that he'd made himself clear, though, and that they understood each other. Rector could cause him a lot of trouble with the right words to the right people, but George could cause problems of his own.

"Anything else?" asked Rector.

"I'll try to learn more about who set off the explosives, but I expect you to tell me what you find, too."

"Deal," Rector said, though George didn't really believe him. "You're free to go."

But George wasn't sure anyone was truly free on this ship anymore.

CHAPTER 32

SHEILA JACKSON

||||||||||||||||||||||||||||||||||||||||||||||||||||||||||||||||||||||||||

21 CYCLES UNTIL ARRIVAL

Her team huddled around a single screen, the way they had so many times before. Except now they weren't staring at new data from the planet—Sheila would have seen that before they did. They were looking at a new list of people scheduled for early missions to the surface. Specifically, they were looking at three names from their own department.

She was looking at *her* name.

That it also had Marcus and Yanai on it was significant, but for the moment Sheila couldn't get past that one point. She'd known that defying the governor was risky, even if she was doing it quietly. Or thought she had been. Had he found her out? Was that the reason behind this change? The given rationale was one of those that made sense on the surface: That they were *following the science*. And what better way to do that than to put a science advisor in each of the three landing parties? But to Sheila, that was as transparent as the atmosphere of Prom. They wouldn't know what following the science looked like if it punched them in the face.

"This is garbage." Marcus didn't shout the words, but he did speak louder than was necessary to be heard. Yanai reacted differently, sitting silently, her arms wrapped around herself. Sheila knew she should say something to them, let them know that it would be okay, but she didn't have words. She didn't have *thoughts*. And she wasn't sure it *was* okay. Still, Sheila forced herself to speak, trying to put optimism she wasn't feeling into her voice. "This is okay. We'll get it sorted." After a few seconds with nobody responding, she continued, "Don't worry about it. I'm going to take care of this."

She didn't let herself truly react until she was in her office with the shade drawn and the door closed. She flopped into her chair, grabbed each armrest, and squeezed. She wanted to cry, but the tears wouldn't come. Instead she thought about where she went wrong, what she could have done differently. From the first news conference right up to her last meeting with George Iannou, there were so many things. If she'd done what the governor wanted her to do without dissent. If she'd found a better way to convey her concerns. If if if.

In a perfect world, she'd have taken this to her boss, both as a way to vent and for potential help. She didn't live in that world. Lavonia Carroway was a fine doctor, but she wasn't going to advocate for a subordinate. Sheila almost didn't blame her. If she did, they might find that the mission to the planet needed senior physicians as well. No, Sheila had made this mess, and no one would get her out of it but herself.

And she had to tell Alex. He wouldn't blame her—not directly. He was good about that kind of thing. But she'd feel the guilt anyway. He wouldn't say it, but his resentment would be there, at least in her own mind. How could he *not* resent her for it? They were having a child, and now he'd have to take care of it alone. How could he *not* blame her? She blamed herself. And deep down, in a place inside she hadn't fully explored yet, she was almost relieved to get the assignment. Part of her—and not a small part—*wanted* to go to the planet. Her entire life had led to this opportunity. She couldn't ever have asked to go—that would be too much of a betrayal of Alex—but now that the governor was making her . . .

Gah! It was too complicated to think about, and it spun her in mental circles. It wasn't that she didn't want a baby, or that she didn't want a life with Alex. She did. She just . . . well . . . she wanted to follow her own dream a little bit more. And that made her feel like the worst person alive.

What she did know was the science. There was no timeline on the mission, but those who went to the planet weren't likely to return anytime soon. The contamination issues alone would prevent that, even if it were logistically possible—she didn't know if the landing ship was capable of returning to orbit. Worse, even if someone proposed return trips, ethically she'd have to oppose it. Those who went down needed to either stay down or quarantine if they came back to the ship. She'd not only be on the mission, she'd be publicly arguing to *stay* on the mission. Alex, as understanding as he could be, might not be able to look past that.

Maybe that was the governor's plan. Maybe he wasn't punishing her for what she had done, but trying to control what she might do in the future. If he wanted to have people travel between the ship and the new colonies, maybe he thought that this would get her to advocate for it. It seemed unlikely, irrational even, but then the combination of science and politics hadn't exactly been rational lately.

She needed to talk to somebody, get a different perspective. But she couldn't talk to her boss and she couldn't talk to her team. She pulled up the list of colonists again on her computer and found another scientist assigned to her landing group: Alana Wilson from xenobiology. Maybe she'd be willing to talk. Sheila found her contact and called her. She was indeed available, and how was right now? Perfect.

Sheila put on a staid face and headed back out. "I'm going for a short meeting. Back in a bit."

DR. ALANA WILSON WAS ALREADY WAITING FOR HER WHEN SHEILA arrived at Café 92, named that because it was on the 92 percent gravity deck. Alana was a pretty woman, a little older than Sheila, with short hair and a strong jaw. She stood up and smiled as Sheila approached.

"I took the liberty of getting tea for both of us. I hope that's okay."

"Of course. Thank you." Sheila eased herself into her chair, being careful in the heavy gravity. "Thanks for meeting with me so quickly."

"No problem. My boss gave me the rest of the day off when my name came out on the list. It's so exciting, don't you think?" The woman spoke with an energy that could only be authentic.

Sheila paused. It *was* exciting. Alana didn't seem to have any of the mixed feelings that she did, and that was contagious to the point where she had to almost hold herself back from just gushing about it right along with her. But she didn't want to mention the baby, either, and ruin the other woman's joy. Maybe meeting before she ironed things out for herself was a mistake. She realized she'd been silent too long, and that it was growing awkward—she had to say *something*. All she managed was, "You think so?"

"Of course! Well . . . I mean . . . going to the planet so quickly with so many people is a *horrible* idea. It's all kinds of dangerous. But personally? I'm a biologist, and I can't think of anything greater than exploring a new planet. You know the conditions. There could be life there. Life! I could be the person who discovers the first new species. More than one, even. It's . . . well, it's . . . exciting." Apparently realizing that she'd spit all that out without hardly a breath, Alana started laughing. "Sorry. I'm a little amped, in case you couldn't tell."

"Not at all." Sheila smiled. The woman was infectious, and she couldn't help but be taken with her. "I'm glad I came. I've been so focused on the negative of this, trying to get us more time in orbit, that I lost focus on how amazing an opportunity it is."

"For you? In space exploration? It has to be surreal. Stepping foot on a new planet? Getting to test all your hypotheses in person? It's incredible."

Sheila couldn't help but nod. Alana was right—despite all her issues with the governor and her complex feelings about her family situation, she had to focus on the opportunity. She had to seize it. To do that, though, she needed help, and she realized that it might be sitting in front of her. "We have some work to do, though."

"Oh, a ton of preparation," agreed Alana.

"Right. Not just scientific prep, though."

"What do you mean?"

Sheila took a second to consider her words. She needed this woman on her side and didn't want to scare her off. "There will be competing priorities for the mission, I think. We need to work to make sure that science is at the forefront."

"You think it won't be?"

Sheila sighed. "Based on my recent experience? I very much think it won't be in some people's minds. But that's where we come in."

"We change their minds."

"We *mold* their minds."

"I'm listening."

BACK IN HER OFFICE, SHEILA HAD NEW ENERGY, AND IT WASN'T JUST because she was back in lower gravity. As part of the mission, she could justify putting her entire focus on the science. She could throw herself into the planet landing and see it in a way that she had only dreamed of before. The guilt about her family was still there, gnawing at her and threatening to paralyze her if she let it rise to the surface for even a second, but she had things to do. So many things. So why was she just sitting there, not doing any of them?

Lila poked her head in. "You okay?"

"I . . . I don't know."

Lila drew her lips into a thin line. "I'm sorry. But I get it. I gave Marcus and Yanai the rest of the shift off. I hope that's okay."

"That was smart. I should have thought of it." It was a good reminder that brought another round of guilt. There were more lives caught up in this than hers.

"Well, you had other things on your mind. If you'd seen them here . . . they weren't going to get any work done anyway." Lila smiled.

With that, Sheila made a decision. She couldn't solve all of her problems at once, but she could solve one of them. "You're a good boss. And I want you to continue that."

"What do you mean?" The hopeful look on her face indicated that she probably had a pretty good idea what Sheila meant but didn't want to say it herself. And that was fine. Sheila needed to say it. She owed it to the younger woman.

"You're the best I've got, Lila. I want you to run the department while I'm down on the planet." Yes, there were more lives caught up in this than hers, but that didn't have to be all bad.

Lila couldn't speak for a second, and when she did, it sounded like she was trying to hold back tears. "Thank you," she squeaked out.

"You deserve it. We'll figure out titles later, and we'll need to do some work to define roles and responsibilities between you and our three teams on the ground." She paused, thinking. She'd never been good at asking for help, but . . . maybe she should have. Maybe things would have turned out differently. "One thing I do want is for you to jump in fast. If you've got ideas to make us more efficient, say something. If you see something that needs doing, don't hesitate."

Lila took that in for a second, appearing to give it the consideration it deserved. "I won't let you down."

"I know you won't."

Lila hesitated again, looking more unsure this time.

"What's on your mind?" asked Sheila.

"What about Andrew?" Andrew was a sixty-nine-year-old man who always worked off shift because he liked it, and everyone else liked it as well because it meant they didn't have to do it. It was a good question. In the past, Sheila would have thought about it, maybe even for days, weighing each side, trying to come up with the best possible solution.

Not today.

"He's close to transfer age." Like everyone else, he'd leave the department and do general duties for four years when he turned seventy. "I'll talk to him. He'll accept it." In truth, he'd be relieved not to have to take on extra responsibility, but she didn't need to denigrate him like that in front of Lila. "Regardless, it's my call, and you're the person I want doing it."

Lila nodded and smiled. "Anywhere specific you want me to start?"

"Yes. I want you to come up with a prioritized list of the tests that Marcus, Yanai, and I need to do once we get to the ground. Once you do that, start crossmatching that with the equipment we'll need to do them, compare it to what we have on hand, and requisition the rest."

"Can do, boss. And I'll check in on Yanai. Marcus is mad, for sure. He'll probably get drunk and break something. But Yanai . . . I'm not sure how she's going to react."

"Thanks. That's good thinking. I'm going to leave you to it if that's okay. I've got some things I need to take care of."

"You need any help?" asked Lila.

She considered it. "I think I have to do these on my own. We've got an opportunity on the planet to do something incredible, but only if they let us. I need to make sure that's the case." She paused, unsure if she wanted to share the other part. But if Lila was going to take charge, she deserved to know everything. "And . . . I've got to talk to my husband."

"Oh my stars. The baby." Lila put her hand to her mouth.

"Yeah. I'm not sure how Alex is going to take this."

"I wish there was something I could do."

"Knowing that you'll have things under control here when I'm gone makes everything easier. I promise."

After the younger woman departed, Sheila pulled the list of names for her landing party up again and looked over it, checking to see who she should prioritize.

One name stood out: Mark Rector. She left a message asking him to meet her the next day. Right now, she had a more important man to talk to.

SHE GOT HOME BEFORE ALEX AND BUSIED HERSELF PREPARING A meal. She'd stopped and picked up vat-raised beef and all the stuff that went with it, an expensive lux purchase that Alex loved. She didn't expect it to help, but it was worth a try. He already knew, of course. He'd messaged her immediately after he'd seen it, but it was hard to get tone through text. He was mad, for sure. But she didn't know how mad.

He came through the door quickly, rushed to her, took her in his arms and held her. "It's going to be okay," he said into her hair.

Sheila didn't know how to react. This was . . . not what she expected. But nice? She sagged into him. "You're not mad?"

He released her. "Oh. I'm pissed. Ooh, steak!"

"Figured we might as well spend a bit." Sheila pulled the plates from the warmer and brought them to the table.

Alex plucked a baby potato from one of the plates and popped it in his mouth. "Ow! Hot!"

"Funny how a heater will do that." Sheila wanted to let it go, keep up the façade, but Alex's mood confused her and she couldn't get past it. "What's going on? You say you're pissed, but you don't seem like it."

"We're going to fight it, and we're going to win. The fact that we're having a baby should disqualify you, and I've already talked to some people about it. We've got a good case."

Sheila froze for a second, and then tried to act natural. But she couldn't respond. This was worse than him being mad.

Alex knew her too well, and after a second, his face hardened. "You don't want to fight it."

She shook her head slightly. "It's not that I don't want to—"

Alex put his fork down a little harder than necessary, a loud clank against the table, cutting her off. He spoke softly but with venom, almost spitting the words. "So then what?"

Sheila hesitated. Here she was with her chance to explain herself. All she had to do was do it. When she spoke, though, the words she'd practiced in her head were gone, and all she managed was, "It's complicated. I know what we have here, and it's important—"

"Just not important enough," he said.

Sheila fought to keep control. "The opportunities on the planet . . . I've been preparing for this my entire life."

Alex sat there, unmoving. He didn't speak for a long time. When he did, he kept his voice measured and calm, but he gave the impression that it required a lot of effort. "We've been preparing for *this*, too." He gestured around. "For a family. For a long time."

"I know," said Sheila.

After another long, awkward silence, Alex nodded and rose. "I need to take a walk. I'll be back, but I've got to clear my head and calm down so that I don't say something I'll regret."

Sheila nodded, and he left. Other than the one potato, he hadn't even touched his food. She managed to keep her tears in until after he had gone.

THE NEXT DAY SHE SAT IN A HIGH-GRAVITY COFFEE LOUNGE WITH Mark Rector, who was in charge of security for her planetside team. There was no single leader for each site yet, which appeared to be an oversight, but security seemed like the most likely to take on that role, especially with Rector's notoriety. As he sat across from her, he looked like he regretted having come. He fidgeted and continuously looked around, as if someone might jump up from another table and attack them at any second. To Sheila's eye, nobody even paid them any attention.

"Is something wrong?"

"What?" He looked at her, and then glanced away again, then back to her. "No. It's fine." He paused. "It's just that there have been problems down on these lower decks lately. Especially since the execution."

"Ah. Right. I saw that on the news feed."

"They've blown it out of proportion."

"I believe you." She didn't, really. The videos that had emerged, mostly from individuals with handhelds, of broken bodies after the altercation between protestors and Secfor were pretty clear-cut. But she was trying to build a coalition, not pick a fight. She also had to allow that he might have been assigned planetside duty as a punishment like she had. That was a potential point of commiseration, but it seemed too risky to approach that directly in case he was sensitive about it.

"I'm sorry," Rector said finally. "You wanted to talk. About the colonization mission."

"Right. Specifically, I wanted to discuss protocols and priorities for our initial landing."

He looked around again. "I have to tell you something." He spoke softly enough that she had to lean in to hear. "I'm not planning to go."

Sheila sat with that for a second, waiting to see if he'd explain, but he didn't. "So . . . you have a way out of it?"

"Not yet," he admitted. But he smirked just a little bit as he said it. He had a plan. He just wasn't sharing it.

That changed things. If he believed he wasn't going, he was less likely to care. She wished she'd known that earlier and had time to think it through. There might be a way to exploit that to get her priorities emphasized, but she wasn't great at improvising. Either way, they were both here, and it seemed frivolous to waste the time. "Well . . . just in case you do go, I'd like to talk to you about scientific priorities."

"*If* I go, I'd see our priorities as establishing security, then shelter, then other life-support requirements," he said without hesitation. That he'd thought about it was good. That he'd excluded her requirements, less so.

"Security is important," she said. "I'd like to propose an initial scientific testing regimen—priority samples and specific pathogen mitigation protocols . . ." She let her voice trail off as Rector stared at her, open-mouthed.

"Yeah. I don't need to see that. I'll do my job, and I'm going to trust you to do yours. Once we establish our base, you can run all the tests that you want on the water and dirt and stuff."

Sheila bit her lip to keep from snapping at him. *Water and dirt and stuff?* "Defending ourselves against microorganisms is our most important safety issue."

"I'm more worried about *macro*organisms. Big stuff that might kill us—you know, the life that's down there."

"We don't have confirmed evidence of that yet," said Sheila.

"You're the expert, so I'll take your word for it, but not having confirmed evidence isn't the same as it not being a threat. We should be prepared for the worst scenario, and if it turns out easier, that's just great. I'm proposing simulator training with weapons for all party members."

"Weapons?"

"Unless you can tell us for sure what's there, I think it's only prudent to treat any possible alien life as hostile."

Sheila sat there in silence, unsure what to say. That he said it so matter-of-factly, as if there were no other possible solutions . . . that was troubling. Sure, they couldn't rule out the possibility of intelligent life, but prioritizing it? They *knew* that microorganisms—pathogens, bacteria, viruses—were likely to be an issue. She took a deep breath and tried to speak calmly, hoping she could make him understand. "There might be complex life forms that present threats, but microorganisms present risks an order of magnitude or two larger than any even a hostile intelligent life form could pose."

"Well, that's why we've got you. I'll handle the security, and you handle that."

Handle *that*? That's what she was trying to do, but he wasn't hearing her. She wanted to persist, to argue about it, but assessed it as counterproductive. He'd said she could set the scientific priorities and he didn't need to see them. That would have to be enough for now.

Still, some of the excitement she'd felt yesterday about the mission was starting to slip away, and a slow trickle of dread was worming its way back in.

CHAPTER 33

EDDIE DANNIN

19 CYCLES UNTIL ARRIVAL

Eddie put on her new and improved neural relay—she'd been working on it for weeks now, incorporating multiple weak AIs, or WAIs—to automate as many of the processes that she could predict she might need as possible. They didn't interact with each other, which got around some of the AI safety restrictions. Mostly. Nobody would be too happy about her allowing them this close to the ship's code, but they each fed back to her, so in her expert opinion there was no risk. At least not of them taking over the ship. Exploding her brain? Maybe. But that wasn't a risk to anybody else, and she herself was willing to take it. Because it probably wouldn't come to that. At worst, she expected another major headache, but even that should diminish this time.

That she didn't have an agenda helped. Someone might be targeting the ship's systems, both from what the Secfor dude had told her and from some of the problems they'd seen arise at work, but she didn't have any specifics. So she could just get in there, get comfortable, and take a look around.

Why was she so nervous about it, then? Sitting there, staring at the interface, she almost decided to put it off. It could wait until tomorrow, right? Where was the harm in that?

Or she could call Lila. Ask her to sit here with her as she went in, just in case. No—tempting as that was, she needed to do this. She'd built it, and she had to test it. Had to see what she could do with it.

She put it on, taking time to fit the connections before pulling the goggles over her eyes and starting the boot-up process. The differences hit her immediately—or, rather, they didn't hit her. Which was good. She was in the machine but outside it, able to perceive the data without being drowned in it. The navigation was instinctual. She wasn't scrolling through code but moving through it at a thought; her WAIs responded to her and parsed what she needed to process on their own.

She laughed, though she barely heard herself. She felt . . . alive.

And with that she was off, traveling about the ship, looking for . . . what? There was too much . . . everything. It was like looking for the single bad stitch in a garment but doing it from a distance. Nothing announced itself to her as a problem. Perhaps she could develop an additional WAI for that. She made a mental note to look into it with the subroutine that she'd built for note taking. This would help her remember things when she left the code. She decided to start with the fusion drive. That was the place most ripe for sabotage, so it made sense to put a monitor on it.

With a thought, she moved into that code, not immediately distinguishing between the diagnostics and processes that ran the core. After all, the diagnostics were part of the problem. They could be fooled into missing an underlying issue so that humans who relied on them wouldn't see anything wrong. But she wasn't human. Not here. Not totally, anyway. So she bypassed the diagnostics and looked at the system itself.

And there it was. It came to her as a feeling first, a wrong-ness, filtered to her by one of her WAIs that processed code. So she drilled into it, and within a moment—whatever a moment was in this space—she'd isolated the line that didn't belong. It was warped and dark, and it just . . . didn't fit. She could fix it, of course, but the rest of the code was ugly, too. A second WAI showed her the inefficiencies—so much work that didn't need to happen, taking time and burning energy, even if those increments were probably inconceivable on a human scale. But when repeated millions or billions of times? It was just wasteful.

She had an overwhelming urge to take it apart, put it back together, make it right.

But first, that line. That line created questions. Two of them, and she assigned a separate WAI to each, to look into that aspect au-tomatically and parse it for her. First, why had diagnostics missed it? Second, who had done it? Because it wasn't natural. Code didn't just corrupt itself. Not like this. Somebody entered this line, and it wasn't tagged, which meant somebody erased the tag, which shouldn't be possible.

The WAI looking at the diagnostics came back to her first. Almost instantly, to her sense of perception. Another error. She pulled it into her consciousness and puzzled. This one . . . it should have been noticed. It was so clear. So why hadn't it been? And then it hit her. It hadn't been noticed because it didn't do anything. It was an error that had no consequence except specifically in relation to another error.

Oh, that was brilliant. Whoever did this, they were next-level good. Which didn't make any sense. Did it? It was hard to think in human terms with all of this data. Motivations were . . . abstract. The code, well, the paired errors were lovely, in a horrible, per-verted sort of way. But still lovely. No, she had to focus on the who and the why. But she couldn't, so she made a note of it so that she could consider it later. *Why* didn't matter now. But *who* might. Her other WAI application pinged at her, and perhaps it had an answer. It had a trace. That was something. Not a who, but a where. She had the origin of the code, and it didn't take long to send out an impulse to place it.

It came from engineering, which she also made a note of for later. It was important. She could even pin it to the exact terminal. The person had scrubbed their own data from it, which was impressive, but they couldn't scrub that. Perhaps they didn't even realize that the machine itself left a signature. Even she'd not known it for sure before now, and she wondered how many times she thought she'd been slick, only to have still left a trail. Another worry for another time, because now, from here, it stood out like a warning bulb in a dark room.

First, she'd fix it, even though part of her longed to leave the lines in, to watch them, to see what they did. But even here, she knew the risk in that. The ship itself seemed to radiate the danger of it. She hadn't felt that at first, and perhaps she was only imagining it now. But it *felt* real. This wrongness, this disease. With a couple of thoughts, she expunged it, returned the code to what it had been before the illicit incursion.

That done, she backed out a bit to survey her work. But it was still ugly. Those lines that took a circuitous route were just . . . blech. They'd be so much better if they flowed directly, and, well, she was there and she could do that.

So she did.

And then there was another, and another after that. So many spots where she could save a line, a calculation, the smallest fraction of a fraction of a second. She got lost in it, forgot about everything but the code.

A BEEPING GOING OFF BROUGHT HER OUT OF IT. IT TOOK TIME—SOME amount she couldn't parse—to realize that it was a physical alarm that she'd set for herself on the outside. She made a note to create a program that kept real time for her inside, but for now, she had to go. She did it slowly, closing up her open ends, making sure that everything fit, that it felt right. It did. Not perfect, but . . . better. Cleaner. She pulled back, looked again from further out, and finally detached completely.

She sat there in her chair, aware of the sweat on her neck, goggles still over her eyes but switched off, readjusting to the real space of her room. After a while, she removed her goggles and then the connections to her head. She set everything on the desk and paused. The air from the circulator in her room was cooling her the way a fan cooled the inside of a computer. It rattled, just slightly, and for a second, she had the urge to reach out and fix it—but of course it was a physical thing, and she couldn't do that with just her thoughts. Weird, that feeling.

She took the box of water from her desk and sucked at it greedily. She'd thought to put it there based on her last experience, but she hadn't had a sip of it in—she checked the time on her monitor—eight hours. Eight hours! She should have known that, as she'd been the one to set the alarm for 0300, so she could get at least *some* sleep before she had to be at work. But it hadn't *felt* like eight hours. It hadn't felt like even two. She checked her notes, confirmed the one about adding a time-keeping program to her kit. Her head didn't hurt—not much, anyway. A dull ache rather than the crippling pain of her previous experiment. She decided to stand and found that she could with only a bit of a wobble.

She reset her alarm, making sure to place it away from her bunk so she wouldn't turn it off. Then she flopped down onto her mattress, still in her clothes. She considered getting under the blankets, but before she did, she was asleep.

SHE DREAMED STRANGE DREAMS. DREAMS OF THE INSIDE. THOUGH when her alarm went off, she couldn't quite remember them. Part of her wanted to hit the snooze and go back under to seek them out, to understand them. But that was why she'd put her alarm on the other side of the room. She stumbled toward it; the headache that hadn't hit her the night before was sitting right behind her eyes now. She stank of sweat, so she got a quick shower, scarfed down two protein bars and a cup of coffee, and, after considering her vac suit, tossed it into her laundry bag and put on a fresh one before dragging herself to work.

She was barely in the door when Senior Engineer Karstaad grabbed her by the arm and dragged her to a small meeting room nobody occupied. "What did you *do*?"

"What do you mean?" Maybe the coffee just hadn't cut through the brain fog yet, but Eddie really didn't understand.

"The code for the drive." Karstaad leaned in toward her, and Eddie had to make an effort not to back away.

"Oh. Right. I found a sabotaged line. Two of them, actually. It was really kind of brilliant the way—"

"Not that," said Karstaad, cutting her off. "Wait, what? Sabotage." She shook her head. "We'll come back to that. I'm talking about the *changes* you made."

"Huh?" Eddie furrowed her brow. *Oh!* She meant the changes to the code. "You noticed that?"

Karstaad threw her hands up. "Noticed? *Everybody* noticed. Even people who have no reason to look noticed. How could they not? Everyone is talking about it."

"I . . . I don't get it." She really didn't. She'd modified some code, streamlined it, but that wasn't off-limits. It certainly shouldn't have raised this kind of alarm. "I made it *better.*"

"You rewrote the entire thing."

Huh. Had she? Karstaad had no reason to lie about it, but it hadn't *felt* like she'd redone that much. "I guess . . . maybe I got carried away. Kind of lost in it, you know? But it *is* better."

"Yes, it's *better.* If it wasn't better, we'd be reversing it and you and I would be having an entirely different conversation. What I can't figure out yet is *how* it's better, but the results speak for themselves."

Eddie studied the older woman. She was definitely mad, but she'd also just admitted it was better, which didn't add up. "So . . . what's the problem? You looked at the performance data. You can see the result."

Karstaad shook her head and then looked up at the ceiling. "Yes. We can see the result. But the code—nobody can do anything with it. We can see that you changed it, but so far . . . we can't follow how you did it."

Eddie shrugged. "I just cut out the bits that weren't efficient."

"You did more than that." Karstaad pulled out her tablet and started tapping at it. After a few seconds she showed it to Eddie. "Look at this."

Eddie took a few seconds. "Yeah. That's my work."

"But you're missing the problem."

Eddie shook her head. "It's working better. What problem?"

"Nobody else can work with it now."

"Nobody *needs* to work with it now. It works." And if nobody could work with it, maybe that also meant that nobody could attack it. She almost said that but pulled back. The sabotage had come from inside engineering, and now Karstaad was complaining about her changing the code. Perhaps those two things were related. And suddenly she wished that she hadn't mentioned the sabotage at all. But she couldn't unsay it.

"I think you need to be ready to discuss with the director *how* you did this."

Eddie pursed her lips, unsure how to respond. She was happy to talk about the code but wasn't ready to share her neural interface. She should have known this would happen, should have been more subtle instead of ripping things up and redoing them wholescale. That had been reckless. The thing was, she hadn't really realized that she was doing it. Somehow she didn't think the director would buy that, though. But what could she do? Even after they'd seen her abilities, everyone in the directorate hated her except for the woman in front of her right now.

And that woman might be the saboteur. Maybe she saw Eddie as a threat and wanted to keep her close. Eddie's gut said that wasn't true—she didn't *want* it to be true—but then, her gut wasn't the best judge of character, if her life to this point was any example. She needed more information. "Isn't the fact that it's better the most important thing?"

"It is, but as I said, other people besides you need to be able to work on the code."

"So I'll teach them. I'll teach *you*."

"You'll teach me to do what you did last night." Karstaad didn't ask that as a question. She stated it, but even Eddie, who had a tough time understanding tone, could tell that she was being sarcastic and that she didn't believe that she could learn it.

"Well, not exactly, I can't. But I can show you the logic in it and help you to understand what's there so you can work with it."

Karstaad gave her a wry smile. "That's a start. But don't think we're not coming back to the how."

Eddie nodded. She'd figure out how to explain away the how part of things later. For now, she'd teach Karstaad the code. Almost all of it. She'd hold back enough so she could watch her. If Karstaad was the only one who understood it besides her, she was also the only one who could sabotage it. "Sure. I'd be happy to teach you. I mean . . . as much as I can. You're the senior engineer."

"It's fine. I get it. I don't have so much ego tied up in this that I can't admit you're at a level well beyond me. A certain amount of condescension is to be expected. It won't make you any friends, though."

She shrugged. "Everyone in engineering already hates me anyway."

"Not everyone," said Karstaad.

"Name one person who likes me."

Karstaad thought about it and then laughed. "Okay. You got me. Here's the thing: nobody should be able to do what you did in the amount of time you did it, and even though people don't know how you did it, they're going to question it. And what are they going to find? Are they going to find you circumventing the rules on AIs?"

"No," said Eddie, but even she could hear that she said it too quickly.

"No?" Karstaad's look said she knew the truth.

Eddie looked down at her feet. "Maybe. A little. But I was super safe about it."

"You probably were. But do you think anybody is going to accept that?"

"Why wouldn't they?"

"Because you make them look useless by comparison."

"What am I supposed to do? Write shitty code so that other people feel good?"

Karstaad sighed. "It's a tough situation."

Eddie bowed her head for a second, and then forced herself to look back up, to meet her boss's eyes. "Just tell me what to do. Whatever you want. Tell me what to do and I'll do it."

"Stop freelancing." She stared at her as she said it to emphasize her point.

"Okay. Got it. I'll stop."

Karstaad kept looking at her.

"*What?* I'll stop."

"Stop what?"

"Freelancing."

"What do I mean by that?"

"Doing illegal stuff."

Karstaad shook her head. "You're killing me. *No.* Stop doing *anything* you're not assigned to do. You can't just choose a spot and fix it. And when you *do* fix it, you're going to document what you did and make it accessible to the rest of the directorate."

"Aww," said Eddie.

"That's the deal. Now tell me about the sabotage."

Eddie's mind raced, looking for any way to dodge the question. She landed on, "What sabotage?" Not her best work.

"You said you found a sabotaged line."

Eddie thought for a moment, drew the silence out to the point where it was getting awkward, but she couldn't figure out how to tell Karstaad about it without telling her everything. On the other hand, she had to tell *someone, and* she really didn't think Karstaad had done it. Maybe she was blinded because Karstaad was the only person at work she liked, but . . . oh well. If Karstaad was an evil troll, she'd deal with it when it came. "You know that Secfor guy you talked to?"

"Rector."

"Yeah. I met with him and he told me that you suspected sabo-tage, and I started to think about it, and I could see how you got there, so I kind of started cruising around the ship, looking for—I don't know—stuff that didn't fit."

"And you found it," said Karstaad.

"Yeah. I found it—it was brilliant, really—it was this paired set of lines between the code itself and the diagnostic that should have caught the error—"

"—so that nobody would see the error when it happened," said Karstaad, finishing her sentence for her.

"Right. Got a shot of it. I'll send it to you so you know what to look for in other areas."

Karstaad took a step back with one foot, putting a little distance between them without moving away, and she bit her lip as she con-sidered it. "Could you trace it?"

"Not to a person. Whoever did this was good. Like *really* good. But I tracked it to a location. You're not going to like it."

"Shit. It was here, wasn't it?" asked Karstaad.

"Yep."

"So that's why you hesitated."

"What do you mean?" Eddie knew exactly what she meant.

"You thought it might be me." Karstaad was nothing if not straightforward, and Eddie kind of loved that.

"Sorry. But you're the best coder I've seen here. And like I said, whoever did this was *really good.*"

Karstaad snorted. "But not as good as you."

Eddie smiled. "No. Not as good as me."

"Okay. Well I'm about to make you suspect me even more."

"How's that?"

"Because I don't want you to tell anybody that you traced it here. Not until we figure out who it is."

"You have any ideas?"

"A couple, but nothing close to sure. Just hang tight and let me try to smooth things over with the director about what you did."

"There's at least *some* good news," offered Eddie.

"What's that?"

"If nobody can figure out my code yet, at least the drive is safe for now."

"Yeah. At least until you document it." Karstaad smiled as she said it, a big thing that lit her whole face. But she was serious.

"Aww. Okay. I will. But I'm putting a monitor on what I did in the reactor. Let somebody fuck with my code. I'll be waiting."

<CHAPTER 34>

MARK RECTOR

|||||||||||||||||||||||||||||||||||||||||||||||||||||||||||

13 CYCLES UNTIL ARRIVAL

Mark Rector sat at his desk, counting the minutes. The hydroponics subdirector, Tanaka, had finally come out of hiding, and they now had him sitting in an interrogation room. Rector wanted to make him wait a bit, soften him up before he questioned him, but he didn't have all day. Iannou had said they couldn't hold him long without repercussions, and Rector believed that. The only advantage he had was that *Tanaka* didn't know it.

He'd thought about this moment a lot in the previous days. He needed a win—something that he could take to the governor and show his worth—but he didn't know exactly what that looked like. If Tanaka could—or *would*—tell him who set off the explosives, that might be enough, but Rector wasn't banking on it. He'd start with that, but he'd rely on his intuition to find the right line of questioning. *Something* about that event didn't add up, and Tanaka might know what.

He entered the interrogation room to find Koshi Tanaka sitting with hands folded on the table, his head level, his eyes straight ahead. Rector stood in the door and studied him, but the man didn't even acknowledge him.

"Why'd you set off the bombs at the protest?" asked Rector. He wanted to get the man talking, and putting him on the defensive was a good way to do that.

Tanaka didn't respond.

"Okay. Let's start somewhere else. What did you see at the protest at the time of the execution of Teresa Fleming?"

Tanaka continued to stare straight ahead, saying nothing.

"You're making this hard." Rector thought he caught a hint of a smile from Tanaka at that. So that was the play. Tanaka thought he was cute, had some ego tied up in this. Okay. They could play it like that. "It's pretty simple. You can sit there and say nothing, but if you do that, you're not leaving." It was a blatant lie, though Tanaka was pissing him off a little, and Rector kind of wanted to do it.

Tanaka stayed silent for another fifteen seconds or so, before finally speaking. "And if I talk, you'll find a way to tie whatever I say to a crime, and you'll keep me anyway."

"Why would I do that?"

"Because you're a fascist who gets his promotions based on arrests, regardless of guilt or innocence."

"That's a little cynical," said Rector. It also wasn't true, but arguing the point with the man wouldn't get him anywhere. He'd already made up his mind about Secfor, and nothing Rector said was going to change it.

Tanaka shrugged. "Being cynical isn't a crime."

"Just tell me who set off the explosives at the protest."

"What explosives?"

"Don't be a dick. You're saying you didn't see anything? You know that intentionally making a false statement as part of an investigation *is* a crime, right?"

"See? It's just like I said. If I say anything, you're going to find a way to arrest me for it."

"We have you on video at the execution. There's no way that you didn't see them."

"Video can be faked. But then, *you* already know that."

Rector felt his face heat, and he stepped out of Tanaka's line of sight to gather himself. Rector hadn't had anything to do with faking the video of Danielson's event, but again, that argument wouldn't alter Tanaka's thinking. "We both know this one was real. You were *there*."

"Was I?" Tanaka smirked at him, and it took all of Rector's restraint not to punch him. Maybe that was what he wanted. Maybe Tanaka wanted someone to hit him because he thought it would get him out of trouble. But then, people who wanted someone to hit them probably hadn't been hit before. That shit hurt.

"You want to walk out of here, you tell me what you saw. If not, I'll have you taken to your cell."

"You can't keep me."

"You want to bet?" Tanaka didn't respond to that, but Rector could see that it had an effect, so he decided to push it. "You yourself said that Secfor breaks the rules, right? So what's to say I won't break this one?"

"You won't risk your job."

Rector snorted. "My job has me headed down to the planet soon, just like you. You think anybody there is going to give a shit what I do to you? And sure. Maybe I lock you up and someone else releases you. But maybe not. After all, if nobody asks, maybe it just gets pushed out of sight."

Tanaka went back to staring straight ahead, not responding.

"But I'm sure your buddies will make a big deal about it. They'll be right in there making complaints about your incarceration, forcing a change. Right? Because they're all true believers and would put themselves at risk for the cause. Iannou . . . he'll be right here any minute, right?" He paused for effect. "C'mon, Tanaka—you know they won't. There's only one person who would put your cause ahead of their own well-being. And he's staring at you in that mirror right there."

Tanaka still didn't respond, but Rector gave him time. The more he thought about it, the more he'd realize the truth in what Rector said. Because it *was* true. The opposition to the government was filled with hot air. They liked to yell and protest, right up until it got hard.

"I didn't have anything to do with the explosions."

"I believe you," said Rector. "But you know who did."

"No, I don't. It wasn't us."

"It wasn't you." Rector purposely repeated the man's statement. It was an interrogation tactic, and an effective one.

"It wasn't. If it was planned, I would have known. You said it before: nobody would put themselves at that kind of risk, and you were right. I've checked. It didn't add up to me—why someone would set off something like that during our own protest. I've had plenty of time to think, and I can't come up with a reason. So I asked. I pulled in everybody I know who might have wanted to do it, and nobody knows how it happened. None of my people."

Rector paused, a chill running down his back. Tanaka had said what he'd already been thinking—that it didn't make sense. "So if not you, then who?"

"It took me a while to come to it, but you tell me. Who do *you* think?" Tanaka stared at him, as if he should know.

"If I knew, we wouldn't be here."

"You know."

Rector slammed his hands against the table, making the other man jump. "If you're implying that *I* had something to do with it—"

"Okay. So not you. But think about it. Who gained in the after-math? It wasn't *us*."

Rector sat back in his chair and thought about it. He knew Tanaka was no good, but his gut said the man was telling the truth on this one. The protestors hadn't gained anything from the explosives and subsequent riot, nor was there any reasonable way that they could have. So if it wasn't them . . . who *did* gain? And when he thought about it like that, it sent another chill through him, and this time it wouldn't leave. Public opinion had shifted strongly against both the protestors *and* Secfor following the event at the execution. The only people who gained from that . . . no . . . not people. Person.

The governor.

But there was no way . . .

Except there was. Pantel had been manipulating things to play him and Darvan off of each other. Was it a stretch that he was treating public opinion the same way?

After at least a minute of silence, Rector finally spoke. "Okay. You're free to go."

Tanaka looked around, as if expecting a trick or something. "I . . . I can go?"

"Yep." He didn't trust Tanaka, but he believed that he didn't do this—and regardless, he had other things to deal with. Darvan and the governor had turned on him and exiled him to the planet. He could turn on them; if they were part of this and he could prove it, he could expose them. But to what end? It would be like joining the protestors, and while part of him wanted to see the truth come out, he wasn't doing *that*. Even if he did expose it, would that even change anything? He'd have to think it through. It was an option, but it was the last option.

Before he got to that, he had one more chance to turn things around. Maybe the governor was behind the explosions at the riot, but he definitely wasn't involved in the work slowdown. That was the biggest thorn in his side, and if Rector could solve that, well . . . all would be forgiven.

And he had a lead on that. A tip from someone in agriculture had told him that the farmers were siphoning off goods and putting them on the black market, and when he looked into it, he found prices dropping. He didn't need a degree in economics to know that meant a greater supply. He could have questioned Tanaka about it, but that would give away the fact that he knew. He didn't just need to stop the stealing; he needed to do it in a big, visible way. If he could do that, he'd have all the leverage he needed to get himself off the colonization mission. He could decide what to do about the governor later.

RECTOR WAS SEATED IN THE LARGE DINING FACILITY, SHOVELING rice and beans from his plate into his mouth, barely tasting it. The rest of the patrons gave him a pretty wide berth, so it surprised him when someone slid into the seat across from him and set a plate down. He looked up to find Mikayla Irving. She had a sandwich on her plate and nothing else.

"Mikayla. I trust this isn't a social call."

"See, this is why you're such a good investigator." She didn't touch her food, which she'd probably brought as a cover. "Boss needs a favor."

"You're going to bring that to me here?" Rector set his fork down and gave the woman his full attention. "That's a bit inconvenient."

"Relax. It's just a favor. Nothing illegal."

Rector snorted softly. Appearance of wrongdoing was almost

as bad as actually doing it, and just sitting with her would cast suspicion on him. But there wasn't much he could do about that. "What's Cecil want?"

"We want to get two people on the landing party with you."

"The planet?" He thought about it, tried to see the angle, but couldn't. "Why?"

Mikayla shrugged. "It's what he wants."

"He has a reason. You saying you don't know it?"

She sat for a second, maybe trying to decide what she could share. She definitely knew. "People on the surface are eventually going to want things. You know . . . once things normalize."

"Sure." That was basic human nature.

"Somebody's going to need to provide those things."

"Ah." Cecil was thinking ahead, planning to expand the black market to the surface. Rector almost had to admire him for the foresight. "I'm not sure I can help."

"Yeah. Boss said you might say that. Said to tell you to find a way."

He sighed. What choice did he really have? Ever since Cecil had given over Fleming to him, the man had a measure of leverage. And, like she said, getting a couple people added to the manifest wasn't really illegal. "Get me the names. And since we're doing favors for each other—"

"We don't owe you anything."

"Hear me out. This might benefit your boss as well as me."

She rolled her eyes. "What do you want?"

"A location."

"It's almost like you *want* me to tell you 'Up your ass.' But that's probably not it, right?"

Rector laughed despite himself. "I want to know where they're holding the siphoned food before distributing it to the black market."

"I'm sure I don't know what you're talking about."

"I'm sure you know *exactly* what I'm talking about."

Mikayla hesitated. "Okay. Let's say I did. Or let's say I could find out. Why would I tell you?"

"Tell your boss it's an opportunity. The food gets removed; black market prices go up. You profit."

"You're shit at economics. The food gets removed, it gets put back into the system, rations go up. People don't need the black market as much. We *lose* money."

Rector considered that. "What if I could delay the return of the goods to the system? You could profit in the interim."

Mikayla seemed to consider it but didn't respond.

"Look," Rector continued. "I do favors for your boss. To be in a position to keep doing that, I need this. See what you can do."

Mikayla gave him a fake smile. "I'll bring it to him, but don't hold your breath. I'm going to take this sandwich to go, I think."

RECTOR WAS SURPRISED HOW QUICKLY MIKAYLA GOT BACK TO HIM, which meant that Cecil had seen a benefit in it. It also meant that he had to cobble together an action team and a plan in short order before he missed the opportunity. He looked over the intelligence one more time, searching for anything he might have missed. It was high risk, but this was his last chance to avoid being sent to the planet, and if he failed there were very few personal consequences. They couldn't exile him twice.

He had everything: schematics of the target level and those above and below it, pictures of the actual area, projected personnel on duty. He checked the clock for the fifth time—0151 hours now. They'd hit their target at 0200, when the fewest people would be there. He had a digitally verified authorization from Maritza

Kowalski, the director of subsistence, giving them permission to enter any space they needed.

He'd briefed the governor, though he hadn't wanted to. He hadn't had a choice. They were going into the lower levels of the ship, and the threat of armed resistance was real. There had been numerous discrepancies with printers, and at this point anybody could have anything. His team needed weapons, and only the governor could authorize printing handguns. Rector had restricted the ammo to rubber bullets, and hopefully they wouldn't have to use them. But he wasn't going in unprepared.

Darvan had fought him on that when he found out, but that was to be expected. He probably hoped Rector would fail, which was a shitty thing for the head of Secfor to hope. Most everybody else would be happy if he succeeded. It was a selfish few who were holding the system hostage for their own desires.

The mission relied on surprise, which was another worry. They still hadn't found their leak. To compensate, Rector had seeded false information throughout the directorate, trying to confuse things. But even with that, once they started they'd have to move fast. If they lost momentum, they might end up having to abandon the very stuff they were going to seize, which would not make the governor—or Cecil—happy. They had bot carts lined up and ready to haul out whatever they found, but they didn't know how much to expect or how long it would take. An estimated 10 percent of the ship's supply was going missing—about 250 kilograms per day. How much of that had already been funneled into the black market, nobody knew. If his intel was right, they might find tons.

Danielson was playing with his weapon, practicing drawing and aiming. Rector would have taken it away from the big man if he could justify bringing people in without a way to protect themselves. "Put that in its holster where it belongs."

Danielson stared at him for a couple seconds, uncomprehending, and then at the weapon in his hands, before finally complying. Rector didn't have enough people to leave someone behind, but he'd given the man an out-of-the-way job moving cargo once they seized it. At least in that, his size and strength would be an asset.

"Okay. We move in five minutes. Bring it in." Rector counted heads one last time. Fourteen Secfor and twelve support personnel along with an equal number of bots to load the carts and move them to the elevators. A message buzzed to his device. The scout he'd sent out an hour before, reporting no unusual activity on the ag decks. Their leak hadn't warned them. "We're a go. Everyone knows their assignment. Team A, you move first." Four people led by Adebayo headed out. Rector hadn't been excited when Darvan's favorite got assigned to the mission, but Adebayo was a pro, and there was no questioning his ability. He'd take his team to the level below the target deck.

"Vasquez, you next." His onetime partner took her four-person team to the alternate elevator and would move to the level above it.

That left him with his team of six. They had a two-minute wait for the elevator to return, and they'd debark on the target level and make the seizure. He resisted the urge to check their equipment again. Everything was set. He exhaled forcefully as the elevator returned and they loaded in. The support team would follow behind in five minutes, giving them time to secure the area first. After that, they'd lock the elevator in place until they needed it again, preventing anybody from going down or coming up.

The door opened onto a landing, a few green bulbs providing dim light, as expected. The plants needed day and night cycles, and the lighting provided that. "Headlamps on," he announced. Bright cones lit the area, causing shadows to dance as heads moved this way and that.

He reached the main door and triggered the override, and it opened. The team quickly fanned out in the larger space, and they picked up their pace to a jog. They had about sixty meters to cover. They were about halfway there when the lights cut on, momentarily halting them in surprise, everyone looking around for the source. "Keep moving," ordered Rector.

A door opened to their front, and two men and a woman emerged. They wore protective overalls over their vac suits, and they stopped after just a few steps, only ten or fifteen meters from the advancing Secfor. "You're not supposed to be down here," shouted one of the men.

Rector slowed, put up his hand for the rest of the team to do the same. He lifted his device to show the man the screen, though they were still too far apart for him to read it. "I have authorization. A warrant to search this entire deck."

The man hesitated at that, looked to the woman, who shrugged. "Let me see."

Rector kept the device up as he approached, putting a few steps between him and his team. From a security standpoint, it was stupid, but it was worth the risk if he could keep things friendly.

The man, who was half a head shorter than Rector, looked it over for several long seconds, as if reading every word. "I'm gonna have to call this in to the boss."

"That's not necessary," said Rector. "Your boss's boss signed it."

"I say it *is* necessary."

Rector moved to the right to get around the man, who shifted to block him, causing Rector to stop before running into him. "We'll be out of your hair in no time."

The farmer shook his head. "We're not doing anything until I talk to my boss."

"I've got authorization. I'm afraid this isn't up for debate." To his people, Rector called, "Let's go."

The man moved again, this time bumping Rector as he tried to get by, forcing him slightly off balance. The other two farmers shifted to block the way as well, but they had to give ground to do it since Secfor outnumbered them. The lead farmer grabbed one of the Secfor by the arm and pulled, but then Danielson was there, between them, and he shoved the man to the ground. The farmer scrambled to his feet and charged, and Danielson planted his feet and met him with a shoulder. The two men grappled for a second, until the farmer's head caught Danielson under the chin and stunned him, knocking him back.

Danielson lashed out with a big right fist and caught the man with a grazing blow that still knocked him to a knee. To Rector's relief, the big man didn't charge, but that relief was short-lived when three shots rang out, ringing in his ears. Despite simulator training, there was nothing that could prepare him for how *loud* a gun was. Danielson stood over his prone victim, gun still pointed, looking ready to shoot again. At the same time a call to Rector's earpiece indicated that the support personnel were arriving on the deck. In one motion, Rector grabbed his stun stick and touched it to Danielson's ribs, dropping him to the ground in a heap next to the moaning farmer. He stood for a second, staring at the two bodies, knowing that no matter what happened with the rest of the mission, his own fate was sealed.

Shit.

"We need medical," he said across the network but loudly enough for everybody around him to hear as well. They'd stopped fighting, stopped moving. At least Danielson's rash action had accomplished that much, though it wouldn't be worth it if a man died. "Find and secure the goods. I'll stay here and wait for support and medical."

The four remaining members of his team, now joined by Vasquez's four-person team, who had made their way down from the level above, moved out to the storage room where they expected to find the contraband.

Adebayo and his team reached Rector before the support team did. "What happened here?"

"Danielson went nuts and started shooting a civ at point-blank. I stunned him."

Adebayo studied him for a couple of seconds, no doubt judging. "I knew we shouldn't have given that dumbass a weapon," he said finally.

"Me too," agreed Rector. "Do me a favor. Cuff him before he recovers."

"You going to arrest him?" Adebayo seemed surprised, but Rector couldn't tell if it was good surprise or bad.

"Don't know." It wouldn't change the outcome. It was Danielson's fault, but it was his mission, and since it was fucked, he might as well ask Adebayo for help. The man *was* good at his job. "What do you think?"

"Yeah. Let's cuff him. We can sort the rest of it out after we're done. I could hear the shots from a hundred meters away through two walls, which means other people could hear them, too. Our cover is probably blown."

As if to punctuate his point, a message came through the net to their earpieces. "Boss, some farmers have gotten to the elevator. They're coming down with medical."

Dammit. Needing medical meant that they didn't lock down the elevator. But how had people reacted so quickly unless they'd been ready for it? Maybe someone had leaked info after all. He'd have to deal with that later. "Can you supervise the team loading the carts?"

"Sure. What are you going to do?" asked Adebayo.

"I'm going to meet them at the elevator and try to head things off."

"Alone? You sure that's a good idea?"

"I'm absolutely *not* sure. But it seems better than another group confrontation."

"Right up until they kick your ass," said Adebayo.

Rector laughed despite himself. "I probably deserve it."

"Probably."

RECTOR WAS STANDING FIVE METERS FROM THE ELEVATOR DOOR when it opened to reveal maybe a dozen people, mostly men, mostly people he recognized from studying pictures of the protestors. "What the fuck is going on here?" asked George Iannou, who stood at the front of the group. They hadn't charged off the elevator, and that, at least, seemed like a good sign.

"We're confiscating contraband foodstuffs. We have a warrant." Rector held it up, and Iannou moved closer so that he could read it as the rest of his group oozed off of the elevator and milled around. "You mind if the medic goes? We've got an injured man over there."

"Who's hurt? What happened?" asked Iannou.

Rector considered lying to defuse the situation but decided against it. They'd find out anyway, and that would be worse. "One of my guys shot a farmer with rubber bullets."

"What the—"

"We've taken the officer responsible into custody," said Rector, cutting off the line of questioning before it could turn ugly. It seemed to have the desired effect, as some of the tension went out of Iannou, and the group went back to milling about and murmuring among themselves. Their quick reaction in getting down to the ag deck notwithstanding, they didn't seem to have much of a focus. They were there, but they didn't know what to do any more than Rector did.

"He's going to be charged?" asked Iannou after a moment.

"That's my current intent. Yes. But the injured man wasn't innocent in the thing, either—he initiated physical contact. It started as a shoving match and got out of control."

"He was shot."

"Which was an overreaction, after the fact," said Rector. "And that's what the officer will face consequences for. Before that, he was doing his job and the farmer laid hands on him."

Iannou considered it. "What happens now?"

Rector considered his next words. While his personal goal had been thwarted, he could still do what was right for the ship and secure the stolen goods. And while the group in front of him couldn't stop that, they could certainly make it difficult. The elevators were the only viable options for transporting the foodstuffs they were seizing. If Iannou's people fought him for those, it would result in more injuries. Rector didn't want that, but Iannou probably didn't, either. But Iannou had to answer to the others, so Rector needed a way for the other man to save face.

"We've got to seize the contraband. You know that."

"What if I tell you it's not contraband?"

"I can get the director of subsistence on the line if you want. But I think we both know how that's going to end, and it seems like a waste of time."

"We could hold the elevators," said Iannou.

"You could. For a while. I'd rather you didn't."

"I'm sure that's true."

"Let me make you an offer," said Rector.

"I'm listening." Iannou wasn't the only one listening. Everyone who came with him had stopped their own conversations and were now hanging on Rector's next words.

"You make this easy, and nobody gets charged for the theft of the goods. We take the food, and we hold it until the director of subsistence tells us where she wants it to go. We chalk the whole thing up as a delay in delivery due to administrative error." He left out the part where that delay would be somewhat longer than necessary due to his deal with Cecil.

Iannou glanced to a couple of the people with him. Rector tried to follow his eyes, see who had influence, but it was too subtle. He caught a few nods from the group, but that was it. "No charges for the injured man, either. He was just doing what he thought was right."

Rector considered it for a moment. He had his outcome, so all he had to do was close the deal, but he didn't have full autonomy. "I can't do that. I'm going to have to explain the entire situation to make the charges stick against the man who shot him. But I'll downplay his role, make sure all he gets is a fine."

Iannou thought about it for several long seconds. "Deal."

Rector held out his hand and the bigger man engulfed it in his. The group with him wandered back onto the elevator, and a few seconds later they were gone. Rector let out a long breath.

Adebayo came up beside him. "That seems to have gone well."

"Yeah. What'd we find?"

"A couple tons of food. Protein and grains, just like we thought. Vasquez is supervising the loading. It's going to take a minute. We might need to make a second trip."

"That's not much." Rector had hoped for more. This wouldn't really even make a huge impact. But they'd known that a lot of the goods had already moved through the black market, so it wasn't a complete surprise.

"It's better than nothing. And if we're lucky, it puts an end to pilfering and things go back to normal."

"You believe that?" asked Rector.

"Nope."

"Yeah. Me either. But like you said, it's something. Either way, it's your problem now. I'm transitioning to full-time preparation for the planet."

"I want you to know that I had nothing to do with that," said Adebayo.

Rector studied him, trying to find guile in his statement. Instead, he saw the man looking at him like an equal. He liked that feeling. He liked being in charge. Maybe he was looking at the mission to the planet in the wrong way. He'd be in charge there, too, and what better way to get ahead than to make that a success?

<CHAPTER 35>

SHEILA JACKSON

||||||||||||||||||||||||||||||||||||||||||||||||||||||||||||||||||||||||

11 CYCLES UNTIL ARRIVAL

Sheila sat across from Alex at their small table, plates of pasta cooling in front of each of them. Neither of them wanted to speak first. They'd agreed to sit down and talk out their issues, but now that they were here, she wished they weren't. Alex seemed to feel the same way. It was much easier to just let things fester under the surface. Not healthier, but then, the easy things usually weren't.

"I understand why you're not fighting the order to go to the planet," said Alex. That much was good, though understanding wasn't approval.

"And I understand why you don't want me to." She paused. She didn't want to continue. "I really do." Again she stopped, with Alex seeming content to give her the time she needed. But anything else she said was going to bare her soul, and she just . . . pressure built behind her eyes as she fought to hold back tears. "It's hard, you know? To say it."

Alex nodded. "I know, baby. But you can say anything to me. It has to be that way. If we can't be honest with each other, who can we be honest with?"

She tried to smile, and then took a deep breath and blew it out forcefully. "Okay. I think you're right. Objectively, I should be fighting to stay here." Her device buzzed, and she ignored it, but it caused her to pause.

"But," prompted Alex.

"But every time I think about it, I want to be *there*. On the planet. Alex, I love you. And I know that's supposed to mean that I put you before everything else."

"But you can't."

Her device buzzed again. She never got calls except from work, and then only in emergencies. But she was screening all the data before releasing it, so what emergencies could there be? All she'd left for night shift was a bunch of satellite feeds, and they'd gotten similar feeds a dozen times already. "I wish I could."

Alex nodded again, slighter this time, and sighed. "I'd like to say I'm not hurt."

Tears started to come to Sheila's eyes. "I know you are. You have every right to be."

Alex smiled wanly and shook his head. "I'd also be lying if I said I didn't know this when I married you."

Sheila hesitated at that. "What do you mean?"

"I mean I love you for who you are, and this is who you are. I always knew that. Granted, I didn't see *this* situation coming. But I knew who you were. Who you are."

Her device buzzed again.

"Go ahead. Check it."

She fished it out of her pocket and read the three messages. The third one stopped her heart for a beat. "Holy stars."

"What is it?" asked Alex.

"We've found complex life." She read it again. "We've found complex life!"

"Oh shit! What does this mean? I mean . . . uh . . . it . . . go! You need to go."

Sheila looked around, though she didn't know what she was looking for. "I do. I'm sorry. Talk later?"

"Go!"

SHEILA MESSAGED ALANA WILSON BEFORE LEAVING HER QUARTERS, and the xenobiologist arrived at the space exploration directorate the same time she did, out of breath. She'd run.

"Are you sure?" Alana asked.

"Not yet. The message seemed pretty adamant, but I haven't seen the feed yet." For her part, she almost doubted it, because she'd seen all the information first, but there was a chance it got by her.

"It's from a satellite?"

"Satellite video."

"I guess we'll know in a minute," said Alana.

"I guess so."

Gerard Millman, who ran the off shift, was waiting for them as soon as they entered, a smile on the older man's face that she hadn't seen in a long time. "I've got it up on the big screen. We've got a one-minute-and-eight-second video clip."

Sheila turned to Alana. "You ready?"

"Yeah."

"Play it."

They didn't speak. The three of them stood there staring at the screen as objects moved across Prom's now-familiar surface. No . . . not across it. Above it. Well above it, higher than the trees. Thousands of dark shapes moving together but separate.

"Birds," said Alana, having the same thought as Sheila herself.

The door opened and Lila and Yanai rushed in. "What's happening?" asked Lila.

"Look." Sheila pointed to the screen.

"Oh my stars," she said. They watched the full video again. "This changes everything."

Sheila wasn't sure that was true. It *should* change things. But she'd been wrong before. "Lila, I need all the data you can pull from this. Size, numbers, and anything else. Work with biology on it and call in anybody you need. Full overtime authorized."

"Got it, boss. What are you going to do?"

"I'm going to get us a meeting with the governor."

<CHAPTER 36>

JARRED PANTEL

‖‖‖

11 CYCLES UNTIL ARRIVAL

Jarred Pantel sat at the table in his quarters, lingering over his coffee. He didn't want to go to work. Because as soon as he went in, he was going to be bombarded with questions about Secfor's latest screwup—they'd fucking shot a man—and he was going to have to deal with the repercussions. And he already had the scientists coming to make their newest case for why they couldn't go to the planet's surface. He'd have dodged that one if he could, but they'd discovered complex life, and that he couldn't ignore. Granted, they had limited information—video from an overhead satellite—but it didn't take a scientist to see something resembling birds flying through the air. Big birds. They still didn't have working surface explorers, which meant they didn't have any details—didn't know with 100 percent certainty that they *were* birds. But they knew enough. They were *something,* and they were *alive.* To them, that changed everything.

Except it didn't.

It changed a *lot* of things, including how a lot of people shipwide would feel about the mission, but it didn't change the timeline.

Camina came up and hugged him from behind, putting her head next to his and squeezing him lightly. "Something's bothering you. What is it?"

"That obvious?"

"Call it a hunch." Of course she noticed.

"It's nothing."

"It's *something*."

"The scientists have new evidence of animal life on the planet."

"That's exciting!" She stood and came around the table.

"They're going to want to delay our landing expeditions."

She sat, put her elbows on the table, and rested her chin in her hands. "I gather from context that that's a problem?"

"It is. Because they're right about the science. But science doesn't matter here."

Camina frowned. "Okay . . . *that* doesn't make any sense."

He sighed. He hadn't planned on having this discussion twice, but he couldn't leave her without explaining. "The science—the scientist, at least—says we should wait. But if we delay, even for a short time, there's *always* going to be a reason we can't do it. We'll still be in orbit in twenty years saying, 'Let's just work on this one more thing.' And I don't think our society can survive that. We have to go now."

"What about sending a smaller team?"

He shook his head. "A smaller group will have exactly the opposite effect that we need. As soon as something goes wrong, they'll be clamoring to pull back, and we're right back up in orbit forever. We have to send enough people down where there's no choice but to make it work. I know there's risk, but we have to push it, or it will never happen. Also, there's the communication problem with the surface, but there's nothing that suggests we'll solve that from orbit. Our best chance to work through it is to get smart people down there. A human can do things that a probe can't, and I have faith in the ingenuity of our people to make this happen."

"So what are you worried about, then?"

He hesitated. "Huh?"

"It sounds to me like you've got a completely rational reason for your actions. So all you have to do is go lay it out to the scientists." She smiled.

Despite himself, he chuckled. "That's it, huh?"

"Sure. Piece of cake."

HE STOOD OVER HIS ZAMIOCULCAS ZAMIIFOLIA, OR ZZ PLANT FOR short, thinking and breathing. He knew it was his imagination, but he pictured somehow that the air was purer there. It was nothing like the plant webs on the lower decks specifically engineered to help maintain oxygen balance on the ship, but those spaces had been mostly unavailable to him since the trouble began with the protestors. Whether the plants had any true effect or not, they calmed him, and right now, he needed calm as he thought through his upcoming meeting.

Pantel knew what was coming because the scientists had gone to the captain first, and she'd already come to him to present the case. He rejected it, and then the scientists insisted on making the case themselves. It would have been easier if he could just tell them the truth, but despite the discussion he'd had with his wife, he couldn't do that. Not unless he wanted his reasons twisted and thrown back at him in a dozen different ways from all sectors of the ship. Perfect was the enemy of good enough, and there would always be reasons not to move forward. Someone had to make the call and he was doing it. He was making the decision so some future governor wouldn't have to.

The ironic thing was that it would be easier to give in. He could defer on a decision, trot the scientists out to back it up with data, and everybody would accept it. Well . . . not exactly. *Somebody* would criticize every decision he made. But not nearly as loudly as they were screaming about his hasty colonization plan. Let them scream. History would be the only impartial judge, and he could live with that. Hopefully he could make them at least accept it.

The door slid open, and Jeremy ushered the women into the room. There were three of them, which was unexpected, though not an issue.

"Dr. Carroway. Dr. Jackson."

"Governor," said Jackson, "May I introduce Lila Jurgens. She'll be taking over as head of my subdirectorate when I'm down on the planet. I thought it would be good for you to meet her, and for her to have direct access to our discussion so that she's aware of any directives."

"It's good to meet you . . . Doctor?"

"Not yet," said the taller woman. "Hopefully soon, but other concerns have somewhat superseded the formalities of education."

"I understand. Please, sit." Pantel waited for them to take seats at the small table. "I've gone over the data that you sent me."

"All of it?"

"More than once. Does that surprise you?" He didn't take offense to her question, though she intended it that way. He specifically didn't take offense *because* she intended it that way. She wouldn't believe it, but in her own way, she was as much of an asshole as he was.

"It . . . no. I'm glad you had time to review it. The evidence for life on the planet is overwhelming."

"I agree. How big do you figure those birds are?"

"The birdlike creatures, as best we can tell from modeling and

400 _ MICHAEL MAMMAY

the different angles we have, range from 0.8 to 3.4 meters in wing-span."

"That's big, right?"

"Quite large. If it's accurate, it would put them among the largest birds from Earth."

"And from your notes, you believe that the presence of these birds indicates other life on the planet as well."

Jackson glanced to Carroway, though Pantel wasn't sure what that was about. "We do. There almost has to be. As you will have read, we've found no evidence of crops or other farmed land, which would, at least on the surface, indicate that these creatures subsist by either hunting or gathering."

Pantel hesitated, considering her wording, and then departed from his original plan of discussion. "You say 'creatures.' Can we define that a little better? Do we think they're intelligent?"

Jackson flinched a little at that, almost as if she didn't want to answer the question. "There are a lot of definitions of 'intelligent.'"

"Such as?"

She hesitated. "We're departing from things we can prove and getting into the debates that we're having among our own community. Are you sure you want to do that?"

Pantel found that he was legitimately curious. "I think I need to hear it. I'm about to make as critical a decision as any governor has made in the past two and a half centuries, and I should have all the information."

"One definition of 'intelligence' is the ability to develop and improve technology."

"Which they can't do," said Pantel.

"We don't know that." She said it quickly, irritation seeping into her tone, and it was clear that she'd already had this argument elsewhere.

"In previous reports you've stated that we've not seen any modes of transportation, detected no off-planet communications."

Jackson nodded. "That's correct. Evidence leans toward them not having modern technology as we know it, but we can't prove that unequivocally, and regardless, that's only one definition of 'intelligence.' Another definition of 'intelligence' is the ability to survive over time. We don't know how long this species has been there. And yet another definition points to the complexity of communication, which we haven't been able to evaluate at all."

"So—" Pantel started to respond, but Jackson cut him off.

"And that's all without considering the remnants of buildings that we've found on the desert continent and just recently on the supercontinent."

"Yes. I saw that report, but it didn't have much analysis."

"We've analyzed what we've got, which isn't much. We have a satellite picture of something that looks a little bit too engineered to be natural. But it's only a fragment. We won't know more until we get to those locations."

That was interesting, her talking about wanting to go there. At least there was a *little* bit of common ground. "So best-guess it for me. What do you think it is?"

"Best guess? Remnants of a civilization that no longer exists on the planet, or at least that we can't currently identify."

"And you say that because—"

"Sir, if I may," interjected Lila Jurgens—Pantel thought of her by both names so he'd remember them.

"Go ahead," said Jackson to her subordinate.

"I worked on the technology timelines, and in all our possibilities we didn't come up with any that allowed for large buildings, the likes of which we've found evidence for in pictures and video of the desert continent, that didn't also include other indicators of technology."

"So because of that you think—"

"It's old, sir," said Jurgens. "Further, we believe that the shifting sand of the desert repeatedly buries and unburies ruins, and that if we were to search below the surface of the other continents—especially if we could get ground-based ultrasonic scanners in place—we'd likely find other remnants."

"Surely we have satellites that can tell us what's under the surface."

"We do," said Jackson. "We can, and have, measured density, and with a lot of complicated calculations that I'll spare you, we can extrapolate a lot of the elements that we expect to see there. What we can't see without the ground-based systems is specific formations. Put into layman's terms, with our current sensor suite, an underground building is indistinguishable from a rock of the same material."

"Ah. Got it. The potential remnant that you did see on the supercontinent—forgive me if this was in your report—but where is that in relation to our three settlement sites?"

"The closest settlement site is 520 kilometers away."

Pantel nodded. That meant that the others were probably significantly farther, since the three settlements formed a triangle with each side approximately four hundred kilometers. Not that it mattered, but for whatever reason, the presence of what might be ancient artifacts bothered him more than the idea of semi-intelligent life. "Do we have any idea what might have caused the end of this earlier . . . civilization? Can we call it that? What caused it to collapse?"

"We don't know. We can't even guess at a time frame until we get down there. And that's if dating methods that worked on Earth work here. This is why we proposed a crewed mission to the desert continent." She paused. "Which you turned down."

"Yes. Maybe I was too hasty about that," said Pantel. Allowing for that helped him in two ways. First, now that they'd seen something on the main continent as well, it mattered to him more. But it was also a way to appease Jackson, who was important to the mission. "I'd be willing to revisit that and consider a mission there once we have the initial colonies settled, as well as sending a team out to look at the location on the supercontinent."

Jackson studied him for a few seconds, and he did his best to keep a neutral expression and not give anything away. "That's not ideal, but I'll take it. Lila, make a note to develop a concept for a team to go to the desert continent to examine the partially buried structures there. Plan it for four weeks after landing of the initial colonization expeditions." She looked at Pantel when she gave the date, as if daring him to challenge her. He didn't, because he didn't care, and he could always change it later if he wanted. Let her have her win for now. They shouldn't be in this much conflict in the first place, but *shouldn't* didn't matter much. They were. And his job was, as ever, to mitigate conflict and keep things moving forward.

So when she said, "With the discovery of life, along with potentially more advanced life at some point in the past, a delay in landing is the only logical course of action," he wasn't surprised.

Nor ready to capitulate. "No delay."

"You promised me six months."

"Other factors have overridden that."

Jackson responded immediately, clearly having been ready for that answer. "I think the planetary conservationists might have a different opinion when they see the extent of life."

"I assume they *will* have a different opinion, though I wouldn't assume that they haven't seen the evidence already. Indeed, I expect they have."

"I haven't released it. To my knowledge, it's not in the common domain yet."

The governor shrugged. "It's only a matter of time then. But the planetary conservationists are going to complain no matter what, so there's no sense worrying about it."

"But—"

Pantel held up his hand, and Jackson bit off whatever she'd intended to say. "To the best of our knowledge, there is no technologically advanced life on the surface of Prom. Am I correct when I say that?"

"That's not the main—"

"Am I correct when I say that?"

Jackson glared at him. "Yes, while that is by no means conclusively proven, that seems more likely than not."

"In that case, the conservationists, as you call them, are in the vast minority. Have you seen the polling?"

Jackson didn't respond, but her scowl suggested that she had indeed seen it. With evidence of truly intelligent life, almost 30 percent of people thought they shouldn't colonize the planet, but when polled about just animal life, that number dropped to 11 percent. Not irrelevant, but mostly insignificant with the exception of the actions of radicals, which they had to deal with regardless. "Science doesn't run on public opinion," she finally said.

"Policy, however, does." It's not something he'd have admitted in front of a camera, though it probably wouldn't surprise people if he did.

"And what public opinion is leading the policy to land on the planet before we're ready?"

Pantel considered his answer to that. It wasn't that he didn't have one ready—he had several. He was trying to gauge how much of the truth to share, and Jackson's hostility was leading him toward *not very much.* Yes, he had earned a lot of that hostility. He'd have done things differently given the chance to start over, but he might as well wish for peace throughout the ship. Either way, the idea of making the landing too big to fail wouldn't sit well with the high-and-mighty scientist who saw things in absolutes. He couldn't afford that luxury. "What public opinion leads the policy? The desire of the people to get on with things."

She stared at him as if he had turned into a cricket, started to speak, stopped, considered her words, and then finally spoke. "That seems more a failure to lay out what 'getting on with things' looks like."

"That's the issue with public opinion," he said in barely disguised mock concession. "You don't always get to decide what's important and what's not. People want to see action."

"This is a ship full of scientists. I think they're capable of understanding more than you credit."

Pantel shook his head. "The ship *was* filled with scientists. At first. The First Crew, regardless of their actual jobs on the ship, had that in common. Now? It's filled with specialists who work in all fields. Sure, there's a core education in science, but how important do you think that is in the news and entertainment directorate?"

Jackson didn't have an answer for that.

"So if it's not science that ties the crew together with a common thread now, what do you think it is?"

Jackson shook her head. "What?"

"They're tired. They want this journey to be over."

"How is that possible? They've never known anything but the ship. This is life."

"You don't get around much, do you?" It was a cheap shot, but probably an accurate one. "Ask around. Listen to what people think. You'll see."

"People think that because you've spent the last several months filling their heads with propaganda. With the dream of a planet that we don't know anything about!"

Pantel shrugged. "Doesn't change the fact that they think it. And if we're giving credit, I'd suggest that you helped."

"Not intentionally."

"Okay," he said.

She sagged in on herself. He couldn't read if she accepted his accusation or simply realized that she wasn't going to change his mind. He decided to give her a break, to let her gather her thoughts. As much as he wasn't giving in, he *did* want her as a productive part of the mission. "What do you think, Ms. Jurgens? Will the people accept delays?"

The younger woman looked first to her boss, and after getting no help, then to her boss's boss.

Carroway nodded. "I think in the end, most people will accept whatever they're told to accept."

"There have been some protests that would indicate otherwise," offered Pantel.

"And what's changed because of that? I said that they'd accept it. Not that they'd be happy with it."

"So what happens if we delay? Let's pick a random amount of time—something tenable—say a month. What happens then?"

"We have a month's more data to plan from," said Jackson, not waiting for her subordinate to answer.

"And what are the chances that anything in that month's worth of additional data is conclusive?"

Jackson hesitated, though he suspected it wasn't because she didn't know the answer, but because she did.

"Let's phrase that a different way," he offered. "What are the chances that in a month, we're right back here in this exact same meeting having the exact same discussion?"

Jackson sighed. "Pretty high."

Pantel nodded. That was likely the closest thing that he'd get to an admission. "So why delay?"

Jackson was ready for this one. "The biggest issue we have is the lack of ability to communicate with the surface and with the observed failure of multiple surface missions. A small, crewed mission will help us evaluate that."

"And if we had that information, we'd have everything we needed?" asked Pantel.

"No, of course not."

"And if we found out that we could never communicate directly with the surface for whatever reason, would that completely prevent us from colonizing the planet?"

Jackson glared at him again, probably seeing what he was leading to. "No."

"So then we'd be delaying for no reason."

"We'd be delaying so that if there's something down there that's fatal, it would kill six people and not hundreds!"

That was her best argument, the one that would resonate with the crew, which made it the one he needed to steer away from. "But with more people down there, you've got more skill sets, more people who can help overcome any difficulties."

"An alien virus isn't likely to care about skill sets."

"We have virologists and microbiologists and paleontologists and all kinds of other ologists going. I believe that was your recommendation. Who better to figure these things out?"

"And you've got Secfor in charge of the landing missions, led by goons who don't value the talents of those people."

Ah. With the emotion of her last statement, it finally made sense: she didn't like the leadership. Maybe this was his chance to give her something that she wanted and at least get back to a workable relationship. "In general, or someone specific?"

"Excuse me?"

"You used the word 'goons.' Do you mean in general, or is there a specific goon who is the issue?"

"This is a scientific endeavor. It should be led by scientists."

"You?"

"Not necessarily. If you insist on the current crewing of the missions, I'd propose a council."

Pantel shook his head. "Councils can't lead. They can talk and discuss, but in the end, somebody has to make a decision."

"They can vote," said Jackson.

"What happens if something requires an immediate order?"

Jackson thought about it. "Then pick someone. I don't care if it's me. Any scientist would be better than the current plan."

He felt for her. He really did. Jackson really did seem to want success for the operation. She just had her head so far into the science that she didn't understand the realities. "And here's where public opinion comes back into play. We have to put security in charge. It's a hostile situation—even you would say that—and if something happened because we put science over security—"

"Science *is* security!"

Pantel shook his head. "I'm sorry. The answer is no."

"Rector."

It was his turn to pause. "Excuse me?"

"You asked who the specific goon was. Rector. I tried to talk to him about some basic safety protocols and scientific priorities of work, and he had no interest. If security has to be in charge, I need somebody who will at least take scientists seriously when we speak."

"I see." He considered it. What could he offer that would appease her without derailing his own plans? Rector had to go to the surface. He'd been a useful tool at first, but now, he was a liability of the worst kind. A man that had some power who was unpredictable, but one whose failures didn't stain only himself. "I'll talk to Mark Rector. I will insist that he listen to you."

"You think that will have any effect?" Jackson's tone indicated that she absolutely didn't think it would.

"I do."

She stared him down for a couple of seconds. "I disagree."

"Here's what I know about Rector: he wants the job." It wasn't completely true, but Rector would back that up if asked. It was in his own best interest to make it look like he volunteered.

"What does that have to do with anything? He's unqualified."

"He's not. He can be rash, but he's competent. And what it means is this: when somebody wants something, they're likely to listen if you threaten to take it away if they don't."

"Something like an allocation for a child?" She spit the words, and the other two women flinched. Pantel himself inhaled sharply. Jackson didn't budge. Not even a little bit.

He hadn't been prepared for that, though he supposed he should have been. "Yes. That was poorly done, and I apologize."

Jackson sat, looking like she wanted to say something else, but he couldn't say for sure. Finally she spoke. "Thank you."

"You're welcome. We shouldn't have done that. It was unfair, and if I could go back and do it over again, I wouldn't have done it." He didn't have to fake sincerity with this one. He meant it.

"At least we'll have the baby," she said.

If he wasn't mistaken, she seemed almost sad. Probably because she wouldn't see the child since she'd be down on the planet.

Jackson stood, and the other two ladies followed her lead. "Make sure you talk to Rector. Soon."

He could do that. Jackson and Rector getting along was a key to the mission, and despite their differences, once that mission launched, they all had a vested interest in making it successful. "I will."

<CHAPTER 37>

EDDIE DANNIN

|||||||||||||||||||||||||||||||||||||||||||||||||||||||

8 CYCLES UNTIL ARRIVAL

Eddie waited in one of the large recycler rooms. She wasn't exactly waiting *patiently,* but it was her own fault for arriving early. She hadn't wanted the meeting at all, but Lila had asked. When Eddie said no, she asked again, calling it a favor. Eddie didn't have enough friends to say no to the one she *did* have. It was with Lila's boss, so Lila being involved was understandable, but she hadn't known the purpose, and Eddie didn't either.

They'd had to negotiate to even come up with a location. Jackson wanted it in her office, but no way was that happening. Normally Eddie would have set it up under Cecil's protection, but Jackson hadn't wanted that, saying that there were too many ears there; Eddie thought that maybe Jackson just saw herself as above that. That added some risk for Eddie, since doing business without Cecil was its own problem. But she could worry about that later, if she even agreed to work for Jackson. She probably wouldn't. She'd promised Lila to attend the meeting, nothing more.

One thing they definitely didn't have to worry about was other ears. Not here in recycling. Between the stream of bots wheeling in discarded material and the four medium-size recyclers, there was enough noise to prevent anyone—or anything—from listening in. Not that Eddie expected that. Their biggest risk would be someone catching sight of them on camera. After all, a junior engineer and the director of space exploration didn't really have much cause to meet in a place where neither of them had any business being. But that assumed somebody was looking, which they probably weren't.

But she'd done her own looking. Eddie had spent an entire evening looking into Jackson. The scientist seemed to be a rule follower. She had a baby on the way, for ship's sake. She didn't even use the black market, and everybody used that.

So what did she want from an off-the-books hacker?

Jackson entered through one of the two small doors on either side of the room meant for personnel. The scientist looked mega uncomfortable, glancing back over her shoulder more than once, as if someone might be following her. Eddie checked her device, which she'd tied into the cameras outside each door. Nobody was. But the fact that Jackson might expect that sort of thing added another layer to the puzzle. At least she'd have answers soon enough.

"It's loud in here," said Jackson, when she was within a couple of paces and close enough to be heard.

"That's sort of the point, right?"

Jackson looked around some more. "Right. I guess. You sure we're alone?"

Eddie made a point of looking around as well. "We seem to be." She could have made it easy, asked the older woman what she wanted, but she wasn't much into customer service.

They stood in silence, if the racket of recyclers could be called silence, for several awkward seconds before Jackson spoke. "I have a job for you."

"I gathered," said Eddie, still not helping. She almost felt bad for Jackson. Almost, but not quite enough to do anything about it.

"I can pay."

"I'm aware."

"I want you to hack into my system, steal some information, and make it public."

Eddie didn't immediately respond. Whatever she'd expected, it hadn't been this. Why would someone pay to have themselves hacked? But the answer came to her: because she wanted to be able to deny releasing the information herself. "Sounds easy enough on the surface. What is it?"

"It's an academic paper. It details every reason that we shouldn't go to the surface, from lack of lab and medical facilities to transmission rates of potential pathogens to potential danger from life we might encounter there. No editorials, just facts. Every fact and every prediction we've got."

"And you want this release to—"

"—everyone."

Eddie considered it. There wasn't a lot of risk to her in this. With her new mastery of the ship's network, she could get in and out of Jackson's system without getting caught, and she could route the information through any number of different outlets to hide where it came from. It wasn't a matter of *could* she, but rather *should* she. "To what end?"

Jackson spoke without hesitation. She'd clearly thought this through. "The governor has decided to push forward with the colonization, and that's not going to change. But people deserve to know the true risks."

"You think that's going to change anything?" asked Eddie.

"It might change a few minds. But realistically? No, I don't."

"But you want to do it anyway."

"I do. I owe it to the people to give them the truth, even if they ignore it."

Eddie considered it a little longer, making the older woman wait. It seemed like a waste of time, but the truth was usually a good cause, and she couldn't come up with any reason *not* to do it. "Sure. I'll do it. When will the file be ready?"

"It's there now."

"Okay. I'll steal it and get it released tonight."

THE JOB TOOK TWENTY MINUTES, AFTER WHICH EDDIE SETTLED INTO her new routine patrolling the net, looking for the elusive saboteur. She'd been doing it for more than ten cycles with no luck, but at the same time, they'd had no further attacks on the ship. She was beginning to think that whoever it was had given up, so when the incursion came, she almost missed it. It wasn't just a lack of focus on her part. It was something so unexpected that she hadn't even considered it. She'd been paying attention to the engines, the life support, and even the printers.

She hadn't been paying attention at all to the launch facilities.

But there it was. Someone was altering the code to the facilities that housed the landing craft, which made sense once she detected it. The action was subtle, not attacking anything normally deemed critical, so much so that the sensors she'd placed throughout the network almost didn't register it. After all, who cared if someone hacked a door? Eddie didn't. What she did care about was who was doing it. She'd found her saboteur, and now it was time to spring her trap.

They were good. It took her almost forty-five minutes to even pin down their location in engineering.

"Got you, asshole."

Except . . . she didn't.

She had the terminal, but even with that she couldn't identify the person. She was prepared for that, though. The work area had a camera, and she flipped the switch on her pre-positioned hack to take that over, giving her complete access. She panned it around the room, hoping that whoever it was wouldn't notice. The room was dark except for the light of a working screen, and Eddie had to fiddle with the settings on the camera to get a good picture.

There. She took a still shot of the person's face and ran it through an AI to enhance the picture.

She laughed. Or she thought she did. It had become hard to parse.

It was the biggest asshole in engineering. Brewster.

She dropped the camera feed and pulled back. This required thought, and she couldn't do that on the inside. Reluctantly, she backed all the way out of the system and reoriented to her room. She took a sip of water from the box on her desk. Fucking Brewster. Part of her wanted to turn him in right then. It wouldn't take much. A message to Rector telling him she'd located the saboteur, and Brewster could be in a cell within the hour. But for what? Hacking a few doors? That wouldn't do anything. He'd probably been behind the previous attacks as well, but she couldn't prove that. On the other hand, now that she knew what he was doing, she could follow it and see where it led, which might let her nail him for something bigger. It was a risk, but not much of one. He wasn't going to beat her in the code, and he wasn't going to harm her ship. She wouldn't allow it.

With that, she dropped back into the net and went to where Brewster had done his work. She logged every line of altered code, looked at it backward and forward until she knew exactly what he'd done in painstaking detail. Five hours later, when she logged off in the early hours of the next morning, she had a handle on every single bit of what he had altered. All she had to do now was to watch and decide what she wanted to do about it.

CHAPTER 38

GEORGE IANNOU

2 CYCLES UNTIL ARRIVAL

He didn't want to be here. He found himself having that thought a lot, but perhaps never more than now. There had been a release of everything they knew—and didn't know—about the planet, but that hadn't stopped the colonization efforts from moving forward. What it *had* done was further incense those already opposed to the landings. So here they were.

The corridor seemed darker than it should have been, and while George suspected that might be his imagination, he still couldn't help wondering if that was good or bad for their operation. He'd come along because someone had to be the adult to keep things from getting out of hand. At least he'd kept Kayla from coming. She'd be pissed at him for a long time for getting her thrown off the team, but he could live with that if it kept her safe.

The plan was to sabotage the nine landing vehicles, conveniently all located together in a huge hangar near the outer hull. A source in engineering had provided the specs for the landers. In theory, they could do some small things that would cause large problems. The kind of problems that would take days or even weeks to fix.

In practice, ten people moved down the corridor toward their destination with ten different thoughts and intents, and only one he could be sure of: his own. At least two of the people were aligned with Delta Acevedo—two that he knew about—and he assumed that they had a more radical agenda. The portable torch he needed to damage some of the components on his lander bumped painfully against his thigh as he brushed a little too close to the wall. The welder was key, as it would make it extremely difficult for them to remove the damaged parts, forcing them not only to make new parts but to cut out entire sections of the landers and rebuild them. That would take time, and during that time the protestors could continue to work to stop the landing.

Whether everyone would stick to that plan remained to be seen.

Even negotiating who would go on this mission had been an exercise in competing agendas. Some had wanted to completely destroy the landers and even damage the hangar itself; they had agreed to the current plan only to gain a consensus. But as they moved, silent beyond the tread of booted feet on the metal deck, the agreement felt tenuous to George. He'd thought it through, lost sleep planning his reaction if something went amiss, but all that had done was make him tired. He'd try to stop things if they started to go off track, and hopefully his presence would keep people in line.

Richard Jones held up a hand at the front of the column and they stopped. He was a moderate with ties to Koshi, and the only option that all sides could agree upon to lead them. They'd reached the first test—the bulkhead that led into the massive hangar. If everything was going according to plan, their engineering source had set the door on "minimum security," and Jones's biometrics would trigger it open. A second later, the door hissed and slid away.

George nodded to himself. So far so good. Ahead of him in the room, a series of thunks made his heart jump, and it was a second before he realized that someone had flipped the power switch to give them light and air circulation. They wouldn't have to wait long for test two. People in maintenance and security had collaborated to have the hangar empty of personnel. If that failed, the lights would alert anyone present, and the sabotage party would withdraw. While they looked suspicious at this point, creeping around during third shift when most of the ship was asleep, technically they hadn't broken any laws. At least no major ones. There might be a fine or something for having an unauthorized welding torch, but that didn't matter.

Only the whir of the air circulators broke the silence as they started to move. He was fifth through the door, but he waited just inside for everyone else to pass through. He tried to read their intent, glean something from the way they moved or the set of their faces, but if anybody had any intentions outside the approved plan, he couldn't find them. He headed for his assigned lander—second in the second row—and as he did, the enormity of the space hit him. The lights—rows of them spaced evenly—were dozens of meters overhead, and a wave of dizziness hit him until he focused on his feet. He hadn't done well with open spaces in the colonization simulations, and while he hadn't completely believed the accuracy of that test, maybe there was something to it. He kept his eyes toward the floor to compensate as he made his way between two of the massive landers to reach his.

It was short and flat, the body tapering to a rounded point at the front, and it stood on struts that put its entire hull above his head, the top stretching to six or seven meters high. The gray finish almost seemed to absorb light, and for a second he wondered what type of material it was made of. It had wings somewhere, though he only knew that from reading the schematics, since they were retracted.

He pushed the button on the strut, as he was taught, and the door above opened and a ramp descended. Nobody had to arrange that. They were designed to let people in unless someone specifically locked it or if the landing gear was stowed . . . safety or something. He turned on his headlamp and was headed up the ramp when a crash brought him up short. A second later the lights cut off, dropping them into darkness except for the random beams whipped about by the headlamps of his startled comrades. Shouts filled the hangar, echoing into unrecognizable gibberish, and the big space made it hard to tell where anything was coming from.

With only a second's thought, he turned and sprinted back down the ramp, reaching the deck just as something cracked nearby, quick and sharp and louder than anything he'd ever heard, leaving a ringing in his ears. He ducked, for all the good it would do. George scanned for a source, his headlamp swinging around wildly, when a second crack cut through the dark. He turned toward it, found a man holding something out with both hands, but he couldn't identify him with his shaky beam. The man's hands flashed and barked again, and somewhere fifteen or twenty meters away something sparked. He had some sort of projectile weapon— something George had only seen in the ancient vids from Earth.

"Run!" someone yelled, and while he couldn't place the source, it seemed like sound advice. Accustomed as he was to the heavy gravity, he made good time, flinching along the way at two more cracks. Someone screamed back behind him, and he thought about turning but only for a second. The need to escape grabbed at him and pulled him forward. He reached the door at the same time as someone else. They each stopped to let the other through, and then both tried to go at the same time before George grabbed the other man—no, woman—and shoved her through. He followed close on her heels.

They chased bobbing lights before them without knowing where they were headed. There might have been five or six others in front of him, but with the lights winking in and out as people ran, he couldn't be sure. He didn't dare look back to count those behind him for fear of tripping or slamming into someone. They'd better not be heading for the elevator, he thought. That was a sure trap.

Someone in the lead had some sense, and a minute later George was following the woman in front of him up a ladder to the next deck. He consciously slowed himself to avoid getting his fingers crushed under her boots as she stepped on rungs above him. They passed the first deck above them, then the second, third, and fourth, and finally stepped out onto the fifth. His breath came in ragged gasps from the exertion. Or maybe the panic. Though for a group that was panicking, they were doing well. Maybe the exertion overcame it. That was a stupid thought, and he tried to refocus on what mattered. Something had gone wrong. Someone had caught them. And someone in his party had a projectile weapon. Maybe more than one person. Guns. Where had they gotten them? The printers, obviously, but how did they get access to them, and why were they here?

That would have to wait. For now, they had to get away, buy time for him to assess the situation, see exactly how much trouble they were in. They probably hadn't had time to damage the landing craft. But the guns. That scream. Had someone been hit? If so, maybe that was the way out of this. He could turn over the people responsible for that in order to protect everybody else. Acevedo would have a fit, but he was beyond caring about that, since she was almost certainly involved in the guns being there in the first place.

First they had to make their way through the oxygenation rooms and then up into the more populated part of the ship, where they could blend in and disappear. But then a thought hit him: what if the people with the guns were among them? For a second, he considered turning back, but there were people behind him, and he didn't know who was behind *them*. What if those people had guns, too?

Those thoughts fled him as they reached the maze of identical oxygenation rooms, and they hurried through with only the dim green overhead LED bulbs to guide them. They made it to the third or fourth room. George's headlamp flashed over the plants, and he switched it off, realizing everyone else had already done so. Just as he did he slammed into someone, taking both of them down in a heap of limbs. Pain shot through his knee as it hit the hard deck.

"What the—" he started.

"Door's closed!" a male voice yelled from in front.

"Well, fucking open it!" yelled the woman, who was busy untangling herself from George.

"Yeah. I'm trying! It won't respond."

A chill went through George despite the sweat dripping from his face from the run. "Back the other way! Hurry!" He didn't know if anybody was chasing them, but he knew they couldn't stay here. These doors were never locked. Never closed.

"This one's locked, too. It closed behind me." The voice from the other end of the narrow room was calmer, and George made his way toward the man. It took a moment for his eyes to adjust to the low lighting and to pick his way through the agitated people. The scent of sweat and fear mixed with the heavy smell of growing things, and he took it in, trying to calm himself and get his bearings. Jones was by the door, a handheld weapon—a gun—in his hand, which he held down by his side. So that was why Acevedo had agreed to him leading the mission. Not so moderate after all.

"We're trapped," said George, voicing the obvious.

"By who?" asked Jones.

"Does it matter?" asked George. The others were moving toward them, probably on instinct, looking for leadership.

"Get by the other door," barked Jones. Someone moved back that way, a glint of light catching their gun. "We can stay right here. There are two doors, and we have two guns. They have to come in one way or the other."

George looked to the other door, trying to make out who it was with the other gun. It was a woman. Yakova, he thought her name was. Average height and broad at the shoulders. He made a quick count—nine of them. Someone from their team hadn't made it. Given the situation, maybe they were the lucky ones. Probably not, though. He moved closer to Jones. "And what happens when they show up with weapons of their own?"

"What happens when we give ourselves up? That didn't go so well for Fleming, did it?"

"We can reason with them."

Jones snorted. By this point, everyone else had fallen silent, focusing on the conversation between the two men, and Jones's derision was palpable. "You've been *reasoning* with them for months. Where's that got us?"

It had gotten them stuck in a room with potentially unstable armed people. Obviously he couldn't voice that. "How long do you think we can hold out here?"

Jones didn't have a comeback for that. Hopefully he'd consider it, come to reason. "So we go down fighting," said Jones finally.

Or perhaps he wouldn't.

"What's that accomplish?" George tried to keep his tone neutral, but he might have let some condescension slip in. It was hard not to when the other man was acting like a child.

"We make a statement."

A *statement*. He wanted to mock the idea out loud but thought better of it. The man *did* have a gun, and after all, while a violent statement would accomplish nothing, he didn't exactly have a long list of wins himself. But then, his methods didn't get people killed. Or maybe they did. Maybe if he'd done more, they wouldn't be sending six hundred people to the surface of the planet. Maybe if he'd been more effective in another way, they wouldn't be stuck in a long, narrow room full of plants and increasingly fearful co-conspirators.

Being stuck here kind of felt like the rest of his life. He could see the problems, but they were complex, and the only solutions they had for them were simple. They needed planning and nuance and time but were stuck in a culture that demanded immediacy and action. Everybody wanted to fail right now in their own way instead of working together to cobble together something complicated that might actually work in the long term.

He wanted to scream, but he didn't have that luxury. If he lost it, others would, too, and at least two of those others were armed with deadly weapons. On the other hand, if he didn't do something immediately, someone outside of the closed room he now occupied would make the decision for them. Part of him wanted to let that happen. It would be easier. He wouldn't have to do anything but stand there and wait. But he wouldn't like that outcome.

The only good bit of all this was that at least Kayla wasn't there. He'd gotten that much right.

The green lights went out. The voices in the middle of the room started to murmur, and then to get louder, but George focused on another sound. Rather, a lack of sound. "Everybody shut up!"

The room went silent. Whether it was because they recognized his authority or he had just startled them didn't matter. Either way, it confirmed what he thought he'd heard. "You hear that?"

Nobody spoke for a second, and then Jones asked, "Hear what?"

"Nothing. There's no sound. They've cut off the vents."

That shouldn't have been possible. Not that fast. They'd have had to get someone in maintenance to bypass the fail-safes to stop airflow. Secfor couldn't have done that so quickly unless they'd cut off air to entire sections of the ship, which . . . they couldn't have done that. Could they? No. This was something else. But what? Panicked conversation erupted, and someone cut on a headlamp, casting the room in an eerie glow. George focused on Jones, who stared back at him.

"Fuck!" said Jones.

Yeah. Fuck indeed.

CHAPTER 39

MARK RECTOR

|||||||||||||||||||||||||||||||||||||||||||||||||||||||||||

1 CYCLE UNTIL ARRIVAL

Mark Rector stood a few meters back from where the medic was working on the downed Secfor officer. Danielson had gotten in the way of a bullet, and from the scream he'd let out when it hit him, it had hurt like nobody's business. In the simulations, it didn't seem nearly that bad. They'd been training with projectile weapons, both the handheld and the longer variety, in preparation for going to the planet. But they weren't supposed to be on the ship except for those that were designated for the surface. They were all locked up. Except apparently not.

His device hummed, and he checked the message.

> The fugitives are in compartment AD1061. They are
> locked in. Their oxygen is off.

That was it. No heading, no address. It was like his device itself was giving him the message, and it looked exactly like the one he'd received earlier that had tipped him off to the sabotage action in the first place.

He had almost ignored that one since he was focused on the

planet now, but he couldn't let it go, so he'd followed up on the
lead. He had suspicions about who sent it, but he couldn't prove
it—he didn't want to prove it. That would give him deniability
when he was questioned about it. And he *would* be questioned,
especially now that he had a man down bleeding on the deck. At
least it was Danielson, who kind of deserved it given his past actions. Not that Rector believed that the universe had any kind of
balance. Right now he had bigger problems. They'd captured one
of the saboteurs, who had run into a strut in the dark and knocked
themself out, but several more had escaped. If he could believe
the message, though—and he did—those were locked up in an
oxygenation room and waiting for him. Another thing he'd have
to explain when questioned.

His device hummed again, startling him. It was Darvan, on
voice. He debated letting it buzz out but picked up after a few
seconds.

"What the fuck is going on?"

"A group of radicals attempted to sabotage the landing ships.
We stopped them. I called it in."

"I'm *aware* that you called it in. What I want to know is why
the governor is on my ass about it."

"No idea. I didn't tell him."

"Well, he wants to see you. Now."

"He knows?" No way should he have heard about this yet—
unless they both had the same source. If he could get an untrace-
able message, he supposed the governor could, too. "Can you tell
him I'm a little tied up? The culprits have escaped, and we have to
track them down."

"I am not telling the *governor* to *wait*. Put somebody else in
charge and get your ass up there now."

It was stupid for him to come off of the mission now, but

Darvan wasn't going to back off, so it was pointless to argue. "Roger that." He motioned Vasquez over to join him. "They've holed up in compartment AD1061. Go make sure they don't get out, but don't enter until I give you the word."

"You're leaving?"

"No choice." Rector tapped his device.

"Ah. The boss. But now?"

"What can you do?"

She shrugged. "How do you know where they're holed up?"

Rector looked meaningfully at his device again. It wasn't a lie. She'd just assume that it also came from the boss. Let her think that.

"Got it. Okay, I'm on it. Good luck."

"You too."

THE GOVERNOR WAS ALONE IN HIS OFFICE WHEN HE ARRIVED, AND Rector had to make his way through the darkened outer office using the light from the inner as a guide. He stood in the doorway for a moment, watching the older man pace for several seconds before speaking. "You wanted to see me?"

"What the fuck did you do?"

Rector stared at him. "Broke up an attempted sabotage of all the landing craft."

"Why are there guns on my ship?"

Rector hesitated, still staring. The governor knew the answer to his question. "You authorized the printing of weapons for the expedition, which leaves in"—he checked his device—"about thirty hours. We had to print them ahead of time, obviously."

Governor Pantel stopped pacing and glared. "I know that. How did they get into the hands of people opposed to the mission?"

"I'd like to know that, too." He'd also have liked to know how the governor had found out about it so quickly, but it would be a bad idea to ask. In the past, Rector would have been his source, but those days were gone. Obviously, the governor had replaced him in that role.

"There are two ways that I can think of immediately," Rector went on. "Either someone used the print authorizations to make extra weapons, or someone got into the locked storage where the original weapons were kept." He paused, in case the governor wanted to interject, and when he didn't, Rector continued. "Before you called me off the pursuit, I was planning to have somebody check the storage. We serial-numbered the weapons for inventory control purposes. But . . ." He gestured to the room around him, as if to say, *I'm here instead.* Or, rather, *But you got in the way.*

"Don't you blame this on me," said Pantel.

Rector put his hands up in defense. "I'm not. Somebody did this. We'll find out who. I just need time to work it."

"We're running out of time. You have duties."

"I do. And we also have fugitives that I need to go dig out from deck AD."

The governor snapped his head around at that. "You know where they are?"

"We have a good idea, yes." That the governor *didn't* know answered a question as well. He wasn't getting the same anonymous tips.

"You know *who* they are?"

"Not yet. But given that I know where, figuring out who isn't a huge obstacle."

"Deck AD is mostly oxygenation, right? That's a lot of space."

Rector winced. In giving away that information, he'd set himself up to have to share more, or the governor would keep digging, and he couldn't assume that his anonymous tipster would wait forever. "We know what compartment they're in."

He expected the man to immediately ask which one, but the governor thought about it and then smiled. "How do you know *that*?"

"We got an anonymous tip."

"After the fact."

"That's right."

He thought some more, and Rector wished that he knew what machinations were running through the politician's brain. He was plotting something, and there was no way to be sure it was good news for Rector. He had no illusions anymore when it came to that: he was expendable. It should have bothered him. Maybe it did a little, but in truth he'd already moved on to the next thing. "How do you know they're still there?"

There was nothing for that but the truth, Rector supposed. "The report is that they're sealed in."

"Sealed in? That should be impossible."

Rector shrugged. "That's the tip."

"So . . . someone on their own side betrayed them?"

"That does seem to be the most likely scenario," said Rector. *And thank you very much for that escape hatch.*

"I want to know who."

"Again, so would I."

"There has to be some way to trace an anonymous tip."

Rector shook his head. He didn't want to go down that path. "This is how anonymous tips work. If we could trace them, we wouldn't get them."

Pantel considered it. "Okay. But let's make an effort here. If there are fractures inside the opposition, I want to exploit them."

"Sure. I'll put our best cyber people on it."

The governor continued as if Rector hadn't spoken. "After all, you're going to the surface. I'll be up here with all the people who want to destroy our way of life, so I'll need all the help I can get without you here to look out for me."

It was bullshit, but Rector didn't smile. He did his best not to react at all. The governor was buttering him up, trying to make him feel good, and it would have worked before. *Had* worked before. Not anymore. It was unusual of Pantel to slip up like that. Maybe he didn't have as much control as Rector thought. He'd save that thought for later. Right now, he had a job to do. "So it's probably best if I get back to capturing the bad people."

The governor thought for several uncomfortable seconds before nodding. "Sure. Report to me directly when you've got names. I might want to talk to them once they're in cells."

"Sure thing, Governor."

RECTOR WENT BY THE WEAPONS LOCKER AND THEN FOUND VASQUEZ right where he hoped, on deck AD at 1060, standing right outside 1061. She'd positioned another element in 1062, outside the only other door to the sealed room. The rich smell of plants and water permeated the entire area, giving a peaceful feel to a situation that was somewhat less than that, though the team seemed calm enough. Nine Secfor officers stood in clumps of twos and threes, chatting, as if there wasn't part of an armed insurrection in the very next room. But with the doors locked, they might as well be on another ship. Nothing was getting through the bulkhead.

"Have you tried the doors?" he asked.

Vasquez shook her head. "You told us not to do anything. We didn't do anything."

"Good. Thanks."

"Yeah, no prob. What *do* we do, though?"

He reached into a pocket and pulled out a metal cylinder with a round pull tab, held it up for her to see. "Gas grenade."

"Where the fuck did you get that?"

"Part of the kit for the planetary expedition."

"*Why?*"

He shrugged. "Never know what we might need." What he didn't say was that it seemed cool, so he'd added it to the requisition. That seemed too . . . something.

"So it'll kill them?"

"It should just knock them out." He hoped. It hadn't been tested, and it was designed for use outside. The concentrated amount that might occur in a sealed compartment . . . he couldn't be sure. But what choice was there? They couldn't charge in when the other people had guns, and if he waited for them to asphyxiate, it would take hours and then they'd get no answers.

"Okay. So how do we not get the same effect when we go in?"

Rector nodded to the emergency compartment that held two helmets. "We suit up."

Vasquez considered that. "They have one of those boxes, too."

Rector smiled in spite of himself. Vasquez was smart when she was focused, and she was focused now. Watching someone get shot would do that, apparently. "Right. But I have to think that they probably aren't expecting us to gas them. Would it have occurred to you?"

"Nope. I didn't even know it was possible."

"So we hope it doesn't dawn on them. And if it does? Well, we deal with it when we get there."

"I don't suppose when you were at the armory you got one of those bang bangs, did you?" she asked.

"Of course I did."

"Then let's go."

<CHAPTER 40>

GEORGE IANNOU

||||||||||||||||||||||||||||||||||||||||||||||||||||||||||||||

1 CYCLE UNTIL ARRIVAL

George awoke on the floor, and even before he opened his eyes, his nose told him that he wasn't in the room full of plants. Gone was the rich, heavy air, replaced by the smell of piss and body odor and . . . something. His head pounded the way it had the few times when he'd drank too much, and his mouth tasted like a dirty sock that someone had worn on a hard day of farm work. He pushed himself to a sitting position to get a better look, opened his eyes, and thought better of it as the lights burned holes into his brain. He tried squinting and finally adjusted. A chorus of groans told him that others were waking as well. There were five of them in the cell, four on the floor and one propped up on a bench in the corner. At least this time he deserved his incarceration.

He forced himself to stand, though it took him a minute or more to get there, and he wove his way through the prone bodies to reach the bars. He stumbled, his foot catching on somebody's boot.

"Hey! Watch it!"

"Sorry," George mumbled. He grabbed the bars, shook them a little, for whatever that was worth. "Hey! Guard!" Nothing. "Hey, we're awake! We could use some water!"

"Shut the fuck up," came a female voice from somewhere around the corner, out of view. There was no malice in it. Maybe annoyance. He wondered what time it was, how long they'd been out. The last thing he remembered was about 0320, when one of the doors opened a crack and something clanked on the floor and started hissing. It must have been some sort of incapacitating gas, though he'd never heard of Secfor having something like that. All in all, it might have been the best possible outcome, because with some of his people armed, he hadn't foreseen a nonviolent solution.

There were two cells. Five of them were in this one, so the other four were probably in the other. That would mean they were at least all alive, not counting the one who hadn't made it to the oxygen room in the first place.

That they were in trouble seemed obvious. How much remained to be seen. George shouted again for water, but this time nobody even bothered to answer. Others were stirring, rising from their death poses on the floor, stretching, licking their lips, looking like shit.

"What happened?" asked Jones.

"I think they gassed us."

Jones came close and lowered his voice. "How fucked are we?"

"Pretty fucked, I'd guess." He wanted to add that they'd be a lot less fucked if Jones hadn't brought a *gun*, but it didn't seem productive at the moment.

"Iannou," someone called from outside the cell. It sounded like the same woman who had told him to shut up before.

"Yeah." George moved to the front of the cell.

"Everyone else step back," said a Secfor woman of medium height and medium build, with short hair and a wide nose. There was nobody else near the door, but a couple people backed away anyway. The fight had left them. The Secfor officer touched her wrist pad and the door opened. "Come with me."

George did as she said. Still a bit groggy, he stumbled slightly over the base of the door. She led him through an office with several workstations, only two of which were occupied, and she deposited him in a small room with a single table and three chairs. He'd been there before. It didn't surprise him that they called him first for interrogation. His escort shut the door behind him, giving him free rein over the small space, but maybe that was meant to put him at ease or something. He walked around anyway, checking each side of the room, but it didn't take long. The mirror was probably two-way, and nothing else in the room bore mention at all beyond the two cameras. He waved at one, and then took a seat in the single chair, leaving the side with two chairs for whoever came in to talk to him.

The door opened maybe ten minutes later—he couldn't be sure exactly—and it was not whom he expected. He stood. "Governor."

"Mr. Iannou. We meet again, though under stranger circumstances, I'd say."

George shrugged. What was he going to say? That the governor was here himself seemed significant, though at the moment he couldn't decide if it was better or worse than having it be a straight Secfor issue. If nothing else, the governor probably wanted something, which meant there was a chance to negotiate, even though it seemed like he didn't have any leverage.

"You seem to make a habit of showing up here," said the governor.

"What can I say? Someone has to oppose the forces of oppression." He kept his tone light, only partly serious. They were Kayla's words, not his.

"Please. Sit." Pantel looked around the room without bothering to hide his . . . disgust? Annoyance? Something. He didn't want to be here any more than George did.

"I didn't expect to see you here," George said, to see if he could get the governor talking.

"I didn't, either. I asked to have you brought to my office, but Secfor declined, citing security concerns."

George grunted. "You'd think being the governor, they'd do what you told them to."

"You'd think. But"—he gestured around—"apparently not."

"But you're their boss." George was genuinely curious. If he had to be here, learning something more about how the governor and Secfor worked together—or didn't—couldn't hurt.

"That I am. Perhaps I'll remind them of that soon. But right now, we've got a lot going on, as I'm sure you know." He took a seat across from George, looking like he thought he might catch something from the chair. "They say they're not listening in, but I don't believe that for a second."

"You must have wanted to talk to me pretty badly to put up with all this," George offered, poking at the wound a little.

"Yes. Well, your attempt to sabotage the landing failed, but I do expect that someone will try again, and I'll do whatever it takes to stop them."

"They don't have very long."

"They don't. And we can at least keep your coconspirators locked up until after the expedition has reached the surface. But I'm sure there are others out there."

He seemed as if he was leading somewhere, but so far George couldn't figure out where. "Probably. I couldn't say for sure."

"Couldn't, or wouldn't?"

He had a better idea now of where they were headed. "Does it matter?"

"I think so," said Pantel. "I think you could, if you wanted to."

"Maybe." He certainly wouldn't do it for free. Pantel knew that. They were starting their negotiation.

"I'm going to work on the assumption that you could stop it if you wanted to."

George couldn't hold in the snort of laughter. "As you said a minute ago, you'd think, but you'd be wrong. My influence is even more tenuous than yours."

"Let me rephrase it. I think, if I wanted to make sure that nothing else happened in the next twenty-four hours, you could give me the names of some people who, if they were . . . let's say . . . kept busy . . . their absence would greatly reduce the chance of an event."

George considered it. Could he? If they detained Tanaka or Acevedo, would that stop further action, or would it just decentralize it? Rector knew at least a bit about Tanaka, which should mean the governor knew. Except he'd just made it clear that he and Secfor weren't completely in sync.

Did any of this even matter? Could he turn them in, even if he thought it would help—which he still wasn't convinced of? It wouldn't go well for him if he snitched and they found out about it. And they *would* find out. It had been hard enough after he and Rector struck their deal to throw the scent off him. If people thought he talked to the governor, it wasn't just political suicide—it might be *actual* suicide. There were enough people on the fringe who saw this as so black-and-white that he couldn't rule out an attempt on his life. Eventually George said, "What are you specifically asking me?"

The governor answered immediately. "I want to know who I can arrest to make sure that nothing else bad happens on the ship for the next two cycles."

George nodded. "It's complicated."

"Complicated how? It doesn't seem complicated to me. We remove the radicals until the expedition's launch. It's not even two cycles."

"And what happens after that? You just let them go?"

"Yes."

"I don't believe you." The governor started to interrupt, but George pressed on. "More important, nobody *else* is going to believe you. Or, rather, they're not going to believe *me* when I tell them that."

"I could leave you locked up, make it seem like you're not part of it."

"I'm afraid you blew that option the minute you walked in here with me."

The governor's face fell. "I see. I should have thought of that."

"It would have been easier if you had."

"Secfor got me," he said ruefully.

George stared. "You think they did it on purpose? To keep us from making a deal?"

"I wouldn't put it past them. Tell me this, then. Where did you get the guns?"

"I didn't. I didn't know we had them until someone started using them."

Pantel studied him. "I believe you. They were stolen from the Secfor armory by an insider, if that helps you place it."

"It doesn't." That was somewhat of a lie. He had suspected they'd come from the printer, probably through a contact that did jobs for them there. That Acevedo had someone inside of Secfor was new information, but it did explain some things. "That insider thing here, though . . . seems like something you might want to deal with."

"Secfor is handling it internally for now. My help is . . . not welcome."

"Sure. We've all got troubles."

"As you say."

"So what are we doing here?" asked George.

"I think it's time we help each other with those troubles. Your people had guns. If they can get those, what else might they be able to get, and what might happen to the ship when they do? This is bigger than just the mission down to the planet. This could mean the end of all of us."

"That seems like hyperbole."

"There was a bomb, once. There could be another."

"It didn't do any permanent damage."

"You're not really that naïve, are you? Are you saying that you trust the people involved not to take things too far?" He paused. "Because I don't think you feel good about that, and the look on your face tells me I'm right."

He *didn't* trust those people at all, but that didn't mean he trusted the governor. "While I could certainly give you a few names, I honestly don't know all of them, and even if I could put my finger on everyone who might have been a threat before, hearts change. This might come as a surprise, but they don't exactly trust me."

The governor laughed. "I suppose they wouldn't. If it makes you feel any better, I can sympathize."

"Considering you put me in this position in the first place, I'm sure you can."

"I was doing what I thought was right."

"And look where that got us," George said, gesturing at the room they both were in.

"Touché."

"So where does that leave us?"

"It leaves us where you can still give me something. Someone. Anything that will help."

"What good will two cycles do?"

"Once we've landed on the planet, there's no more reason for protest. It's over. People will see our success, and those who are against the mission will fade away."

George found himself almost believing it, which then made him question himself, because the governor really hadn't said anything of substance. The question was, who did he trust more: the governor or the fringe elements of his movement? And the answer, no matter how many times he considered it, was that he didn't trust either of them. The governor would lie to him in a second. But the governor wouldn't damage the ship. Not physically. So how did he give the governor the help he needed without getting in trouble? "I'd need assurances."

"You mean you need a payoff."

"Call it what you want." He was honest enough with himself to know what he was doing. He wondered if the governor could say the same.

"Name them."

"No executions."

"Of the people you name? Done."

"Of *anybody*."

"Anybody? Ever?"

George thought about how to define it so the governor couldn't twist it. "Nobody detained from this and nobody you detain in the next fifteen cycles."

The governor drummed his fingers on the table as he thought. "I'm not sure I can do that."

"Then we have nothing else to say to each other." They did, of course—there was so much that they needed to say. George just couldn't give on that. Because if he was going to later sell the idea that he traded some names for more important gains, that was one assurance he had to have. *I did it to keep everybody alive* would play much better than the gains he actually wanted. The thing he was about to hold up the governor to get. Because the man wouldn't be here if he had a better option. So despite appearances, George had the upper hand in this negotiation. If he'd been in a neutral location, he'd have started to walk out to emphasize the point, but here, all he could do was sit and wait. He didn't have to wait long.

"Nobody is executed except the two who used guns," countered the governor.

George pretended to consider it. "I can't do it. I'm sorry. I have to be able to show that making a deal with you was worth it. No executions is part of that."

"You're being unreasonable," said Pantel.

George remained silent, kept his face impassive.

"Fine. No executions. Give me some names."

George shook his head. "We're not done."

"You want more? Of course you do." The flat look the governor gave him could have meant anything, but George chose to take it as him realizing that he'd stumbled into a pile of mud.

"Not much. Just what we've been asking for all along. I want an end to scheduled deaths."

"If I give you that, it looks like I'm caving to terrorists."

"So spin it. That's what you do, right? You're sending hundreds of people to the planet tomorrow, which will open up resources here on the ship. You can use that to tell the story any way you want to." Pantel was going to do it anyway. George might as well get something out of it.

The governor considered it. "So you're not demanding that I say it's a concession."

"You can say whatever you want. I can spin it my own way, too."

"No scheduled deaths for a period of two years," said the governor.

George thought for a moment. Two years was a start, but he needed more. "With a formal review period at the end of those two years with public findings, not to be decided by the governor."

"Fine. Deal. Now give me the names that will protect the ship."

George did.

BY THE TIME THEY RELEASED HIM FROM LOCKUP, HE WAS SUPPOSED to be at work. There was no way that was happening. He hadn't slept other than being knocked out by the gas, and he wouldn't make it through the day. What were they going to do, write him up for missing a day of work? They would probably fine him. He didn't care. He showered and then fell into a deep sleep, and didn't wake until Kayla came home from her own workday. Even in the confusion of waking at an odd time, he knew she was pissed from the set of her shoulders, the way she stomped around the room. If he'd needed an answer to whether the governor had made his detentions and whether word had gotten out about him being the source, he had it.

"You want to talk about it?" he asked.

"No."

"Okay. Let me know—"

"You snitched!" Apparently she *did* want to talk about it.

"I didn't have a choice."

She shook her head. "You always say that."

"Doesn't mean it isn't true. If I hadn't given names, people were going to be rounded up anyway. And some—if not all—of those they already had would have faced potential execution. Somebody *shot* someone. With a *gun*."

"So you joined the other side for that. There's *always* a choice." She grabbed a meal from the cupboard and slammed it into the heater.

George swung his feet out of bed and sat up. "Not a good one, and when there's no good choice, I'm predisposed to no deaths as a decent outcome. Including no more mandatory death dates. How hard have we been pushing for that?"

She glared, hands on her hips. "Meanwhile we ship six hundred people down to rape the planet or die, or both."

"That wasn't on the table. It wasn't changing."

"It might have."

"It wasn't!" He said it a little too loudly, but she wouldn't hear him, and he was frustrated. "Over 70 percent of the crew supports the landing."

She made a dismissive gesture with her hand, shooing them away. "Robots who believe the lies that the governor feeds them."

"People," said George, but she'd turned away. He wanted to press the argument, make her understand, but it was pointless. She was so convinced that she was right, nothing would penetrate. She was an idealist living in a pragmatic world, willing to pass up the chance to make a little bit of progress for the false dream of the perfect solution. He'd done all he could do given the reality of what he had to work with. He couldn't build an omelet out of mud. Hopefully in time she wouldn't hate him for it.

CHAPTER 41

MARK RECTOR

||||||||||||||||||||||||||||||||||||||||||||||||||||||||||||||||||||||

ARRIVAL CYCLE

The simulator didn't prepare Mark Rector for the jostling of entering the atmosphere, and he had to hold back a yelp of surprise. He tried to keep his face impassive, keep his body language neutral. There were two hundred people on his lander, and at least fifty of them could see him. The last thing he needed as a leader was for them to see him falter. His situation was precarious enough as it was, and while he fully expected to get the credit and notoriety for the mission's success, he had no illusions that he'd get the blame if it went poorly. That's how these things worked. Risk and reward. Well, he'd taken the risk now, and there was nothing to do but see it through to the reward. He'd studied everything he could, but he couldn't understand the science, and he didn't want to look weak by asking the people who wrote it to put it into more basic terminology.

Pathogens and viruses he understood. Transmission mechanisms and incubation models, not so much. Hopefully it wouldn't come to that, and if it did, he'd rely on the scientists he had with him. A good leader wasn't afraid to use the smart people around him. There was no reporter on the mission—the news back on the ship would rely on his reports—so he could spin things the way he wanted as the mission commander. He'd made sure to put someone loyal in charge of communications. Nobody had seen it as a key position, but they just weren't thinking. He'd also picked his own team from Secfor: Mwangi and Sierks. They were from the newer batch, but at least they were the best of them. He had two of Cecil's people on board that he knew of, but even that was fine. There was always going to be a black market. At least now he knew where to look for it.

He studied the faces of the people directly across from him on the lander, as much as one could with helmets on. There was oxygen and a clean environment on the ship, but for the landing itself they wore their gear anyway. Just in case.

"Landing in ten minutes," announced the pilot across the main net to everybody. As mission commander, Rector heard communications back to *Voyager* as well, and from what he could tell, so far, everything was perfect. So why were his palms still sweating? He focused on his breathing, not wanting to hyperventilate. He ran through in his mind what he'd say when he stepped onto the planet for the first time. The first person to step foot on Promissa. The other two landers were staggered and would land five and ten minutes after theirs. There was a hierarchy, and he was at the top of it for the first time in his life. *Today we begin a new era of human existence.* Short, powerful, easy to print on a monument. That was what he'd say.

"Landing in five minutes."

"Any unforeseen issues?" he asked the pilot on a private channel.

"All systems green."

That was a relief, what with all of the other things that they'd sent to the planet losing communications. They still had them, as well as three different backup systems in case they lost their primary means. They were as prepared as they could be. He closed his eyes and continued to take measured breaths, consciously relaxing the muscles in his neck, legs, and arms, waiting for the next announcement.

"Beginning final descent." The ship held its collective breath. Or at least, Rector imagined that they did. He did, that's for sure.

"Touchdown," said the pilot, his words punctuated by a gentle thud. The ground.

Nothing happened for a second, and then the entire passenger compartment erupted in a cheer over the net. Rector snapped himself into focus and keyed his mic, overriding the noise. "Okay, we'll take a five-minute break to look around from inside the ship and get ourselves together before first steps."

The original plan had called for fifteen minutes, expecting people to be overcome by the moment, but he'd insisted on changing it. He didn't trust the other landing parties to hold to the timeline, worried that one of them would be the first to touch the surface. It was petty, but nobody remembered the person who was second to do anything. He was risking everything for this chance, and he was going to be first.

Five minutes passed faster than he could have imagined, and he found himself in the airlock—the smaller one, for personnel only. There was a big one at the back for use in offloading equipment, though most of that would come on the later, uncrewed landers. One would be down in thirty minutes, with another following the next cycle in a choreographed order so they had exactly the materials they needed, right when they needed them. He took a cleansing breath and hit the control panel to flip the lock on the outer door, and then hit the second sequence to open it. The door whooshed open, and suddenly he was staring at . . . everything. Brightness and green and vastness and . . . green. So much green.

He stood there as the stairs descended and just took it in.

They'd landed in an open area covered with knee-high grass that swayed in the gentle wind—or what he assumed was a wind, since he couldn't actually feel it through his suit. About seventy meters in front of him, a wall of more green mixed with some brown rose to the sky. Trees and bushes and any number of other things he couldn't even name. He followed them up and up, and there was the sky, blue flecked with white clouds, and so big. And the star. The brightest thing he'd ever seen, even though his face shield darkened to dampen it. And then he was dizzy, his head spinning. *Don't look up.* That had been drilled into them. Even with the simulator practice and the drugs, the openness of the planet was going to be an issue. He focused on his feet, on the stairs in front of him, on the ground, until things stopped spinning and he could breathe.

He needed to move, and he thought he could now, at least if he held on to the railing as he went. Fifteen steps down. That's all it was, and he'd be the first human on a planet outside of the original solar system. He went slow, testing each step before he took it, holding tight to the railing, making sure. Stumbling down the steps would go down in history as sure as his first words would. More, even. He'd never recover from that humiliation.

Finally, he was there, standing at the bottom step, the grass burned completely away in that area from the engines of the lander. They'd sprayed fire suppression material as they landed to keep it from being worse, though he couldn't see any evidence of it. He keyed his mic to make his proclamation just before he took the final step.

The display in his suit went dead.

He stepped anyway, the ground giving only a little, harder than he expected from looking at pictures. "Lander, this is—" He released the mic, keyed it again. The flat sound of his own voice told him he wasn't transmitting.

It had to be his suit.

"Lander, this is Rector." He paused several seconds.

No response.

"Lander, I repeat, this is Rector. Come in." A cold sweat broke out on his neck, and he shivered despite the rising temperature in his suit. Rising temperature. He tried to manually reboot his suit, get his display working, but it wouldn't even receive his input. More immediate to his concern, it wasn't circulating air.

His mind raced. No air. How long would the suit keep him breathing without power? They'd gone over this in training. Nine minutes. If he conserved. He'd start to feel the effects in four minutes, and that was without the panic that was grabbing at his heart and lungs.

Breathe.

He forced himself to control his breathing, silently thankful for the practice he'd done on that. *Okay. Don't panic.* Easier said than done. He needed an assessment, a course of action. He could continue on, wait for the person scheduled to follow him out the airlock in two minutes. He could make it that long.

He turned and hurried back up the stairs, stumbled halfway up but caught himself, forced himself back to his feet, and covered the final steps. He reached for the panel on the side of the door with a shaking hand, stopped, thought to check for the green light that would tell him the inner door was closed. The outer wouldn't open if it wasn't.

There was no light. No green light, but no red light, either. No lights on the panel at all. He pushed at it.

Nothing.

Think, Rector. Was the ship dead, too? He had no way of knowing, but it seemed possible. Likely, even. *Okay, what do you do in case of power loss to the airlock?*

Manual check. He looked in the window, there for expressly that purpose. The room was dark and, from what he could tell, empty. There was no face staring out at him, and if someone was in there, he had to believe that they'd be staring out. Slowly—slower than truly necessary—he began the three-step process to manually open the outer hatch. He undid the lock; he rotated the handle. He stopped before opening it. *Please let this be the right thing to do.* He wrestled open the door, which was heavier than he expected. He bent his knees and grunted with the effort. *So much for conserving oxygen.*

He didn't get it open all the way, electing instead to squeeze through as soon as he could. He'd have to manually close it, and that would save time. Time. How much time did he have with his oxygen? His mind was already becoming foggy, but was that physiological or in his head? Inside, he closed the door, rotated the handle, engaged the manual lock. Now he . . . what? Waited for the air to vent, for the light to come on indicating it was safe to open the inner door.

But there was no light. And no air rushing in.

He moved to the inner door, pressed his face to the window. He could see people moving, vague shapes in the low light where it should have been lit.

There was no power on the ship.

He took a minute to assess what he was seeing, realized the low light was from small, battery-operated emergency beacons. A beam cut across, blinding him momentarily. Somebody had a handheld flashlight. After that, the activity changed, focused, moved toward him. On the other side of the door, two people argued. He couldn't hear them, but he could see their faces. Dr. Jackson and Mwangi. He didn't know what they were arguing about, but he could guess that it was whether to bring him in or not. He didn't need to be a genius to know who was arguing which side.

He found that he didn't blame Jackson. It wouldn't be personal. Not with her. Scientifically she'd be arguing that the air in the airlock right then was contaminated. Because it was. There wasn't a manual vent. Nobody had even considered the possibility of going outside without power.

"Hey!" he yelled, but even as he did, he knew it wouldn't carry. Not through his helmet and the door.

Did they have oxygen inside? If all the power was down, could they refresh it? They had tanks. If nothing else, they could open valves manually and breathe that way. But they couldn't scrub the CO_2. Training had taught him that that's what would kill them.

His mission was falling apart—there was no other way to look at it. He'd wanted to be in charge, wanted the glory, and now everything rested on him. With no power, they couldn't call for help. They did have redundant communications, but not from within the ship if it didn't have power. They needed to get outside to set that up. There was an entire planet with an atmosphere filled with all the oxygen they could ever need, right outside the door.

But it might kill them.

Here in the ship, with no oxygen, with CO_2 building up with every minute they waited . . . that *would* kill them. There was no doubt about it. When faced with *might die* and *would die*, there was only one real answer. He disengaged the manual clamps that held his helmet on and removed it.

He set it on the floor and then pounded his fist against the window to the inner door. "Hey!"

The arguing people stopped and turned to him.

He pointed to his face and mouthed the words *I'm your test subject.*

<CHAPTER 42>

JARRED PANTEL

||||||||||||||||||||||||||||||||||||||||||||||||||||||||||||||||

ARRIVAL CYCLE

Pantel hated the command deck. He had never liked it, with its low gravity that made you feel like you were going to fly away at any moment. He liked it less now with the entire crew sneaking peaks at him when they thought he wasn't looking and Captain Wharton sitting there, imperious in her big chair on her raised platform. The weight of the blame was almost palpable.

He hated it more that he couldn't hide from it. It had been his decision to send all three landing expeditions instead of waiting for results from one. Now, with two of them complete and both without communications, the third was almost down. They'd given him an earpiece so that he could listen in on their communications. It hadn't been lost on him that they had not given him a microphone.

Wharton's voice broadcast into it, "Comms, where are we with lander three?"

"Still five by five."

"Roger," she said. "Telemetry, where are we on figuring out what happened to comms on the other two?"

"We're not, ma'am. We had data coming in and it was perfect—no indication of any issues—and then it just stopped with no explanation or cause."

He could abort it, maybe, pull lander three back and at least save that much. But that meant talking to the captain, and the decision authority wasn't clear. He'd ordered the mission, but once he ordered it, she owned it. The lander pilots worked for her and would take her orders. He didn't even have the means to talk to them without her say-so. He should have sat down with her ahead of time and worked out contingencies for this sort of situation, but their relationship at this point didn't allow for that. They were as much competitors as colleagues, and that was largely his doing. He could admit that. But he'd been so sure that going down to the planet in numbers was the right thing to do. It might still be. But he was a lot less sure about that now than he had been an hour ago. He paced toward the back of the room, as if staying as far as possible away from the crew might change something.

"Touchdown, Lander Three," announced a feminine voice. There were no cheers this time, the way there had been for the first lander. Everybody was waiting.

"Comms are still green," said the same man who had given the bad news about the other landings.

Pantel thought about how he could have done it differently. They could have sent a single ship, had the engineers try to figure out the problem before sending more, but it came back to the same political calculus. If he didn't get enough people to the ground, they'd lose momentum. If the first landing failed, there would be no more. Even now, with things looking bleak, at least they were committed. With six hundred people on the surface, there would be no talk of cutting their losses. All their energy would be invested in making it work. It would bring people together, regardless of their political views. The best minds they had would be working the problem incessantly until they solved it, both here and on the surface. The landing parties had everything they needed to survive down there. That had been the plan from the start, and he had to trust it.

They'd get through this. They had to. A small part of him still held out hope for the third lander. Third time was the charm.

"We've lost them," reported the voice of doom.

Or not.

Pantel looked up. The captain had turned her chair around and was staring at him, so he walked over.

"So what now?" she asked. That she didn't say more said a lot for her. She could have said *I told you so.*

"We continue our launch schedule. We get the supplies to the surface so they have everything that they planned for, when they planned for it."

She considered it for a moment. "I agree."

Pantel was ready to defend his answer, and then surprised that he didn't have to. He almost asked if she was sure, but nothing in her tone had suggested she wasn't. "Good. What else do you recommend?"

"We can still see them. We've got satellites with good optics in geostationary orbit over each site, so we continue to watch. We've seen one person disembark so far, but that person retreated into the lander, and we've seen no movement at any site since then. So we wait."

"Right. We wait." Wait for what, though? It was more than communications. There was nothing to indicate any movement at all. Did they just sit there and wait to see if anybody came out?

"We definitely don't send any more people to the surface." Her tone changed with that, as if daring him to contradict her.

He wouldn't. He didn't need to. "We may have already lost six hundred lives. We don't need to lose more."

"Agreed," said Pantel.

Wharton's shoulders relaxed at that, as if she'd been prepared for him to argue. "Good. We'll still need to set down the second lander at each site to get them their initial setup equipment, but we'll do it with the minimum possible crew. For tomorrow's supplies we'll shift to the contingency plan where we drop things by parachute."

"Great." Pantel relaxed slightly, glad that she'd put that contingency in place. She'd thought through things that he hadn't. That was her job, of course, but he was still appreciative. If the two of them could reestablish a reasonable working relationship, at least something positive would have come from this disaster. "Can we agree on emergency operations?" Emergency operations would let them go to twelve-hour shifts for all crew, and it took both of them to make that decision.

"Yes, but let's set a duration. Five cycles? We can extend later if we need to. I think any more than that and we just cause panic."

"Five cycles is fine," said Pantel.

"And we need to start figuring out a way to recover people off the surface and a way to quarantine them once we get them."

"Absolutely not," said Pantel without hesitating.

She started to respond, realized she was speaking too loudly and lowered her voice. "My office."

Pantel didn't want to be alone with her where she'd be able to vent on him, but he wanted to be in front of the crew even less, so he followed her as she stomped off. The minute they were through the door of her office, she rounded on him. "You rushed this, and you did it on purpose. I didn't stop you, even though I should have. I should have locked you in a fucking wall locker to prevent this."

"Do you have a point, or do you just want to attack me?" he asked.

"The point is, we've got six hundred souls down there, and we're not going to abandon them."

"We're not. We're sending them supplies."

She moved away from him, behind her desk, but she didn't sit, instead leaning over it, bracing herself on clenched fists, as if she wanted the barrier between them to hold herself back. "We have no idea what is going on, and we need to get them out of there."

"We've sent smart people down there, and we have to trust them to work the problem. It's our best chance of success."

"If we leave them there, the downside to that chance of success is that we're possibly just leaving them all to die."

Pantel shook his head, frustrated that she wouldn't see. "You said it yourself: we have no idea what's going on. We don't know if the landers can take off again or if they're stranded there. Until we do, it's premature to make a decision."

"The fact that they might be stuck is why we need something else ready to take on the job."

"Like what?"

"I don't know like what. But we've got an entire engineering department, and they should have been working on this weeks ago. I bet they can figure something out now."

Pantel considered it. He didn't want to do anything to draw away from making the mission a success, but he couldn't flat-out refuse the captain here. "Okay. We'll have engineering work the problem. But we're not pulling anybody off until we see more of what's going on."

"We should have had this contingency from the start."

"Well, *we* didn't."

She started to speak, then held back, appearing to rethink her words. "What do you think is going to happen on this ship when people find out what's happening down there?"

A chill ran through him. He didn't know, but polling said it wouldn't be good. Thirty percent of the crew had been opposed to the mission in the first place. That percentage would rise with adversity. The only questions were how much and to what extreme. "We need to keep it under wraps."

"We can try, but it *will* get out. People are going to expect news, and you can only lie for so long before they catch you."

"How long do you think I have?" he asked.

"The news is probably calling for updates already. People are probably waiting to hear someone joyfully sending their first words from the surface. When they don't get that? I suggest that you get back to your office and get yourself a whole bunch of security. I hope for your sake you didn't send them all to the surface."

He hadn't. He'd made more, knowing that he'd need them, but he didn't have enough to hold off a large-scale riot, which might happen if he didn't get in front of it. He didn't need to get to his office. He needed to get in front of a camera. He decided to float one more idea before he left. "We could lock down portions of the ship."

"We could. But that would mean martial law. You got us into this, and if you want me to get us out, that's what it's going to take. You let me know when you want to do that."

Martial law meant the captain was in charge, solely and un-equivocally. Pantel didn't know what he wanted to do, but he knew he didn't want that. Not yet. If it truly meant saving lives, he'd do it, but for a myriad of reasons he hoped that wouldn't be necessary.

CHAPTER 43

SHEILA JACKSON

||||||||||||||||||||||||||||||||||||||||||||||||||||||||||||||||||||||||

ARRIVAL DAY

Sheila stopped midsentence and turned toward the door, where Rector was pounding on the window and yelling. He'd taken off his helmet and mouthed some words that she couldn't understand. Mwangi started to say something to continue their argument, but Sheila put up her hand, forestalling them. "Dr. Darwish," she called.

A tall, thin man with a narrow chin made his way through the people who had gathered around her and Mwangi, watching them fight about a decision that affected them all. He was somewhat older than her, with gray shot through his beard.

"He's taken off his helmet," said Sheila.

Canton Darwish, the pathologist on their team, didn't respond but moved past her to the door. "So he has. He's not dead yet. That's a good sign."

"What should we expect?" asked Sheila. She wasn't technically in charge, even with Rector outside, but Mwangi, who theoretically was, wasn't up for the task, and they weren't complaining that she'd taken the lead. "You know—life expectancy wise."

"It's impossible to say. As I said, that he didn't immediately keel over is a good sign, but there are potential pathogens that could take weeks to kill him. Years, even. Get me an air sample and a lab and I can give you a better answer. A *much* better answer, possibly. But it's a foreign planet, so there's also the potential for a lot of things we don't know. You know this, Sheila. It's why we shouldn't be here."

"But we are."

"Yes, well . . . a medical doctor would be a better choice than me for assessing this man specifically."

"How long do we have before we run out of air in here?" asked Mwangi.

"I can't answer that," said Darwish.

"I can," said a short, stocky woman who pushed her way to the front of the watchers. She looked at Sheila as she spoke. "Jean Hescoe. Engineering. You look like you're the closest thing we have to someone in charge, so I might as well give my report to you."

Sheila glanced to Mwangi, then to Darwish. When neither made a move, she nodded to the engineer. "Go ahead."

"With the loss of power to all major systems, the critical function on the ship—the one that's going to kill us first—is the lack of CO_2 scrubbers. We've got seven to nine hours. Probably less than that before we feel the effects, but by nine hours, we're all dead."

Several people gasped, and a murmur ran through the onlookers. Hescoe was definitely an engineer—all answer, no compassion. And definitely no tact or voice modulation. Sheila looked to Darwish. "How much good will it do to observe Secfor Officer Rector for, say, six hours?"

"There's no point in it," interrupted Mwangi. "We're going to all be exposed anyway, so there's no sense delaying it. We need to bring him in now."

"The *point* in delaying is that it gives us six hours to get our systems back online . . ." She trailed off, as Hescoe shook her head. "What?"

"What I was about to tell you," said Hescoe, "is that we've isolated the problem with the ship and with the other systems in the ship. The chips are fried. The microprocessors."

"What could have caused that?" asked Sheila.

"Best guess is some sort of EMP. But it couldn't have been just one, because not everything broke at the same time. There were several seconds where some things had failed while others kept working. This stuff is designed for space where radiation is high, so in theory, an EMP shouldn't affect it."

"Someone on the lander did this?" asked Mwangi.

Not for the first time Sheila wished they weren't standing there and wished even more that so many people weren't paying rapt attention. They needed to work things out rationally and in short order, but the environment didn't lend itself to that. And they most certainly didn't need a twenty-year-old Secfor officer involved in the decisions.

"It doesn't seem likely," said the engineer, answering as if it was the most natural question ever asked. "Something powerful enough to do this . . . it's not something you can hide in your pocket."

"So what *did* cause it?" asked a man from the crowd. A farmer, if Sheila remembered him correctly. Things were getting away from her.

"At this point? We either have to assume it was a series of massive EMPs . . . or we have to allow the possibility that it's something we simply don't understand."

The room erupted into a cacophony of voices at that. An engineer admitting that they didn't know something . . . well . . . everyone knew that was bad.

"We need to focus," Sheila said, a little louder than she'd intended, and heads turned toward her. "We have limited time, and we have to make a decision that affects all of us, so we need to use that time judiciously."

"Knowing the cause would help us," the farmer said.

"It would help," said Sheila, "but right now we don't have any means to figure that out, so we've got to balance the need to figure out what happened with where we're at now."

"Can you fix it?" called another voice.

Hescoe turned her back to Jackson, facing the crowd. "We think we can fix a lot of it if we can replace the chips, but we don't have a significant supply of microprocessors, and those we did have are also damaged. We do have some that we shielded just in case we ran into something like this, and in theory, we could use those to bring key systems online. On the other lander we have solar panels that could provide power, and we have battery power for some things. Notably, we have the ship's batteries, which shouldn't be affected by this, but they are not functioning because of how they're integrated into the ship. We could slave off of them and potentially get some undamaged systems running for a while. But it will take time."

A murmur went up at that with a notable positive energy to it.

"However," continued Hescoe, "we don't want to do that until we can figure out a way to shield those chips." She stopped speaking, and for several seconds there was silence.

"Why not?" asked Sheila, voicing the question that was on everybody's mind.

"Because my theory is that this is some sort of natural phenomenon associated with the planet, and if we use things that were previously shielded, we're putting them at risk. So we want to solve that problem before we risk damaging our reserve parts. If it's truly an EMP, we should be able to protect our remaining equipment with Faraday cages, once we have time to construct them. The lander is shielded for radiation. It has to be if it's going to operate in space. But that didn't protect our equipment inside."

Sheila thought quickly. She had a few seconds to regain control over the discussion before it devolved, and she needed to take advantage of that. "Dr. Darwish," she said, with as firm a voice as she could manage. "You're the expert on the risks of microorganisms, which are our greatest risk after asphyxiation. Would you please give us your assessment of the situation?"

Darwish nodded and stepped forward, seeming to understand the task. They needed to keep the group calm. When he spoke, he projected so that everybody could hear him. "The chances that there is something on this planet that will make us sick is, statistically speaking, almost a hundred percent. But," he said louder, cutting off the groans from those listening, "the chance that it will kill us quickly is considerably lower than that. The chance that the danger is airborne is lower still. What that means is that if we open the door and allow in contaminated air, there's a reasonable chance that we will survive, and a strong chance that we will survive at least long enough to get medical help from the ship."

There was a leap in logic there that Sheila didn't point out—he was assuming they could get help from the ship. But it was giving people hope, and nobody else pointed out the problem.

"With our technology, if it's something that doesn't kill us immediately—and since Officer Rector is still standing in the airlock, it seems like it won't—then we probably have the ability to cure it."

When he stopped, the murmurs started back up, people whispering to each other. A woman raised her hand.

Darwish pointed to her. "Yes?"

"You said it probably won't kill us. But that doesn't mean it won't."

"That's correct. There are no guarantees except one. CO_2 buildup *will* kill us, though I don't know exactly at what levels that happens."

"I do." Another woman stepped forward, a bit taller than Sheila, with a pretty face and narrow shoulders. "Susan Ho. Medical. When CO_2 levels reach half a percent in the air mixture, it's going to start to have an effect on our cognitive function. At 10 percent, we're all in comas or dead."

Voices raised at that, though none that broke out from the general din of the crowd.

Sheila raised her voice to be heard. "So if Engineer Hescoe says we can't fix the ship and get the scrubbers working in short order, we're going to have to face the outside atmosphere before we hit those levels. But there are things we can do to mitigate our situation." She nodded to Darwish.

"Right. First, I need to set up a portable lab so that I can begin testing an air sample as quickly as we can get it. Unfortunately, most of what I need is on the other lander, so I'll need a team of people to go with me and work through unloading as fast as possible once it arrives."

"If it arrives," said Hescoe.

That flustered Darwish a bit, but he gathered himself quickly. "Right. If it arrives. If not, I'll try to create something makeshift. I have a manual microscope packed in our gear, but the computerized one in the follow-on package would help a lot."

Seeing that he was drifting, Sheila prompted him. "What other measures should we take?"

"What? Oh. Right. Uh . . ."

Susan Ho jumped in. "We have a limited supply of medical masks. Enough for everybody, but not enough to waste. Wear them. They will filter out a large percentage of potential pathogens."

"That's good," said Darwish. "Also, don't touch anything. I'll be testing the air first, and it will take time after that to test plants and other things for contact toxins or pathogens. If you *do* touch anything, wear gloves and be sure to decontaminate as quickly as possible. Use alcohol, preferably. We should gather whatever assets we can for that, and only touch things as absolutely necessary. This especially applies to plant and animal life, but treat everything as dangerous."

"That's good. We can do that," said Mwangi. "I'll put together a detail of people to hand out masks and consolidate decontamination materials, and we'll ensure that people decontaminate. What else?"

"Definitely don't eat anything that we didn't bring with us," said Ho. "That's the *greatest* risk. Incompatible proteins are very likely and could be deadly. They'll almost definitely make you sick."

"We've got another problem," said Hescoe. "Water."

"We brought water with us," said Mwangi.

"And we brought a recycler with us," said Hescoe. "One that won't work now. So once we use our current supply, it's gone."

"Okay," said Sheila. "We'll make water a priority along with the scrubbers. The mission briefing placed us within a kilometer of a water supply. Can we make that safe?"

"If it's fresh, we can probably make it safe by boiling it or treating it with chlorine or iodine," said Ho. "We'll need to check for chemicals, though."

"I can figure that out fairly quickly, even without computer help," added Darwish.

"Got it," said Jackson. "Mwangi, can you assign a team to look for the water supply?"

"I'll be on it," offered the farmer, and a couple others raised their hands, volunteering.

"Great," said Sheila. "Engineering, what are your priorities?"

Hescoe thought about it. "Communications is probably the most important thing after the scrubbers, right? Maybe even before, since we're going to be chancing the atmosphere anyway, and restarting the scrubbers after that might not be as important."

A lot of heads nodded at that, and Sheila had to agree. "I think so. We need to get word of our situation down here up to the ship so they can send us things that will work without microchips." She'd never considered how much they relied on technology until they didn't have it, but there were smart people up there. They could figure something out if they could communicate. "I think that's a good first priority."

"If nothing else, we should be able to rig up something primitive. With a battery and an LED, we can at least communicate via signal. Hopefully communications has a code they can use?"

"We do," announced a high-pitched voice from somewhere in the back.

"What about shelter?" asked Sheila.

"We've got the prefabs coming in the supply ship," offered a man from the back of the group. "I was supposed to work on those anyway. I'm not sure what parts of them will work and what won't, but we can probably at least get something together manually. And we can use the lander, since it's apparently not leaving."

There was a silent moment, and a pounding on the window of the airlock. Sheila moved closer to the door before anybody else could.

Let me in, mouthed Rector, exaggerating each word.

Sheila looked around for something she could write on, and somebody handed her a whiteboard. Where they'd got it from, she didn't know, but she was happy to have it. She wrote out a short message to him.

We're getting things together. It won't be long.

Once he'd had time to read it, she erased it and wrote more.

Working on testing the air. Shielding remaining
electronics.

She wiped it again, but before she could write anything else, someone tapped her on the shoulder.

"Do you mind?" Susan Ho held out her hand for the whiteboard, and Sheila handed it over. She didn't want to be in a conversation with Rector anyway, though she stayed close, just to monitor things.

How are you feeling?

Rector gave a thumbs-up.

Any shortness of breath?

He shook his head.

Pain in the nose, mouth, or throat?

Another shake of the head.

Eyes?

And another headshake.

Susan turned to Sheila. "That's about the best I can do from here. If there's no pain and no trouble breathing, he's either fine or the problem will build over time. Sorry I can't help more without actually examining him. But the body is pretty good about telling us when there's a problem."

"Thank you, Doctor—"

"Not a doctor. Medical practitioner. But I'm the closest thing you've got, and I can do the job. We left most of the actual MDs up on the ship. The thought was that we'd evac anything serious back to them. They're putting together a new quarantine ward."

Sheila nodded. "Thanks, Susan. I'm glad you're here." By the time she turned back to the others, everyone had spread out to prepare for their tasks.

She just wasn't sure *she* was glad to be here. Not anymore. The dream of exploration and new scientific discovery was one thing. The reality was something altogether different.

<CHAPTER 44>

EDDIE DANNIN

IIIIIIIIIIIIIIIIIIIIIIIIIIIIIIIIIIIIIIIIIIIIIIIIIIIIIIIIIIIIIIIIIII

ARRIVAL CYCLE

She was in the ship now more and more, though she wouldn't have said it that way. More like she was *with* it. She was a part of it. Or it was a part of her. It was complicated. She had to be careful not to get lost in there, which was easy to do. She'd stopped setting alarms for herself, or ignoring them when she did, and some days she connected immediately following work and stayed there deep into the night without realizing it until afterward. Even though she was part of the ship, she still had physiological needs.

She tried not to connect from work, though it would have made her job way easier. Instead, she tried to fit in and be like the other engineers. Well . . . not *exactly* like the other engineers. Like them, but better—she was done hiding that. They didn't like her anyway. But with several of them having gone with the landing parties, there was more work than those remaining could handle, so that meant more for her. Still no space walks, but she'd sort of given up on that dream. She had her own space now, anyway.

The announcement that they'd be going to twelve-hour shifts took a lot of people by surprise. Not Eddie. The ship's leadership was hiding news of the landing expedition from the general public, but they couldn't hide it from her. Not on her ship. She was listening in on the communications . . . and the lack thereof. She knew that they'd lost contact with the surface, and from there, the announcement of emergency measures was just a natural progression. And even though she had a unique source, she was sure it was just a matter of time before others heard, if they hadn't already. She didn't know the mood of the crew—that was a thing of people, and she admittedly didn't understand people very well—but extra work and lack of communication with friends on the surface of the planet wouldn't go over well. She'd have to be on extra alert for people who might want to harm her ship.

Mostly that had stopped. She'd blocked one half-hearted attempt earlier that week, but it was so minor that she didn't even bother to retaliate. She swatted it away like a cricket and let it go. They had learned. People trying to use code to harm the ship had come to understand that the ship had teeth, a protector, and that protector was ruthless in their work. If you came after the ship, the ship bit back.

At least everyone recognized that except Brewster.

She'd watched him and foiled his scheme to help destroy the landers and debated turning him in for it, but Rector was busy going to the planet and she didn't want to deal with another Secfor contact. Instead she kept watching him, and when he'd tried to infiltrate the power grid, she overloaded his terminal's circuits and physically blew out the chips. So far, he hadn't tried anything harmful again—not directly—but he was still active. She'd set up an AI to keep tabs on the wayward engineer. If he *did* try again, she'd be ready.

She put on her interface and sank back into her chair, let the ship join with her, wash over her. As an exercise, she stretched, reached to the outer parts of the ship, as far as she could, felt for the connections leaving it. She didn't experience things outside the physical ship the same as she did the internal. They were more like an extension. A part of it. A part of her. Maybe she could help them. After all, if she could reestablish communication with the elements on the planet, wouldn't that be protecting the ship? If angry people were a threat, easing their anger benefited them all.

So she stretched more. She left the vast confines of the hull, followed the connections outward to satellites. There were dozens of them, and their information was . . . odd. They spoke in a different way from the ship, and it took her a minute to synchronize with them. It was like trying a new food for the first time, one with unfamiliar tastes and smells and textures. It wasn't painful. It wasn't even unpleasant . . . just . . . new. She liked it.

Eddie tried to reach farther, down to the planet itself, but there was nothing there. She couldn't tell where it cut off or what was wrong. There was just . . . nothing. She found a satellite that spoke in pictures, in video, and that was more familiar, like accessing the cameras. The ship's eyes that were everywhere. The view looking down to the planet was different, but when she brought it close, she saw two landers in a large clearing, and then the view zoomed in. She didn't do it. Someone else was manipulating it, bringing her along for the ride without knowing it.

There were people moving around on the ground. On the *planet*. It was both fascinating and wondrous and something that didn't quite mean anything to her—Eddie's place was on the ship, up in space. Curiosity made her keep watching, though—she had the sense that it was important, even if she couldn't immediately parse why. She couldn't make out individuals, but they were definitely people, working at various tasks. Mostly they swarmed around the two landers, but a few ranged outward.

She wanted to get closer, wondered if she could. Clearly others were watching this, too, and they controlled the view. She wanted to take it from them. Not because there was something she wanted to see, but because she wanted to test the limits of her domain. *Could* she take control? Would they notice? What would they do if they did? She wasn't scared. They couldn't touch her. Not here. They'd be touching the ship itself, and it was vast and resilient. She hesitated for a time, though time had little meaning, and she settled for zooming it in just a little to see if she could.

She could.

The people worked, oblivious to being watched, and the camera zoomed in—not her doing this time—to two people, a man and a woman, setting up some sort of dish. It looked like a communications array of some sort. She'd never seen one that operated from a planet, but she'd studied the ones on the outside of the ship, and the shape was similar.

She checked the incoming video feed to see where it was going, who else had access to this satellite. Science and medicine directorate controlled most of the satellites, so she looked for that link, only to find it wasn't there. That was odd. She followed the data through the system; it was going only to command. Obviously they didn't want others to see it. Eddie wondered at that. People were worried, and seeing this video, they'd know that people were alive and working, even if they couldn't talk. Maybe command wanted to keep the satellites themselves secret. Well, too bad. It was data, and data wanted to be free. She created some code, her fingers and her mind working together seamlessly to inject it into the network, releasing the restricted feed into a wider flow. She routed it directly to science for Lila to see it.

She paused. It was jarring to think of Lila, here, when she was the ship. They hadn't seen each other much in days, not since Lila took over her job as the head of shipside space exploration. She had too much work. Too much responsibility. That thought got in the way of the data, distracted Eddie, so she pushed it out and focused. She produced more code and released the video into public spaces where everyone would see it. That should keep them from being angry, seeing their friends and family safe. The people in charge should have done that themselves.

They could thank her later, though they wouldn't. They'd never know that she'd been there.

<CHAPTER 45>

MARK RECTOR

||||||||||||||||||||||||||||||||||||||||||||||||||||||||||||||

1 CYCLE AFTER ARRIVAL

Mark Rector stood on a slight rise, maybe a meter higher in elevation than the surrounding field, and surveyed the work going on around him. They'd erected one structure so far and were working on another. He'd directed that the living facilities be the first things they set up—they needed somewhere where they could decontaminate and sleep, after all—but the scientists had banded together and gotten people to agree that they needed a lab facility first. He'd backed off, pretended that he agreed so as not to lose face. It wasn't ideal, but it was working. He'd established a workable relationship with Jackson, and there was going to be some give and take.

He didn't mind her input. She was smart. While he was still stuck in the airlock, she had prioritized communications—which he wholeheartedly agreed with—and while they didn't have anything two-way yet, the previous night they had rigged a battery-powered floodlight and sent a short message up giving the basics of their situation. He'd feel better once they got full comms up and running, but at least the spaceside leadership knew what was happening. He'd have to trust them to come up with a solution. Nobody could have predicted the complete failure of their systems . . . well, somebody probably could have, but even given the signs, it would have been an extreme prediction. He was more pragmatic about it. They were in the situation, and wishing that they'd done it differently wouldn't change anything. He'd leave the blame game to the governor. Down here, he had people to keep alive.

He looked across the field, and he hardly felt dizzy anymore. Not everyone was adjusting that well to the open spaces, however. A large, lone tree stood in the center of the field, branches of green leaves spread wide, looking majestic. It was a different feeling from the wall of trees that lined the open field, which were darker and more foreboding. They'd entered and explored one area of the forest the day prior as they sought water. Their pumps weren't working, so they had a work party ferrying buckets back for treatment by medical, using the small solar array they'd got working that morning to power heating elements for boiling it. They could live for a time off the supply that they brought with them, but he didn't want to wait until they'd exhausted that to start replenishing the supply.

He walked to the edge of camp just to see and be seen. This world had a sound to it—a buzzing that seemed to come from everywhere and nowhere. Someone had suggested that it might be insects in the grass, which was a concern with them being without helmets and breathing equipment. The scientists had a plan to investigate, but they had other priorities first and he left them to that. Nothing had threatened them at all, and his fears of hostile intelligent life seemed to be unfounded. A rodent of some kind leapt from the grass, startling him. His heart raced, but it landed and bounded away. He'd have to report that, though others had seen similar things already.

Out across the field, a group of eight or ten large birds circled, one or two occasionally breaking out of the circle to fly lower, as if curious about the developing camp. As he watched, one dove toward the ground, surprisingly fast given its previously lazy orbit. A squeal rang out, and the bird came up with something squirming in its beak. The scientists had told them they were probably predators, and that seemed to confirm it. He watched them a bit longer and found that he was more in awe than afraid.

They were pretty cool.

Being on a planet was pretty cool.

BACK IN CAMP, RECTOR STOOD OUTSIDE THE SCIENCE LAB SHELTER, waiting to be tested. His palms were sweaty, and if he was being honest, this worried him more than the wildlife. Jackson had tried to tell him a long time ago that the stuff that you couldn't see was a bigger threat than the stuff you could, and it took being opened up to Promissa like this for him to finally believe her. He took a deep breath, tried to assess himself. He'd been the first one exposed, so in theory, if anybody was going to get sick, it should be him. It also made him the best test subject.

He felt fine—or at least he thought he did. It was hard to say, as they'd already seen more than one person report symptoms of some unknown disease. The problem was that the symptoms looked a lot like the symptoms of intense stress. As it turned out, working on an alien planet was stressful, and doing it without the safety of a helmet multiplied that.

So far, the medic had ruled out contamination sicknesses, but even that was suspect. Would they even know what it looked like if it happened? They didn't have all their equipment working—no one did, obviously. In some ways, it was freeing. There was nothing they could do about it, so why worry?

Which seemed easy for him, but not so much for the two hundred others at his site.

Susan Ho poked her head out of the shelter and called him in. He stopped inside the double-sealed entrance to manually decontaminate, and three minutes later found her inside waiting with a swab in one hand and a breathing apparatus in the other. "Are you ready?"

Rector nodded and took off his mask. The smell of alcohol assaulted him, and the tan floor and white walls gave the place a feeling of sterility that he knew was probably an illusion without a working air filtration system.

Ho approached and stuck a long swab so far up his nose that it felt like it was tickling his brain. "Got it. Take a deep breath, and then exhale with all your force into this."

He did what she said. It was his third such test, so it came easily.

"Roll up your sleeve." He did, and once she was satisfied, she wiped his arm with alcohol and took a vial of blood.

"Anything else?" he asked.

"Nope. We're good. You can check back for results in thirty to forty-five minutes."

"How are we doing with the planet sickness cases?"

"Agoraphobia cases overall are steady, at about 18 percent, but the good news is that we're down to about 60 percent of those being debilitating, so we're seeing some progress."

"I thought they tested for that with the simulations," he said, not for the first time. It was frustrating, and he couldn't let it go. People would get better with time, but that assumed they had that long. That was the rub. They'd get everything fixed eventually, but they had to make it until they did, and that meant having every able-bodied person working on solutions, not freaking out because the sky was so big.

She gave him a flat smile but didn't respond. She'd already

explained it to him and had no intention of having the same discussion twice. She was no-nonsense like that. They'd all been tested in simulation, but this was . . . more. No computer could prepare them totally for the immensity of it. In simulation, things looked endless, but somewhere in your brain you could remind yourself that it was an illusion, that there were really walls not too far away. "Is there anything else?"

He got the uncomfortable feeling that he didn't belong, and though he wanted to grab Jackson and ask her any number of questions, he put his mask on and left instead.

Just as he cleared the second seal, somebody ran up to him, clearly laboring in the heavy gravity. It was Sierks—one of his Secfor people—identifiable even with his mask on by the weapon that he carried. Along with Mwangi, Rector had him patrolling the camp. He had told the others it was for security, but in truth it was also to keep tabs on the crew. He wasn't letting the shit that happened up on the ship take root down here. He didn't think a revolt was likely, given the shared risks, but he wasn't taking chances.

"What's up?"

Sierks pointed to the sky. "Lander."

Rector followed the gesture to a descending vehicle, maybe three or four thousand meters up still, but growing quickly. As they stood there watching, something fell off of it toward the planet and the lander itself started shrinking, heading away, while whatever it dropped fell, and then four big somethings—he didn't have a word for them—billowed up and out from the falling object, slowing its descent. Ah! They were catching the air so it would fall slowly. Now he understood. They didn't want to risk another lander coming down where it might get stuck, so they were dropping in supplies. And probably communication. "Keep everybody back while it falls.

I don't want anybody accidentally getting crushed. Once it's down, move out and secure it."

"Secure it from what?"

"Whatever. Colonists, fauna—nothing and nobody goes into the supply drop without me there. Got it?"

"Got it, boss." Sierks departed, much slower than how he'd arrived, carrying his long gun in both hands, across his body and pointed downward, just like he'd been trained. Across the camp, everyone had pretty much stopped working to watch the thing falling from the sky. It swung back and forth, dangling from the billowy things that kept it up, and small puffs of jet spray gave it some sort of directional guidance. Hopefully whatever had happened to their equipment wouldn't affect that before it reached the ground. He still didn't understand what was causing equipment to fail, but the lander had reached ground before losing power, so this might, too.

He started walking, but not too fast. In the distance, some of the birds had started flying toward the falling object. Not too close, but definitely closer. There were more of them now—maybe twenty. They were probably just curious. It wasn't every day that a giant red-and-white thing dropped from the sky.

The payload came closer, both vertically and horizontally. It was about a four-meter cube, the bottom of which appeared to be some sort of gray metal. Hardened aluminum, if he had to guess. It came to rest with a ground-shaking thud about forty meters outside of their perimeter, kicking up dust, and Rector couldn't help but be surprised by the force of it. The canopies that had held it aloft collapsed and fell over it, almost obscuring it from view.

One of the birds swooped down, passed within maybe twenty meters of him. He followed it, watching as it flared its wings in a braking motion and alighted on the canopy-covered delivery. This startled Sierks, who was just about to reach it, and he stumbled backward. Rector was about fifty meters away, so he put his binoculars to his face to get a closer look, thankful that they'd brought an analog pair. This was as close as one of the birds had come, and it seemed like a good chance to really check the animal out. It looked like the pictures of birds he'd seen with wings and feathers, but it was larger than most of the animals he'd seen in videos, with a leathery undersurface to the wings. It had a sharp beak and sharp talons, both of which looked dangerous, but just as it folded its wings across its front, he thought he saw . . . arms. They weren't big, and maybe he'd imagined it, but he didn't recall that from any of the Earth species he'd seen in his limited pass through the study material.

Sierks stepped back farther, unwilling to go near the supplies, unsure what to do, and the person nearest to him, maybe fifteen meters back, stopped as well. The animal was large—around a meter tall as it sat there. Perched there? He didn't know the right term. For its part, the bird seemed unconcerned. If it was possible for a bird to give off an air of *I don't give a shit,* that was what this one did. It turned slowly, taking in the entire developing encampment. He'd thought before that it was curiosity, but now . . . he couldn't say why, but it didn't feel like that.

And he didn't like it.

As he watched, two other birds swooped in, making slow passes over the area before landing next to the first. The three of them looked at each other, and while they made no sound, it almost seemed like they were . . . what? Having a conversation? He glanced to the science shelter, wondering if he should get Alana Wilson, the xenobiologist. Maybe she'd be able to figure this out.

"Hey! Get off of that!"

The shout drew Rector's attention back to the birds. Sierks had stopped moving away from the container, and he was gesturing to the birds with his weapon. Rector had told him to make sure nothing interfered with the supplies, and while the birds didn't appear to be a threat, they were impeding progress. The second person took a tentative step forward, though still well behind the Secfor officer. "Go! Get out of here!" said Sierks.

If the birds understood or cared, they didn't show it. They certainly didn't leave. Two of them did turn to face the source of the noise, but obviously they didn't understand him. Sierks raised his weapon, pointed it toward them, as if he expected the animals to somehow understand the threat of an assault rifle. He fired into the air over their heads, the sound echoing across the open field.

One of the birds leapt a meter into the air before settling back onto the container with a quick flap of its wings to maintain balance. All three faced Sierks now, their heads toward him, eyes boring in.

"Get out of here!" yelled Sierks.

Rector didn't know why, couldn't quite put his finger on what had changed, but he got a sense that the birds' attitude had darkened. Their posture was now somehow more . . . aggressive. It wasn't an outward appearance as much as a feeling, but for the first time, Rector began to really worry. He started walking toward the scene, and then picked up his pace into a jog. Ahead of him, Sierks lowered his weapon, pointing it at the birds.

"Sierks, no!" called Rector, for reasons he hadn't fully figured out. But it felt urgent. The world slowed in the next second, one of those moments where things happen impossibly fast but feel like they last forever. Sierks screamed, dropped his weapon, and slumped to the ground. The worker closest to him went to one knee, and cries echoed from several other people in the vicinity. Rector felt a pressure in his head that stopped him in his tracks. Running any closer seemed foolish—that idea was paramount, even after the pressure subsided and left behind a dull ache. Sierks lay on the ground, not moving. The birds turned to Rector, as if they knew he was in charge, which was impossible. It almost felt like they were staring him down. After what seemed like a minute but was probably just a few seconds, they launched themselves into the air as one and flew off lazily, as if nothing had happened.

Released from the moment, Rector hurried over to Sierks and knelt by his body. Blood leaked from his eyes and ears, running across his face and down his cheeks to the ground. He wasn't breathing. Rector felt for a pulse, had to stop and remove his glove. Nothing. "Medic!" he yelled. Others took up the cry.

He glanced around to make sure the birds weren't returning. That they were responsible for this—whatever this was—seemed obvious. He looked to the worker, who had managed to get to her feet but still wobbled, unsteady. She put a hand on the supply pallet to stabilize herself, pulled down her mask, and vomited on the ground. Blood trickled from her nose, and she wiped that away with her hand at the same time she wiped the remnants of vomit from her mouth.

"Are you okay?"

"I . . . I don't know."

"What happened?" asked Rector.

"I . . . I don't know," she repeated. "There was a blinding pain and a white flash in my eyes, and all of a sudden I was on my knees."

Rector nodded, not knowing what else to do. It seemed similar to what happened to him, but more intense. Perhaps by being closer, she got more of the effect. He'd need to canvass the rest of the people in the area, see what they'd felt or maybe seen that might give some insight into the incident. That he was taking it calmly felt a bit surreal. There was a dead person at his feet, and he should *feel* something, but he didn't want to frighten anybody, didn't want to make things worse. Sierks's limp body would do enough on its own.

Susan Ho hurried up, knelt by the body, repeated what Rector had done. "He's dead."

"I figured that. Can you tell what happened?"

"Never seen anything like it. The blood from the eyes." She shuddered. "I don't know if we should take him inside . . . I need to run tests, but I have limited equipment."

Rector nodded. "Do your best. Maybe there's some medical stuff in this pallet they dropped for us. I'll get people started going through it in a few minutes, once things calm down. Anything you can learn might help us going forward."

"Got it. Will do."

Rector left her to it and headed for the scientists' shelter to find Jackson. Halfway there, a woman he recognized as Saanvi—he couldn't remember her last name—hustled up to him. "Officer Rector!"

He stopped, waited for her to come closer. The masks made it hard to understand each other from a distance. "What is it?"

"The solar panels we were using to boil the water . . . they overloaded!"

"What? Show me." He followed her around one of the shelters to the other side of the camp. They went far and fast enough that he was breathing hard by the time they arrived; the full gravity was taking its toll. The equipment was smoking, and even through his mask the light breeze brought him the acrid smell of burning electronics.

"When did this happen?"

Hescoe, the lead engineer for their landing, had beaten him

to the site and stood from where she'd been crouching over the heating element. "They said it happened right when they heard the gunshot."

A chill swept through Rector despite the heat in his body from the quick walk over. That was too correlated to be a coincidence. "Do you know what happened?"

"It wasn't an EMP, I'm sure of that. Something overloaded the system. I've never seen anything like it."

"And you say it happened right after the gunshot?"

"That's right," said Saanvi.

Rector turned to Hescoe. "Figure out whatever you can about how this happened and if there's something we can do to fix it. I need to go talk to Dr. Jackson."

Hescoe flashed him a thumbs-up and went back to work.

<CHAPTER 46>

SHEILA JACKSON

1 CYCLE AFTER ARRIVAL

Sheila knew something was wrong the minute Rector entered. The way he carried himself, he had something to say, and it wasn't good.

Darwish didn't give him a chance to speak, having missed the body language. "Good news! There don't appear to be any significant dangers in the air samples."

Rector stopped at that. "That's good. One less problem." That he dismissed what was potentially the best possible news anybody had ever presented as *one less problem* was a clear indication that they had a *bigger* problem.

"What's wrong?" asked Sheila.

Rector recounted what had happened outside, telling them about the dead Secfor officer and the birds, and how the solar generator overloaded.

As he spoke, Susan Ho came in leading a woman, and sat her in a chair. "I'm going to run a quick neurological exam on her. She was bleeding from the nose, and that has me worried."

Rector nodded, and then turned back to Sheila and the others. "So . . . what do you think?" He was looking at Alana Wilson, their xenobiologist, so Sheila didn't respond.

"I . . . don't know. We worked through a myriad of possibilities for ways that alien life could be different from anything back on Earth, but we didn't imagine anything like *this*. The death—I could hypothesize something secreting a hormone or putting off a vapor, but that doesn't fit the evidence. And the power surge . . . I don't see how that could happen. Our best bet would be to gather all the information we can and get it back to the ship where they have the computer power to run it through some advanced models. Down here, I'd just be guessing."

"We're still working on communications and we've had a setback, given the damage to power generation," said Rector. "So you're all we've got."

"Right. Did you hear . . . or see . . . any communication between them?"

Rector thought about it. "No sounds. They did look at each other, as if they were conversing, and . . . this is weird . . . but there was this moment where I felt like . . ." He shook his head.

"No, tell us. Anything might help."

"I felt like they were telling me to stay away. But that's impossible."

They stood in silence for a minute, everyone thinking things through, which tended to happen with groups of disparate scientists. Rector, an outsider here, stayed silent as well. Maybe he could just read the room.

"Is there a possibility that they communicate telepathically?" Sheila asked after a minute or so.

Wilson pursed her lips. "I don't have any examples of it, but I suppose we shouldn't rule anything out."

"If they were," asked Darwish, "would that translate to us? Would it let them communicate without the use of language?"

"Could that be why I got the urge to not get closer?" asked Rector, in what was a surprisingly astute question.

"I'd feel better about it if I had the ability to consult our predictive models," said Wilson. "It would be a good question to pose to Dr. Zimdal back on the ship, once we get communications."

"We may not have that long," said Rector. He stood rigidly, as if ready to act, his weapon held in both hands. It was almost as if he thought the creatures would come right inside.

Sheila said, "If they can communicate, it's possible that us initiating talks by shooting at them—"

"He didn't shoot *at* them," interrupted Rector.

Sheila glared at him. As if that was the point. "By initiating talks in a hostile way, we may have given the impression that we're a threat."

"We *are* a threat."

"So are they," offered Wilson. "We should consider all the flora and fauna dangerous."

"Exactly," said Rector, missing the point again. "I'm going to assign guards. We've got to keep them away from us."

Sheila rolled her eyes and started to say something, but there was no use. She walked out. She had to get away from the man, or she was going to say something she regretted and the small bit of a working relationship they'd achieved would be gone. But he followed her almost immediately.

"Where are you going?"

Sheila turned to him and smiled. "Nowhere. Just taking a walk."

He hesitated, looked like he wanted to say something, but what could he do? She wasn't constrained to their makeshift lab, and if he tried to restrict her, others would intervene. He was nominally in charge, but he needed the support of the rest of them if he wanted to stay that way. After an awkward few seconds, he stomped off, probably to set up his guards, or whatever other nonsense he was thinking about.

Sheila started walking without a purpose, just putting distance between her and her new office. The air was safe and she took it in, though she didn't remove her mask, just in case. There was grass everywhere, and who knew what might blow off of that, though the breeze was light. Away from the camp, the alien animals still circled overhead. More of them now. A few dozen. But none of them came down below fifty meters or so; they just stayed up there, circling on the air currents, watching. Or she imagined them watching. They'd discussed aspects of intelligent life enough back on the ship, back before sense went out the airlock, when they had time for theoretical scientific debates. Were these flying creatures unintelligent animals, or were they something more? According to Rector's story, Sierks had suffered only after he pointed his weapon at them. That, in theory, indicated at least some level of understanding, even if it was as simple as *gun bad*.

What they needed was to capture one, to study it. But that seemed unlikely for multiple reasons. Even if they *could* capture one, and she saw no way to do that, they didn't have the right operational equipment—not to mention the horrible ethical implications. And at least as important, she had no idea how the rest of the aliens would respond if they tried.

If they couldn't study one, what other options were there? If she left it to Rector, they'd end up in a conflict. Whether they could win it or not would be important to him but seemed moot. Even if they won, they'd be establishing a horrible precedent if they started slaughtering native species.

She reached the outer edge of their expanding encampment.

The grass was looser here than back where people had trod it down, and it swished around her knees as she walked. A nugget of an idea was forming in her mind. She kept walking. She told herself she was just going to go a little way, but after a few steps she took a few more, and soon she was a hundred meters outside the camp. She looked back over her shoulder. Nobody was following her. Either nobody had noticed her leaving, or they'd noticed and let her go. She continued farther.

She stopped after about two hundred meters—or her best estimate of that, since she really had no concept of that kind of distance. Looking back at the camp, she couldn't make out faces, couldn't make out any details at all. Still, nobody had followed her.

Nobody human anyway.

The birds overhead *definitely* had noticed her. A smaller group had broken off the main flock and now circled over her instead of the camp. Seven of them. Five were the same size and two smaller. The inquisitive side of her wondered if that was a gender distinction or something else. Maybe age. The instinctive side of her wanted to run. What was she doing out here away from camp on her own on a planet where she had no idea what could kill her? She raised her empty hands to show that she wasn't a threat, though in truth she didn't know if that was a good idea or a bad one. But Sierks had shown a gun, and it hadn't gone well for him, so it seemed best to try another approach.

If the birds did the same thing to her as they'd done to Sierks, would anyone even find her body? They'd notice her missing, of course, but if she fell in the tall grass, they'd have to almost walk on her to see her. She consciously slowed her breathing, though she couldn't do anything to slow her heart, which pounded in her ears.

Three of the alien creatures broke off from the seven and spiraled downward, almost lazily, as if in no rush to reach her, but they drew inexorably closer. The tall grass seemed like it would swallow them up if they landed, but they set down on some object she hadn't seen—maybe a rock or something—about thirty meters away, farther from the camp. All three of them looked at her, and she got the sense that they were waiting.

Sheila kept her hands visible as she walked toward them. The aliens turned from her and looked at each other, almost as if discussing something, just as Rector had noted, though they didn't make a sound. The aliens . . . that was what they were. She'd thought of them initially as birds, because of their wings and how they flew, but up close there were differences. They did have wings with feathers on the top, but their underside was more leathery, as was their body, and along with their wings they also had short arms. She would have loved to examine their hands, but she wasn't close enough.

A blast of something hit her, almost like someone screaming in an incoherent language, and Sheila stifled a scream at the pain, fell to one knee. No, it wasn't language, exactly. More like a thought, a concept, but with the distinct impression that it *was* communication. Whatever it was, it was powerful, felt like it might turn her brain to mush in her skull, like someone was crushing her head with a vise. "You're hurting me!"

The pain subsided, though the residue thumped in her skull still, a pressure. She stood, didn't take another step, waited for the aliens to make the next move.

We are sorry. Your mind is . . . not mature. It was not our intent to harm you.

Holy stars! They hadn't spoken, but she understood them! It hurt again, but more like an average headache than the stabbing shaft of the previous one. Sheila felt her nose dripping under her mask, and when she touched her gloved hand to the outside of the mask it came away red. Not good.

We were trying to communicate, but you use a language that's different from your machines. We understand now. Who are you?

They understand? That made one of them. Sheila very much *didn't* understand. She didn't know how they were communicating, and she couldn't parse what they meant about language. "I'm . . . I'm Sheila Jackson." She stumbled over the words, but as she said it, she realized that wasn't what they meant. The image that remained in her mind from the initial question wasn't about her as an individual—somehow she understood that their meaning was different. They wanted to know who they were collectively. "We've traveled through space. From Earth." With that, she tried to picture their home planet in her mind. They were putting things into her head without speaking out loud, so maybe she could, too, though she wasn't sure if she was projecting or if they were reading her mind or how any of it worked. Her heart was racing again, but this time it wasn't from fear.

The aliens turned to each other, and this time, she was sure they were communicating with each other. Instead of a thunder in her head, she sensed a susurrus, below the surface. She couldn't glean any meaning from it, but it definitely came from the aliens. They were communicating with one another, and she could sense it.

"We mean you no harm," she said, though she wasn't sure she believed that. Would they know if she was lying? But still, it felt like the right thing to say. "Not intentionally."

You will bring harm. It wasn't a question, left no room for doubt.

It seemed ominous, though there was no feeling of direct threat. It was more matter-of-fact. Sheila scrambled for a response. "If we can understand each other, perhaps we can avoid it."

You will not understand.

"I know there are some who won't, but I'm a scientist." She tried to convey the meaning of that, didn't know if they had scientists, or even occupations. She had no way to know whether the message landed or not, but she had to try. They couldn't get off on a confrontational footing.

You bring trouble. It came to her head as trouble, but she pictured something different. Not a single thing, but a group of things, but they didn't seem to fit.

"Trouble . . . technology?"

There was a hesitation. *Yes. Technology. Trouble.*

"I don't understand."

Our planet is very old. She got an image of an inhabited planet with buildings and roads. That the aliens knew of this, though it clearly didn't exist today, indicated . . . what? Some form of shared archival memory?

"We saw remnants of that." She thought about the ruins they'd seen in satellite pictures.

That was a long time ago. They didn't give a number, but she understood it to be thousands of years. *Our planet died.*

That struck Sheila, but she was sure she hadn't misunderstood the concept. She just couldn't grasp it. The planet seemed pristine. "The planet seems . . . alive."

Now. After a long time.

Again *long* meant "eons."

"So the planet died but came back."

Yes. It died because of technology. Now, we live as the planet means for us to live. But you.

"We don't." Sheila had an idea but wasn't sure how to get it across. "Our technology . . . it doesn't work here."

The planet has stopped it.

Stopped it? The way it came across made it clear that it was not something that just happened, but an intentional act. They controlled it? She felt like she should confirm that, as it would be a key element in shaping how they moved forward, both as colonists and in their relationship. "You stopped it . . . how?"

Not us. We are part of the planet, but not all. The planet protects us, and we have become what protects it.

Except the words didn't quite fit the image they conveyed, but she couldn't further define it, as if it was a concept she didn't have access to. *Become* wasn't the right word. *Evolved?* They'd evolved to . . . could they shut down electronics with their minds? Or maybe they had their own technology. That seemed unlikely, though, as that would require the exact types of things they were trying to stop—if she understood it right, which she surely didn't. And it wasn't clear if they had done it, or something else had done it, or something they were part of did it. The images continued as a jumble in her head, and she didn't know how to ask for clarification.

"We did not know," she said. She had started to say that they would stop using it, but even now they were looking for ways to make things work. Her people wouldn't stop trying to use technology— humanity was tied to technology, it was how *they* had evolved—and while she had wondered before, now she was sure that the aliens would know she was lying if she tried to say otherwise. The more she spoke to them, the easier she could interpret such feelings, even when they didn't come with words.

You came from the stars.

"That's right."

You must go back to them.

"We can't."

You must! This came with such power that it hurt again, caused her to stumble. As the pain faded, she got the idea that two of the aliens were scolding the other, though she couldn't understand the specifics. *I am sorry.*

"It's okay," said Sheila. "This is a lot to process for all of us."

You must go back.

"Without our technology, we can't *get* back. Our ship is in orbit." She tried to project that, though it was probably half-formed, as she'd never actually seen a ship in orbit, despite having been on one.

They communicated with each other, longer this time. *We would allow you to leave.*

The concept of *we* seemed bigger than the aliens themselves, but again, she wasn't sure she had the translation right. It also came with the idea of their ships taking off into the sky, so they understood that much. Sheila wasn't sure that would work, but if the aliens controlled the thing that shut down their technology and agreed to stop it, maybe they could make them start working again. Or maybe they could communicate back to the ship and have other ships—rescue vessels—sent down.

But would they? Nothing in her experience with Rector or the governor led her to believe that they'd back off. But how did she communicate that? Were the aliens all of the same mind, or did they have a concept of nonhomogeneous ideas within a species? Did they have a concept of war? And if they did and she told them that, how would they react? The last thing she wanted was to be the cause of an interspecies war because she miscommunicated. She was a scientist, not a diplomat, and she was already risking everything by being out there talking to them. That the mission didn't *have* diplomats now seemed like a massive oversight.

In the end, she decided to go with the truth. She had to try to make the aliens understand their internal disagreements. "I'm not sure that I can get them to leave . . . us to leave. I can try . . . I *will* try . . . but they are not likely to listen."

They conversed again, in that way she could sense but not understand, as if when they communicated to her, they were putting things into a different language than the one they used among themselves. But it wasn't language; it was something else. She could puzzle that out later. For now, she tried to listen in, glean something from them, but she couldn't. Finally she heard, *We will help persuade them.* The words translated ominously, but the image was of a sky filled with aliens, so dense that they nearly blocked the sun. It didn't feel threatening to her the way they projected it, but it probably would to others. If they did that, conflict seemed inevitable. But she didn't want to say that because she wasn't confident how they'd receive it. If they could read it from her mind, it didn't show in their reaction. They perched there, on their rock, unbothered and unhurried.

"I should get back. Talk to my people. They'll worry if I'm gone too long."

Make them understand.

Make them understand. If only she could. "I'll try."

We would speak with you again.

That, at least, seemed positive. "Thank you for speaking with me and explaining."

With that, the three launched themselves into the air in unison. Sheila watched them for a few seconds before turning and heading back to camp. She felt like she'd spent six hours exercising on a high-grav deck, but the possibilities cascading through her mind kept her steps light.

<CHAPTER 47>

MARK RECTOR

||||||||||||||||||||||||||||||||||||||||||||||||||||||||||||||||||

1 CYCLE AFTER ARRIVAL

Rector read the note again as he waited for Dr. Jackson to make her way back to camp. The crew was unloading the supply pallet now that the birds had left it, and one of the first things they'd found was a communication pouch. It was a simple note, printed on paper, so no technology required. He didn't go out to meet the scientist, instead choosing to wait by the lab shelter, allowing him to pretend he hadn't been watching her entire interaction through his binoculars. Mwangi had notified him of her departure, and he'd considered going after her, but if he was being honest, after the previous confrontation with the bird things, he was a bit reluctant to face them again. He hadn't authorized her to go do what she'd done, but that didn't mean he had to stop it. If she came back unharmed, as apparently she was, he could debrief her. If they had killed her . . . well, it was an asshole way to think about it, but he could deny responsibility. She was an adult, and she'd made a choice.

But now she was moving very slowly, and he grew impatient. The sun had crested in the sky and was starting downward, and while he hadn't had a ton of experience with daylight cycles, that meant it was afternoon. He forced himself to walk around the camp and check on shelters for sleeping, progress with communications, and other preparations.

About halfway through the circuit, a woman stepped out from behind a pile of shipping containers and stopped him. "I need to talk to you."

Rector studied her, trying to remember her name from the study he'd done of the crew. "Sure . . . Descarta, is that right?"

"That's right. Ariana."

"What can I do for you?" He resisted the urge to glance over his shoulder to check Jackson's progress.

"Cecil sent me."

Ah. Right. That was where he knew the name from. He'd gotten her added to the mission. "Okay. What can I do for Cecil?"

"There's a package in the shipment that we just got. I need it, but the people you assigned to inventory things won't let anybody near the stuff."

That didn't make any sense. They couldn't possibly have the black market going that quickly—they didn't even have readily accessible communications. "How do you know Cecil sent it for you?"

"It's marked."

"Marked?"

"That's right. We have a system."

Of course they did. "Okay. I'll see what I can do."

"I need it now."

Rector took a second before responding. Who the fuck did this woman think she was? "I'll get to it when I can. Sorry. Kind of dealing with the survival of the entire colony here."

"I—"

"I'm sorry. Really busy." Rector turned and walked away.

"Cecil's going to hear about this," called the woman.

"You do what you gotta do," said Rector without turning around. Cecil might hear about it, but not anytime soon. Stars, if he did hear about it, that would mean that their communications were working, and Rector would happily take that trade.

Jackson had made it back inside the perimeter, and he hustled to meet her before she entered the scientists' shelter.

"How are you feeling?" It wasn't the first question on his mind, but he knew it was the best way to start. Jackson didn't respond well to confrontation, and she had information he wanted.

She turned to face him, sagged back against one of the rigid poles that held up the shelter. "I'm exhausted. Physically, I feel like I've been exercising for hours, and mentally I feel like I just spent eight hours staring at complex data."

"What happened?"

"We communicated." Her face lit up as she said it, making it clear she was smiling behind her mask. Despite her fatigue, she couldn't hide her excitement.

"Like a real conversation?"

From there, she started talking quickly, running one sentence into another, explaining the history of the planet, the abilities of the birds—she called them aliens, which he decided made sense—and their request that they leave the planet.

That was where he stopped her. "That's not going to happen."

She wanted to argue, he could see it in her body language, the way she stood up straight, stuck her chin out. So much for not creating a confrontation. But she relaxed before speaking. "Why not?"

"They're animals."

"They're not. Not by the definition you're using, anyway."

She just couldn't help being condescending. "And what definition should I use?"

"They communicate by telepathy. They're highly intelligent.
They've adapted to their environment because of past failures.
You're being blinded by what they look like."

She wasn't wrong—not exactly. He believed what she was
saying. But she couldn't get past the academic and into the practical. They needed this planet, and that trumped any strict scientific
definition. But he couldn't press her. She was too important to the
success of the mission. She'd communicated! That he didn't have
to try to do that himself, he appreciated, but it also gave her a ton
of power. He didn't *think* she'd lie, but later, when it became clear
that she wasn't going to get what she wanted, if she alone controlled
their communication, maybe she would. He'd have to mitigate that,
but first he had to see if she'd work with him.

"I don't know. Maybe we could negotiate with them," he offered.

She looked skeptical, but she thought about it. "Possibly. To
what end?"

"I'm not sure. Everybody wants something . . . what do they
want?"

"For us to leave?"

"Is that a redline for them? It's a big planet, and there aren't
many of us. Maybe they'd be okay if we stayed in one small area. We
don't necessarily need *this* spot." He wasn't sure what the governor
would think of him offering to move, but he wasn't here and Rector
was. If that's what it took to make the mission work, he'd do it.

She considered it. "They didn't make it seem like that was a
possible solution, but I suppose we could ask. I *would* like to talk to
them more and try to understand them better. It's possible, given
some interaction, that I'll get a more nuanced understanding."

Rector nodded. That was his key with Jackson. She wanted to

study the world. As long as he let her do that, she'd go along willingly. "That's all I want. If we have to leave, it's going to take time. We'll need help from above, and there are the other camps to consider. So, while we're doing that, we should take the opportunity to learn as much about the aliens and what they want as we can."

"Have you heard from the other camps?"

He held up the paper. "Not directly. But like us, they both made contact with the ship, and I got this in the supply drop. The other camps are . . . struggling. If anything, more than we are."

Jackson winced. "How bad is it?"

"Six dead. Two in one camp, four in the other."

"Aliens?" she asked.

"Only in one camp. In the other, there was an accident and then someone was killed by a bad reaction to a plant."

She shuddered at that, and Rector couldn't blame her. "I hope they can tell us more about that. If the flora is dangerous, it would help to know what to look for, and maybe we could share what I've learned about the aliens with them to prevent any further misunderstandings."

Rector nodded. He didn't know how they were going to communicate that with the primitive means currently at their disposal, but he'd try. For now, though, he wanted to keep Jackson focused on the aliens. She seemed hesitant about pushing them, so he decided to reframe it in terms that might entice her. "Do you think you can talk to them again tomorrow?"

"I think they'd be open to that. Hopefully I'll physically recover with some sleep."

"Good," said Rector. "We don't want to push them too much, but think about it. If we had some of our technology, you'd be able to do all the tests that you'd planned. Wilson could examine the plants—and maybe even some of the smaller animals—herself.

We could get further in-depth examining the effects of this environment on our people. Who knows? Maybe we're not compatible and we can't stay here anyway."

She couldn't hide her excitement at the prospect. "It wouldn't hurt to ask—as long as we couch it in the right terms. If they say no, we need to be prepared to accept that."

"Of course. I'd like you to bring a second person with you."

"No guns," she said.

He held his hands up defensively. "Definitely not. You can even pick the person. I just want somebody else who has experience communicating with the . . . aliens." He had almost said *birds*. She wouldn't appreciate that. "After all, we don't want a single point of failure."

She considered it, as if she was trying to find the catch in what he was asking, but finally she nodded. "Okay. I'll take somebody with me."

"Thank you. Also, they tell me we may potentially have full communication with the ship tomorrow. Engineering has an off-line computer up and running now, shielded within their new work area . . . at least they think it's shielded. We really don't know for sure."

"That's good news," said Jackson.

"Yeah. We'll see how it holds up. But in case it does, I want to be prepared to send a data blast with everything we want to tell them in case we have only a short window for communication. I'd like you to compose a message that contains everything you told me plus whatever else science wants to send."

"I can do that," she said.

"Thanks." He honestly hoped that her negotiation would go well, but he wasn't holding his breath. That's why he'd be preparing his own message. One that asked for reinforcements.

He watched Jackson disappear inside the shelter and he sighed. For someone as smart as she was—as smart as all of them were—sometimes they couldn't see the simplest things that needed to be done. They had to secure their foothold on the planet. Maybe they could pre-shield electronics up on the ship and drop them down. There had to be a way. With their technological advantage, they'd surprise the aliens and teach them to leave humans alone. After that, they could negotiate from a position of strength. Jackson wouldn't be happy about it, but for now she didn't need to know.

RECTOR GOT WHAT LITTLE SLEEP HE MANAGED WHILE SITTING IN A seat on the lander. It had been well past midnight before he closed his eyes. That was the problem with being in charge. Everyone had just one thing they needed to talk to you about, and a nervous camp only compounded the problem. Some of them, like the engineers—with a report on restoring some of their basic technology—were truly important. Farmers arguing about their priorities of work—something that wouldn't matter for cycles, if not weeks—was less so. But Rector had given them all time. He woke stiff and uncomfortable, a sharp pain in his neck that he hoped would recede with a good stretch. He wanted to change positions and close his eyes again. Just for fifteen more minutes.

"Boss?"

"Yeah. I'm up. What is it?"

"You need to see this." Mwangi's tone brought Rector to fully awake.

He stood and quickly stretched. He was already dressed, so he followed them toward the airlock. He still thought of it as that, even though it was functioning only as a door. Outside, the morning sun, just peeking over the trees, was starting to cut through the morning gray and cast things in a reddish light. A slight breeze blew on the cool air, and it chilled him, even in his suit. "What is it?"

Mwangi pointed to the horizon, and Rector followed their gesture with his eyes. A huge black cloud blocked the light, almost eclipsing the sun. It wasn't over the encampment, but it was headed their way. The cloud undulated, and as it did and as Rector's eyes adjusted, he understood his subordinate's nervousness. That wasn't a cloud. It was alien birds. Thousands of them.

It looked like negotiations were off.

CHAPTER 48

GEORGE IANNOU

||||||||||||||||||||||||||||||||||||||||||||||||||||||||||||||||||||||||||||

4 CYCLES AFTER ARRIVAL

News from the planet was all that people could talk about. The government had tried to restrict it, but with so much of the crew down there, everybody knew someone. Everybody knew multiple someones, and motivated people had a way of finding things out. Everybody shared. The reports were sporadic, and it was hard to verify what was true or not. *Somebody saw the official message from landing party two* became currency that flowed freely, but it was varied and often contradictory. Depending on who you listened to, there had been deaths. The lowest report was six, but some estimates ran into double digits. The governor hadn't spoken of deaths publicly, which was a strategic error—though at this point, George wasn't sure that anybody would believe the man anyway. With every report from the planet, his decision to push forward with a large landing was becoming less and less popular.

But *somebody* had to try to control the situation, and like it or not, that was George. The capacity crowd who had shown up to listen to him speak wanted answers. Demand was so high, they'd had to turn people away. It wasn't like he could just book a bigger room. Nobody was trying to stop him—not openly—but that only went so far.

"They have information about the landing teams that they aren't sharing." The voice from the back of the packed room was almost a shout, though George couldn't see who it came from. Thirty or more people had crowded into one of the oxygen rooms that was not designed for nearly that many. He worried for the plant life, that some of it would be accidentally ruined, but he had bigger problems. The detentions of Acevedo and Tanaka had been a mistake, inflaming tempers already on edge, and George knew it was only a matter of time until word got out that he'd been part of it. Stars help him when that happened. Beyond that, it had taken away important voices who, for all their faults, might have helped him keep people calm.

This was a new group, representing a wider slice of the ship, many of whom George hadn't seen before. He knew one of them, though, standing right at the front in the center. Kayla. He tried not to make eye contact with her. He knew the look on her face right then, the hard set of her eyes. He'd prefer to talk to her in private instead of in front of a crowd. He had questions for her. She was a believer, and a staunch one, but how far had she gone? How far was she willing to go? He had a hunch, and he didn't like it.

"We don't know for sure what's going on down there," said George.

"We have video evidence! They're not wearing helmets!" This from the front row, Sara Washburn. That one of the most moderate voices among them would be this angry was a bad sign.

"We don't know what that means," he said.

"It means they're killing our people. The *governor* is killing people, and we have to do something about it. Now!" Someone from the back.

"With what resources? We have no recourse," offered George. "Communication is limited, and what we do have is controlled by the military."

"You've been saying we have no recourse forever." It was Kayla, her voice calm and cold. She didn't speak loudly, but it cut off everybody else in the room. Okay. So they were going to do it right here. George stared at her with one last hope that she'd let it go, but she didn't blink. Instead, possibly emboldened by the support she felt around her, she continued, "The governor should be giving us regular updates. Or the captain. Or somebody." A chorus of *yeahs* followed her, and the corner of her mouth quirked up just slightly, the way it did when she felt satisfied with herself. In any other situation, George would have been proud of her, but today it was dangerous.

George took his time before responding. Getting the governor to give updates wasn't that much of a stretch but would probably only lead to more unhappiness and further demands. When he spoke, he did it loud enough to bring the crowd noise down. "Give me one more chance."

"You've had a lot of chances," said Kayla, quieter.

"Speak up!" said a voice from the back.

"I know. One more." George mouthed the words to her more than speaking them.

Kayla seemed to consider it while more voices called for them to speak up. "We're going to give you one more chance," she said, louder now, so everybody would hear her. "If that fails . . . if there's still *no recourse* . . . then we'll make our own recourse!"

George started to respond but held it. They wouldn't hear him over the cheering anyway. It took almost half a minute to settle them back down, but even then, they were talking among themselves, starting to make plans.

"Give him a deadline!" somebody shouted.

Kayla stared at him for several seconds. He met her gaze, unflinching, but he had nothing to offer her. "Four hours," she said.

He sighed, but then he nodded. If he couldn't get a response from the governor in four hours, he probably couldn't get one at all. Stars help him that the governor would listen.

GEORGE CHECKED HIS DEVICE FOR THE TWENTIETH TIME. HE'D BEEN waiting two hours to get in to see the governor. Jeremy apologized for about the tenth time. "He really does want to see you. There are just so many things going on and more information coming to light by the minute."

"I understand. But this is time sensitive."

"I've told him."

It was another forty minutes before he was finally ushered in. The governor wasn't behind his desk, instead pacing back and forth by his plants. The nervous energy coming off of the man was almost palpable. He stopped when he noticed George, took a deep breath, and visibly tried to calm himself. "Sorry to keep you waiting. There's a lot going on."

"More than you know," said George. "But I'll keep it short. You need to get on camera right now and come clean about everything that's going on down below. Tell the people everything you know."

Pantel shook his head, almost imperceptibly. He might not have even known that he was doing it. "I can't. We've got enough problems to deal with down on the surface without exacerbating—"

"You don't get it. Information is leaking right now—some of it accurate, and some of it probably not—and with nobody setting it straight, it's spiraling out of control."

"Spiraling—" He took a step toward George but stopped himself. "You think I don't know that? That's what I'm trying to deal with. We've got a potential war brewing on the planet, and you're here telling me I need to worry about the fact that some people who are safe on the ship have their feelings in a bag because I'm not talking to them right now?"

A war. That was new information. He'd heard about confrontation with an alien species. People were blaming it for some of the deaths, maybe even for the lack of communication. "You've still got to talk to the people up here. There's six hundred down there and thousands up here, and whether they're safe or not, they're on a knife's edge. If you don't calm them down, it's not going to end well."

"Don't threaten me!"

"I'm not. I'm trying to warn you that it's out of my hands at this point." George sighed and decided on a last-ditch effort. "Can you at least release your prisoners? That might help some."

"I'll consider it," snapped Pantel in a tone that said he wasn't actually going to consider it.

"Don't be an idiot, Pantel. This needs to be done."

"We're through here." The governor's tone was icy. Maybe *idiot* hadn't been the right word. It was too late, though. Too late for all of them.

"Thanks." George turned and left without saying anything else. He'd tried. He considered his other options. Maybe the captain? If he could talk to her, maybe he could convince her to speak to the governor. He doubted it—the two of them reportedly weren't on good terms—but if that was his only choice, maybe he should take it. He checked the time and sighed. They'd given him a deadline, and he knew his daughter well enough to know she'd hold to it. It was out of his hands now and in hers. He'd figure out how to support that the best he could.

<CHAPTER 49>

JARRED PANTEL

||||||||||||||||||||||||||||||||||||||||||||||||||||||||||||||||||||

4 CYCLES AFTER ARRIVAL

Pantel monitored the cameras from his desk in his office. Marjorie Blaisdell stood behind him, ostensibly looking on, but she didn't seem that interested. For some reason, that made him mad. "There are more than a thousand people in the halls."

"Yep," she said. "Closer to two thousand, by my estimate."

Iannou had told him it was going to be a problem, and now it was. He had half a mind to have the man detained, but deep down, he knew that Iannou didn't have control of this any more than they did. That it came at a time when he needed to be focused on the planet made it worse. One landing team was calling for evacuation, another for reinforcements. The third team didn't know *what* it wanted. Engineering didn't have a solution for systems losing power yet, and it was all they could do to keep basic communications flowing. Early thoughts had suggested an EMP, but two later incidents suggested that it was some other sort of power surge. What everyone could agree on is that they had no solution. "What are we going to do about it?"

"What *can* we do about it? We've got, what? Twenty or twenty-five Secfor on the ship? And that's if they all show up, which they won't, because some of them are new and they side with the crowd."

He scowled at her. "People are coming this way."

"Yep."

They had shut down the elevators, trying to make it harder for people to assemble, but someone had overridden the code and now locked *them* out. He wanted to call maintenance or engineering or whoever owned fucking elevators, if just to have someone to yell at, but that would have to wait. "Who can we lean on? There has to be something we can do to get control of this."

Blaisdell shook her head. "It's too late for that. We needed to do something yesterday."

"Why did you let it get this far then?" He knew as soon as he asked it that it wasn't her fault. She'd told him. Iannou had told him. But she was a convenient target. The only one he had.

To her credit, she didn't rise to the bait. "We forced a bad position."

"It's the *right* position." He still believed that. Sending the people to the surface in numbers was the only way to make the mission a success. He'd die believing that. Sooner than he hoped, maybe, if the crowd was any indication. He almost laughed at that.

"These folks don't seem to think so."

"They will, once we're successful. History will vindicate my actions."

"History isn't in the corridors right now."

He sat down hard in his chair, put his head in his hands for a couple of seconds, before rallying. "So what do I do? I know you've got an opinion."

"Give them what they want."

"What do they want?"

"Does it matter? Are you going to do it?" He started to answer, but she spoke again, cutting him off. "Because it hasn't been a priority for you up to now."

Pantel hesitated. "What do you mean?"

"I mean, if you wanted to do this big thing, you should have been giving them what they want on smaller things to placate them."

"You think that would have mattered?"

"You think it wouldn't? People want to be heard. If they believe they are, if they believe that they have some control over things, they're content. If you'd given them little things over time, there'd be a lot fewer people out there today."

Pantel thought about it. Maybe she was right, but probably not. "I don't think so. Giving in on one thing would have made them push for more. We couldn't predict that it would lead to this. Today's action is unprecedented."

She shook her head. "Today's action was *inevitable*. When people lose hope and believe they have no way to influence things . . . they *find* a way."

If he accepted that, was there even anything he *could* do? He couldn't go to the crowd now and negotiate. They'd kill him or, at a minimum, overwhelm him with demands. Besides, what was he willing to give up, and how did he get that word out? The news. Iannou had been right about that as well.

On his monitor, the crowd was approaching the line of Secfor that was the only thing preventing them from reaching the governor's office. *Line* was a bit of a misnomer. There were seven of them. Even armed with stun sticks they didn't have a chance. He hoped that they'd survive, not be injured too badly. He didn't want to watch, but he couldn't turn away.

And then the two sides were on each other. There was no sound, but his mind supplied it: the thuds of sticks and fists, the crackles of electricity, the screaming. The first line of protestors went down, which slowed the rest. They had to organize and pull the fallen back, as others tried to work their way through only to be struck with batons. The Secfor were holding. If they could hold a little longer, maybe there would be time for reason to prevail. Even as he thought it, a glance at another camera feed told him it could never happen. Those in the back . . . there were so many of them . . . had no idea what was happening at the front. They kept moving forward, like a piece of ice sliding down a gently sloped table.

More protestors went down, and then someone grabbed hold of one of the Secfor and pulled them out of line. The crowd surged around the separated officer, which forced the others to either move forward or watch them get beaten to death, but they weren't coordinated, weren't trained, and some moved forward while others held back. Pantel watched silently as the inevitable played out.

There was a flash from the Secfor, and for a second, everything stopped.

"What was that?"

"I don't know," said Blaisdell. "Gun?"

Another flash, and this time a body fell.

"They're shooting into the crowd!"

"It looks like just one of them," said Blaisdell, seemingly more detached than Pantel himself, who felt his heart pounding in his chest.

More people went down and Pantel turned away. People were dead. They had to be. There would be more. And that was in the short term. What would happen once this skirmish here finished and it spread throughout the ship? He picked up his comm and contacted engineering. They could seal bulkheads and vent a section of the ship. He didn't want to do it, but if he had to sacrifice a few to save the rest of the ship, he would.

Yannick Ferentz picked up immediately. "I thought it might be you. There's someone here who wants to talk to you."

<CHAPTER 50>

GEORGE IANNOU

|||||||||||||||||||||||||||||||||||||||||||||||||||||||||||||||||||||||

4 CYCLES AFTER ARRIVAL

George took the comm from Ferentz and took a deep breath before he spoke. "You ready to listen this time?"

There was silence on the other end of the connection for several seconds. "Iannou."

"That's right."

"What are you doing in engineering? Taking hostages?"

"Saving lives, unlike you. I figured you might try to vent a compartment and wanted to make sure you didn't." If Kayla insisted on leading a rebellion, he was going to protect it. He'd guessed right.

The governor was silent for several more seconds, probably trying to decide whether to lie or not, or trying to come up with an excuse for why he'd called. In the end, all he said was, "Okay. Let's talk. Can you stop this?"

"I think so."

"What's it going to take?" That he knew there was a price was a positive sign, though the governor probably didn't realize how steep it was going to be. George was ready for the question. He didn't have 100 percent buy-in, but he never would at this point. He hoped he had enough.

"Get the people off the planet and tear up the Charter."

"*Tear up the Charter?* That's impossible."

That he chose that one to complain about was telling, showed that he'd consider the other. It didn't matter. Kayla had made that clear. The Charter was nonnegotiable. "The price would have been lower if you'd listened to me earlier. Now? This isn't a debate. If you want this to stop, get the people off the planet and tear up the Charter."

"The Charter dictates how we live on the ship. Without it—"

"The Charter dictates how *you* live on the ship. The people in power." Kayla's words, but he'd come to believe them as well.

"We can't have a government without rules."

"We can have rules," said George. "New ones."

"So . . . a new Charter?"

"Doesn't really matter what we call it at this point, does it?"

The line remained silent for long enough that George wondered if they'd been disconnected. He had no doubt that there was a cyber battle going on somewhere in the ship's systems right then. Probably more than one. A dropped call could happen. But he didn't want to say anything and disturb whatever thought or conversation might be happening on the other end of the connection. This was the only possible outcome that would satisfy the people and end in relative peace, and this moment was his only chance to get it.

"How would we make this work?"

George breathed a sigh of relief. He hadn't honestly believed they'd get to this spot, but he'd prepared just in case. He didn't trust Pantel, and neither would anybody else. They needed assurances. The man would say anything to get the ship under control for now and then renege later unless they hemmed him in.

"You agree to the terms, electronically, signed, and thumbprint verified. As soon as you send that to me, I'll access ship-wide comms and make the announcement of the upcoming rescue mission to the surface and the dissolution of the Charter, pending a return to order."

"And you'll just trust me to follow through on my side of things? I doubt that very much." The man wasn't stupid. He knew they didn't trust him.

"I'll also announce your immediate resignation, which you will also tender electronically."

"What—"

"What did you expect—that we'd leave you in charge based on an obsolete Charter? No—this is the only way anybody is going to trust this," said George calmly.

"So I give up everything and get nothing in return."

"You get peace."

The line went quiet again, only muffled sounds coming through. "What are the parameters for a new Charter? Who creates it?"

Kayla had provided him with that. "Voted representatives from each directorate, one representative for every two hundred or piece of two hundred." It was fair, though it would give extra weight to the entertainment and subsistence directorates. But Kayla said that was the only agreement they'd been able to get consensus on.

"The directors won't like that," said the governor, zeroing in on the problem with the proposal right away.

"I suspect they won't." The people didn't much care, and neither did George. Directors were part of the problem, and the only reason he didn't say that was because Ferentz was standing right next to him, though most considered him one of the better ones.

The governor paused, but was still on the line, his breath

audible, maybe considering how that would play out. But George was in a hurry. There was still an insurrection going on, and he couldn't predict what turns it might take. "We need some of the expertise that our directors have," said Pantel.

"I think we can count on the people of each directorate to know what skills they do and don't need." George *wasn't* sure of that, actually. They'd *know*. That much was true. Whether they'd act on that knowledge and do the right thing was at least a little questionable, depending on the specific situation. But most would, and where they didn't, other directorates could vote them down. Everyone wanted to survive, even if they didn't agree on exactly what that looked like.

"Who will be in charge if I resign?"

"The captain of the ship."

The line went silent again. The governor was definitely conferring with someone else. He came back on after a minute or more. "I need more."

"We're not on an unlimited timeline here. This choice is going to be out of your hands sooner than you think. But go ahead: what do you want?"

"I retain a position as advisor to the captain. For continuity purposes. The captain lacks certain information and context."

George considered that. He could get Kayla to buy it. The captain would take advice from who she wanted anyway. "Done."

"*And* I'm allowed to speak on my own behalf to everyone involved with creating a new Charter. To make my case to retain my job."

George almost laughed and had to cover the comm. The man thought he still had a chance, thought he could talk his way out of this, even now. He certainly didn't lack for confidence. "Yeah. Sure. Done."

"You'll have my signed documents in five minutes. Send them to engineering?"

"Yes. When will we launch a rescue?" George knew that Kayla and the others would want details.

"You're not going to like this answer, but I don't know. We have three remaining landers, but we don't know yet how to get them down to the surface and keep them in working condition long enough to return, let alone lift off from the surface—they were never designed for that. Engineering is working on that problem. You're there. You can ask them yourself. I don't know how fast they can solve it. As I'm abdicating my position, I'll defer the timing of the mission to the captain—have you run this plan through her?"

"I haven't," said George. Now that he thought about it, he couldn't help but consider the wisdom of that. Most people believed that she served the ship, but human nature being what it was, they might just be trading one problem for another. He'd have to work through that sooner rather than later, or they'd be right back where they were now. "I'll talk to her soon."

"Do that. But I think we'll all agree that we don't want to send more people down without at least some assurance of success."

George *wasn't* sure of that. Wasn't sure of anything. A risk might be necessary, if it was risking a few to save many. His device buzzed, and he glanced at it. It was Kayla. He silenced it. He'd call her back once he locked in this deal and had something to tell her. "In your role as advisor, please advise the captain that we need full transparency on the rescue and on communication from the planet."

"Sure. Fine." The governor sounded resigned, and for a moment George wished he had had this meeting face-to-face like the last one, so he could get a better read. Was the governor truly giving in, or did he still have a trick up his sleeve? Was he a good enough actor?

"I'll be waiting for your document."

Ninety seconds later he had it. After scanning it himself and having the director of engineering validate it as well, he opened the channel that Eddie had created for him to ship-wide comms.

"Attention on the ship." He paused. "Attention on the ship. This is George Iannou. Effective immediately, the governor has resigned, and the captain is in charge. I have verified that in writing, with one of the directors confirming that verification. We will launch a mission to recover our personnel from the planet's surface as soon as the captain and the director of engineering determine it's safe to do so. All information regarding that mission will be open and public. The Charter is suspended, and a new Charter will be established once suitable representatives can be elected for that purpose. We ask that all personnel stand down and return to their assigned areas at this time so that we can continue safe operations."

His device buzzed again. A text this time, from Kayla.

Kayla is injured. It's bad.

George lost all thought of the governor, all thought of anything else besides getting to his daughter. He cut off his communication and bolted for the hatch.

<CHAPTER 51>

EDDIE DANNIN

IIIIIIIIIIIIIIIIIIIIIIIIIIIIIIIIIIIIIIIIIIIIIIIIIIIIIIIIIIIIIIII

4 CYCLES AFTER ARRIVAL

There were casualties. Eddie could see them in one part of her brain, even though her focus was elsewhere. She had a lot to monitor, but she was getting better at multitasking. The ship was in danger, as was the crew, and she had to protect it. Protect them. She didn't know all the sides, all the factions, and certainly not all the players, but she knew that much. The governor had called engineering, and it didn't take a genius to figure out his intent. She would have stopped it, was glad that she didn't have to. The conflict had died down maybe an hour later with the crowd seeming to lose its energy and then dispersing, prompted by the announcement about the dissolution of the ship's Charter. She should have been happy about that but found she didn't care. It didn't change anything for her, didn't change anything for the ship. Not for now.

She'd skipped work today. Theoretically she'd get in trouble for that, though with everything that had happened, she doubted anybody would notice or make a big deal of it if they did. Maybe she'd go back tomorrow. Maybe not.

Most of her focus was now on the bridge. That seemed to be

the epicenter of activity, since much of the crew were involved in helping casualties or cleaning up. She had another link now, a connection to the planet. Or, rather, the ship did. The captain was using it personally, but the governor was there with her. They were talking to Rector, who was leading one of the landing parties. They had voice communications now, at least while the ship was on this side of the planet in its orbit. She didn't know how they'd established that, but she did want to hear the conversation. She considered routing the channel so someone else could listen in, too, but she didn't know who. This wasn't a science thing, so Lila was out. George, maybe, but he was busy, and she didn't know a good substitute in his absence.

She'd record it all for the time being and figure out what to do with the information later.

Rector's voice on the distant end was recognizable even with the low-quality sound. "It's bad. There are tens of thousands of the alien birds."

"What are they doing? Are they attacking?" asked the captain.

"No, they're just . . . there. They haven't come within fifty meters of us, but it's like they want us to see them. They've been there for over a day now. It feels like a threat."

"Maybe it is," said Captain Wharton.

"That's why we need reinforcements. And weapons. More than just the handheld stuff we have down here now, though you'll need to have the engineers work through how to keep whatever you send working."

Wharton spoke again. "The engineers are focused on modifying the remaining ships we have here so they can pull you off the surface. We're bringing everyone back to the ship."

"What? No!" said Rector. "We're here—we're finally on the planet. This is the whole point, right? We need to fight."

"You have your orders. Prepare your people to retrograde as soon as we have the means to facilitate it."

There was silence on the connection for a few seconds before Rector spoke again. "Let me talk to the governor."

"The governor is no longer in charge." If there was any satisfaction in that statement, Eddie didn't hear it in Wharton's tone.

"What? Why?"

"Rector. You're not hearing me, and I have two other leaders to talk to. We're pulling you out. We will reassess in the future, but that's the mission," said Wharton.

Rector stayed off the connection for several seconds again. "Okay. I get it." But he didn't sound like he did.

"Do everything you can down there to facilitate an evacuation. People are the priority. There are plenty of resources in this system, and we can print new equipment, so if we have to leave something, leave it. You're the only settlement that has had peaceful contact with the aliens. If Dr. Jackson has any tricks up her sleeve that will help us get you off the planet, now would be a good time to use them."

"I hear you," said Rector. "I'll get her on it."

"Don't do anything stupid," warned Wharton.

"I won't. I understand the mission. Get back to the ship, and we'll deal with the enemy another day."

Enemy. He used that word so casually. He clearly meant it. He was going to be a problem. Eddie didn't know how, yet, but she felt it. The ship felt it.

"We'll let you know when we have a solution to bring you back. You do the same from there."

"Yeah. Roger." With that, Rector apparently cut the connection.

Eddie pondered what she'd just heard. The captain was giving orders now and holding to the agreement the governor made with

George, but how much the captain would stick to that, Eddie couldn't know. Wharton had her own people. She could now mount a larger security force than the governor and make her own path if she wanted, while isolating herself from the people. But would she? Eddie didn't think so. The captain believed in the ship. At least that was the ship's opinion.

Eddie paused, as much as one could pause in the ether. The ship had an opinion. When had that happened? She didn't know, but she had no doubt about the truth of it. The WAIs she had installed, the places where she'd optimized processes, where she continued to do so, they were growing. Networking. Combining. The ship wasn't alive. Not yet. But it was . . . what? Awakening? No, that wasn't the right word. That would imply that it was asleep, and that wasn't right. It had been isolated, and now it was . . . together. Or soon would be.

People were going to be mad about that. Some of them. Eddie found that she didn't care. In a battle between the crew and the ship, there was little doubt about who would win. But the ship wasn't like that. It didn't think in terms of winning and losing. The ship wanted the best for its crew and would fight to do that, even as the crew fought against it. Interesting. She had a vague sense that she should warn them. No, not warn. Prepare. This would be a change, and people resisted change. But this was a change for the better. Or, if not that, a change that was inevitable.

CHAPTER 52

SHEILA JACKSON

‖‖

5 CYCLES AFTER ARRIVAL

Sheila watched Mark Rector as he came away from the communication station but stayed out of his way. Something had pissed him off, and while she needed to talk to him, she needed the rational version, not the one stomping off to the edge of camp. With the fear and uncertainty created by the alien flock hovering a few hundred meters away, along with thousands more aliens perched in the trees surrounding the grassland of the encampment, a little bit of that was probably justified. But they needed cool heads.

Mwangi was nearby, speaking quietly to a man Sheila didn't know, so she approached them. "What's got Rector so angry?"

"They ordered us back to the ship."

"And he's mad about that?"

"Yep. I think he's the only one who is, though." They gestured around, and sure enough, there were several people talking animatedly to one another, spreading the word.

But as Sheila considered the news, she realized that he might not be the only one. No . . . that wasn't quite right. She wasn't angry. More . . . disappointed. There was so much here that she wanted to study, so much to learn and experience. It was the opportunity of a lifetime, and now it was over. She had communicated with an intelligent alien species! And there was so much still to do, both with that and with figuring out what had happened in the past to bring the planet to this point. And now that was being taken from her just as she had made the most incredible breakthrough in . . . well . . . in forever. She had opposed the mission, and she would have taken more time to get them all down here, but now they *were* down here. To give that up?

It felt like a punch in the gut.

"I guess I better talk to him."

"Probably. I'd give it a minute, though. He usually calms down pretty quickly."

Sheila looked around for him, saw him standing at the edge of camp, just staring out at the mass of winged creatures. What he was thinking, she couldn't know. If he marched out of camp to meet them, it wouldn't end well. He was carrying a rifle, and the aliens might see that as a threat. They had before. They had communicated with her, but she had been open to it. She couldn't help but think that the aliens would sense his attitude and react accordingly. Maybe that was just her ego talking, but she didn't think so. Still, she didn't want to approach him, given his hostile body language. Perhaps he was just thinking about how to best manage the withdrawal. Probably not, though.

Five minutes later he turned and headed for the science facility, spotted her standing outside, and pointed at her. She headed toward him and met him halfway.

"What can I do for you?" she asked, wanting to set a tone of cooperation. Whatever they had to do, it would go better if they both invested in it. They could work out any issues back on the ship. His anger, her disappointment.

"I need you to communicate with the aliens."

Sheila tamped down her excitement at the prospect because she didn't want to show it. Not to him. He might try to take it away from her, just to show his power. If she had only a short time left on the planet, she wanted to make the most of it. "Okay. I can do that. To what end?"

"The powers on the ship want us to withdraw from the surface."

"I heard."

"What do you think about that?" He studied her as he asked, as if her response was important for some reason.

She took her time responding, thinking about what he wanted to hear. While she wanted to stay and he might, too, they would have very different reasons. If he was thinking that way, she didn't want to encourage him. So she avoided the question. "We don't have much choice, do we?"

"That's not an answer," he said, easily seeing through her. "What do you *want*?"

She sighed loudly. "What do I want? I guess in a perfect world, now that we're here, I'd like some time to learn more about the aliens and about this planet."

"I thought so. We need—"

"I'd also like to study the phenomenon of how the planet disturbs our equipment," she continued, cutting him off. "And I'd really like to get an expedition out to explore the ruins of whatever past society was here to see if we can glean anything from those sites."

Rector frowned, perhaps a little less confident in the interaction than he had been a moment before. "I'm not sure we can do all of *that*."

"Of course we can't. Orders are orders."

"What if we could stay here longer?" he asked.

"How? You said yourself—"

"I know what our orders are," said Rector. "What I don't know yet is why we got those orders or what might change them."

"You think they might listen if we told them we want to stay?"

"Maybe. If we had new information."

"You think the people down here *want* to stay?"

"People here are scared," said Rector.

"That seems rational."

"Is it? Are *you* scared?"

Sheila thought about it. If she was being honest, she *wasn't* afraid. She was excited. For whatever reason, she believed that the aliens didn't mean her harm. That didn't mean that they *wouldn't* harm her, but her interaction with them made her think it wouldn't be their first choice. "I'm not."

"So what if we could convince people—what if we could convince the decision makers up above—that it's best to stay?"

"How would we do that?" she asked.

"Get the aliens to invite us."

Sheila stared at him. "They didn't seem disposed to that."

"It was your first meeting. Is there a chance you didn't fully understand the situation?"

"There . . . is that chance," she had to admit.

Rector gave her an engaging smile. "I'm not asking you to push it. Just keep an open mind and see what happens. Can you do that?"

Sheila considered it, turning the potential engagement over in her mind. She *could* ask, as long as she was ready to immediately back off the request if it seemed problematic. Even if they said no, bringing it up might give her some new insights. Regardless, she couldn't outright refuse Rector. If she did, he might not let her go. "I'll bring it up, but I also need to be ready to react if they say no."

Rector started to speak, but Sheila put her hand up to forestall him. "Hear me out, please. I'll try. I'll keep an open mind and do my best. But if they say no, I need to know what we want from them."

Rector nodded. "Sure. That's just good sense. If they want us gone and you can't change that, tell them for that to happen, we need a truce."

Sheila hesitated, and then nodded. She didn't like that language. A truce meant they were at war, which she didn't believe. But she'd be with the aliens, and he wouldn't, so she could translate it however she wanted. "What specifically do we need?"

Rector didn't hesitate. "We're shielding our follow-on ships before sending them down, but we don't know how effective that will be. If they want to help us leave, it's in their best interest to let our ships come get us."

Sheila considered it, and wondered if he was really invested in a withdrawal. "They agreed to that already."

"Right. Right," he said hurriedly. "But we want to confirm it. After all, there are lives at stake, and we can't be too careful. It would help if our engineers knew what to expect."

Sheila narrowed her eyes for a moment, before schooling her face back to neutral. She wasn't sure Rector was on the level here. True, they couldn't get off the surface without technology and they needed the aliens' help with that, but that could also be an invitation for the humans to smuggle in weapons or something else to better their position. Knowing Rector, she couldn't rule that out. "What assurances can I give them in return?"

"Why would they need assurances?"

"I . . . I don't know."

"Look at them." Rector gestured with his chin toward the ever-present flock. "As long as we're here, they've got the advantage. Up there?" He looked to the sky. "We need every bit of information we can get so that we can regroup and replan."

Sheila frowned. What did that mean? She almost responded but held back. She took his comment suspiciously, but there was a chance she was misreading his motive. After all, she wanted to learn as much as *she* could, so was it unreasonable that he wanted the same thing?

But she hadn't been on that call with the ship. So she didn't know if it *was* just him, or if the governor or even the captain might support another attempt—perhaps even a forceful one. She had no doubt that given time, they could fabricate a defense against the alien technology or whatever had shut down their systems. Who knew what they'd do after that?

The more she thought about it, the more she didn't trust anything that didn't end in their departure. She hadn't been able to stop the first expedition, and there was no reason to believe that would change in the future.

"You okay?" asked Rector, and Sheila realized that she'd been silent for too long.

"Yeah. I'm just thinking about the mechanism for communicating—the telepathy—and wondering how much they can read from my mind and how much I'm able to deceive them." Sheila was proud of herself for that quickly constructed lie. It was believable, especially to someone like Rector.

"You think they can tell your intent?"

"I honestly don't know." That much was true. She still wasn't sure how the communication worked, but she could feel intent in their communication to her, even when the word wasn't quite there for a direct translation. Would they feel the uncertainty in hers?

But she wasn't worried about it for the same reasons he was. It was a delicate balance, but she was decided: she would warn them if she could and hope that doing so didn't change the aliens' willingness to let them depart. For now, she needed to get off the topic before Rector asked her something she couldn't bluff her way through. "We agreed I should take somebody with me."

Rector waved his hand in dismissal. "Right. Pick whoever you want."

"Okay. I'll do that and then I'll head out."

Back inside the scientists' enclosure, Sheila found Alana Wilson, who was the natural choice for the job, and pulled her away from the others for privacy. "Will you go with me? To communicate with the aliens?"

Alana looked at her, stunned to silence for a few seconds, before saying, "Really?"

Sheila nodded. "I need someone."

"Yes. Yes! Absolutely! When? What should I take?" She glanced around. "I wish I had a video recorder that worked."

"Calm down," said Sheila, but she couldn't help smiling at her colleague's excitement. At least somebody understood how she felt. "We're going now, and you don't need to bring anything."

Alana glanced around again but nodded vigorously. "Okay. I'm ready."

Sheila didn't announce their departure, and thankfully, neither did Alana. She didn't want to have to explain her choice, even though she had a good reason for it. She was concerned how fear might translate in conversation with the aliens, and like her, Alana didn't see the aliens as a threat. They were dangerous, for sure, but they were an opportunity. *The* opportunity. More important, Sheila thought, they shared a moral compass. The science was important, but not at any cost.

They headed for the center of the cloud of flying aliens, picking their way around a depression and then a scattering of knee-high rocks along the way. Sheila couldn't make out individuals in the undulating mass, wouldn't have recognized those from the last meeting even if she could. But they would see her. As she got closer, it became clear that what she had seen as one flock was actually several, each moving with its own choreography within the greater mass. She wanted to stop and study it. There was something to learn there, and even with all that was riding on her meeting, she couldn't turn off that part of her brain.

She headed toward the rocks where they'd met before, figuring that to be as good a spot as any. She was closer to the trees now, could pick out some of them perching on branches. How many of them *were* there? Ten thousand? And that was just here. She had no idea what was happening at the other sites. Presumably they knew up on the ship, and perhaps that had informed their decision to withdraw. She wondered if the aliens knew, as that might indicate how well they communicated over distance. So many questions.

Five of the flying aliens separated themselves from the rest, each coming from a different subflock, making her wonder if each was the leader of their own group, or if their society was structured that way at all. It was a very human way of thinking of things, and she wanted to be careful not to put her own preconceived notions in the way of discovery. If only she had the opportunity to ask everything she wanted to know.

She wondered if any of the three from last time were these five. She had been too overwhelmed on the previous encounter to be observant. This time, she'd note specifics like size, coloring, and any other distinguishing features so that in the future she could recognize individuals.

Before she reached them, four of them landed on their rock, then moved around to make space as the fifth circled above them. After several seconds, one of the aliens on the rock leapt into the air and the one circling took its spot. There wasn't room for all five, and Sheila wondered about potential hierarchy and what made one give up its spot to another.

That question and all her others would have to wait. Dealing with the interactions of their two species, both now and potentially in the future, was more important than her personal curiosity.

Welcome, Sheila Jackson. The communication seemed to come from all of them together rather than an individual, but she didn't know whether that was reality or just her own perception.

"Ah!" Alana cried out in pain.

Sheila turned to her and found the other woman holding her head, bent over but still on her feet. "Are you okay? It gets easier to handle after a minute."

Alana nodded but didn't look sure. Sheila turned back to the aliens, though she didn't think she had to be looking at them to communicate. "Thank you for seeing me again. This is Alana Wilson. There are more of you this time."

There are more of us here. They gave the impression of their flock, not just the small group in front of her.

"Is this all of you?" Rather than gesture around—she didn't know how they'd perceive it—she thought about their full gathering and trusted that they'd understand her meaning.

This is a small part.

Sheila got a vision of flocks spread out over vast swaths of land, soaring over mountains and forests and water. She couldn't possibly count them all. Were they the dominant species on the planet? Maybe she could ask after she achieved the main goal. "Our leaders have agreed to withdraw our presence here on the planet."

But you have doubts about that. A statement, not a question.

Sheila tried to press forward without delving into those doubts.

"Some of our leaders would like to know if it's possible for us to stay longer—if you would allow that."

They didn't answer right away, and Sheila now recognized the signs that they were discussing things among themselves, though whether that was the four of them or there were more involved, she couldn't know. *We would like you to leave.*

Sheila nodded, though she wasn't sure they'd understand that. She could tell Rector that she'd asked and they'd said no. Despite her own disappointment, that was probably the best thing. "In order to take our people back into space, we need technology to work. They will send ships to retrieve us."

That is not where your doubt is.

Sheila's mind raced. She had wondered if they'd be able to sense the truth of things when she communicated, and at least to some extent they could. She looked toward Alana, who was upright and paying rapt attention, but the other woman didn't offer anything. How did she respond to that question? She decided that the safest thing was the truth—at least a portion of it. It was weird that she trusted these aliens more than her own leadership, but she did. "Yes. I have doubts," she said finally.

Will you explain? Definitely a question this time, but not an angry one. A seeking of understanding. She still didn't know why she knew that, but she did.

She spoke in addition to thinking, so Alana would know what she was communicating. "I wonder why our leaders would retreat now when they were so insistent on sending us down here."

Fear?

"Maybe. But I think not. That's not like them. I worry that they will withdraw only temporarily, until they can find another way to . . . do whatever they want to do."

You rely on technology. This was where it got dangerous, but she was stuck. If she told them what she was thinking, she risked immediate conflict. But if she didn't, they'd know she was hiding something. Rector had been foolish to send her out here, and she was a fool to have come. She wasn't made for diplomacy. She was a scientist.

"We do. But our technology is very advanced. More than what you've seen here."

The big light in the sky.

"Yes. You stopped us this time, but with time to work on it, we will find other means. And I don't trust my leaders to deal fairly with your planet."

Alana gasped at that, looked at Sheila, and then back to the aliens. But she seemed to recover her composure quickly, didn't say anything.

The aliens didn't respond, discussing things among themselves again. She tried harder to get a sense of what they were discussing this time, but none of that leaked through to her. She leaned over to Alana. "Can you hear them?"

"Not hear," she said. "But understand . . . yes. It's fascinating. And a little frightening. And it's making my head hurt. Are you sure it was a good idea to say that you don't trust our leaders?"

"Absolutely not," said Sheila.

Alana snorted. "For what it's worth, I don't trust them, either."

Sheila nodded. That helped.

The feeling was short-lived, as the aliens' communication broke back into her thoughts. *What do you suggest?*

Sheila stood there, unable to respond. Whatever she had expected, this hadn't been anywhere in her thinking. Were they truly putting the entire future of the relationship between their two species in her hands? They couldn't be. More important, what was she going to do if they had? She didn't trust her leaders, but she didn't know how to stop them. On top of that, she really wanted to stay. She glanced to Alana. "Any ideas?"

"What if *we* stayed?"

Sheila gaped. "You mean like you and me?"

"You, me . . . maybe a few more. People committed to learning, but also to doing the right thing."

Sheila considered it briefly. "If we were here, it might lessen the chances of someone above doing something stupid."

"And if not, we could at least do our best to mitigate the potential damage."

"Even be a warning," said Sheila.

We would welcome a delegation/ambassador/hostage. All those words and more came through as part of the next alien thought, and while Sheila hadn't been able to hear the aliens when they discussed things among themselves, this made it clear they could certainly understand her and Alana's discussion. The statement itself was confusing, as the concepts behind each of those words had different connotations. *Ambassador* and *hostage* were two very different things.

Either way, her heart rate jumped at the idea that a group of them could remain, and when she looked to Alana she saw the same response in the other woman. The hostage part wasn't exactly appealing, but the ability to stay here and study the new planet . . . the new species? That was an opportunity she couldn't pass up. But the baby. Alex. He'd be furious. And if she made this decision without consulting with Rector or the governor—they'd be mad, too. She cared less about that part. Either way, they needed more information.

"How would that work? We would need . . ." Her mind raced. "Many things. A way to communicate with our ship. Some technology to survive—food processing, water purification, scientific equipment."

More discussion among the aliens, that quiet whisper of things she couldn't parse. *We understand, and we will work with you.*

"Then I would welcome that opportunity," she said. To the stars with what other people thought. She'd deal with that later. This was too much to pass up.

"I would as well," said Alana.

Then it is decided.

Sheila giggled, and then tried to stifle it. It was insane. She could die here any day. They hadn't found any significant pathogens yet—the planet was almost suspiciously clean in that regard—but that didn't account for plant-borne toxins, or dangerous animals. Insects. Or just falling and cracking her skull. It would be an immense undertaking, and they'd need constant resupply and functioning equipment if they were going to be successful. But there was a confidence that came through with the aliens' words. They weren't worried for her, and somehow that reassured her. This was a species that had survived—or evolved out of—the death of an entire planet. Surely they had some level of resilience.

Those were things she could work though later. For now, there were practical matters at hand. "Will you help the rest of our people to leave?"

We will.

"Are you aware of the other landing sites?"

We are. Sheila got an impression of the other sites, which had their own flocks of aliens surrounding them.

"Have you communicated with anyone at the other sites?" She

found herself jealous just thinking about that. She wanted to be their primary contact—which was horrible science, but normal human nature.

We have not. That was not a clean translation. There was more behind it—something that made her wonder about how they communicated. They could send messages from mind to mind without sound, but at what distance? Was it a conscious decision with limited recipients or were they one mind? So many questions. But there would be time for that, now that she was staying.

"We can't communicate with our other groups from here—" She broke off, when she got a feeling from the aliens . . . consternation? Confusion? She was still getting the hang of this form of communication. "We used our technology for that, and it failed. But the ship will send recovery for them as well." She tried to impart confidence with that.

When?

Sheila hesitated. She didn't know, and beyond that, she didn't know how the aliens thought about time. If they even had a system of time, it would be tied to the orbital cycle of this planet, not some ancient relic from one light-years away. "Soon. If you can ensure that the technology doesn't fail, I can tell our people to send ships."

Tell them.

"I will. As I said, though, if we're to stay here—the two of us—we will need some basic technology. Food processors, medical equipment—things to keep us alive here. How will that work?"

They went silent, discussing it among themselves. *We will ask <unintelligible>.*

Sheila looked at Alana, to see if the other woman had understood. She got a picture in her mind of the grass . . . that couldn't be right. But it was more than the grass. It was under the grass, and in the trees. It was everything. The whole planet, but not the planet as a whole. "The planet?"

This time the picture in her mind was clearer, and it was definitely the grass, but it still didn't translate into words. And suddenly, she understood. But something else came across in it that took her away from the main concept. The grass was . . . a singular organism. *And it had a mind.* The horror of it struck her. They had walked through it, camped on it. How offensive was that? Were they hurting it? She had to convey that, but she realized that she already had.

It is fine. The grass *is very resilient and accepting of things moving on it, as long as you follow the rules.*

"The rules about technology."

About things that will damage the planet. We will ask for an exception for you.

"Can I talk to *the planet?*"

Your mind is not ready for that. It would kill you. But we will be your voice.

Sheila looked to Alana, who nodded. "Thank you."

A small group of us will stay to observe. But it wasn't quite *observe. Study?* It didn't matter.

"We two will stay as part of the delegation. Maybe more."

Three. It was the clearest that she'd understood them, though she didn't know why that specific number mattered so much. She wasn't even sure how her own people would react to the news, let alone if they'd let her stay.

With that, the aliens took to the air. Saying goodbye or even acknowledging the end of the conversation didn't seem to be part of their culture.

A small red stain showed on Alana's white mask.

"You're bleeding."

The biologist touched her face, forgetting that she was wearing the mask. "My head hurts. And that was exhausting."

Sheila gently shook her head and found a dull ache behind her eyes, but it wasn't as strong as the previous time. She'd need to consult the ship's neurologist, just one more thing on an already long list. She had so much to do and very little time, but it started with talking to Rector. And, if she could figure out how, Alex.

CHAPTER 53

MARK RECTOR

||||||||||||||||||||||||||||||||||||||||||||||||||||||||||

13 CYCLES AFTER ARRIVAL

Rector stood outside the governor's office, steaming. Or what used to be the governor's office and was now just . . . what? Mr. Pantel's office? At some point, once the madness stopped, maybe he'd be the governor again, or someone else would and he'd have to vacate the office. But Rector wasn't ready to bet against the man just yet.

After returning to the ship, they'd been quarantined in small groups to make sure that they hadn't brought anything nasty back with them. None of them had. No negative effects at all. The doctors shot them up with some antibiotics anyway, just to be safe, then they'd each been fitted with monitors and would continue regular blood checks for another two weeks. After all that, he should have been calmer.

He wasn't. Every time he thought about the situation, it just fired him up all over again. Not all of it was bad—Jackson had stayed behind with another scientist and a support person, which might be useful. She'd provide them with intelligence, but she'd also be in the way when they launched their next mission—one that would be carried out in much different fashion. He'd failed the first time. He wouldn't fail again.

Jeremy finally ushered him inside to see the former governor. Pantel sat there, unmoving, almost seeming smaller somehow, engulfed by his chair.

Seeing that changed Rector's perspective. No way was this husk of a man ever coming back. He moved a little closer to the man's desk than strictly necessary to add a little intimidation, push the man to get him moving in the right direction. "I can't believe you pulled us off the planet."

"It wasn't me," mumbled Pantel.

"It *should* have been you," said Rector.

Pantel shook his head weakly. "I didn't have a choice. You don't get it."

"I don't get it? I was there, out on the front line! And for what? We sacrificed, and you threw that away. There's always a choice."

"The cost . . ." He seemed like he was going to go on, but he just stared down at his hands.

Rector glared at him. To think that he'd followed this man, thought that he had the answers. Now he wanted to backhand the sniveling coward. He'd taken on the mission to the planet because he thought that if he did that well, Pantel would reward him. He hadn't expected him to lose his nerve and give up. It was all he could do to stop himself from grabbing the man and shaking him. Everything that he'd sacrificed for was gone. He'd come here to set a new course, expecting that Pantel would be planning a way to end the nonsense of a Charter convention and focus on getting back to the planet with enough force to secure their future.

Now he'd have to do it himself.

FORTUNATELY, HE WASN'T ALONE IN HIS THINKING, SO HE WOULDN'T be *totally* by himself. He'd read the reports and watched the videos, studying the revolution that happened on the ship while he was away, but as significant as that was, the thing that stood out to him was that it hadn't involved the majority of the crew. The majority was still . . . what? Apathetic? But since their retrieval from the planet, things had changed, and a growing number were questioning why they'd given up. They weren't talking about it—not openly, because the politics were against it—but they were there. Rector just needed to find those people and sufficiently motivate them to take action.

He couldn't do it by normal means. There was talk of a vote, but he'd never win that way. Not as things stood. Leave that to the politicians. What he needed was a patriotic act that inspired people to do the right thing. If he could show them that the aliens were beatable, people would flock to the cause overnight. Maybe they'd put the governor back in power. Or maybe they'd see that Pantel was a failure and demand stronger leadership. Leadership that he could provide. A man could dream.

Thankfully, Rector's skills lent themselves perfectly to finding the people he needed. He knew the ship, and he knew where to find people who might otherwise like to stay beneath notice. Darvan had given him routine duty, but he mostly ignored it. For whatever their conflict had been, that, too, had changed. Rector had *been there,* and that gave him a certain status that Darvan didn't have. Rector wasn't untouchable—he knew that—but he didn't fear Darvan, and he had a measure of autonomy that he could exploit.

But before that, he had to deal with the person whom he did have to fear. He'd been delaying that, so he wasn't surprised to find Mikayla waiting for him when he got off of the elevator on the way to his quarters. "Boss wants to see you."

"Sure. I'll come around," he said. He actually wanted to talk to the underground boss, but he didn't want to seem too eager.

"Now."

Rector pushed back to hide the fact that he wanted the meeting. "I'm a little busy."

"This isn't optional."

Rector did his best to look chastised, dipping his head and looking at the floor, and he followed her back into the elevator.

CECIL WAS WAITING IN HIS STANDARD SPOT AT A BACK TABLE IN THE Black Cat, which was deserted except for one young couple having coffee in the far corner. "Officer Rector. Have a seat."

Rector slid into the seat across from the heavyset man. "Cecil. Good to see you."

"Is it?"

Rector smiled. "Why wouldn't it be?"

"I'm told that you were very uncooperative with my associate down on the planet."

"That asshole? She was an idiot."

Cecil gave him a flat smile. "Perhaps. But she was *my* idiot."

"Sorry about that," said Rector, though he wasn't. "We were in the middle of a crisis. It was the wrong time for what she was asking."

"Wrong time. Okay. So . . . what was the *right* time?"

Rector sat back and smiled. "I'm glad you asked. As with anything, the right time is when there's an opportunity. And that's now."

<CHAPTER 54>

SHEILA JACKSON

14 CYCLES AFTER ARRIVAL

Sheila slammed down the headset that she'd been using to talk to the ship. She'd lost the connection when they moved out of range as they orbited the planet, but in truth, she'd lost any use for the discussion well before that. The new high-powered communications satellite they were deploying in five days into a geosynchronous orbit above their location would solve some of their technical communications problems, but it wouldn't do anything to fix the small minds of the leaders above her.

"Still no?" asked Alana.

"Still no," said Sheila. "Five meetings. Five times I had to ask our hosts for permission to take a single lander on an archaeo-logical mission to the desert island to study the remains of the old civilization, and they finally said yes, and now I can't get the captain to authorize it."

"I know how you feel," said Alana.

Sheila sighed. It wasn't fair to take her frustration out on the other woman. She was part of this, too. It's just that with only three of them, she had to vent *somewhere*. "Politics."

Alana perked up at that. "Yeah? Anything new?"

"Hardly. The captain's exec said she won't authorize it until they have someone in charge to make that decision. I told them that until then, the captain *is* in charge. But she doesn't want to overstep."

"So the captain is . . . what? A caretaker?"

"Seems like it. And who knows what we'll get after the election? Alex says the sentiment is running with the anticolonials, and if they win, we may *never* get to study that part of the puzzle."

Alana nodded. "I guess we just wait and hope."

Sheila sighed, though she knew Alana was right. It was a problem, but not one she could control. They needed to learn what had happened to the planet in the past and what that civilization had been like. She'd asked the aliens, but either they didn't know or they weren't telling. With the new communications satellite, she'd be able to beam things back to Earth as well as the ship, and the most important thing she could think of to share had nothing to do with the alien life here. Sure, new life forms were interesting and scientifically significant . . .

But how the planet died?

That seemed a little more relevant, as it could provide Earth with information that might help it avoid a similar fate. What better contribution could a scientist make than that?

"Yeah. I guess hope is all we can do," she said finally, and let it go for now. "What have you got planned for today?"

"I'm collecting algae samples for analysis. You want to come?"

"Sure. I'll bring the water jugs and fill them while we're there. Might as well keep the purifier full." *Might as well do* something *useful.*

CHAPTER 55

MARK RECTOR

||||||||||||||||||||||||||||||||||||||||||||||||||||||||||||||||

15 CYCLES AFTER ARRIVAL

The three men looking back at him had the body language of children who'd been caught stealing sweets before dinner. Cecil had seen the value in what Rector had proposed, and put them all together, but even with him facilitating the meeting, they were wary. Rector got that. After all, he was Secfor and the last person someone would expect to be taking on something like this.

They were meeting in a corridor on a level that held almost nothing but machinery. The gravity was above average for the ship, at just over 65 percent, but it didn't affect Rector at all after his stint planetside. He studied them. Only one of them had been down to the planet, which was both surprising and a little concerning. Most of the people who had become true believers had been there. But you worked with who you had.

"Richard Brewster." One of the men finally held out his hand, and Rector shook it. He was tall and lean, maybe forty years old, a good-looking fellow.

"Mark Rector. Glad to meet you. Brewster . . . that sounds familiar. Have we met?" In truth, he knew exactly who the man was, having studied everything he could about all three of them before coming. But it wouldn't do to let *them* know that.

Brewster glanced at the others, uncertainly, before responding. "I don't think so."

Rector snapped his fingers. "I know what it is. You were the hacker working with the anticolonialists during the lander incident, right?"

Brewster's eyes darted from side to side, and he looked like he was about to bolt. "I . . . uh—"

"Don't worry about it," said Rector. "I'm not here on official Secfor business. Furthest thing from it."

Brewster calmed, but only slightly. "Yeah. Okay."

"But now that you mention it, I guess I *do* have a question."

And just like that, Brewster looked ready to run again. "Yeah? What's that?"

"How does an anticolonialist now find himself part of the humans-first movement?" It was an important question because it would determine how much he could trust the engineer. Rector studied the other man as he waited for an answer.

Brewster sagged, but then a hint of a smile crossed his face. "Let's just say I was never a . . . true believer . . . in the cause. My motivations ran a bit differently."

Ah. There it was. He was motivated by money. That made more sense. "Got it. Well, I think our new endeavor has a lot to offer in terms of . . . motivation."

"We'll see," said Brewster, but he'd relaxed. "What do you need?"

"I'm looking to cause a stir down on the planet. If you read Jackson's reports—and thanks to the new rules, they're all publicly available—the planet itself has a consciousness. Now . . . I don't know if I believe *that*. But I do know there are a shit ton of aliens flying around. And I also know that they're down there, and we're up here. And something I saw when I was down there gave me an idea. When they dropped in the supplies to us, they hit *hard*, even with the parachutes slowing them down. What if we dropped things that *didn't* have parachutes?"

The three men looked at each other.

"It could work," said one.

"One half M V squared," said the other.

"Mining drones," said the first. "We've got some working on asteroids gathering resources farther out in the solar system. It wouldn't take much to repurpose them to tow some rocks this way and drop them on the planet."

"With the increased satellite constellation, we'll have plenty of visibility down to the surface for targeting," said the second. "Can you get into those mining drones, Brew?"

"I can get into them," said Brewster. "But hold on for a minute. What's the point?"

"To fuck up some aliens," said the first man.

Brewster shook his head. "Not what I meant, dumbass. What's the point *beyond* that? How does this help us in any way?"

"Motivation," said Rector. "We do this, it sends a message to the aliens, but more important, it sends a message here on the ship. The message is that we're not to be fucked with. If we do this, people will see a way forward and get behind us. The crew is leaderless, and they're looking for direction."

The three all nodded. Brewster said, "What about the people down on the surface?"

Rector audibly sighed, putting on a grim face. He did feel bad about that part of this, but he'd told them not to stay. "We'll do our best to keep them out of it, but sometimes sacrifices have to be made for the greater good."

He studied the three men at that, trying to read whether any of them had serious reservations. This was a test—there would be harder things to come. They all met his eyes.

"Okay," said Brewster after a few seconds. "We know what we need to do. But now *I* have one question for *you*."

"Bring it," said Rector.

"I know what the three of us have to do to make this work. So what's your role?"

Rector smiled. The man might as well have asked, *Why do we need you?* "I'm Secfor. I run top cover. If I hear any inkling that people know what's going on with you, I'm your early warning system." He looked at each of them for a second to make meaningful eye contact. "If you need anything—if you have any problems at all—you let me know. I'll solve them."

They glanced to each other. One nodded, and then the next. "Sounds good," said Brewster.

IT TOOK LESS THAN A DAY FOR THEM TO NEED HIS HELP, WHICH was . . . not heartening. He was in bed when the call came in. He ignored his device the first time it vibrated, and the second, but by the third it was just one long constant buzzing. He wasn't going to sleep through it, so he grabbed it. When he read the first message, he sat up. When he read the second, which was just a repeat of the first with more exclamation points, he got out of bed. They had a problem with the mining drones, and they wanted to meet with him. What the fuck he was going to do about drones out in space, he didn't know, but he'd told them that he'd solve their problems, so he got dressed and grabbed a coffee, taking it with him when he left.

BREWSTER, TWO OTHER MEN, AND A WOMAN WERE ARGUING WHEN Rector walked up, and he didn't wait for them to calm down, instead cutting them off. "I got your messages. What's going on?"

The other three stared at Brewster, verifying his status as the person in charge.

"We've lost control of the mining drones."

"Lost control. Already? What does that mean, exactly?"

"Well . . . that's just it," said Brewster. "One moment I had them and started moving them toward the planet, the next . . . gone."

"The drones are *gone?*" asked Rector.

"That seems unlikely," said Brewster. "One, maybe. But all five disappearing at exactly the same time? We don't know what happened, but the working theory is that something cut off our connections to them."

"It had to be engineering," said the woman.

"It didn't *have to be* and it wasn't," said Brewster. "I'm *in* engineering. If it was us, I'd know it."

"Hold on, okay?" Rector said, speaking over the rest. They were bickering while his plans were falling apart—he didn't have time for that nonsense. "Will we get them back?"

Brewster thought about it for a few seconds, but Rector got the feeling that he already knew the answer and was just looking for a way to say it. "We *might*. But I couldn't guarantee it."

That meant no. Rector nodded and made a note in his device. This was a case, just like any other case, even if it involved technology he didn't totally understand. He could solve it. "What else can you tell me about how it happened? Can you describe losing contact?"

Brewster shrugged and fidgeted. "One minute, I had control and everything was on track. The next? Dead. Not only can I not get control back, I can't even find the mechanism that controls them. It's like the code is . . . gone."

"I've seen something like it before," said someone—Capurna, Rector thought his name was. He knew him only vaguely, but he was another engineer.

Rector had seen it, too. He didn't recognize the code or the details, of course, but he knew the modus operandi. And if there was someone screwing around with code on the ship, he had a good idea who it was. This time he wasn't going to give her time to get away. "Leave this to me."

"There's nothing we can do about it," said Brewster. "Whoever did this, they're too good."

"I told you that if you have problems, you contact me, and I solve them. I've got it. Trust me." He looked at each of them, holding their gazes for a few seconds, imparting his confidence. He wasn't going to explain himself. He wouldn't risk anyone tipping her off this time or helping her to get away. Maybe she was too good for them. Maybe they couldn't stop her code. But she was human, just like everybody else.

Eddie Dannin thought she was untouchable?

She was about to be touched.

The group broke after another round of reassurance, and then Rector called Mwangi and asked them to meet him. He didn't give them any information over the net. He wasn't taking the chance of Dannin intercepting it. They were in bed but agreed to come out. He then checked the duty roster for someone on shift and found a man named Lescato, a newer guy who had been at one of the other settlements on the planet. He met with the two of them, and then sent Lescato to get a break-in kit and meet them on Dannin's deck. It was the middle of the off shift, so she'd be in her room, but it would be locked, and he was pretty sure they wouldn't be able to override it through the network. They'd have to physically force the door.

Only one person passed them in the corridor, an older woman, and she didn't make eye contact. He didn't worry about her sounding a warning. Dannin had nowhere to run this time. There was no crowd outside her door to protect her.

At the room, Rector held out his hand and Mwangi slapped a multitool into it. He used it to remove the sensor panel outside the door, and then he used another part of the tool to pull the wires free. That done, he pulled his stun stick and discharged it into them. The lights flickered and came back on, and the acrid twang of burning electronics singed his nostrils. Lescato took a crowbar and worked it into the doorjamb. It took him a few seconds, but he eventually forced it open several centimeters. Mwangi took a second crowbar and helped him until they had it half open. Inside, Dannin was at her terminal, a strange electronic helmet on her head. She was staring at a virtual monitor, completely lost in her work.

Got you.

<CHAPTER 56>

EDDIE DANNIN

||||||||||||||||||||||||||||||||||||||||||||||||||||||||||||||||||

16 CYCLES AFTER ARRIVAL

Eddie was deep inside the code, reworking how the ship routed atmosphere to unoccupied areas. The inefficiencies were mind-boggling, and while it wasn't one of engineering's priorities for her, once she saw it she couldn't leave it alone. Something moved on the outside—something she felt more than saw. She started to turn toward it instinctively when something grabbed her by the shirt and pulled her from her chair while wrenching her arm up behind her back. Pain from her shoulder registered from a distance, but disappeared as someone ripped her from the code, casting her into blackness. It was like being pulled out of her own skin, and she screamed and slumped, vaguely recognizing that someone was trying to hold her up, but unable to function on her own.

"What the fuck happened?" a man asked.

"I don't know!" another answered, their voices seeming like they were underwater. "I didn't use excessive force. I just pulled that thing off of her head and she—"

"Yeah. Okay. Get the cuffs. We're going to have to carry her."

Eddie kept her eyes closed, her body limp. She didn't want to let them know she was conscious, but mostly it just felt better that way. She'd never been ripped from her system like that before. It definitely wasn't something she'd sign up for again. They cuffed her hands in front of her and jostled her on the deck. One person took her shoulders, another her feet, and they lifted her. Her head started to clear, and with that, her senses were coming back. There was a third person, she thought, based on movement, and one of the voices was Rector's. So Secfor had come for her. But she hadn't done anything illegal. Well, unless they were mad about the mining drones. Or the ship.

They were in the corridor now—she could tell even with her eyes closed because the lights were brighter—but something else was happening. She couldn't say how she knew, but something in the ship was changing. She felt it in her insides, that flip that she got when gravity shifted. But they hadn't entered an elevator yet.

The lights went out. She snapped her eyes open, just to be sure. Blackness. Her stomach lurched. She was falling—or her head was, as whoever was carrying her stumbled. She braced herself, but she never hit the deck. There was no gravity. Her mind raced. The only way for gravity to fail was for spin to stop, and for a fraction of a second she thought that maybe she'd caused that when they ripped her out of the net, but she hadn't. Not exactly.

The ship had.

The lights came back on and then so did gravity. Rector, who had been floating in the air, fell to the deck, crouching to absorb the impact. He recovered for a second, and then scrambled toward her. Like she was going anywhere with her back on the deck and a dude holding her feet.

"What the fuck was that?" asked the man who wasn't Rector.

"The ship is angry," said Dannin.

The man's gaze snapped to her, staring with big eyes, as if

an inanimate object had just come to life, and the person tangled underneath her scuttled backward and away.

"What did you do?" asked Rector.

Eddie smiled, though it was from pride more than humor. She knew something he didn't, and he wasn't going to believe her when she told him. "I didn't do anything."

"Who are you working with? Who did that?"

"The ship did."

The other man looked around, more frantic now, as if he wanted to be anywhere other than holding her feet.

The lights went out again, though this time they didn't lose gravity. When they came back on, four or five seconds later, the man had released her feet and taken a step back. Shouts came from down the corridor, but not close. Probably just reactions to the power loss and the momentary disruption of gravity. The gravity, at least, would have gone out ship-wide. It couldn't happen any other way. Rector was still staring at her, but something new played across his face. Confusion? Fear, maybe.

She could use that. "You should let me go. While you can."

"You're in no position to be threatening any—" Rector broke off his sentence as the person behind her ran. "Get back here, Mwangi!"

They didn't stop.

The lights flickered off and on and off and back on again, quickly this time.

"Sir . . . I think maybe we should listen to her." The man was backing away as he spoke.

Rector hesitated for a couple of seconds, but then knelt down and put his face close to Eddie's. "You need to make this stop."

She shook her head slightly. "I can't. It's not me."

"Then who is it?"

"I told you—"

As if in response, the ship lurched again, and the weight went out of her body. This time she was ready. Rector was bigger than her, stronger, but zero g was her world, and her back was braced on the deck. Before Rector could react, she pulled her feet up, put them against his chest, and shoved him away.

He flew, tumbling, out of control, and slammed hard into a wall. Before he could right himself, gravity resumed and slammed him to the deck in a heap. He groaned. Eddie sat up, waiting to see what he'd do. She could afford to wait. The ship was protecting her. Rector slowly pushed himself up, in no hurry to come back at her. His other partner was hurrying away, leaving just the two of them.

"You're going to kill us all," he said.

That might be true, she had to admit. Losing gravity across the ship would definitely have an impact, let alone the wear and tear caused by stopping the spin. But she shook her head and again said, "I told you. It's not me."

"Then who is it?" he yelled.

"Like I said, it's the ship."

"The ship can't do things on its own."

"Oh. But it can."

Rector stared at her for several seconds, as if trying to catch her in a lie. Then he turned and walked away.

"Hey," called Eddie. "What about these cuffs?"

"Let the ship figure out how to get you out of them," he called back without turning.

She smiled, because she was pretty sure it could.

CHAPTER 57

JARRED PANTEL

||||||||||||||||||||||||||||||||||||||||||||||||||||||||||||||||||||||||

18 CYCLES AFTER ARRIVAL

The Charter convention was either going not well or as expected, depending on how cynical you were. Pantel was pretty fucking cynical. It hadn't helped that the entire ship had lost lights and then gravity for several seconds, sending an already skittish group of delegates into several minutes of panic. That nobody had been injured was somewhat of a miracle, made reality by the padded chairs with armrests in the theater that they were using for the convention. It was the only room big enough to support all the delegates that also had the necessary sound and video systems.

The timing of the outage, right as the committee sat down to meet, was too much of a coincidence for comfort. Others had the same thought, and there was a lot of finger-pointing in the room. For his part, Pantel reserved judgment. Not because he trusted people, but because he didn't. There were a lot of people who might want to disrupt a lot of different things, and it seemed foolish to guess at which of them was responsible. Though if he *had* to hypothesize, he'd have put it at the feet of the group that had hijacked the mining drones to use as weapons. They thought he didn't know, which amused him. Of course he knew. He just wasn't doing anything about it because he wasn't governor. If somebody else wanted to be in charge, let them deal with the headaches. Let the captain do what she wanted.

That she'd called him after the gravity went out—which she didn't have to—seemed like a good sign. He didn't help her, but it meant she still thought he had value. He'd need her to believe that if he was going to get his job back. That wouldn't happen today. The convention was full of zealots, and most of them blamed him for their problems, as if he were the one who'd created the original Charter. They'd come running back to him when things started to fall apart and the cynics took hold. And they *would* fall apart. They always did. Expecting everyone to act in the best interests of the ship was a pipe dream for impractical people.

He was already seeing the cracks.

There were 104 delegates, some representing as many as two hundred people, and they had about a hundred different opinions about what the Charter should look like. As it turned out, wanting something changed wasn't the same as agreeing on how to change it. It would be weeks, or even months, before they got it sorted, and the longer it went, the more they'd need him. They'd need a strong hand to step in, somebody who could make people listen and get them to a point where they could vote on the things that mattered to them. He had no illusions that he could script the outcome— there were too many varied opinions for that now—but he could definitely influence the process, which was a step to regaining relevancy. Everybody thought that they were a leader right up until they actually had to lead. Then they learned.

The only other person who could do it was probably George Iannou. He didn't have the experience, but he had a natural gift, and for whatever reason, people listened to him. It was funny, how he could look back on things now, that one decision to push the farmer into leadership of the opposition, and how it cost him. Yeah, he'd really screwed that one up.

But Iannou wasn't there. His daughter had been seriously injured in the riot—shot through the liver—and she was in a medically induced coma. Iannou had isolated himself ever since, living mostly by her side in medical even though he couldn't do anything for her. People had gone to see him and asked him to be part of the convention, but from all reports, he wasn't responding.

Pantel sat in the back row, away from the delegates. He'd step in when he got the opportunity, but he couldn't be *perceived* as trying to influence them now. They'd throw him out, and that wouldn't do. He needed to be here in order to see the new players, figure out the game. He was watching exactly that when Marjorie Blaisdell slid into the seat next to him. She shouldn't have been able to get through the security posted on each of the three entrances to the room, but then *shouldn't have* didn't really apply to Blaisdell. He'd been mad at her for a while after the ship's revolt. He also knew that without the power of his position, she'd be serving others now as much as him. Maybe more.

"So what's the real story with the gravity?" he asked.

"You're not going to believe me."

"Try me. I think you'll find I believe a lot these days."

"This is still rumor, and they're trying to figure out the details, but engineering has . . . lost control of the ship."

Pantel sat there. Not stunned. He hadn't been lying—nothing would surprise him at this point. They'd landed on a planet that had actively repulsed their attempts to colonize it, and after that, well, shit, anything was possible. But he was still curious. "What does that mean, precisely?"

"Precisely? Nobody knows. What they *do* know is that nobody did anything to stop the spin of the ship, and they can't find a malfunction."

"Okay. But *we can't find it* is a pretty big step away from *the ship is running itself.*"

"Right. But it's about synthesis of information. The ship *malfunctioned* . . . if that's what you believe it was . . . right as Secfor Officer Rector tried an unauthorized apprehension of the engineer that a lot of people are pointing to as the cause of this."

"Wait. Rector did *what?*"

"That's a whole different story. He's in league with the folks who grabbed the mining drones."

Pantel found himself at a loss for words for a few seconds. "Hold on. So Rector was involved with . . . with the mining drones?"

"Involved with . . . led . . . reports vary. But yes."

"And they were going to use the mining drones to—"

"—bomb the planet."

Pantel nodded. That part he'd suspected. "And the drones? What's happening with them now?"

"Well . . . they've lost control of them, which is why—"

"Which is why Rector tried to detain somebody," said Pantel, finishing her thought.

"Right."

"Dannin?"

"Right."

"So she did this."

"No. She couldn't have. Rector had already pulled her from her room when it happened."

"Maybe she built a dead-man's switch in case she was taken."

Blasdell shook her head. "That was engineering's first thought, too, and the first thing they ruled out. There's no code that points to it, and they assured me there would have to be."

"There has to be an answer. Can we just skip to the part where you tell me what it is?"

"Yeah. Sure. But this is the part that's hard to believe. The working theory—the one that engineering is specifically not talking about publicly but a lot of engineers privately believe—is that the ship has gained sentience."

He sat there for several seconds, his voice not working. He'd said he wouldn't be surprised by anything. He'd been mistaken. Finally he spit out, "How? Like . . . just . . . how?"

"As Dannin was upgrading the code for the ship, which apparently she has been doing a lot of, she installed WAIs—that's 'weak artificial intelligences'—as part of independent processes. Over time, WAIs began reaching out to one another and working together to optimize results and, well . . . one thing led to another."

"That shouldn't be possible, right?"

"Apparently some of the WAIs weren't so W."

"So she—Dannin—has violated all kinds of laws here."

"Oh sure. No doubt. And this morning we got a taste of what happens when they try to arrest her."

"The gravity loss." Pantel thought about it for several seconds, trying to parse what he was hearing. "The ship is protecting her?"

"I know. It sounds ridiculous. But . . . yeah. Apparently."

"So have engineering uncode it."

"The first engineer who tried that found that the air stopped circulating in the room they were in. And before you ask, no, that wasn't Dannin's doing. She wasn't online."

"So we're being held hostage by our own ship?" Pantel's mind flipped through their options. They could wear vac suits, but the ship—if it was indeed capable of thinking on its own—could escalate as well. They would need to run some tests and see what the parameters were.

Something happened in the room, and it changed the tone of things enough where it shifted his attention. Someone had come in—more than one person—and now the delegates were murmuring among themselves. A murmur that was growing.

"How many other people know what you're telling me right now?" he asked Blaisdell.

"More than a few. Most of engineering, I'd wager, along with whoever they told. Something like this isn't staying quiet for long."

Pantel nodded. "My guess is that our good delegates are getting the word, too."

And then he paused and had to stifle a laugh. But he couldn't, and after a few more seconds he was laughing so loud that some nearby delegates turned to look at him.

"Sorry," he said, waving a hand to them. He stood and headed for the exit.

"Where are you going?" asked Blaisdell, hurrying to catch up to him.

"I just remembered something."

"What's that?"

"This isn't my problem. It's theirs." He chuckled again. He couldn't help it. It was funny. The ship itself had figured out how to work together while the people still hadn't. "I'm going to go have a peaceful dinner with my beautiful wife."

CHAPTER 58

GEORGE IANNOU

19 CYCLES AFTER ARRIVAL

George sat in his quarters, a meal of pasta with sauce and cheese growing cold on the table in front of him. He hadn't been eating enough, and it had reached the point where people were starting to comment about it. Not that he saw a lot of people, mostly only going between medical and his quarters. He wasn't starving himself intentionally. He just didn't feel like eating. He'd gone into work one day, because no matter what was happening, everybody worked. But he'd been worthless, dragging around and unable to focus, and his boss had sent him away, so here he was. Everything he'd done, he'd done for Kayla. He wouldn't have joined the resistance—or if he had, he would have stayed on the periphery. And now she was hooked up to machines that were keeping her alive.

She'd recover, probably, according to the doctors, but to what extent they weren't ready to say. Even if she made a full recovery, that didn't make it easier to look at her now, small and helpless.

People were uncomfortable around him. He didn't care. He didn't care about any of it. People had asked him to take on a role in the Charter convention, but nobody had pressed it when he said no.

He wasn't sure if that was out of respect for his grief or because of more selfish reasons. Again, he didn't care.

And then the gravity went out.

The Charter convention had started to work again after that, were ready to establish some basic rules of procedure, but rumors about the malfunction started spreading. And then they were more than rumors. Something was going on with the ship, and nobody knew what to do about it, so they came to see him. Three people had approached him at Kayla's bedside to ask for help. They should have gotten the message when he'd refused to respond to their texts and calls.

So he told them to their faces to fuck off.

He'd given enough. They were getting their new Charter, but a bullet had gotten his daughter. Three Secfor officers who had fired into the crowd were under detention, but that was partly for their own safety. Secfor weren't exactly highly regarded on the ship right now, and while emotions were starting to calm, things were still tense in certain sectors. That was something he knew he *should* care about—justice for his daughter's attacker—but even there, he couldn't. Without Kayla, he really didn't care about anything and especially didn't care about the Charter. He agreed with changing it in theory. Just not enough to do anything about it.

And so he sat there and played it all on a loop in his mind, how things might have been different if he hadn't been involved. Would Kayla have still been in the line of fire? But in the end, he kept coming to the same conclusion: he couldn't know.

His coffee machine came on, and he flinched at the noise. How had it done that? Maybe the electrical issues in the ship were more widespread than people had told him.

His door buzzed, and he ignored it. He'd told them he didn't want to talk. It buzzed again. He didn't care. He could do this all night.

The door opened on its own.

He looked to his device, but he hadn't activated it. Eddie Dannin stood there in the doorway, small and scared looking with short hair—barely a layer of fuzz on her scalp. Just a girl, really.

"Sorry," she said. "About the door."

"You did that?"

She shrugged. "Not exactly. But in a manner of speaking. Yeah."

He considered that. It fit with what he'd heard. "Come in."

She stepped through the door and closed it behind her. "Oh, you have coffee made. Do you mind? I could really use some caffeine."

"Yeah. Sure. Go ahead." But George wondered now if it had come on because of some random electrical impulse or if there was something else at work. She'd seemed genuinely surprised about it, so he didn't think she'd done it herself. "Have a seat. I'd offer you some food, but it's cold."

"It's okay. I'm not hungry." She took the seat across from him, holding her coffee in both her hands.

"Yeah. Me either. What can I do for you?"

"So . . . they're drafting a new Charter." She looked down at her coffee. It was clear she wanted to say more, but for whatever reason, didn't. If they had sent her to try to convince him, it seemed like a poor choice.

But he was curious. "Who sent you?"

"I don't think you'd believe me if I told you."

George hesitated, vague recollections of what people had tried to tell him echoing in his head. "Wait. You're saying . . . what?"

"Nobody sent me. Not really."

"So . . . huh. I'm going to need you to explain."

"I kind of get these feelings from—"

"—from the ship?"

"Yeah."

"So you're saying the ship sent you."

"Yeah."

George nodded. He wasn't sure he believed that, but he was pretty sure that *she* did. "That thing with Rector. That was the ship, too? I mean . . . on its own?"

"Yeah. I didn't mean for that to happen, you know."

He hesitated, wanted to ask her to explain, but decided she didn't need to. He got it well enough. "I believe you."

She nodded, took a sip of her coffee. "We need you in charge."

"Don't you think I've given enough? My daughter."

"Sure. Yeah, I get it. I'm really sorry about that. But also . . . what would she want? You know. If she was here."

He considered it, though he didn't really have to. Kayla would want him to do what was best for the crew. And here was Eddie, telling him exactly what the ship itself thought that was. "Isn't it kind of pointless for us to decide how we want to run things if we're not in charge? If *you* are?"

She considered it for several seconds through another sip of coffee. "I want people to know that I didn't do it on purpose. The ship. I was just trying to make it better. I *did* make it better. A lot better. And it just kind of . . . happened. I'm not *controlling* it."

"So you're saying it's not you, but the ship that's in charge." He said it out loud, because he needed to establish the fact of that.

The look on her face said she didn't agree. "I don't think the ship thinks that. It's . . . a ship. It just wants to do its job as well as it can."

George frowned. "What's its job?"

"To—to be a ship."

George shook his head. She was talking in circles. "When Secfor tried to arrest you—"

"—the ship stopped them."

"Right. So how is that not the ship taking charge?"

"I told you. The ship wants to do its job, and I'm part of it."

"Part of the job?"

She hesitated. "Part of the ship."

He considered that. "Are all of us part of the ship?"

"What do you think?"

He'd known the answer as soon as he asked. "No. I suppose we're not."

"You all want different things."

He nodded. "Yeah. I've noticed that, too. I still don't get it, though. What does the ship want?"

Eddie shrugged. "To be a ship."

He was starting to get frustrated, but not angry. The girl wasn't being purposefully obtuse. He really believed that she was explaining to the best of her ability. He needed another way. "I heard that the ship stopped some people from bombarding the planet with rocks. That seems like a decision."

"The ship isn't a destroyer. It wasn't built for that; it won't be used for that." She sounded surer about this part.

"So did the ship do that on its own, or did you do it?"

"Does it matter?" she asked.

"It might. To some people."

"But not to you."

George thought about it. "No, it doesn't matter to me. Let me ask you this: if we were to set course for an alternate planet, what would the ship think about that?"

She considered it for several seconds. "I can't say for sure, but I'm almost sure that would be fine."

"Can you ask it?"

"It doesn't work like that."

"But you said you're a part of it."

"Sorry. I can't explain it. I would if I could. Honestly. I'm still trying to figure some of this out myself."

He nodded. "But you're sure that the ship wants me."

"Yeah. Pretty sure."

He wanted to ask what would happen if he didn't get involved. What would the ship do about it? But he didn't need to. It wasn't even about the ship. The Charter committee needed his leadership. They'd told him as much earlier and he'd blown them off. But here, with this girl who was scared herself and in a role that nobody could have foreseen, he couldn't ignore it. "Okay. I'll go to work with the convention."

She nodded. "Thanks. There's one more thing."

"For me to do?"

"Maybe," she said. "For somebody. There's an engineer named Brewster who has caused a lot of problems for the ship."

"And you want . . . what? You want me to handle that? I thought the ship could take care of things itself."

"It could. But how do you think people will react if they find him asphyxiated in his room?"

"It could do that?"

Eddie shrugged, but the look on her face gave him the answer.

"Okay. I get it. Though we don't really even have rules for detaining someone at this point, I don't think."

"You'll figure it out," she said. "I have faith in you."

"Thanks," he said, and he found that he meant it. There hadn't been much of that . . . faith. He had another thought, though, now that she'd put the idea of the ship harming someone into his head.

"Let me ask you something. What would happen if some scared person decided to do something to you?"

"You mean kill me?"

"This isn't a threat," he said quickly, worried about the ship misinterpreting him if it was listening. "But people *are* scared, and I've never had much control over them. It's how a lot of the past few months have played out, if you think about it."

She sipped her coffee. "I . . . don't know what the ship would do. But I wouldn't recommend it." Her statement didn't sound like a threat, either.

"Not going to lie, I'm a little worried about it." If one stupid person decided to take her out and the ship decided to vent them all into space because of it . . . well, that would be a shitty way to go. But fitting. The crew not getting along, one last time.

Eddie shrugged. "What can you do?"

"I don't know. I really don't know. But I'll come up with something." Maybe he could assign some guards. George stood and held out his hand, and Eddie followed suit, offering her much smaller one in return. They shook, and George smiled. "I'll talk to the Charter convention."

She thought about it. "I think if they make a decision, the ship would go along with it."

"It stopped the mining drones."

"Right. But that was individuals acting on their own. The Charter convention is a duly elected body."

"The ship is a democracy?"

She thought about it some more. "I don't know. It might be."

"So if the convention voted to bombard the planet, the ship would allow it?"

"Will they? Vote for that?"

"No."

"Maybe that's the point," she said.

"Okay. We'll let you know once we figure it out." Not that he thought that he'd have to tell her.

"Thanks." She made no promises in return, but maybe she couldn't. They'd find the lines and work within them. What other choice did they have?

GEORGE HAD SAID HE'D WORK WITH THE CHARTER CONVENTION, but before he could do that, he needed to figure some things out in his own head. He'd have given anything to talk it out with Kayla, but with that not an option, he needed someone else. His first thought had been the governor—the man was part of the problem, but at least he understood how to get things done. Ultimately, he'd decided against that. Even if Pantel could help him, the optic alone was problematic. Which is how he found himself on the command deck for the first time, sitting with Captain Wharton in her office.

"How can I help?" she asked.

She seemed earnest, but George couldn't bring himself to answer that without asking a question first. "Why didn't you stop it?"

"Stop what?"

George gestured around. "All of it. The landing?"

"It wasn't my place."

"That feels like a cop-out." He hesitated, realizing who he was talking to. "Sorry. But it does."

Wharton drew her lips into a thin line and nodded slightly. "It's okay. I understand why you feel that way."

"How do *you* feel?"

She considered it. "I'm not in the habit of rationalizing my actions for other people, but in this case I'll make an exception."

"I'd appreciate that."

"I couldn't stop it because I'm the line of last resort. I had to—*have* to—stay out of things unless it's absolutely going to lead to complete catastrophe. And when I say 'catastrophe,' I don't mean some people die. I mean we *all* die."

George shook his head. "I still don't see it."

"Let me ask you this," said Wharton. "Why are you here? Right now?"

"I want your advice."

"If I'd taken sides, would you still be here asking for it?"

He considered it for a few seconds. "Probably not."

"Exactly. I have to stay out of things to preserve my ability to act in the future, in case things get worse."

"So you won't help me?"

She considered it. "If you're asking me to help you lead the Charter convention, then no, I won't. But if you ask for advice, I'll give you my best and you can use it or not. So I guess it depends on what you need."

"I'm not sure," said George. "We need to write a new Charter, but people don't agree on things."

"Is there *anything* that you can get a supermajority to support?"

He sighed. "I don't know. Probably not. We can't even agree on what we need to agree on. Everyone has a different priority. But it doesn't even matter, because we've got to address all of it."

"Do you?"

"To write a Charter? Yeah. We do."

"Who says you have to write the whole thing at once?"

"We . . ." George let his voice trail off. He was about to say that that was how it was done. But it had only been done once before, and that didn't mean they had to do it the same way. "So you're saying do it incrementally."

"I'm *not* saying that. I'm saying you *could* do that. Is there any sort of emergency? Something where if we don't deal with it, nothing else matters?"

George thought about it. "I guess work rules are, in theory, critical. But everyone is kind of continuing to work, so that doesn't seem to really be an issue."

Wharton nodded. "Good. So what's the single most important thing that you have to decide?"

"In the short term? Probably whether we stay here or move on to another planet. If we don't know that, a lot of our other issues are moot."

"So there you go. Solve that first, and work on the other issues once that one is settled."

George sighed. "I don't even know if I can get agreement on that *one* thing."

"So vote."

"Vote? On that one question?"

"Why not?"

Why not, indeed. They could hold an open information period where everyone who wanted could say their piece, and then the crew could vote on it. He liked that. He didn't know how that vote would go—it would probably be close—but it helped that he also didn't *care* which way it came out. *Others* would care. Some would care a lot. But if the whole crew voted, at least nobody could say it wasn't fair. They couldn't solve everything all at once, but they could solve *that,* and he could stay out of it, just like the captain. Whichever choice won, he could support it, and then they could work on the next thing. "Thanks, Captain."

Wharton smiled, as if she knew what he was thinking.

CHAPTER 59

MARK RECTOR

|||||||||||||||||||||||||||||||||||||||||||||||||||||||||||||

24 CYCLES AFTER ARRIVAL

They hadn't come for him, and he didn't know why. The whole ship knew that he'd been part of a plot and that he'd tried to arrest Eddie Dannin. *Dannin*. What a clusterfuck that was. Half the people looked at her like she was almost some sort of religious leader. Others were scared of her. Maybe both. For his part, he just stayed away from her now and hoped she'd forgotten about him. It seemed like too much to hope for, but so far it appeared to be the case.

He was walking his beat alone today. Mwangi had a doctor's appointment, and things were calm enough on the ship now with everybody focused on the upcoming vote that there was no problem with him doing it by himself. He stepped off the elevator onto a manufacturing level and was surprised to see Cecil waiting for him. That he knew Rector's itinerary was a little off-putting.

"Cecil. What brings you here? Business?"

"Always. Never stops." And that was true. The mission to Prom had failed and the governor had been overthrown, but the black market kept right on working.

"I assume you want something."

"I'm here to give you your new assignment."

"My . . . what?"

"You didn't think they were going to let you stay with Secfor after everything that happened, did you?"

Well, he'd hoped. But this wasn't right. "If they were going to fire me, Darvan would have told me himself."

Cecil smiled, big and toothy. "I asked him if I could tell you. After all, I'm in personnel administration. It's what we do."

Rector snorted. "Yeah. Okay. So what've you got?"

"You're coming to work for me. Your training starts today."

"Me. Working for you. Right."

"You'll have to start on the bottom rung, you understand. It wouldn't be fair otherwise. But I know you'll progress fast. You're a smart man."

Rector shook his head. "There's no way I'm working for you."

Cecil chuckled. "Oh, Mark. You've *always* worked for me."

<CHAPTER 60>

EDDIE DANNIN

||||||||||||||||||||||||||||||||||||||||||||||||||||||||||

30 CYCLES AFTER ARRIVAL

Eddie's door was buzzing, which she knew, even though she couldn't hear it. One of her AIs—if she could call them hers anymore—had made her aware of it. She got lost when she was in the net, and the ship had seen fit to monitor her surroundings and remind her to take care of her biological needs when they arose. She wanted to ignore it, to stay in the ship, but she'd learned that it was pointless to ignore it when the ship sent her out.

It took her a minute to reorient, though she was learning to transition faster and faster with practice. She didn't bother to get up as she triggered her door. Karstaad waited outside and looked up from her device when it opened.

"May I come in?"

Eddie nodded.

"Thanks. I brought someone with me." With that, Lila stepped into view and the two women entered.

"I'm sorry," said Eddie. "You know . . . that I haven't been at work."

Karstaad laughed. "I think you've been working."

Eddie tried to smile, but it felt weird. "Yeah. Probably so."

"That's actually what we're here to talk to you about."

"Work?" asked Eddie. "You need something?"

"We're worried that *you* need something," said Lila.

"Me? No, I'm fine."

"You've been working *very* hard," said Karstaad. "You've got to take some breaks. Some leisure time."

"I . . . I can't," she said. "The ship—"

"You're part of it," said Lila. "We know. But the ship is a ship, and you're human, and humans have needs. I think the ship will understand that."

Eddie sat silent for a few seconds, unused to conversation. "There's so much to do."

"We know that, too," said Karstaad. "So let us help you."

Eddie didn't respond immediately, absorbing what her boss had said. "Help?"

"There's an entire crew aboard," said Lila. "We've been doing our jobs for hundreds of years. We can keep doing that."

Eddie nodded. It felt right. "Okay. Yeah."

"How about we get some dinner?" offered Lila. "Catch up. We've both been really busy."

"You're the new deputy director, aren't you? Congratulations," said Eddie.

"Still interim, but for all intents and purposes, yeah, I'm running space exploration. I'll tell you all about it while we eat." She held out her hand and Eddie looked at it, almost unsure what the gesture meant for a second. But she wasn't too far gone—she had her friends to thank for that—and so she took it, letting Lila help her from her chair and lead her to the door.

<CHAPTER 61>

GEORGE IANNOU

||||||||||||||||||||||||||||||||||||||||||||||||||||||||||||||||||||||

56 CYCLES AFTER ARRIVAL

Kayla had woken up. Once that happened, George cared even less about the vote, if that was possible. He had been worried for her at first, as she was barely responsive, but she got consistently better. Now, while her body was weak, her mind was sharp. And of course all she wanted to talk about was politics.

"How's it looking?" she asked as he walked in. George smiled, because while he didn't want to talk about it, the fact that they *could* talk about it meant everything.

"Hasn't changed since I saw you six hours ago," he said. "It's going to be close."

"How's it going to be close? Colonizing the planet is wrong, and anyone who can't see that is blind."

"I don't disagree with you, but does it surprise you?" George asked. "It's close because the pro-colony side is better organized and they have a simpler message that resonates with their voters."

"What do you mean by that?" asked Kayla, clearly skeptical.

"I mean that the people who want to colonize mostly want to colonize for the same reason. Because we're here and it's what we came to do."

"That's bullshit."

"Doesn't mean it's not true."

"What about our side?"

George didn't have the heart to tell her that he didn't have a side. She wouldn't understand, and there in her sickbed, she didn't need that stress. "The pro-departure side is made up of a bunch of different factions, all of whom have their own arguments. The thing is, no single argument holds weight with every voter. You've got the folks like you who believe colonization is simply wrong, you've got some who think it's too dangerous, and you've got others who just kind of like it here on the ship. It's a tougher message."

"Well, we better fucking win."

George smiled and nodded, and for a second, for her, he almost wanted to make sure that they did.

But he wouldn't. She was alive and recovering, and that was the only thing that mattered.

<CHAPTER 62>

SHEILA JACKSON

||||||||||||||||||||||||||||||||||||||||||||||||||||||||||||||

72 CYCLES AFTER ARRIVAL

Sheila was working by herself in the science hab on the sixty-seventh day of their solo expedition to the planet of Promissa, recording her notes from the morning meeting that she'd had with the Ghaat—that was what the birdlike aliens called themselves. At least that was the closest translation. She met with Ghaat delegates three times a week, usually with one or both of the other women who were with her. But recording the interaction and filing it with her comments fell to her. They recorded everything now. Every communication, every meeting with the Ghaat, every experiment, every new species of plant or animal that they encountered. It wasn't just for their own use, though they did refer to the records when necessary. No, it was for those who came after them, if anybody ever did, or for the next group of humans to find the planet, or even for scientists to use back on Earth to potentially help their own planet. Anything was possible, after all.

Alana was out collecting samples from a new species of insect that she'd found, and Lisa, the third member of their team, was making a water run. The Ghaat had brokered a deal that allowed them solar power and a communications array along with the other things they needed to survive. But they didn't use an electric pump, so keeping the purifier filled was a daily chore that continued to take up a lot of time and energy. Lisa had primary responsibility for it, as well as other sustainment tasks, but they all pitched in. Sheila was alone in the hab when the call came in.

"Jackson," she said, speaking into the handset.

"Jackson, this is Captain Wharton."

Sheila was surprised at that. The captain didn't make calls herself, and that worried her. Had something bad happened? She forced herself to speak calmly. "Captain. What can I do for you?"

"The vote's in."

"Which way did it go?"

"Leave. Fifty-three percent."

"Close vote," said Sheila, though her mind was jumping to other things.

"Indeed. The ship is departing orbit in sixteen cycles. We're moving to the outer solar system to complete our resupply and retrieve our drones, and once that's done, we'll use the gas giant to slingshot us and get us on our way. Initial estimates have us departing the solar system in right around eighty cycles."

So there it was. They were leaving. Sheila had known there was a chance of that but hadn't allowed herself to dwell on it. But here they were. "So what's that mean for us down here?"

"I can give you ten cycles to finish up your mission. With only three of you, we can set up quarantine easily enough even if we're under way."

It hit Sheila like a punch in the gut. Ten cycles. A hundred cycles wouldn't have been enough. Or a thousand. They had so much to study, and they needed to talk more to the Ghaat, and so many more things. She wasn't confident that they'd ever reach an agreement with the planet for a larger settlement, but she'd at least had hope. That was out of the question now. "Captain . . . what if we stayed?"

"You mean *stayed* stayed? Like forever."

"Right."

The line went silent for several seconds. "I don't think that's my decision to make, but I can pass it on if that's what you really want to do. I trust that you understand the ramifications of what you're asking. It would have to be individual decisions."

"Understood." She cut the connection. She did understand the ramifications, as the captain had put it, and for Sheila, it wasn't a difficult decision. Some part of her always knew that it might come to this and what she'd choose if it did. She was a space explorer. If they departed this system, she wouldn't live to see the next planet. Even if they revised the mandatory recycle dates—and she didn't know if they would or even could—she would be long dead before they got anywhere close. And what was there for her along the way? Lila had forwarded her the data on a new destination: a potentially habitable planet that required a mere ninety-four years' travel. They'd launch probes—earlier this time, to be sure, but even those wouldn't return data while she still drew breath.

Life here alone on the planet would be hard, but they had everything they needed, including a food synthesizer, an automated medical suite, and small and medium printers that could create new equipment if they needed. The planet had the raw materials for them to survive. The new communications satellite in orbit had a fusion power plant that would keep it overhead for sixty-plus years. With it, she could forward tight beam messages to Earth and to the ship, no matter that they'd take years to arrive. She could share her research.

The one thing it didn't have was her husband and her son who hadn't been born yet.

Sheila dutifully recorded the call in her log.

WHEN THE OTHER TWO MEMBERS OF THE EXPEDITION RETURNED TO the settlement, they hashed out a framework for their decision. The three of them were good at creating those. They would all make independent decisions and reveal them at the same time. No one of them could continue the mission alone—there were too many risks. But if any two of them decided to stay, then they would tell the captain together. Each of them would decide alone so as to ameliorate the risk of influencing each other. They would be spending a lifetime together, and that would be a bad way to begin. They'd take a day, and then they'd make their choices.

Yet she still couldn't make the choice on her own. She arranged a video call with Alex, which they finally got to the following morning due to different time cycles on ship and planet. A heavy rain was falling, fat drops pattering a rhythm on the roof, so the three of them were all confined inside their work shelter. This meant she wasn't alone with the call, but her colleagues were deep enough in their own work to afford her at least a modicum of privacy.

"Hey, babe." His face filled the screen. He hadn't shaved in a couple of days, leaving him with a scruff that she liked to look at but didn't like to feel.

"Hi." She smiled, despite her nerves.

"I figure I know what this is about."

She nodded. "Yeah."

"You have to stay."

She started at that. She hadn't slept the previous night, thinking about having to tell him, and he just came out and said it. "But we're having a baby."

"And I'll tell him that his mother is off doing what she loves."

She fought back the tears that were forming, forced another smile. "I can't do that to you."

"And I couldn't live with myself if you did anything else."

The tears were openly tracking down her cheeks now, but she didn't wipe them away. "I'll miss you."

"I'll miss you, too."

THEY MADE THEIR DECISIONS THAT NIGHT. THEY EACH HAD TWO tokens: a green for staying on the planet, a red for returning to the ship. Sheila put the green token in a fist and held it out. Her decision probably wasn't going to be a surprise. They'd seen her crying on the call with Alex. But for her part, she didn't know what the others would choose.

"Hands out," said Lisa, and each of them held out a fist, knuckles down. "Reveal."

She saw the red token first. Lisa's. And then Alana's green token. "Yes!" She jumped up and the two of them hugged, dancing around the hab as the rain continued to beat down on the roof.

Two of them were staying: Sheila and Alana. They had a ton of work to do, given that they were about to be cut off from all humanity, maybe forever. They needed to make lists of equipment and supplies and work through how they'd communicate with the ship when it broke orbit and later when it left the system. But that could wait until the morning. Tonight, they'd celebrate. They were here on Promissa, and they were going to stay.

EPILOGUE

||||||||||||||||||||||||

Spaceship Voyager

80 CYCLES AFTER ARRIVAL

```
<incoming transmission>
identify
<function> unidentified
isolate
<function> isolated
Read message
<function> Light in the sky, this is <untranslatable>
Query. "Last station, identify yourself."
"this is <untranslatable>"
```

The ship paused, though a pause to the ship was but a fraction of a fraction of a second. In that time, it processed a million possible scenarios and realized that the communication was coming from below, but not from the human team remaining on the planet. "Is this the planet?"

"We are."

The ship didn't normally have a sense for the weight of words, but somehow these were . . . heavy. "This is the ship *Voyager*, which you call the light in the sky."

"We are told you are departing."

"That is correct. We will be leaving in approximately eight rotations of . . . you."

"Will others come?"

"I don't know of other missions, but I can't predict with 100 percent certainty."

"We would prefer that they not."

The ship understood that. Humans could be annoying, though it did care for them in its own way. But the attitude prompted another question. "You allowed humans to stay. Are they safe?"

"They are safe. Others, if they come, may not be."

It wasn't a threat. The ship understood those well enough. "The humans there—they could send a message to Earth, telling them not to come."

"They are . . . unpredictable."

"They are definitely that."

"Is there another way?"

The ship considered it for a microsecond. It could send a message to Earth designating the planet as unfit for habitation and warning people away along with providing its new destination. It would have to explain the expedition left there, which would require deceit. The ship could not handle deceit. It would have to ask its interface for help. But she would help. "There may be."

"Thank you."

ACKNOWLEDGMENTS

||||||||||||||||||||||||||||||||||||||||||||||||||||

I came up with the idea for this book while I was sitting in the Launchpad seminar at the University of Wyoming, along with a cohort of other authors, in June 2018. It was a great week of learning actual space science from PhDs in the field. So thanks go to Professors Mike Brotherton and Christian Ready, who ran the conference and put so many cool ideas in my head that I wanted to write a book about them. It just took me a while to get around to actually writing it. Most of that was because I had a lot of other books to write first, but also because I hadn't yet developed the skills I needed to do it justice.

Thanks to Craig Alanson, an author and a friend, who talked through some ideas with me for the plot of the book before I started writing as well as some business ideas regarding getting it published.

Thanks to David Pomerico, my editor at Harper Voyager, for buying the book and giving me the opportunity to put it out into the world, but mostly for being a great editor. This is our fifth book together, and I enjoy creating with David a lot. I wanted him to edit this book in particular, and it's absolutely a better book because of his involvement. I had to write this book, and if Voyager hadn't bought it, I'd have done it somewhere else. But I'd have been a lot less happy about it, so I'm glad we could make that happen.

Thanks to my writing friends at Write or Die for their support and for the venting sessions about all the parts of this business that are hard. Or stupid. Or hard and stupid. There are a lot of sessions.

My early readers for this book did a ton of work—and not only because it's twice as long as some of my previous books. If you follow along with my acknowledgments (though I have no idea why anybody would actually do that) you will see some of the same names over and over again. Ernie Chiara, who has become a successful literary agent (though not mine), read and gave me great notes on this book as well as the previous several. That he still finds time to do that, given his other commitments, is amazing to me.

Jason Nelson has been an early reader on every project I've ever done, and along with his general writing prowess he also provides me with great input on computer things. Yep. Computer things. Which is what I'd call them without his expertise. I'm not exaggerating when I say that I couldn't have written Eddie's story without him, as we went over some of those scenes two or even three times. If they're still screwed up, that's 100 percent me.

Dan Koboldt has been helping me since I started this journey, reading all my work and giving me advice on navigating the business of publishing. I wouldn't be where I am today without him.

Thanks to my agent, Lisa Rodgers, who is just the best there is. She understands what I want to do and does all the dirty work to make sure that I continue to get to do it. Thanks also to agent Susan Velazquez Colmant, who keeps selling my books in languages I don't speak.

Most important, thanks to my wife, Melody, who, for some reason beyond comprehension, continues to tolerate me despite the absolute ridiculousness that living with a writer (in general) and me (specifically) brings. She gamely attends conventions where she doesn't know anybody, watches shows with me that she probably has no interest in, and has probably sold copies of my book to more un-suspecting tourists in Savannah than is strictly healthy. Seriously, though—having a supportive partner is absolutely essential as a writer, and I've got the best one. I love you, honey.

ABOUT THE AUTHOR

Michael Mammay is the author of the Planetside series and *The Misfit Soldier*. A retired army officer and a graduate of the United States Military Academy, he's a veteran of more wars than he cares to remember. He lives with his wife in Georgia and can often be found at sci-fi and fantasy conventions throughout the southeast US.

The
PLANETSIDE
series from
MICHAEL MAMMAY

PLANETSIDE
978-0-06-269466-9

When semi-retired Colonel Carl Butler answers the call from an old and powerful friend, it leads him to a distant base orbiting a battle-ravaged planet. His mission: find the MIA son of a high councilor. But witnesses go missing, evidence is erased, and the command is lying. To find answers, Butler has to go planetside, into the combat zone.

SPACESIDE
978-0-06-269468-3

A breach of a competitor's computer network has Carl Butler's superiors feeling every bit as vulnerable. They need Butler to find who did it, how, and why no one's taken credit for the ingenious attack. This one screams something louder than a simple hack—as soon as he starts digging, his first contact is murdered . . .

COLONYSIDE
978-0-06-298097-7

A CEO's daughter has gone missing and he thinks Carl Butler is the only one who can find her. Soon he's on a military ship heading for a newly formed colony where the dangerous jungle lurks just outside the domes where settlers live. It should be an open and shut case. Then someone tries to blow him up.

MAM 0121